THE NEXT TRACK

THE BROTHERS' BAND, BOOK 2

LIZA MALLOY

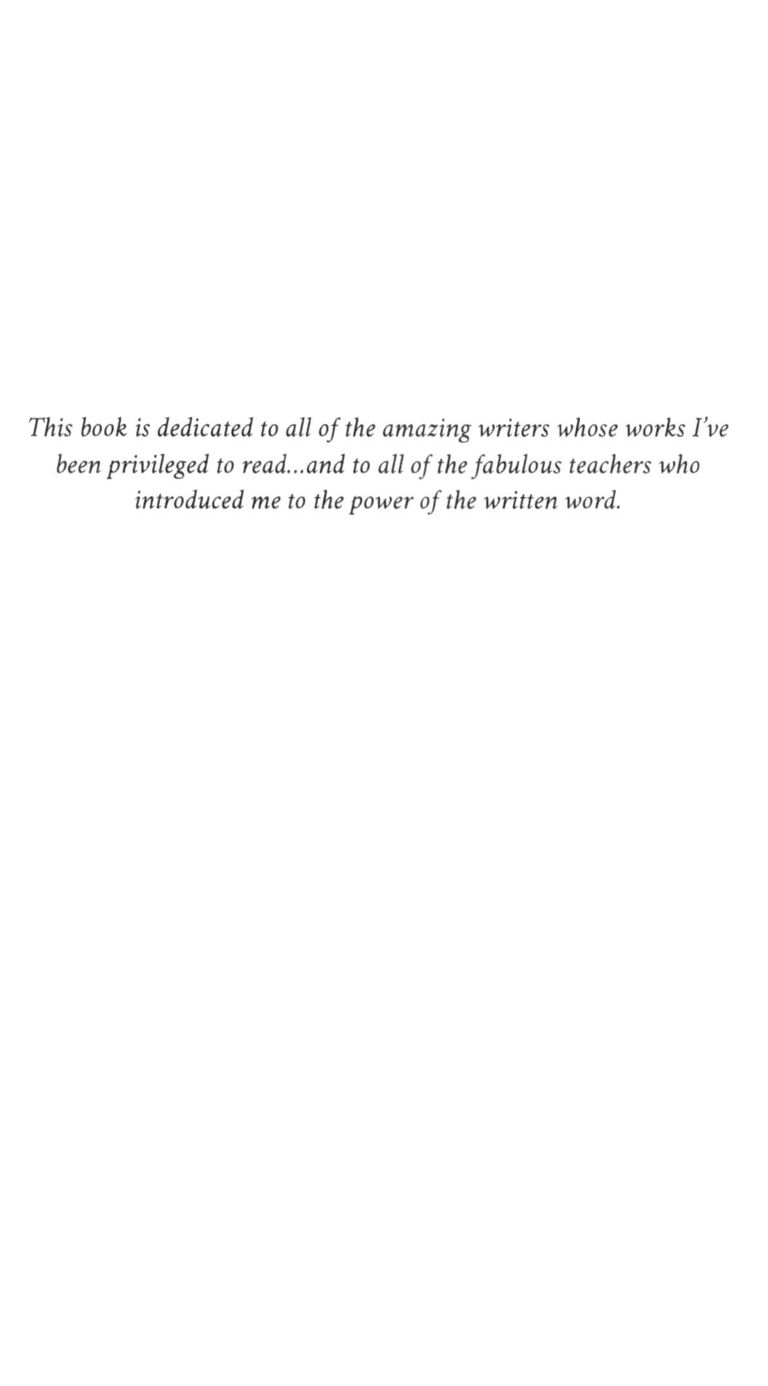

This book is dedicated to all of the amazing writers whose works I've been privileged to read...and to all of the fabulous teachers who introduced me to the power of the written word.

CHAPTER ONE

"To love or have loved, that is enough. Ask nothing further. There is no other pearl to be found in the dark folds of life."
Victor Hugo, *Les Misérables*

LILY

I thanked the doorman as he stepped out of the elevator. The doors slid shut with a dignified clang, signaling it was too late to turn back. Swallowing the lump in my throat, I lifted my daughter into my arms. Feeling the weight of her warm little body and her rapid heartbeat against my chest offered me a slight sense of security. She quickly thrust her small finger into the center of my earring, tracing the inner loop of the silver hoop.

"Lucy, be gentle with Mommy," I cautioned. She tapped her foot lightly against the wall behind me, giggling as the contact caused flashing lights to erupt from her sneakers.

I smiled. Whoever thought of light up children's shoes was a genius.

I focused on Lucy's small pink backpack to steady my breathing. The fact that I was already this nervous couldn't be a good sign. I hadn't set foot in this building for nearly four years, but the mix of emotions that I felt even just being near the Parker brothers' floor hit me like a wall of water, assaulting me on impact and then forcing its way into my lungs, suffocating me.

The elevator dinged softly as it jerked to a stop. I clutched Lucy tightly to my chest and stepped into the hall. Though the building was large, there were only two apartments on this floor. I was intimately familiar with both apartments and with the men who lived inside each one. Out of habit, my feet angled towards Dylan's apartment, but I quickly pulled out of that current and knocked on Thomas' door.

He opened it instantly, having been alerted to our arrival by the doorman. His long-sleeved olive Henley clung pleasantly to his biceps and echoed the green of his eyes. Even though I'd already seen Thomas once since returning to town, the sight of him still paralyzed me momentarily.

The four years hadn't aged him a bit, but he was different from the Thomas that had plagued my dreams during our separation. He seemed taller, for one, and perhaps a bit more muscled. But his deep chocolatey hair looked as soft as ever, and his velvety smooth voice still gave me shivers.

I assumed my response would be the same to Dylan. The cliché "tall, dark, and handsome" fell short when describing the Parker brothers. They were all of those things, and so much more. They were mesmerizing, enchanting, magnetic.

They were also addictive and dangerous.

As Thomas smiled calmly, leaning forward to kiss me gently on each cheek, I shooed away the intrusive thoughts telling me I hadn't waited long enough to return. I inhaled the surprisingly familiar scent of his cologne, relaxing slightly.

Thomas turned to my daughter, who was now burrowing her head into my chest. "How do you do, Miss Lucy?" he asked. He eyed her fondly, even when she refused to answer. Then, he stepped back and motioned for us to enter the apartment.

I quickly obeyed, eager to exit the hall before Dylan might chance upon us. I set Lucy on her feet in the entryway and she took off like a greyhound, dashing about the apartment. Although she was typically shy with new people, she was overly adventurous in unfamiliar places.

I'd always been uneasy with her curiosity, and now I felt my face flush at her audacity. But before I could call her back to my side, Thomas pressed his palm against the small of my back.

"She's fine, Lily. There's nothing she can bother."

Unless he'd redecorated, that claim was hard to believe. His apartment was massive by Manhattan standards, and filled with treasures a three-year-old could quickly destroy.

"Would you like some tea?" Thomas offered.

My throat was painfully dry already, so I nodded, then set off to find Lucy. The apartment was identical in layout to the one down the hall that I'd shared with Thomas' brother Dylan many years ago. At the time, both apartments had been furnished in similar modern, clean-cut styles and neutral colors too. From what I could see thus far, Thomas hadn't changed much.

"Lucy, don't touch that!" I shrieked, seeing her lunge for a guitar.

"It's fine," Thomas said softly. He handed me a mug of tea and crouched beside Lucy. "Have you ever played a guitar?"

She shook her head, her eyes widening with intrigue.

"This one's a little big for you, but it'll do for now," he said. "Soon we'll have to get you your own guitar." He glanced at me as he spoke, his eyes twinkling.

I lowered myself into the chair across from them and watched in awe as Lucy clambered onto Thomas' lap the second he sat on the floor. Thomas placed her tiny fingers over the strings, her face filled with delight as he helped her strum.

They played together, my breath quickening whenever

Thomas sang. I'd hadn't been able to avoid Sierra's music since I'd been away, nor had I tried. I'd sought out their songs for my daughter, letting that slight connection assuage some of my guilt for having kept them from her. Besides, they were on the radio often, and occasionally popped up in the news. But hearing the smooth, soothing voice in person brought back a colossal wave of memories I wasn't yet prepared to surf.

Lucy eventually moved to the piano, a more familiar instrument for her. My paternal grandmother, with whom we'd lived back in Michigan, owned a piano. When she passed away, we kept the piano. I'd never been very musical, but Lucy adored banging on the piano.

I wandered back to the kitchen, granting them some privacy and giving myself some much-needed space. Seeing Thomas again was hard; there was no surprise there. But it wasn't fair to deprive Lucy of everything he and Dylan had to offer just because of my past mistakes.

Lucy was a constant reminder of what I'd done, how I'd threatened to tear apart the delicate balance between the brothers. I'd never claimed to be perfect, but I generally considered myself to be a good person. I didn't cheat or steal, I went out of my way to be kind to others, and aside from harmless white lies, I was honest.

And truly, I'd never been unfaithful to a lover, aside from *that* night.

Logically, Lucy had to be Dylan's child. The chances she'd been conceived during my one night with Thomas rather than the many times I'd been with his brother—my fiancé—were slim to none. Still, it was always in the back of my mind, that toxic *what if* line of thinking. I wondered if Thomas entertained similar thoughts. He was being exceptionally gentle and caring with Lucy now, but that could simply be an extension of his past feelings for me, or the fact that she was a mirror image of his deceased sister. Then again, the look in his eyes as he watched

Lucy tap out "Chopsticks" could be described as parental. He wasn't an idiot; he had to have at least considered the possibility that she was his child.

Before seeing Thomas the week before, I'd always assumed Dylan had told him about Lucy. Even though Dylan had no reason to doubt Lucy was his child, there was still no explanation for why he hadn't said something to Thomas. The brothers shared everything, so why had Dylan chosen to keep his daughter a secret?

I stared into my nearly-empty tea mug, suddenly overwhelmed with exhaustion. After a moment, I sensed a presence near me. I turned, and Thomas was watching me. Lucy was still in his music room, now thrumming on the keys like any untrained three-year-old.

"The student is growing restless," he murmured.

I nodded. "Thank you so much for your time, Thomas."

His brows dipped. "I need to speak with you. Alone."

I'd expected him to have questions, to need to talk…but I just couldn't give him the answers he deserved yet. He was entitled to hate me—they both were—but there was nothing I could do about that now. And I knew myself enough to realize my limits. Letting him spend time with Lucy was hard enough. Until I'd been back longer, until I trusted myself to be alone with him and not let myself think about…everything…

My breath hitched.

"I can't, Thomas," I finally said, swallowing the lump rising in my throat. "I know what you must think, me coming back here and… I really just wanted you to get to know Lucy, if that's something you want. I can't get involved with you or Dylan on any level." I paused. "And if you want to see Lucy, then…"

"Of course I want to keep seeing Lucy," he snapped. "You've already kept her from me for three years. Wasn't that enough?"

I blinked, struggling to hide my shock at his tone. "I was only going to say that once she gets to know you better, you two could spend time alone, without me. I can't let myself get caught up with you and Dylan again. It's better for Lucy this way."

Thomas' face softened. "I'm sorry. I didn't mean to raise my voice. I only thought, well…" He sighed loudly, stroking his chin with his thumb and forefinger. Lucy scampered up to join us and Thomas' lips curled up into a wide, natural smile. He gazed at her for a moment, then turned back to me. "I really do need to talk to you alone, and soon. It's about Lucy. After you hear what I have to say, you can avoid me like the plague."

I cringed, but I couldn't say no. He had a right to ask his questions. "I'll need to find a sitter," I said. "When are you thinking?"

"Tonight? Or tomorrow morning?"

As much as that seemed like too soon, I'd only stress about whatever he had to say until he'd said it. And Lucy could go to church with my parents in the morning. "Okay. I can meet you tomorrow morning. Maybe 10?"

He nodded, so I suggested a coffee shop about halfway between our respective neighborhoods.

"You could just come here," he said. "I'd rather speak with you in private."

I shook my head. I absolutely could not be alone with him, not when my pulse still raced at the sound of his voice.

Thomas furrowed his brow, but relented. Then he crouched down to Lucy. "Miss Lucy, it has been a pleasure. I'll see you again soon."

She stuck out her tongue, then giggled hysterically. I clasped her fingers in my own and tugged her towards the door. It was obvious she already liked him, and for some reason, I found that unsettling.

* * *

THOMAS

I paced listlessly after Lily left my apartment. Nervous energy filled me, so I retrieved my journal, eager for the serenity writing brought me. I sat in the wingback chair by the window, my pen poised above a fresh page in the notebook. After a moment's thought, I scribbled the date in the upper corner, then I began.

"Today, I met my daughter," I wrote. Then I paused. Technically, I'd met her a week ago. Only then, I hadn't known she was my child, so perhaps it didn't count. I rubbed my strained eyes, then flipped back to the last entry in my journal, which was from two weeks before. I'd written when Lily had first returned to town.

At the time, I'd been filled with hope. Lily was back, and she'd called me, not Dylan. That had to mean something. I hadn't anticipated that she wouldn't be alone, or that she didn't even realize my brother hadn't mentioned Lucy's existence to me. And I certainly hadn't yet known that Dylan had kept my own child from me for years.

What kind of a monster did something like that?

Probably the same kind of monster that sleeps with his brother's fiancée.

We truly were cut from the same cloth, Dylan and I, in every possible meaning of the phrase.

Dylan hadn't apologized for his transgression, but he was sorry. I didn't think he so much regretted doing what he'd done, but that he felt he had no choice. He had to punish me for what I'd done and, I had to admit, the punishment fit the crime.

As for myself, I had already spent years regretting my actions. Every time I'd looked at my brother, hell, every time I looked in a mirror, guilt flooded me. I hated myself for betraying him. As much as I'd treasured every second of my night with Lily, I would've gone back and done things differently if I could. I would've talked to her longer, would've walked away when she kissed me. I would've left the apartment when she stripped naked.

But now—now I couldn't regret it. Thanks to that night, I had a daughter. Thanks to that night, Lily had a reason to return to me.

Dylan and his wife, Patty, had left for the West Coast the previous day. The first I'd heard of the trip was after Lily returned, so I suspected he was leaving to give me space. I appreciated that. He'd had years to hate me for my betrayal, but I'd only now learned of his. It would take me some time to forgive him. And navigating the next step with Lily would be easier without Dylan looming over my shoulder.

I moved from the armchair to the piano, lightly tracing the ivory and smiling at the memory of Lucy seated at that very piano. She hadn't been very good. She didn't know her notes, and she watched her fingers as they moved across the keys. But the way her eyes lit up when the piano rewarded her efforts with music—well, that gave me hope. She was too young to be technically skilled anyway, but loving the music meant a lot at this point.

Lily had always appreciated music but never played an instrument. I once asked Dylan if he'd tried to teach her and he'd scoffed at the notion. Maybe someday I could teach her, too, and not just Lucy. I pressed my foot against the pedal as I decided what to play, then closed my eyes and let my fingers take over.

I focused on the melody, trying to shake away the vision of Lily seated beside me at the piano. She'd asked me to teach her daughter. Our daughter. Not herself. Lily wanted nothing to do with me. She had every right to hate me, or at least to distrust me. I'd known what Dylan was like, never doubted that he could pull her in and then utterly destroy her, and I hadn't scared her off.

Years ago, when I'd first seen the signs that Dylan was abusing cocaine, I'd kept it from her. When she raised red flags, I'd dismissed her concerns.

I hadn't been willing to risk Dylan losing Lily because I had wanted to keep her in my life.

That wasn't love; that was…selfishness. Fear, maybe.

But whatever I'd felt for Lily, it hadn't disappeared. Before her return, I'd thought it had faded. I'd dated other women, and I'd enjoyed vast periods of time where I considered myself happy. But as soon as I saw Lily again, I'd felt it again—that overwhelming, crushing desire. I needed to be near her, to see her, to hear her voice, to touch her skin. Even her scent still drew me to her.

After all these years, I wanted Lily Mitchell so much that it physically pained me. My chest ached when I saw her and couldn't touch her, my stomach churned, and my throat tightened.

I couldn't deny the truth—after four years, I was still hopelessly in love with Lily.

But just as before, there was another person standing in the way. Another person that I also loved. Except this time, it wasn't my brother, but my daughter. Lucy. I barely knew anything about the child, but already I felt this primal urge to protect her and to do anything to bring her joy. Maybe it was the simple biological response or maybe it had something to do with Lucy's resemblance to her mother or to her namesake, my sister, the original Lucy. I hadn't been able to protect my sister, who had succumbed to a tragic accident in childhood. But with this Lucy, I had a chance to redeem myself. My brother and I both did.

Whatever it was, I couldn't do anything to risk hurting this precious child or to jeopardize my ability to stay in her life.

I was so close to having it all that it hurt.

I slid my hands off the piano, opening my eyes. I rose to my feet. No amount of music would clear my mind. With nothing else to do that evening, I decided to head to the gym.

CHAPTER TWO

The next morning, as promised, I went to meet Thomas. I hadn't slept well the night before, plagued by memories of Thomas and Dylan, regrets flitting through my brain like ants parading across a picnic table. I'd given up trying to sleep around five, gone for a slow jog to clear my mind, and even practiced yoga. I straightened my hair, tried on half a dozen outfits—hating myself for even caring what I wore—and finally decided on a simple mustard-colored dress with three-quarter length sleeves. I paired it with a chunky necklace and knee-high boots the color of coffee with two creams.

By the time Lucy awoke, I was already exhausted, but at least the fatigue helped tame my nerves. I left for the coffee shop early, heading out the moment my parents took Lucy to Sunday School. I'd brought a book to read, although it was more for work than fun. Having read *Jude the Obscure* at least four times before, it didn't matter that I repeatedly tore my gaze away from the page to stare at the entrance to the coffee shop.

At five till ten, the shop's bell chimed. I was sure it was Thomas even before I peered up to confirm my hunch was right. His head was down as he entered, but still I'd recognize him anywhere. His dark-wash jeans clung to him in a way that I wished I hadn't noticed, and he'd rolled up the sleeves of his plaid button-down shirt, revealing muscular forearms. I forced myself to look away as soon as he spotted me.

"Can I get you anything?" he offered, eying my existing coffee cup.

I shook my head, hating that I could smell his tantalizing aftershave even with the strong coffee aroma permeating the small cafe.

"I'll be right back," he promised.

I watched Thomas as he waited in line, comforted that I wouldn't be caught staring since he was focused on his phone. When he finally returned, he held up his paper cup and chuckled, his emerald eyes twinkling.

The barista had written "Tomás" on his cup.

I smiled, wondering if she'd simply misinterpreted the accent. My eyes drifted back to his wrist. A single knotted gray band tied to his wrist proclaimed "grace" on a rugged-looking placard.

"Grace," I read aloud. "Is that your girlfriend?"

He flinched but quickly recovered his composure. "It's a word. A reminder I need to see throughout the day. I don't have a girlfriend," he added, almost as an afterthought.

I didn't have a response for that, so I focused on my coffee.

"Are you staying with your parents permanently?"

"No, only until I find an apartment for Lucy and me."

"Can you afford that on a teaching salary?"

No. "We're looking for something small and outside the city."

Thomas didn't look convinced, but he moved on. "So you're teaching now?"

"Mmm hmm," I chewed the inside of my lip, wishing he'd just get to the point already. After spending the night awake trying to imagine what he could possibly need to tell me so urgently and in person, I wasn't in the mood to wait longer.

"I'm glad. You had too much passion for literature to sit inside a cubicle all day at a travel agency. Were you teaching in Michigan also?"

"No. I took a few courses I needed to get my teaching certification and then did my student teaching and some substitute work. This is my first year with my own classroom."

"I always thought teaching would be a fun profession. Challenging, but rewarding," he said awkwardly. "I certainly don't have the qualifications for it myself, but…"

I stopped listening to his actual words and focused on his fidgety demeanor. He'd been sipping his coffee every time I spoke and when it was his turn to say something, he tapped his fingers against the paper cup. He was clearly nervous. Thomas wasn't one to waste words, and this was definitely the first time I'd seen him ramble. I couldn't handle it.

"Thomas, you said you wanted to talk about Lucy. We're not here to catch up. What did you want to discuss?"

His bright eyes widened at the interruption. He took his time before speaking. "I'm sorry. I'm not certain how you're going to react to what I have to say. I don't want to upset you."

I avoided the temptation of saying, *then don't*. "What is it?"

"Have you spoken with Dylan since you returned to town?"

I shook my head.

Thomas frowned. "Why not? I thought you wanted both of us to get to know Lucy."

My stomach muscles clenched. I did want that, in theory. But if it was this hard seeing Thomas, I wasn't sure I could handle seeing Dylan. "I do," I began slowly. "I mean, I will. I've just been waiting. We have so much history, and he's got a wife now. For all I know, he still hates me."

"Dylan doesn't hate you," Thomas quickly replied.

The brothers shared everything with each other. If Thomas

said Dylan didn't hate me, it was probably true, although it was hard to imagine why Dylan wouldn't feel that way. I ran away at the start of his tour and didn't let him see his daughter for three years. And if he knew about me and Thomas…

"If he knew the truth…about us…, he'd hate me," I said, glancing down at my coffee. Thomas didn't speak for a moment.

I looked back up and saw Thomas' jaw twitch, his mouth tightening into a firm line. "He does know. And he still doesn't hate you."

There was a tightening in my gut. "What do you mean, he knows? Did you tell him?"

"No." Thomas reached across the table and placed his hand over mine, his fingertips lightly resting on my knuckles. My heart raced from the contact, or maybe it was from Thomas' words.

He took a deep breath, then blew it out slowly. "Lily, he knows everything, and he always has."

I shook my head frantically. "No, that's not possible. No. He…"

Thomas shushed me. "I went to speak with Dylan after I first saw you at the playground. He told me that he can't have children."

I squeezed my eyes shut, replaying his words in my mind. If Dylan couldn't have children, then…

"As soon as he saw the photo of Lucy, Dylan knew about you and me."

The first few tears snuck past my eyelashes and began trickling down my cheeks. I had so many thoughts rushing around in my head that I wasn't sure where to start. "That can't be," I finally said. "He sent money. He assumed he was the father."

"That was my first thought too. But he said the money was for Lucy. He wanted to send what he thought I'd send."

"Then why not just tell you? Why keep if from you for all of those years? Why not let you send your own damn money?"

"Dylan didn't want me to know," Thomas said, his voice cracking. "He was punishing me."

I glanced around the room, suddenly feeling the walls closing in on me. "I need some air. I have to get out of here." I pushed away from the table, knocking my chair to the ground with a crash.

I rushed out the door and down to the end of the block before stopping, panting and dizzy. I bent over, placing my hands on my thighs as though I'd just run a marathon.

After a moment, I felt a hand on my back.

"I'm going to be sick," I said, hurtling myself to the nearest trash can and emptying the contents of my stomach in front of all of New York. When I was done, I felt better.

Thomas handed me a tissue, then led me down a mostly deserted side street. "I'm sorry," he said. "I shouldn't have told you here."

"It's fine, Thomas. It isn't your fault. Dylan should have told me, should've told us both, three years ago." I sat on the edge of the curb, weary from my newfound knowledge.

I interpreted Thomas' silence as agreement.

"What kind of jerk keeps that to himself?" I asked.

Thomas took his time answering. "A heartbroken one." He rested his hand on my knee, then quickly pulled it back. "He loved you, Lily. And he trusted me. And then we…"

"I know what we did," I snapped.

We were both quiet for a long time. At first, I counted the cars as they passed, focusing on the normalcy of it all. My world had just changed, but on the outside, everyone else was still continuing about their usual business. I closed my eyes, relaxing and letting my ears pick up the slack.

I'd missed the sounds of the city when I was gone. We'd lived in Ann Arbor, Lucy and I, so it wasn't exactly the country, but it might as well have been for how quiet it was compared to this. No place was quite like NYC. Even when I'd traveled to other major metropolitan cities—Paris, London, Los Angeles, none of them sounded the same. None of them echoed the same level of buzz from conversations, whistle of wind whipping around the buildings, or hum and beeping of traffic.

It's good to be back, I thought.

I slowly opened my eyes to face the world again. "What was Dylan like when I left?"

Thomas hesitated, but I wordlessly pleaded my case with him until he conceded. "How do you think? He was a mess, Lily. He kept calling you, calling your parents, even calling Jill. We had to cancel four concerts."

"I saw that."

"Ari or I stayed with him all the time. We let him drink, but nothing else. After a few months, he seemed fine."

"Months?"

Thomas shrugged. "He got over you faster than I did," he finally said, his voice soft.

I pretended I hadn't heard his last statement, focused on the past, trying to recall anything I could about that critical time. "Lucy was nearly a year old before he sent that first check. I guess that was about eighteen months after I left."

Thomas nodded, apparently agreeing with my math. "After I met you at the park, when Dylan told me Lucy wasn't his, I went back over the past couple years in my mind. I tried to remember if there was any time he acted strangely around me, any hint at all of when he found out that I'd betrayed him, but there was nothing." A breathy, disgruntled chuckle escaped his lips. "It's ironic really, the man who got so worked up over you even talking to a coworker can learn that his own brother committed the ultimate betrayal, and somehow not even let that affect him at all."

"Oh, Thomas. You didn't betray him. I'm the one who was engaged to him."

"He is my brother, Lily. My behavior was inexcusable, unforgivable, even. But he'd been terrible to you. You owed him nothing."

I didn't agree with any of that, but was not surprised to hear Thomas say it. Thomas was nothing if not loyal to his brother. Sure, he messed up once, but the amount of stress he'd been under at the time… And it *was* my fault. I'd been the instigator.

"I always thought he'd kill you if he found out." I paused. "Or himself."

Thomas nodded. "Me too." He stood slowly, offering me his hand. I wasn't certain my legs would support me yet, but he tilted his head towards an empty bench down the street. I rose to my feet and lumbered in that direction.

"He almost hit me when I confronted him," Thomas said as we reached the bench.

I slumped onto it and Thomas sat beside me.

I raised my gaze to his face, which showed no signs of a physical confrontation. Years ago, when I'd been with Dylan, they'd fought twice. Both times about me, I recalled.

"I was quite angry with him initially," Thomas continued. "For not telling me about Lucy sooner."

"You're not still angry?" I couldn't imagine ever forgiving someone for such a cruel act.

"I am, but…" Thomas shrugged and tapped his bracelet. "I bought this originally as a reminder to not be so hard on myself, to recognize that while I'm possibly the bloody worst brother out there, I'm not always so dreadful. Usually, I do right by Dylan. But then it seems if I'm going to forgive myself for what I've done to him, perhaps I should extend the same compassion to Dylan. He shouldn't have kept Lucy from me, but we can't change that now. Nothing good comes from focusing on what he took from me, or what I took from him."

I raised an eyebrow, but didn't comment. Thomas had always impressed me with his deep, philosophical viewpoint on the world, but that was a little too zen even for my tastes. I was furious at Dylan for not telling me the truth, and I wasn't the one deprived of three years of my child's life.

Suddenly, I realized I'd been focused on the wrong facts since his surprising news. "So you're Lucy's father," I said abruptly.

"Seems that way," Thomas said.

I felt my lips tug upwards at that.

"Is that, I mean, are you okay?" he asked.

"Yes. I'm relieved."

"Relieved that you know now?"

"Yes."

He looked disappointed.

"And relieved that it's you." I added.

Thomas raised his eyes to gaze at me again. My pulse increased almost instantly under the intensity of his stare, and that terrified me. He shouldn't have had that effect on me, not after so much time had passed, not when we had Lucy to think about.

"You and I were only together those two times, and Dylan and I…" I didn't want to recount for Thomas the numerous times I'd made love with his brother, but he knew nearly as well as I did that Dylan and I had an overly physical relationship. "I just figured that statistically, Lucy was more likely Dylan's."

"Wouldn't that have been better?"

I understood what he meant, and in some ways, it was true. I had let people assume Lucy was Dylan's child, and that was easy, since everyone had known we were engaged at the time I'd gotten pregnant.

Dylan had called my parents countless times to try to search for me, and when I'd confessed the pregnancy to them, I'd feared my mother would tell him. She insisted I was wrong, keeping his child from him, and she warned me that he'd just take me to court to enforce his parental rights. I'd assured her that he wouldn't do that because of his drug problem, but I'd never once mentioned the possibility that Lucy wasn't even his child.

Now, if I had to tell anyone that my daughter actually belonged to a man with whom I'd never had an open relationship, and who was a blood relative of my then-fiancé, well, that was going to be a tough conversation. But if Lucy wasn't Dylan's child, I never had to worry about that connection to him. I could cut off all direct ties with Dylan and never look back. And since I'd spent four years in Michigan hiding from practically everything and everyone familiar to me just to avoid being tangled in his web again, that was a good thing.

"Because of the drugs?" Thomas said, catching me off guard. "You're glad Dylan's not the father because you're afraid he might start using again, right? And because you don't want Lucy to have any genetic predisposition to addiction?"

I smiled despite myself. Of course those things were both true, but that certainly wasn't what I'd been thinking. It surprised me that Thomas didn't get it. I was quiet for a moment while I decided how to best explain.

"Thomas, when I discovered I was pregnant, I knew I had to get away from Dylan. I couldn't just break up with him, I had to physically leave town and sever all ties."

"You were afraid he'd hurt you or Lucy," Thomas said.

I shook my head. "I was never afraid of Dylan."

"But he did hurt you. Several times. He hit you, he pushed you, he raped you."

"He never hurt me on purpose. It was the drugs," I snapped, a tone of finality in my voice. "But I knew we weren't good for each other. I couldn't imagine raising a child with that kind of drama."

"Then why did you leave your phone at the airport? You know they called Dylan and said they found it there?"

"Thomas, if I had seen Dylan… God, if I had even spoken to him, I would've gone back to him. I couldn't say no to him. You know he had that power over me. And I couldn't let myself risk getting sucked in again once I had Lucy to look after."

"But you're back now. What changed?"

Hopefully everything. "He's married, he's clean. I missed the city. And I missed my family. I was lonely in Michigan, especially after my grandma died. It's hard being a single mom without any family nearby. I thought enough time had passed that I could come back here and risk seeing him." I paused, but Thomas didn't speak. "I figured I'd always have some tie to him, because of Lucy, but now that I know I don't, I'm free."

"You still love him," he said it like an accusation, one that disgusted and alarmed him.

I shook my head. "No. I don't think I do. And it doesn't matter anyway."

"Of course it matters," he said.

I gazed out to the street. We were along an alley, so there wasn't much traffic, but several cars were parked along the curb. I wanted to tell Thomas that it didn't matter because I'd changed. I wasn't the same naïve, optimistic girl who'd daydreamed on subways and blew her paltry salary on designer shoes. My priorities were different now, and I'd grown. Learned. Now I knew that love—the kind of love I'd thought Dylan and I shared—existed only in fiction. The reality wasn't so idyllic.

"What about me, Lily? Do you still have feelings for me? Did you ever?"

I closed my eyes and inhaled slowly. When I opened my eyes again, Thomas was still there, eying me expectantly.

"I'm glad you're Lucy's father, Thomas. And I want you to be a part of her life. But that's all I can handle now." I avoided eye contact with him, and I didn't ask if he still had feelings for me. I didn't need to, anyway. I'd seen it all over his face.

He was quiet for a moment, then reached for my hand. "Come, I'll walk you to your car."

"We still have a lot to discuss. If you're Lucy's father, I mean, as Lucy's father, you have rights."

"And I owe you money," he replied matter-of-factly.

"I'm not worried about that," I said. "Of course, I need to pay back Dylan."

"I wouldn't," Thomas snapped. "He knew Lucy was mine when he sent you that money. It was a gift. Keep it."

I shook my head.

"You have a lot to process," Thomas said after another long pause. "Why don't we meet to discuss the rest another time?"

I nodded and started off towards my car with him. "Thanks. That sounds good."

CHAPTER THREE

*L*ily arrived at 4:59. I was intrigued by her promptness. Not that I'd ever have described her as flighty, but the old Lily wasn't known for her timeliness. I wondered if it was motherhood, maturity, or teaching experience that had changed her.

I greeted them both with a warm smile.

Lucy turned her head abruptly, avoiding my stare. Lily cringed, then jostled the child in her arms.

"Lucy, sweetheart, you remember Mr. Thomas. You had so much fun playing piano with him last week."

The child made an incomprehensible sound that I'd best describe as a fuss but could've possibly been an actual word. Her message was clear though.

I awkwardly patted her arm then stepped back to let them enter.

"Sorry," Lily mouthed, adding in a regular voice, "She just came from daycare. It takes her a little while to transition."

I shrugged. "It's fine." It was, really. Although, I supposed it shouldn't have been. My own daughter didn't know me, let alone like me. I couldn't blame her—I wouldn't trust some strange man with a funny accent I hadn't seen the first three years of my life, either. Except I hadn't exactly chosen to be absent from her life...

"Can I get you guys a drink or something to eat?" I offered, annoyed by my own bitterness.

"Lucy just had snack," Lily said.

"Do you want something? Water? Tea? Wine?"

Lily perked up a bit at that last suggestion, but she politely shook her head.

I lowered myself onto the piano bench, giving Lucy some space while her mom wrangled the multitude of warm layers off of her. It was a brisk autumn day, but the bulky coat, scarf, hat, gloves, and sweater seemed overkill to me.

"What is your favorite song, Lucy?" I asked.

She didn't answer.

Lily addressed her daughter, making some suggestions for what she could tell me. Lucy remained silent.

I listened to the possibilities, then chose the theme song to a recent princess movie. I searched the sheet music on my tablet, then began playing. Having never played the song, I needed to keep my eye on the music to actually hit the right keys, so my first chance to glance in my daughter's direction was after the chorus repeated a third time.

As I'd hoped, she was now enthralled. She still sat on her mother's lap, but she was watching me, an eager look in her eyes. She was happy, and possibly even proud.

I finished out the song, then patted the bench beside me. "I could use a second set of hands with this one," I said. "Could you help me?"

Hesitantly, Lucy slid off her mum's lap and joined me at the piano.

I tapped a key. "Okay, I want you to be in charge of this note. Whenever I say 'go,' you press that key. Got it?"

She nodded, her expression serious.

We attempted the duet for a few rounds, then I played *Twinkle, Twinkle Little Star* and made her guess the title. We practiced that one, singing the *Twinkle, Twinkle* lyrics, then repeated it all with *Baa, Baa Black Sheep*, finally ending on the *A, B, C* song.

Lucy appeared happy while playing, and she wasn't terrible. Well, technically, she was, but I supposed that it was to be expected that she wouldn't remember which notes came when at her age. I switched directions for a moment, playing a few other nursery rhymes I'd looked up after our last lesson. I'd play the melody, then ask her to guess the song. The game worked well for a few rounds.

Lily had pulled a stack of papers out of her messenger bag and was hunched over the coffee table. Judging from the red pen in her hand, she was grading, and by the looks of the paper in front of her, the student wasn't doing too well. I smiled, entertaining a fleeting vision of this being our new normal—Lily grading papers while Lucy and I played piano. After a while, Lucy would head off to play and I could offer Lily a shoulder massage to release the tension she was clearly holding in her torso.

"I'm hungry," Lucy said suddenly, interrupting my fantasy.

She hadn't spoken loudly, but Lily gazed up as though she'd been paged. "Okay, sweetie." She turned to me. "It's getting late. I should get her home for dinner."

I nodded, reluctantly standing from the bench. As soon as I stood, Lucy took over, pounding on the keys with unrefined glee.

Suddenly, the thought of them leaving so soon pained me.

"Do you cook?" I asked, certain that was not a skill in her repertoire years ago.

She laughed. "Sort of. Lucy doesn't have the most sophisticated palette yet. We do a lot of plain pasta and chicken nuggets."

I stood and walked out of the music room, heading straight to the fridge. Lily followed.

"It's not a chicken nugget, but I do have grilled chicken I can warm up. And plenty of pasta."

She smiled apologetically, her chestnut hair cascading over her shoulders. "I can't ask you to cook for us, Thomas. Thank you so much for the piano instruction though."

I hesitated, then said what I was thinking. "I want to spend more time with her. And this way, you don't have to cook. Please? It'll only take fifteen minutes to make and you can get her home right when we are done eating."

Lily seemed tempted, but still didn't agree.

"Traffic will be much lighter by then, too," I added, certain that would cinch the deal.

It did.

"Where's the pasta? I'll make it while you watch Lucy."

I retrieved a box of pasta, filled a medium saucepan with water, and lit the stove. "There is olive oil in the cabinet there with the spices," I said, pointing, "And some vegetables in the fridge."

Lily laughed, sending flutters through me. "Lucy eats hers with a pat of butter. I'm not sure olive oil and fresh mushrooms will do the trick for her."

"That's for you and me," I said, smiling. Then I went to rejoin Lucy, even though she seemed perfectly comfortable alone in the music room.

I played with Lucy for about ten more minutes, then suggested she join me in the kitchen. She scampered over to her mother, ferociously hugging her legs.

Lily stumbled, then smiled down at her. Slowly, she gazed up to me. "Can you take over here? I want Lucy to use the bathroom before dinner."

I nodded, curious if she was still of nappy-wearing age or if potty training was underway. I knew nothing about such things, either the norms or the particulars of my daughter's situation. I had a lot to learn, it seemed.

I poured Lily and I each a small glass of wine, then searched my cabinets for a suitable cup for a child. I didn't have any of those small cups with lids, so I selected a plastic cup I'd gotten from some pizza delivery place instead.

Lucy and Lily emerged from the bathroom, and I couldn't help but notice that Lily appeared to have touched up her makeup. I forced myself to wait until they were gone to ponder the significance of that fact.

"I have water or milk for Lucy," I began.

Lily hesitated, glanced at her bag, then turned back to me. "She'll take a little milk, thanks."

I poured a small amount into the cup and set it at the table, then froze. "I'm sorry, I don't have a highchair. Will she be okay at the table?"

Lily nodded, a smile peeking out behind her cheeks. "She'll be fine."

I nodded, then handed the serving spoon to Lily. "I'll let you dip hers," I said.

She prepared a plate for her daughter. *Our* daughter. She plopped a small amount of pasta on the plate, slathered it with butter, then began cutting it into smaller noodles. She similarly cut a piece of chicken breast, then squirted ketchup beside it.

"The ketchup's for the chicken, is it?" I asked, astounded.

Lily chuckled and nodded. "Any chance you have any strawberries?"

I shook my head, then checked the fridge. Lily reached over my arm and grabbed the pint of raspberries.

"May I?" she asked.

"Of course."

She washed the fruit then placed about half the container on

Lucy's plate. She carried the plate to the table, then lifted Lucy up to her seat.

I dipped Lily's food and my own, then carried them over to the table. I felt like I should say something poignant as we all began our first meal together, like a real family, but the words didn't come to me. Lucy attacked her berries with an enthusiasm that brought a smile to my face.

"She really likes fruit," Lily said, her tone apologetic.

My smile widened. "There's more if you want it," I said to Lucy.

"After you eat your chicken," Lily added.

I nodded for Lily to eat, then began my own food, more for the distraction than anything else. It was hours before my usual dinner time, and I really had no appetite anyway. I lifted my wine glass to my lips, wishing the liquid could instantly relax me.

Suddenly, Lucy seemed to spot the decorative tiger figurine in the middle of the table. Her arm jutted forward, knocking into her cup and sending milk spraying everywhere.

She immediately drew back, and Lily flew to her feet.

"Whoopsie daisy," I said, smiling while shaking my head at Lily, motioning for her to sit. I retrieved some paper towels and a damp cloth, cleaning the mess quickly.

As I gazed over at Lucy, I realized she was now staring at me, her lips parted, a mixture of confusion and concern on her face.

"You okay?" I asked.

She closed her mouth and eyes, shaking her head. "I'm so sorry. I should've given you her sippy cup."

"It's not a problem."

I sat back down at the table, then handed Lucy the figurine. I asked her if she'd ever been to the Bronx Zoo. She gazed to her mother, who shook her head.

"You should go sometime," I suggested. "We all should. The gorilla exhibit is fantastic. What is your favorite animal, Lucy?"

She answered, and the conversation flowed smoothly until we finished eating.

After dinner, Lily offered to wash the dishes, but I declined. I would've enjoyed her presence longer, but she was clearly exhausted. She probably needed to get home to put Lucy to bed anyway. I had no idea what time children, or Lucy in particular, even went to bed. There was so much I simply did not know.

CHAPTER FOUR

"And all should cry, Beware! Beware!
His flashing eyes, his floating hair!
Weave a circle round him thrice,
And close your eyes with holy dread,
For he on honey-dew hath fed,
And drunk the milk of Paradise."
Samuel Taylor Coleridge, *Kubla Khan*

THOMAS

The loud clanking in the hallway outside the apartment alerted me the moment Dylan returned. I peered out the peephole and confirmed it was him and Patty. My stomach tightened. I hadn't been alone with Dylan since his admission about Lucy, but now that he was back, we'd probably have to face the truth at some point.

I returned to the armchair where I'd been attempting to write lyrics for a new song. We already had the melody, but the words weren't flowing easily. I poised my pen above the page again, but after a moment, I shook my head and dropped it.

I was too distracted to write, so I changed into athletic shorts and a tee shirt. Exercise was the only thing other than music that would clear my mind and calm my nerves. I grabbed my headphones and cellphone, and started out.

As soon as I opened my door, I nearly slammed into my brother's fist, poised at eye level as though about to knock.

We both froze, awkwardly.

Slowly, Dylan lowered his hand.

We stared in silence.

"What, no welcome back hug?" he teased.

"I was on my way out," I said, lamely.

"Headed to the gym, I see," he said. "Are you simply avoiding me or still in your dating drought?"

I sighed, not about to take the bait. Not when it already took so much effort on my part not to strangle him. "Did you need something?"

"I thought we should talk."

"Can it wait?"

He considered this for a moment, then nodded.

I started to brush past him to make my way to the gym, when he spoke again.

"I'll meet you in the gym in a few minutes. We can talk there. Multitask, you know?"

I rolled my eyes as I stepped onto the elevator.

I began my workout with a brisk jog to warm up, and by the time I stepped off the treadmill, Dylan was there, seated on a weight bench.

I wasn't sure how long he'd been there, but decided to start with small talk. "How was your trip?"

He shrugged. "Eh, fine. Patty shopped. I read. Nothing too thrilling."

I adjusted the weight plates on the chest press and lay back beneath the bar.

"Need a spot?" he offered.

"No thanks." I wasn't planning on trying anything too heavy. And if I did let him help, well, he'd probably just drop the weights on my face anyway.

"How was your piano lesson? Is she any good?"

My chest tightened. We couldn't avoid talking about Lucy forever. And nothing I said would ever let him know how much he had ruined for me. I was still learning everything I'd missed the past several years.

"We've had two so far, and not really. But she does seem to enjoy music." I paused. "The resemblance is uncanny."

Dylan took his time answering. "To our Lucy or to Lily?"

As he spoke, I couldn't even recall which I'd actually meant. "Both, I guess," I said.

I finished my first set, acutely aware that my brother was simply watching me.

"They stayed for dinner after her last lesson," I told him.

"They? You mean Lily too?"

"Yes, of course. You think she'd leave her child alone with me? Lucy doesn't even know me."

"You're her father."

"Lucy doesn't know that, and I'm not sure it matters anyway. I'm a stranger to her," I said, omitting *thanks to you*.

"How does Lily seem?"

I turned to Dylan, needing to see his expression to decipher the meaning of his question. He was married now, so surely he couldn't be interested in her. But he was too big of an ass to realize that he should be worried about her after betraying her for years.

"Fine."

"You told her?"

"That you knew about us all along and lied to punish us?" I clarified. "Yes. I told her. She was literally sick at the news."

"Hmm."

He actually looked remorseful. Again, I tried to think back in time, to recall when he might have learned the truth about my tryst with his ex-fiancée. Had *he* been sick when he learned? Had he avoided me? And if not, how? How had he faced me, interacted with me, treated me like everything was normal, when secretly he knew that I had betrayed him in the worst possible way?

"We aren't even, you and I," I said suddenly. "Lily and I hurt you, but you hurt us *and* Lucy. She didn't deserve that."

Dylan considered that for a minute. "True. But would it have been any different if she'd known?"

He had a point. Lily left to avoid him, to avoid us. Even if she'd known I was the father and not Dylan, maybe she wouldn't have returned any sooner. Surely I could've insisted on visiting my daughter, but would I have done so? If she'd asked me to stay away, I probably would have.

"You're a dick," I said finally. "Spot me on the second set."

Dylan nodded and stood, coming to help with my weights.

* * *

LILY

I decided to stop by Dylan's apartment on my way to talk with Thomas the next day. Since he lived down the hall from Thomas, it was inevitable that I'd see him at some point, but now that I knew he wasn't Lucy's father, I had no obligation to let her spend time with him. But I couldn't put off our conversation forever. I needed to let him vent about my betrayal, and then I needed to pay him back all the money he'd sent me the last two and a half years. I didn't want to owe Dylan anything.

I held my breath after knocking on the door.

"It's open!" called a familiar voice from within the apartment.

I hesitantly pushed the door open a few inches, certain Dylan thought his visitor was Thomas, not me. I popped my head in a few inches and immediately saw him.

Dylan was standing in the kitchen, leaned over the granite countertop reading something while gnawing on a Twizzler clutched in his hand. He wore jeans and a dark printed tee shirt and his hair was messed. He had several days worth of stubble and was barefoot. All of these observations told me Dylan was relaxed and comfortable.

I felt myself smiling by the time he glanced up at me. His face registered the shock I'd expected, but then he smiled, too. He pulled the licorice from his mouth and dropped it on the counter before approaching me.

"Lily," he said, still grinning. He kissed each of my cheeks, lingering long enough on each side to make me nervous. He smelled delicious and unexpectedly familiar.

"Dylan," I said, my voice coming out much calmer than I'd expected.

He glanced around me. "Where's the little one? With her pop?" His tone was bitter, but his face conveyed a different message altogether.

I cautiously shook my head.

"You should bring her by sometime. I'd like to meet my niece."

"Of course." I smiled politely, but his words had shocked me. I hadn't imagined he'd want to get to know the child who literally embodied the betrayal of his former fiancée and brother. "You look well," I finally said.

"I look *well*? Bloody hell. I was just thinking you looked stunning, as always."

Heat rushed to my cheeks. Dylan had always been a charmer and a flirt. He stepped closer and I sensed it—the slight electric buzz of energy still between us.

His hand grazed my cheek. "Don't blush Lily, I know what you meant. And you're right. I am well." He turned, crossed the kitchen, and opened his refrigerator, bending to glance at its contents. "I'm sure you knew that before you returned to town though. Drink?"

I nodded and he pulled out two local beers. It was far too early in the day for beer, and I'd assumed he meant water when he'd offered me a beverage. But, now that I saw the alcohol, I had no interest in saying no. He opened both bottles and slid one down the counter to me.

"Where's Patty?" I asked, more to gauge his reaction than anything else.

"Work," he replied.

I swallowed, wondering if he hadn't pressured her to quit her job like he had to me, or if she'd just been wise enough to refuse. "What kind of work does she do?"

He flashed a quirky grin. "Thomas didn't tell you?"

I shook my head. "We really haven't spoken much since I've been back."

"Patty is our publicist. Well, she was. She doesn't represent the group anymore. Conflict of interest."

I considered this for a moment. "Did I ever meet her?"

Dylan shrugged and motioned for me to join him on the couch. "Probably. She wasn't really on my radar until after… well, after I got over you."

"And when was that?"

He snorted, probably at my audacity. "I was desperate to find you, Lily, to hear your voice, to know that you were okay. You were one tough cookie to track down."

"That was intentional."

"Why?"

"Oh, Dylan," I murmured. "You know why. If I'd seen you or spoken to you even, you would've convinced me to come back. And then we'd have been right back where we were then instead of…" I couldn't decide how to finish my sentence, given that technically, we were side by side in his apartment…in the same apartment we'd shared, years ago.

He sighed. "Anyway, I finally found you, or the guy I hired did anyway, and you had a baby. At first, I just assumed you'd moved on, that you'd met someone quickly after you left. I couldn't tell how old the baby was in the photos anyway." Dylan lazily swigged his beer.

"That's when I first noticed Patty flirting with me," he continued.

I winced. Somehow I'd forgotten that this was the story of how Dylan met his wife, not a story about me. Despite everything, it still hurt to know I wasn't the center of his world anymore. It should've been a relief, and the fact that it wasn't disturbed me.

"When did you know though?" I asked, and thankfully, he knew what I was asking.

"The private investigator had mentioned the girl's name was Lucy, and I just couldn't shake the odd feeling, even months later. So I asked him to get another photo." Dylan closed his eyes momentarily. "Then I could tell. The resemblance is striking, you know. They look like twins."

I nodded. I'd seen photos of the original Lucy Parker, Dylan and Thomas' younger sister, the one who died as a child. There was an uncanny resemblance, right down to the surprisingly blue eyes.

"You must hate me," I mumbled.

Dylan's face hardened, but he shook his head. "No. I did much worse to you," he said. "Of course, I was faithful, at least." A whimsical look crossed his face. "To think you're the only woman I never cheated on, and you got up the duff with my own brother."

"What?"

He chuckled. "Knocked up."

"I'm sorry, Dylan," I said, and I was. I mean, I wasn't sorry it happened because it gave me Lucy, and she was definitely the best part of my life, but I was sorry I'd hurt him. "It wasn't a long-standing affair, you know. It was just one night."

He finished the last of his beer, tipping his head back to drain the final drops. "I should've seen it coming," he mumbled. "I practically drove you to his arms, and I knew he was in love with you."

"You did?"

"Of course. The whole bloody band, even our manager Ari, knew Thomas was in love with my fiancée. I've never seen Thomas so smitten with someone before. I'll never comprehend how you were oblivious for so long."

I sighed.

"He never moved on," Dylan said.

I swallowed uncomfortably. "I should go. I just wanted to give you this." I reached in my purse for the envelope and handed it to him.

He accepted it and curiously peered inside. He laughed, then handed it back.

I shook my head. "No, keep it. I can't pay you back everything you sent yet, but I will."

"It's yours, Lily. I don't want any of it back."

"But she's not your child to support."

"I knew that at the time I sent it to you."

I sighed. "Why did you do it, Dylan? Why didn't you just tell me?"

A lengthy silence stretched between us and the energy of the room shifted.

"Because I'm not the good brother," he said, his eyes sparkling in contrast to his devious tone.

"You are a good man, Dylan." I stood, setting the money on the counter. "And it isn't right for me to keep the money."

He stood and snatched the envelope, placing it forcefully

in my hand. "Lily, I need you to keep this, and every cent I gave you. Put it in a college fund if you don't need it." He gradually loosened the grip on my hand. "This is my way of apologizing. This is how I assuage my guilt. Please let me have that."

I nodded slowly, placing the money in my purse. I started for the door.

"You're happy now, right?"

He seemed to consider my question before nodding. "Yes."

"And you love her? Patty?"

Dylan shuffled towards the door after me. His closeness made me nervous. "Yes, Lily. Don't worry, I do."

"You seem different, calmer."

He laughed. "You drove me crazy, you know? I loved you so much and I just didn't know how to contain it all. I wanted so badly to protect you and not let you down, and then I ended up losing you anyway." He glanced to his feet, then back up to me. "I do love Patty, but it's different. I don't feel so compelled to guard her."

"You didn't have to take care of me either Dylan."

"I know. It wasn't you; it was me."

I shook my head as I stepped out of his apartment. *It was a little bit me too*, I thought.

I walked down the hall towards Thomas' apartment then paused. What was I thinking visiting Dylan right before heading to discuss custody with Thomas? Could I have picked two more stressful activities to pair back to back? Probably not. Now that I was in the same hallway, though, there was no place to run and hide. Not even a bathroom I could duck into at the end of the hall. I panicked and made my way to the elevator, pressing the Down button a second time, even though the light illuminated the first time.

"Lily?"

I swiveled around quickly at the sound of my name, mortified by the fact that I legitimately did not know which Parker brother had said it.

There stood Thomas, wearing dark slacks and a long-sleeved button down that looked ridiculously soft. Not that I was going to touch it. He eyed me warily.

"Did you leave something in your car?" he asked.

I shook my head. "No, I was…heading out for coffee. I thought it would be nice to bring you coffee."

He nodded slowly. "I have coffee. Although you seem…jittery. You want decaf?"

I blew out a sigh. "I'll get it. Can I get you some?"

"Sure," he said, still looking at me like I was a poisonous snake. "Pods are in that top drawer."

I tugged the drawer open, rolling my eyes at the predictability of Thomas having all of his coffees sorted by type. Organization was definitely more his thing than Dylan's. He had infinitely more Colombian than any other variety, so I assumed that was his favorite. I asked and that was what he wanted. I decided decaf was a good idea for me.

"You went to see my brother, didn't you?"

"Yeah." I opened his fridge, trying to locate cream. Finding none, I pulled out a quart of milk.

"I thought you drank it black."

"I did. Now I don't. I gave up trying to be skinny. It was pointless after pregnancy."

Thomas raised an eyebrow. "You're still skinny."

"Do you want milk in yours?"

"Yeah. And sugar please."

I spotted the sugar bowl behind the coffee pot and dropped a sugar cube into his mug.

"How was Dylan?"

His question piqued my interest. "Haven't you spoken to him since he returned?"

He nodded. "Yes."

Nothing good could come of me discussing Dylan with Thomas. I carried our coffees over to the end table between the couch where he sat and the armchair where I'd left my notepad. I set them on the wood. Wordlessly, Thomas slid a coaster under each mug. Another reminder that he was nothing like his brother.

I gazed down at my notepad to get focused on the important topics at hand.

"So," I began, focusing on keeping my tone as business-like as possible, "In light of Dylan's admission, what do you want to do? If you're amenable to the idea, we could try to figure out an arrangement without attorneys."

Thomas bit his lip, but the dimple in his right cheek revealed his struggle not to laugh. "Yes, I'm amenable to that idea."

I tilted my head. "What is so funny? This is a serious discussion."

He smiled. "I know that, Lily, but we're friends, aren't we? Or at least we were, and I'd like to think we could be again. We don't need to be this formal."

"Of course we're friends, Thomas." I paused, painfully aware I could never truly be friends with him, at least not anytime soon. "So what do you want?"

"Pardon?"

"Well, you want to spend time with Lucy, right?"

His eyes widened. "Certainly."

"Okay, do you want to say once a week, or every other weekend, or what?"

"Lily, this is completely unnecessary." His face wrinkled up as he turned to me. "I want to spend time with her when I can, not on some stupid schedule. Why don't we all hang out together so she can get comfortable with me and then when you're both up for it, I can spend some time alone with her?"

I hadn't expected that at all. I'd been prepared for a tedious discussion, and now, I began to realize how illogical my worries had been.

As if determined to prove to me how ridiculous my fears were, Thomas continued. "You know, I'm home some during the days. I could probably watch her some while you're working. After she is more accustomed to being alone with me. Unless that makes you uncomfortable."

"Uh, no, that's…fine." My mind started to whirl already. If my mom and Thomas could split care of her enough that I could drop from daycare to just a regular preschool, that would be really helpful for my finances. And since he was technically her parent too, it wasn't like I was accepting a handout to let Thomas watch Lucy while I worked.

But we weren't there yet. Thomas barely knew Lucy, let alone how to care for her.

"Where are you guys living?"

"We're still staying with my parents for now. I've been looking at apartments near there."

"But the school you work at is in Jersey City?"

I nodded.

"Why not get a place there? They have some great areas downtown, and it's a quick commute to Manhattan."

"It's a little out of our price range." Okay, it was *a lot* out of my price range. "And I don't want to put Lucy in full time day care or spend all day in the car shuffling her back and forth from my parents."

"Fine, I'll stay out of that. But if you need a good realtor, let me know." He pulled out his checkbook. "So about the money. How much was Dylan sending you?"

"He sent me a check for five thousand every few months."

Thomas glanced up as though he was doing mental math.

"Look, Thomas, I really don't need your money. I get health insurance through my job and my parents watch Lucy for free."

"I'll probably need Lucy's social security number," Thomas

said without acknowledging what I'd said. "I'm adding her to my life insurance and will, and getting a college fund set up. I was thinking about a trust fund too, since we both know my income will probably slow down at some point here."

He scrawled on the check, tore it loose from the checkbook, and slid it across the table to me. I took one glance at it and slid it right back to him.

"Thomas, that's way too much."

"I haven't given you a cent for three years, Lily. It's nowhere close to what I should be giving you, but I just don't want to muck up either of our taxes before I speak with my accountant." He pushed the check back to me.

"What am I supposed to do with this?"

He shrugged. "Use it for a deposit on a new apartment or a down payment on a condo. Enroll Lucy in one of those fancy private preschools. Buy clothes, purses, shoes, whatever."

"You can't spend child support on purses and shoes," I snapped.

He sighed. "You and I both know you will spend it responsibly. I only mean that I don't need an accounting of what it goes for."

"I don't feel right about accepting this," I said, shaking my head.

Thomas rolled his eyes. "Do you have any idea how much money Dylan and I make these days? I want my child to be raised with any benefit that money can bring her. I'm not saying you have to spoil her, but I don't want to argue every time I give you a check."

I clenched my teeth together, trying to figure out how to make him understand. "Thomas, with everything that happened with Dylan, it's important to me that I be able to support myself and Lucy. You have no idea how terrifying it was to have to decide which was worse for my child—trying to raise her on my own with no job, no income, and no apartment because I gave it all up for Dylan, or staying with someone who could support her financially but might ruin her emotionally."

His jaw tightened into a hard line. "You could have asked me for any amount of money, Lily, and I would've given it to you, no questions asked."

I swallowed hard, hating the way it made me feel to know that he was telling the truth. "For Lucy's sake, I can't be completely financially dependent on a man. Any man."

He seemed to consider this. "Fine, then start up a savings account. Put whatever money you don't need there, and then if anything ever happens, you'll have it."

I chewed the inside of my mouth while I considered this. It did make sense. I would still have my own income, but I wouldn't be increasing our debt each month. That could only be good, long term. "Fine."

He leaned forward, pretending he was trying to see my notepad. "What else is on the agenda? Shall I be taking notes or will you be typing up the minutes?" he teased.

I firmly shut the notepad. "I just don't want to mess this up. I've already made enough mistakes with Lucy, and you, and…"

Thomas reached forward and placed his hand over mine. "Lily, give yourself some credit. You uprooted your entire life to protect our daughter. You've raised a smart, funny, and precocious child. And you were willing to give up the love of your life —and his no-good younger brother—just for her."

Heat rushed to my cheeks from the compliment before I fully put together the implication of his last sentence. Once I did, I had to look away. Surely, he was kidding. Thomas didn't actually think he was the love of my life…did he?

His phone buzzed, snapping us both out of the moment.

"I can go. You must have things to do."

"Please don't," he quickly replied. "I want to talk more about Lucy."

I swallowed the lump in my throat and started to reach for my pen.

"No, not that stuff. I want to know more about her. What was she like as a baby? When did she walk? What was her first word?"

An uncomfortable laugh escaped my lips at the unexpected questions.

"Bubble," I said, answering the last question first. "Her first word was 'bubble.'"

"What? Not mama?"

I laughed and shook my head.

He asked a few more questions, but before I could answer, he waved his hands. "Wait, wait. Don't tell me about this stuff yet. Lucy should be here when you do. Maybe you could bring some pictures next time you two come 'round and we could look at them together? I'm sure she'd love hearing the stories about herself as a baby just as much as I would."

Thomas was right about that. Lucy's favorite line of stories were the 'Little Lucy' ones, as I called them. "I kept a pretty detailed baby book, actually. Recorded every little detail and took tons of pictures. And I have detailed emails I sent my parents."

He smiled, but I detected a distinct hint of sadness at that. I tried to think of something else to talk about, but he beat me to it.

"How was your pregnancy?"

I shrugged. "Not terrible. I had morning sickness at the start, but I was so miserable and stressed out about the move, that it's hard to say how much of my exhaustion and nausea was the pregnancy and how much of it was the pitiful state of my life." I paused. "I got a job waiting tables right away and then found a librarian position by third trimester, which was good timing. That way I wasn't on my feet the entire time."

"Any strange cravings?"

I cringed, visions of Dylan in his kitchen flitting through my mind. "Licorice, actually. I couldn't get enough of it."

"Hmm. I'll have to remember that," he said.

"Don't bother. I can't stand it now."

"How odd."

"I didn't eat poultry the entire pregnancy. The smell of it—no matter how it was cooked—disgusted me. And then, the first thing I ate in the hospital was chicken tenders."

Thomas cocked his head to the side, smiling.

We talked more about those first several months we were apart. I had completely lost track of time when Thomas' phone buzzed again and I realized it was already an hour past the time I'd told my mom I'd be home.

* * *

THOMAS

I'd accomplished nothing between the time that Lily left my apartment and when I was due to attend a band meeting. We had a hefty list of topics to discuss at the meeting, but I still hadn't cleared my mind. Since the meeting was at the office of our manager, Ari, I decided to walk. Hopefully, the fresh air would calm me.

Apparently, Dylan had opted for a different method of self-medicating, as he reeked of booze when he arrived. I didn't comment on it, nor did anyone else. Since checking out of rehab nearly four years prior, Dylan hadn't touched a single illegal drug to my knowledge. But he'd resumed drinking and occasionally smoking the second he was home. From what little I knew of addiction, that wasn't the right approach. Even though his problem had been with drugs, I suspected he was supposed to avoid all addictive substances, including alcohol.

Still, as long as he kept the drinking under control and it didn't affect the band, I'd never seen a reason to complain.

"Well, Thomas, why don't you share your news with everyone?" Dylan suggested, smiling drunkenly.

I gazed around the table, noting the entire band was already there. Ari and one of his interns were also at the table.

The guys all turned to me. I cleared my throat and glanced at Dylan. They'd find out eventually, but this didn't seem like an appropriate time to share. Unfortunately, my brother didn't share my sense of timing.

"He's a father!" Dylan said.

They all looked predictably surprised, but congratulated me.

"Uh yeah, thanks," I said, ready to move on to relevant band business.

"Was I the only one who assumed that, between the two of them, Dylan would be the first to knock up a girl?" Owen asked.

Gavin and Dave chuckled and nodded in agreement.

"Well, it's funny you should mention that," Dylan said. "Because especially if you knew who the mother is, you'd probably have guessed I'd be the father of her child. But nope."

My bandmates' faces were a mixture of curiosity and confusion now.

Trying to dispel the awkwardness, Ari asked if I had a photo. Luckily, I did. I showed the photo on my phone and everyone commented on how adorable she was.

"How old is she?" Owen asked.

"Almost three and half."

"And you just found out about her?"

I nodded.

"No denying that girl is yours though," Gavin said. "What's her name?"

"Lucy."

"Named after our sister," Dylan added.

"Wait, so who is her mother? Anyone we know?" Owen asked, his eyebrows furrowed. "I can't even remember who you were dating four years ago."

"He wasn't dating the girl's mother. I was," Dylan said.

They all fell silent for what seemed to be a full minute. Every passing second was painfully awkward.

"Wait, so you had a baby with…Lily?" Dave finally asked, pointing to me.

"While she was engaged to me," Dylan added unnecessarily.

"Yes," I said, clearing my throat.

"Shit," Ari mumbled, rubbing his temples like he was getting a migraine.

I'd never been on the receiving end of judgmental stares in my life and I didn't enjoy it. I was accustomed to Dylan being the disappointment to everyone. I shifted the burden as quickly as I could. "Dylan knew Lucy was mine for years and didn't even let me know I had a child."

Now the glares switched to him.

"Okay, enough. I can't handle any more of this soap opera." Ari said. "We need to finalize your performance schedule and discuss some ideas for the music video."

Slowly, everyone's attention shifted back to work. I knew the guys now viewed me differently, though, and I couldn't even say it wasn't deserved.

CHAPTER FIVE

"If I loved you less, I might be able to talk about it more."
Jane Austen, *Emma*

THOMAS

The next week was idyllic. On Monday, Lily brought Lucy over after school. We played the piano briefly, then flipped through the baby book together. Like a family. Lucy giggled uproariously at the plethora of pictures of herself as an infant and we both listened, enthralled, as Lily shared every detail of Lucy's various misadventures.

I cherished every story, adored every picture, hung on Lily's every word. I felt a warmth and a deeper happiness inside that wasn't my usual sentiment. But at the same time, every bit of it was a painful reminder of everything I'd missed. And I had missed a lot.

Sure, it was just three years, but it was a busy three years. Lucy had experienced her first smile, her first step, her first tooth, and her first birthday, and I'd missed it all. She'd said her first word, gotten her first hair cut, and attended her first day of preschool. I wasn't there for any of that, either.

"My mother is expecting us for dinner," Lily said, much earlier than I would've liked. "I can leave the album here, though, if you want to borrow it."

I nodded.

"We could come back Thursday, if you'd like?"

I clicked on my calendar. "Band stuff. Friday?"

Lily hesitated before agreeing.

"We could order pizza. Do you like pizza, Lucy?"

She nodded vigorously.

I stood and walked closer to Lily as she collected their coats. "Dylan mentioned wanting to meet her. I told him I thought it was too soon. But if you disagree, he could maybe drop by just to say hi on Friday, not to stay for pizza or anything."

Lily rubbed her forehead along her eyebrows and I wished I hadn't said anything.

"Let me think about it, okay? I mean, I know he'll meet her eventually, but…"

I placed my hand on her shoulder. "Hey, it's fine. Either way, no worries. My feelings certainly won't be hurt." I, of course, couldn't say the same for my brother, since he didn't seem to have human emotions most of the time. But when it came to Lily, he'd always had an excess of feelings.

"You should invite Dylan and Patty for pizza," she said.

That sounded horribly awkward, but Dylan dropped by a few minutes later as if on cue, asking if I had plans Friday.

"Lily is bringing Lucy by for pizza. You can come by if you want to meet her."

Dylan looked intrigued by this idea. "What kind of pizza?" he asked after several moments.

I flung my hands into the air.

"Jesus bloody Christ, Tom, I'm kidding," Dylan said. "What time? Like uh 7:30?"

I sighed. "She's three, Dylan. She goes to bed at 7:30. We'll be eating around 5:30."

"Do you want me to?"

"I don't know," I answered honestly. "You'll meet her eventually, so I suppose you might as well."

"And Lily is okay with this?"

I nodded.

"Who does Lucy think I am?"

"Nobody," I said. "She doesn't even know who I am yet. She calls me Mister Thomas."

"You haven't told her?" His tone was filled with accusation.

"She barely knows me. She just moved to a different state and is attending a new preschool and she already has a lot of other adjustments. I'm not going to add something else to her plate right now."

Dylan pursed his lips. "So she won't be calling me Uncle Dylan?"

"Not just yet."

He shrugged. "Okay. Save me some pizza."

On Friday evening, Lily brought Lucy over right after school ended for the both of them. Lucy immediately scampered into the music room, but having already practiced once that week, she grew bored quickly. When the pizza arrived, I cleared my throat and opened my cupboard, making a big show of gesturing to the two brand-new sippy cups positioned front and center on the bottom shelf.

"Thank you," Lily said, turning to Lucy. "Do you want the pink one or the purple one?"

"Pink," Lucy said.

I filled Lucy's cup with milk then offered Lily some wine. Surprisingly, she accepted. Perhaps she was as uneasy about Dylan's impending visit as I was.

Lucy picked up her slice of pizza in both hands and ate just like a grown up, albeit smearing considerably more sauce around her face than an adult would.

I chuckled and handed her a napkin. She eyed it suspiciously.

"Lucy, did you know that I have a younger brother?" I began.

Lucy shook her head.

"His name is Dylan. He looks a lot like me, only much less dapper."

She frowned and turned to Lily, who explained, "That means handsome, or pretty."

Lucy giggled. "Boys aren't pretty."

"Well, anyway, when you come over here, you know how you ride an elevator to this floor, and then you go down the hallway to my apartment? If you go the other direction, you'd reach my brother's apartment."

I paused to let all of this sink in.

"He might come by and say hi later. I told him I've been getting to spend some time with a sweet little girl and he wanted to meet you, too."

Lily smiled, signaling her approval. Lucy clearly was unaffected by all of this. She peeled the rest of the cheese off her pizza and then made a face at the saucy, crusty remnants.

Lily removed the offending pizza parts off of Lucy's plate and offered her a new slice.

"How was school today?" I asked.

"Are you asking me or her?" Lily said after a lengthy silence.

"You."

"Oh. Um, it was okay, I guess. I really like the school, it's just a lot different from the one in Michigan where I subbed. I've had to start from scratch with my lesson plans, so it's a lot of work after hours."

"I'm happy to watch Lucy in the afternoons or evening so you can get more work done. I can pick her up from daycare if you like, or you're welcome to work here while she plays. I was thinking I'd get some toys for my apartment."

Lily's expression softened and she parted her lips as though about to speak. Before she said anything though, there was a knock at the door.

"Speak of the devil," I mumbled, even though we hadn't actually been speaking about Dylan just then.

I peeked out the peephole before opening the door to my brother.

He offered me a casual nod, but I could've sworn he actually looked nervous. He peered past me to the table, staring for a moment before stepping fully into the apartment. The tension in the room was palpable.

I waited for him to say something, then realized I was the one who should speak. I stepped back, motioning for him to enter, then turned to Lucy. She eyed him with a slight hint of curiosity, then quickly turned back to her pizza.

"Lucy," I began, waiting until she faced us again. "This is my brother. His name is Dylan."

Dylan stepped closer and smiled awkwardly.

Lucy made a funny face, then giggled. "You don't look the same," she said in a silly voice. "Do you have a sister?"

Lily leaned over so quickly that her bracelet clanged into her wine glass, causing a loud chime.

I cringed, grateful she recognized how uncomfortable her daughter's question could've been, but wishing she'd just let it go.

"Lucy, when you meet someone new, you say 'nice to meet you.' Remember?"

"Nice to meet you," Lucy repeated, looking serious for about a nanosecond before sticking out her tongue and blowing raspberries then laughing uproariously.

Dylan shrugged. "A lady after my own heart, I see." He bent down beside her. "It's a pleasure to meet you too, Miss Lucy."

She didn't respond, so he walked away to help himself to the pizza. Even though I'd set a plate for him, he grabbed one slice in each hand and began eating one while walking over to the table. Lucy watched him curiously now.

He finished his first slice in record time, then wiped his hands on his jeans and leaned forward. "Has your mother told you about our sister?"

I shook my head rapidly, certain this was not a safe topic of discussion for the evening, but Dylan's eyes were squarely focused on Lucy. She too shook her head, but in the intrigued way that simply encouraged him to say more.

"When our sister was your age, she was so beautiful. In fact, she looked just like you."

"Was she a princess?"

Dylan chuckled. "Technically no, but she acted like one. She loved wearing skirts and she played the piano."

Lucy gasped. "I play the piano."

Dylan nodded knowingly. "I'd love to hear that after we eat." He started on his next slice of pizza, carrying it with him to the kitchen and helping himself to a beer from my fridge. He held it up, turning to confirm Lucy was still watching him. "Do you drink beer Lucy?"

Now she laughed even harder. "No, silly, I'm a kid."

I wiped my mouth on a napkin and reached for my wine. I drank thirstily, focusing on the deep burgundy of the wine rather than the jealousy rising in my chest. She'd only just met him and already *my* daughter liked Dylan better. Why shouldn't she? Lily chose him over me, it was only fitting for Lucy to do the same. Only this time, I wasn't going to sit back and let it happen. He wasn't going to take my own daughter from me. Not again.

"Tom?"

I jolted out of my thoughts, realizing the wine glass I still held to my lips was now empty. I turned to Dylan, aware he'd asked me some question I hadn't heard, but he simply nodded to Lily.

"Do you want more wine?" she asked. Her voice remained

calm even though I assumed she'd already posed the question at least once.

I nodded and slid my glass closer to her. She poured a sizable portion, then smiled. The way her eyes focused on me, I wondered if she could read my mind, if she suspected the heinous thoughts I'd been entertaining about Dylan. I stared back, but she quickly averted her eyes. I was about to do the same, then stopped. If I had an opportunity to watch Lily, I might as well use it.

For the most part, whenever I'd seen her lately, I'd been preoccupied with Lucy. Now that Lucy was entertained by her new favorite person, though, I was free to admire her mother. Time really had been generous to Lily. She'd always been gorgeous, but she'd only become more striking with age. The sharper angles of her face had softened, leaving her beautiful and prominent cheekbones, but protecting her from any hint of wrinkles and making her already idyllic lips even fuller.

Her hair was still long, but now seemed even glossier than before. I suspected she no longer had the same amount of time to dedicate to her style, and that this hands-off approach had resulted in healthier, shinier hair. She also wore less makeup now, which also suited her well. She was still thin, but I couldn't help but appreciate the more feminine curves accenting her figure.

Mostly, though, she seemed to carry herself differently now. She'd never been shy, but I wouldn't have described her as confident four years ago. Now, she didn't walk so much as sashay. Her steps were purposeful. And she meant business.

She turned back to me, raising an eyebrow, and I couldn't help but smile. Somehow, just by staring at her, all the tension, anger, and jealousy I felt towards Dylan had melted away, at least for the moment.

"Do you know the most interesting part of it all?" Dylan was asking.

Lucy leaned forward, hanging on his every word.

"My sister's name is Lucy," he said.

"Our," I interrupted, correcting him. "Our sister."

He nodded as though that were an insignificant distinction. Lucy's jaw literally dropped. She gazed from Dylan to Lily then back to Dylan.

"That's my name!" she squealed.

Dylan nodded eagerly. "Your mummy has excellent taste in names. And a beautiful, talented girl like you should have a beautiful name." He pushed his plate to the middle of the table. "Now, are you going to show me how you play piano?"

Lucy jumped eagerly from the table. I peered at her plate, noting she hadn't touched her fruit.

"You didn't finish…" I began.

Lily shook her head, waving her hand in the air with a smile. She stood and began clearing the table. Not sure I could stomach watching the nauseatingly sweet display of affection between dear uncle Dylan and Lucy, I quickly helped. Once the dishes were all in the kitchen, I told Lily I'd finish up. She worked so hard already, she shouldn't have to help when she came to my place. She deserved a break.

But as I watched her take a seat by the piano, smiling admiringly at Dylan, I wished I'd kept my mouth shut. I didn't want to see her with him, certainly not looking at him.

Even after all these years, I was still haunted by visions of it, that twinkly doe-eyed look Lily got whenever my brother was in the room. She'd been a fan of the band before they met, and right up until the bitter end, she still gazed at him with that same innocent obliviousness of a mere groupie. He'd been perfect in her eyes, even when he so clearly wasn't.

A wine glass slid out of my hands as I rinsed the soap, clanking loudly against the side of the sink without shattering. Lily didn't even glance up. Her eyes were glued to the piano, staring at my brother like he was playing a Stravinsky movement and not *Three Blind Mice*. She was so enamored with Dylan that the whole fucking house could probably burn down, and she wouldn't even notice.

It was too much for me. I finished rinsing the glass and flipped it upside down on a clean towel draped across the counter. Then I walked to the door and left my own apartment. As I reached the elevator, a flash of regret washed over me at the awareness that I'd forgotten my jacket, but I didn't care. I wasn't going back in there. Not now.

I punched the Down button, then winced, hearing my apartment door open. I had nothing to say to Dylan now. Nothing nice, anyway.

"Tell Lily I had to run out," I mumbled gruffly, inching closer to the elevator.

"Tell me yourself."

I swiveled to face her, already feeling the heat rush to my cheeks. I quickly tried to think of an excuse for my quick exit, something other than a tantrum over the fact that she kept choosing the wrong man.

I opened my lips to launch into my explanation, but no words came to me. A crease formed along her brow as she pulled my apartment door shut behind her and stepped closer.

"Are you alright?"

Again, I tried to say something, then gave up, shaking my head. The elevator beeped to signal its arrival and I exhaled. "Dylan can lock up. I'll um…we'll talk later," I said, stepping on to the elevator.

Lily rushed forward, thrusting her hand over the door. "Thomas, wait."

The intensity of her voice startled me enough that I actually looked up at her.

"I don't understand what happened," she said.

I swallowed the lump in my throat. "I'll call you tomorrow."

She moved her hand as the high pitch buzzing of the door

sensor signaled its wish to close. I stared at my shoes until I reached the lobby.

* * *

LILY

Lucy and I stayed at Thomas' apartment, with Dylan, for over a half hour after Thomas left. Not because I had any hope that he'd return that night, but because Lucy was enthralled with her uncle. I was tempted to text Thomas, to ask for some explanation, but I stopped myself. He had a chance to tell me and had chosen not to.

When Lucy had finally tired of Dylan, he'd turned to me and quirked an eyebrow. "Where'd Thomas run off to?"

I shrugged, shaking my head. "He said for you to lock up."

"A moody bugger, isn't he," Dylan mumbled. He leaned in to hug me then crouched down to bid Lucy a more enthusiastic farewell. "She's delightful, Lily," he said as he rose to his feet. "Thank you."

I forced a smile, then focused on getting Lucy home and to bed.

By morning, I still hadn't heard anything from Thomas, and my mom wanted to take Lucy shopping, so I decided to return to the scene of the crime.

I didn't call first, telling myself I'd just do some shopping in the neighborhood if he wasn't home. But when I reached the lobby of his building, the doorman greeted me cheerily. It was the same man who'd been on duty the night before. A twinge of guilt hit me for not knowing his name, since he clearly knew who I was.

"Where's the little one?" he asked.

"She's, uh, with her grandma," I said, unsure how much he knew about our situation. "Is Thomas in? He's not expecting me."

The man shrugged. "I believe so. You can head on up."

I hesitated, noting he hadn't even called up. Was I already on the list of approved visitors? What did that even mean?

When I reached his door and knocked, it was several minutes before I heard any noise inside the apartment. Finally, Thomas answered the door, wearing a pair of thin, grey sweatpants and nothing else. He looked every bit as surprised to see me as I was to see his attire.

My eyes automatically drifted to his chest, and I fully drank in the sight of him before turning away. His skin still bore the remnants of a summer tan and his entire torso appeared to be chiseled out of some exquisite rock. A light dusting of soft brown hair led from his belly button downward.

"Lily," he said, prompting me to talk.

"I'm sorry," I said, squeezing my eyes shut and not reopening them until I had angled my head upwards. "I thought the doorman would've called up."

He shook his head, running a finger through his messy hair. "No, I told them you're welcome whenever. Is everything okay?"

"Were you sleeping?" I asked, ignoring his question. It seemed a ridiculous notion. I'd been up for hours already, having taken a brisk jog, fed Lucy breakfast, then graded papers while enjoying my own oatmeal and coffee. But gazing down at my watch, I saw that it was only 9:45. "Shit. You were," I realized.

He nodded towards his apartment. "Come in."

I did.

"No Lucy?"

"She's shopping with my mom."

He ambled over to his coffee maker, handing me the first cup he prepared.

"Thanks." I sat on a barstool with my mug, wrapping my fingers around it and absorbing its warmth. Thomas kept his back to me while he waited for his own cup to fill, letting me observe that his back was every bit as muscular as his front.

My hands flew back from the mug as, suddenly, I was too hot.

Thomas offered me milk and sugar then gazed down, as though just realizing he was shirtless. "Be right back," he mumbled, almost sheepishly.

I wanted to protest, to let him know he didn't need to dress on my account, but before I could think of a tactful way to phrase it, he was back, wearing a sleeveless undershirt. He sat beside me, staring straight ahead. I bit back a smile, wondering if it was possible for a man to look even sexier like this.

"You've been working out," I said, cursing my lack of filter as soon as the words left my mouth.

Thomas followed my gaze to his biceps then frowned as though confused. "Yeah. I guess so."

He guessed so? His arms were nearly twice the size as the last time I'd seen him without a shirt. And he was hot then, but this was...

Jesus. I needed to get to the point before I said something even stupider.

"When you left last night, I was worried."

Thomas sipped his coffee, then set his mug gingerly on the counter. He said nothing.

"Was everything okay?"

He nodded.

I waited, taking a deep breath in and exhaling fully. But still he was quiet. Fine. I reached for my own coffee. Two could play the silent game.

After another minute, though, I gave up. "I'll get out of your hair. I'm sorry I woke you, and I'm sorry for whatever I did to piss you off last night." I stood, then paused. "Although, if you won't tell me what I did, I really don't know how I can make sure I don't do it again."

I reached for my purse but the strap caught on the chair, nearly toppling it over as I tugged. Thomas steadied the chair with his hand, then brushed his fingers across mine.

I stiffened at the unexpected contact, my eyes rising to meet his. He looked tired. Or maybe just hungover. But I could've sworn there was a hint of sadness too.

"You didn't do anything, and I'm not pissed off."

I didn't have an answer for that, since he was still avoiding eye contact and treating me like he was mad.

"Then why did you leave?"

His eyes drifted shut as he blew out a sigh. "I couldn't handle seeing you look at him like that," he said.

I was about to ask who I was looking at and like what, but there was only one possible explanation. "Dylan?"

Thomas thrust his hand through his hair again. "He's no good for you."

I felt my temper start to flare. Was he seriously accusing me of hitting on his brother? His married brother? With my child right there? "How exactly do you think I was looking at him, Thomas? What are you trying to say?"

"It's your life, Lily. But I'm telling you now that I can't handle watching you fall for Dylan all over again. I won't."

I flung my hands in the air, nearly knocking over my coffee mug. "I wasn't looking at Dylan any particular way. When they were playing piano together, I was watching Lucy. I was thinking about how happy Lucy was, how much she reminds me of you already, and how stupid I was to keep her from you for so long."

I paused, clenching my teeth together to keep from crying. "I wasn't looking at Dylan. I'm not falling for Dylan. I have no interest whatsoever in your brother."

Our eyes met as I finished talking and I watched his expression change. He didn't speak right away, though.

"You don't have feelings for Dylan," he repeated.

"No," I said, even though he hadn't phrased it like a question.

"Because he's married?"

I sighed. I had no intention of ever sleeping with a married man, or cheating on anyone in any capacity every again, but that wasn't the main reason. "I just…don't feel that way about him anymore. I can't explain it, but the feelings are gone. And I'm glad."

Thomas' relief was palpable.

"That's seriously why you stormed out? You thought I was still in love with Dylan?"

He chewed the inside of his lip then cast a sideways glance at me. "The way you were watching…Lucy…last night. That's the same way you used to look at him. It just felt a little too familiar, me standing on the sidelines while you ogle him, blinded to reality."

"Thanks," I mumbled, rolling my eyes.

"You know what I mean."

I did, and it still was offensive.

"It wasn't just that," he finally said, standing to help himself to more coffee. "The way he was with Lucy. She loves him. She warmed instantly to him."

I cringed, having noticed the same thing. "She loves you, too,' I said, painfully aware of how lame that sounded. "Besides, that's how it's supposed to be. He's supposed to be the fun one. The one who just drops in for these little chunks of time where everything is pizza and candy and games. You're her father, so you get to deal with all the serious stuff. But that's the more important role."

He seemed to consider that for a moment before shaking his head. "I get it, but that doesn't make it any easier. After watching you choose him over me, it's not easy to see my own daughter do the same thing."

I nudged my coffee cup across the counter until he took the hint and made me a second cup as well.

"I don't get why you're so insecure. He's not even the one I'm attracted to now," I said. Then I snapped my lips shut, acutely aware of what I'd just implied. I quickly tried to think of a new, innocuous topic, but Thomas had already stopped what he was doing with the coffee. Actually, he might have stopped breathing altogether.

Shit.

He swiveled around slowly, his eyes fiercely green as they locked on me. I drew in a shaky breath and dropped my gaze to the counter.

"What did you say?" he asked, his voice deep and husky.

"I…nothing." I paused, feeling stupid for even pretending to think he hadn't heard me. Obviously, he already knew what I'd said. "You know what I meant."

He crossed the room in two large strides, overbearing me with his sudden proximity as he leaned down, pressing his elbows onto the counter. I inhaled sharply. For someone who'd just woken up, he smelled…enticing.

"I'm not certain I do," he said. "Care to explain?"

I could feel the intensity of his gaze burning into me, so I raised my eyes, determined to bravely meet him head on. I paused at his lips, his soft full lips, surely still warm from his last sip of coffee.

"You know how you look," I finally mumbled, tearing my eyes from his mouth just as his lips twitched, signaling his efforts to fight back a smile. They sold posters with his photo on them for Christ's sake. Thomas couldn't possibly be oblivious to the effect he had on women.

"I've seen a mirror, but what I'm asking is how *you* think I look."

How *I* thought he looked? Hmm… seductive, arousing, delicious? He was so close now that I could kiss him if I dared. I could taste his sweet lips, feel their warmth as his tongue swept through my mouth and his palms pressed against my skin, working their way up…

Shit. Shit. Shit.

"I should go," I said, swallowing the excess of liquid that had gathered in my mouth while I fantasized about kissing him.

He stared at me for another moment, his eyes scanning me, searching for…something. Then he stood upright and the spell was broken.

"Have dinner with me tonight," he said.

"We had dinner with you last night."

"Just you tonight," he clarified.

I stood, bracing myself on the counter until I was certain my legs would actually support me. "It's not just me anymore."

He didn't answer and didn't seem surprised or upset at my response. He watched me walk to the door, but said nothing as I let myself out. I waited until I was alone in the hall to exhale the tension with a dramatic whoosh.

I pressed the button for the elevator and gazed back at his apartment door. If there was one thing I knew about Thomas Parker, it was that he was a patient man. He could bide his time like nobody's business. As far as I could tell, he'd waited for me for years. And now, thanks to my big mouth, I'd just given him reason to keep on waiting.

Crap.

CHAPTER SIX

THOMAS

I didn't think I'd hear from Lily before our scheduled piano lesson on Tuesday, so when she called Monday, my first thought was that she was cancelling. I knew what I'd seen in her eyes that weekend. Lust. She wanted me as much as I wanted her. She'd basically said as much. But I'd also seen regret and fear. She wasn't going to give me a chance anytime soon, nor would she acknowledge her feelings. Probably she'd just avoid me like the plague until enough time passed for me to have forgotten.

As if I could.

"Are we still on for tomorrow?" she asked, quickly amending, "You and Lucy, I mean?"

"Yes."

"Do you think…I mean, would it be okay if I left for a little bit, while Lucy is at your place?"

I frowned, replaying her words in my head until I was confident I'd heard her correctly. "You want to drop her off?"

"Well, I'd come in, of course. I can stay until she's comfortable," she said.

Apparently I'd underestimated her. "So you *are* avoiding me."

"No!"

The speed of her reply confirmed my statement.

"I thought you wanted time alone with her," she said after a pause.

Lily was the one I wanted to be alone with. I wanted time with Lucy, yes, but I wasn't sure it mattered if we were alone or not.

"There's an apartment I'd like to see. Their office closes at 7," she said, finally offering a legit excuse.

"Where is it?"

She told me the cross streets. It was a good location, not too far from her school and not too far from Lucy's preschool.

"I thought you couldn't afford that area," I reminded her.

She breathed heavily into the phone. "It's a nice apartment," she finally said, not exactly addressing my question.

"Sure. Drop her off whenever. We'll be just fine. You could join us for dinner after, if you'd like," I added, grinning at the image in my head of her nervously biting her lip.

"I…um…it'll probably be late, so…"

"Of course. I'll just plan to feed Lucy then."

She thanked me and hung up.

Come Tuesday, Lucy scampered into my apartment without a care in the world. I didn't think she would've noticed if her mother had simply dropped her at the door, except that Lily came in, hovered for several minutes, and repeatedly told her she was leaving. Lily handed me lengthy note about caring for Lucy, essentially read the entire dossier aloud to me, then confirmed twice that I had her cell phone number.

By the time she finally left, I was actually nervous that I wouldn't be capable of keeping Lucy alive the full two hours Lily anticipated being gone, let alone manage to entertain her. Of course, my worries were unwarranted. We played piano for a few minutes before switching to the violin. I let her strum with her fingers, rather than a bow, and delighted in the screeches she produced almost as much as she did.

When Lily called to say she'd be back shortly, Lucy had finished dinner and I was reading books to her on the couch. Though I suspected the reason for her call was to give me time to get Lucy ready to leave, I made no such efforts, determined to force Lily inside for a few minutes.

My plan worked. Lily looked exhausted when she arrived, but smiled seeing Lucy happily seated on the couch wearing the adorable nightgown and slippers I'd found in her bag.

"She dribbled some ice cream on her shirt," I said, explaining the change of clothes.

"Thank you," Lily said, still staring at Lucy.

I wondered if she'd just missed the child that much or if she was avoiding eye contact with me.

"Can I get you a glass of wine?" I offered. "Or tea?"

Lily hesitated before shaking her head. "I should get her home."

I nodded. "How was the apartment?"

"Gorgeous, but…" she shook her head. "We can find something in a better price range. The rent alone was at the top end, and I hadn't realized there were so many extra fees. I actually haven't ever rented something on my own. There's a lot I didn't know."

Before I could say anything, she started over to Lucy, tickling her before lifting her up in her arms. She carried her into the kitchen and confirmed everything was back in the bag. I wrestled Lucy into her coat and hugged her, my heart nearly skipping a beat when she pressed a quick, slobbery kiss on my cheek and then giggled uproariously.

The feeling was indescribable. It would be one thing to know the child liked me because I was her father, but this was different. She liked me for me. She didn't even know who I was to her.

I turned to Lily and saw she, too, was smiling.

"We should go," she said. "Thanks again."

I was so distracted by my happiness over Lucy's farewell kiss that I let them leave without saying anything else about the apartment. But when I floated back to earth a while later, I sent her a text.

"You should get the apartment. I'll pay for it all. For Lucy."

I clicked 'send' then stared at my phone. After a minute, the little dots appeared, indicating she was typing a response. But then, shortly after that, the dots disappeared, and no answer ever came.

* * *

LILY

The following Saturday, Lucy and I went to my friend Jill's house. Even though we were absolutely nothing alike, Jill and I had been close for years. And now that she and her husband Scott had finally welcomed their first child into the world, Jill and I had something in common—motherhood.

"God, she's just precious," I said, sniffing Elise's nearly-bald head for the billionth time. "Almost makes me want to have another."

Jill wrinkled her nose. "I can't imagine ever doing this again. Pregnancy wasn't that terrible, but the whole delivery..." she shuddered. "And this newborn stage is rough. That sleep deprivation is no joke. I don't know how you did it all alone."

Words couldn't express how hard it had been. Hard in every possible meaning of the word. So, I never attempted to explain it. "I wasn't completely alone. I had my grandma. And my parents came to visit some."

Jill tilted her head to the side sympathetically. Even though I'd left town without leaving her a forwarding address or decent explanation, we'd stayed close. When I told her that I didn't want to talk about Dylan or why I was leaving or where I'd gone, she hadn't pressured me.

I switched positions to hold Elise more upright and a loud belch escaped her delicate lips. Jill and I both laughed.

"I actually wanted to run something by you. Other than the apartment lease, I mean," I clarified, having been so distracted by her adorable baby that I nearly forgot that was the reason for my visit. Jill wasn't a realtor or attorney, but as an accountant, she had a decent understanding of finances. I figured she was a good person to have look over my new apartment lease before I signed it.

"Okaaaaaay…" Jill's drawn-out single word response reminded me that she knew me well enough to recognize I was nervous about what I was about to confess.

"I want you to tell me your honest reaction about something."

Jill glanced at her infant, then leaned forward, looking intrigued.

I swallowed nervously. "What if I told you Dylan wasn't Lucy's father?"

Her face remained unchanged for a moment. "I'd say your math is wrong. Didn't you say Lucy was 7 pounds 2 ounces? That sounds like a full-term baby to me, and you were still with Dylan forty weeks before her birth."

Leave it to an accountant to go the math route.

"What if I told you I cheated on Dylan?"

Jill shrugged. "I'd say he probably deserved it, but that doesn't mean Lucy isn't his. She looks just like him." She leaned forward and wiped a drop of drool from her daughter's lip. "I'd also be curious about this other guy and why the heck you never mentioned him before."

I inhaled slowly, bracing myself to tell her the truth, but she continued before I had a chance.

"The only way you could convince me Dylan wasn't Lucy's father was if you told me you'd slept with his identical twin," Jill finished. The moment the words left her mouth, her jaw dropped.

"Oh Lily… you didn't…" she said, wincing as though my scandalous behavior physically pained her.

I didn't answer at first because, well, I had done exactly what she was thinking.

"How did… I mean, did he…force you…?"

"No, no." I shook my head at the preposterous thought of Thomas using force against a woman ever, and at the equally preposterous idea that he'd ever *have* to force any woman to sleep with him. From what I'd witnessed, women literally jumped at the chance to go out with Thomas.

"It happened when Dylan was in rehab. Thomas had been watching out for me since Dylan's overdose and we went to dinner one night and drank way too much, and one thing led to another…" I lowered my voice. "It was my fault. I knew he had feelings for me and I was completely the instigator."

"But Lily, even if you did sleep with him once, you know Lucy could still biologically be Dylan's."

"It was twice," I mumbled. "And Dylan can't have children. Which actually explains a few comments he made back when we were together, but I didn't know that at the time."

Jill's face was pained. "Why didn't you tell me?"

"About Dylan?"

"No, about Thomas. It had to be stressful for you to carry all this around by yourself."

I nodded. "Yeah, but I deserved it. And how could I tell you? It's hard enough to know in my heart that I did something so horrible, but to actually admit it out loud…I was already struggling to explain to you and my parents why I was leaving and I needed you guys to think I was the victim because I never could've left if you were all still supporting Dylan."

"Lily, you were the victim," Jill interrupted. "We only liked Dylan because we didn't know what he was really like."

I rolled my eyes.

Jill's hand shot out and covered mine. "Stop, Lily. Listen to me. You are the victim. Nothing you did or didn't do made you deserve what he did to you. Even if you slept with the entire band, he was not justified in hitting you."

I swallowed hard. I'd heard those words before, but that didn't make it any easier. "It was his brother, Jill. The only other person in the world he could depend on. When I slept with Thomas, Dylan lost both of us."

"Dylan was abusive and a drug addict. Dylan made bad choices with his own free will and his choices led to the circumstances you found yourself in when you made your own less-than-stellar choice." Jill was speaking to me like I was a child, slowly enunciating each word. "If Dylan wasn't unpredictable, violent, and high—if he never overdosed or went to rehab—would you have still slept with Thomas?"

I shrugged.

"Does Thomas know he's the father?"

I nodded. "He was the one who told me. I haven't told my parents yet, though. Or Lucy."

"That's tough."

"Yes."

"Oh my God. This is like a soap opera. I mean, really. I might need a flow chart to keep up," she teased.

"Those midnight feedings really are taking a toll on you, huh," I replied.

"Have you seen Dylan since returning?"

I nodded. "He was friendly with Lucy. He seems calmer than before."

"Wait, I don't understand something," Jill said with a frown. "Why did he send you money if he knew he wasn't her father?"

"He didn't think Thomas or I deserved to know the truth, but he apparently isn't a big enough jerk to penalize Lucy."

"Hmm. That's disturbing. I mean, that's a really long time to hold a secret grudge against someone. But I guess sort of nice that he sent the money anyway?"

I shrugged. There was no logical way to wrap my head around the situation, let alone explain it to an outsider.

"How did Thomas react to the news?"

"Hard to say. I mean, he seemed thrilled about Lucy, but not nearly as pissed at Dylan as I'd expect. And he was upset with me for keeping her from him this whole time."

"He has to understand why you did, though."

I shook my head. "He says I could have told him, that he would have protected us no matter whose child she was."

Jill seemed skeptical. "Really? That seems pretty extreme for a one-night stand."

I shrugged. Elise fidgeted then fussed, spotting her mother in the corner of her eyes. I snuck in one final squeeze, then handed her back to Jill. She quieted immediately.

"So how do you think my parents will react when they find out Thomas is Lucy's father?"

Jill contorted her fact into the most pained expression I'd ever seen.

"That bad, huh?"

"I'm sorry, sweetie. It won't be good, though."

I groaned and tickled Elise's tiny toes.

"Thomas seems to be processing it all. He seems…good. I guess he's still mad at Dylan, too, but he'll get over it faster than I will, I guess. He was excited to spend time with Lucy. And I got the impression that he's…"

"That he's what?"

"I think he still has feelings for me," I admitted sheepishly.

Her eyes widened with horror. "No. Lily, no! I forbid it. You will not get involved with either Parker brother ever again. I forbid it! Stay far away!"

"First of all, he's Lucy's father. I can't avoid him completely. Second of all, he's nothing like Dylan. Nothing. But I'm not going to date him anyway."

"No, Lily. I can tell. You're thinking about it!"

I covered my face with my hands. "I'm not, really. It's just, well… he's hot. And I can't help thinking, you know, how perfectly everything could have worked out if I'd just met him first. He's funny and thoughtful and responsible in all the ways Dylan isn't, and he's really hot."

"You already mentioned that part," she said with an eye roll.

I shrugged. His hotness merited at least two mentions.

"Look, I get it. He's an attractive guy, and he wants to take care of you and your daughter and so you can't help but envision this perfect nuclear family." Jill finished, shaking her head. "Not gonna happen, Lily. This is not a fairy tale. You won't live happily-ever-after with the brother of your abusive, junkie ex-fiancé."

"I'm not dating him. I'm letting him get to know Lucy, and that's all. If there's anything I've learned, it's that I can't trust my feelings. I followed my heart last time and it landed me in Michigan. This time I'm thinking with my head." I glanced down at my drink, hoping my voice sounded more convincing than my internal monologue.

Skepticism oozed from Jill's eyes. "No. I forbid it."

"There's nothing to forbid. I've just been thinking about him. That's nothing new. I can handle it."

"What do you mean? You were thinking about him before?"

I chewed my lip. I hadn't stopped thinking about Thomas since the night we spent together. Mostly, it was dumb, fleeting thoughts, fantasies about an easy life with him by my side during pregnancy, childbirth, and the first years of parenting. When I slept, the thoughts were juicier, mixed with actual memories of our time together, the feel of his hands all over my body, the taste of his tongue, the warmth of his breath on my inner thighs…

"Thomas has been a frequent flier in my imagination for years," I finally said.

"Not Dylan?" Jill looked skeptical.

I shrugged. "I had closure with Dylan. We gave it a go, and I know how it turned out. With Thomas, there was so much potential. So much we never explored."

Jill shook her head slowly.

"I know, I know. I'm not going to explore it. I promise."

"Good." She wiped off the coffee table with Elise's blanket. "And of course you've been fantasizing about Thomas. There are literally no other men in your life. What you need is to date someone else. Once you see that there are men outside the Parker family, it'll be easier to put Thomas behind you."

"Let me guess—you have just the guy for me?"

"As a matter of fact, I think I do! His name is Andy. He's a lawyer I've consulted with on a few cases. He's super cute."

"Does he have kids?"

She shook her head. "No. But he's divorced."

I sighed reluctantly. Jill would be relentless now that the idea was in her head, but I had no interest in a blind date.

"I already showed him your picture and he really wants to meet you," she added.

"Jill!" I scolded, surprised at her audacity.

"I also snuck a photo of him when he wasn't looking," she said mischievously, slipping her cell phone out and holding it for me to see.

The man in the photo was turned to the side, so I couldn't see his eyes, but he had short, dark blond hair and a seemingly decent body. From the side, he did look attractive, in the generic sort of way.

"You won't regret it," Jill said.

"I already do," I said, "But fine. Give him my number."

She squealed gleefully. "Okay, now go change her diaper so I can look over this lease," she said.

I laughed at the tradeoff, but happily reached for the baby. The diaper change only took a minute, so then I played with her, shaking various toys above her. I pulled her to a seated position, smiling at how tightly her tiny hands clutched my fingers. We made silly faces at each other until Jill called out that she was done with the contract.

"What do you think?" I asked, bouncing Elise on my hip.

"I'm no lawyer," she began, "So maybe you should ask an expert, like Andy."

I stuck out my tongue and she smiled.

"It looks pretty standard to me. I don't see any red flags from a financial standpoint, anyway. Except, have you actually put this into your budget and made sure you could afford it? I know you have savings from when you were working and living rent-free in Michigan, but when you factor in the amenity fees and utilities, isn't it more than your teaching salary?"

I hesitated, then nodded.

Jill scowled. "Then what are we even doing here? If you can't afford it, you can't afford it."

I knew she was going to hate what I was about to say, but I needed her opinion.

"I can't afford it, but Thomas can. He offered to contribute."

"How much?"

"All," I said sheepishly.

"He's just going to pay for the whole thing? Full rent on an apartment he doesn't even live in?"

I shrugged. "For Lucy."

"That's not how child support works."

"Well, we both agreed we didn't want to overcomplicate things by getting lawyers involved and coming up with some rigid agreement. He has plenty of money and I trust him to take care of Lucy, so…"

Jill rolled her eyes in slow motion. "The reason for the rigid agreements is to keep it simple and standardized. And to keep emotions out of it."

I considered that. "I don't want to become dependent on him either, but it's different now. If we need to get an official agreement in the future, we can."

Jill took her time answering, but eventually nodded. "Do you know what you're getting yourself into?"

I bobbed my head up and down as convincingly as I could. But really, we both knew I had no clue.

CHAPTER SEVEN

"Perhaps, after all, romance did not come into one's life with
pomp and blare…perhaps…love unfolded naturally out of a
beautiful friendship,
as a golden-hearted rose slipping from its green sheath."
Lucy Maud Montgomery, *Anne of Avonlea*

THOMAS

When Lily brought Lucy by on Monday, she immediately made herself at home at the dining table. She spread out two stacks of papers, retrieving a highlighter, a red pen, and a blue pen. I assumed she was planning to grade papers while I entertained Lucy. That was fine by me. Better than fine, really.

I was careful not to let her see my smile, but when Lucy insisted on a bathroom break—then kicked her mom out of the bathroom, I couldn't help but tease her.

"Gave up on avoiding me already, huh?"

"What? I'm not avoiding you. I just…she told me to leave. She's in this independent phase."

I laughed, shaking my head. "I only meant that you seem content to hang out here today. Last week I was pretty sure you weren't going to let yourself get near me for at least another month."

"I wasn't avoiding you," she insisted, her eyes darting to the side and betraying her words.

"So you signed the lease?"

Her lips parted, then closed. "I'm supposed to tomorrow," she finally said.

"But?"

"I feel bad taking your money."

I turned, starting back towards my office. Lily had always been hung up over money. I'd bought her a plane ticket once and she'd acted like I'd never forgive her when she couldn't immediately repay me.

I retrieved my checkbook, then returned to the hall just outside the bathroom, where Lily still stood, her ear pressed against the door.

"You worried she's got a boy in there? Or smoking pot perhaps?" I teased.

She didn't give me the satisfaction of a response, so I moved on.

"How much did you need again?" I asked, filling in the remaining parts of the check.

Color flooded her cheeks. "I can show you the lease if you want. And then we should sit down with an accountant or at least try to calculate everything using the standard child support charts."

"I'd rather not. How much is the apartment?" I asked. "Including the amenity fees and insurance and whatever."

"I don't need you to pay it all. You're only responsible for Lucy's portion, and only half of that."

I suppressed an eye roll. "Could you just give me a number so I could write the check before our kid finishes taking a crap?"

My words came out harsher than I'd intended.

"I have enough in savings for the deposit. But one thousand a month after that would help immensely. Since you've already given me some, though, I don't need anything for a while."

I wrote the check for five grand and ripped it free from the checkbook.

She accepted it, then scowled.

I raised my hands defensively. "I don't want to argue, Lily. The last check was backpay, for what I already owed you."

"You don't owe me anything."

My chest tightened. I owed her so much, her and Lucy both. I'd failed to protect her when it mattered. But she was right that it was her choice to keep Lucy from me.

"I already spoke with my accountant. She said this was fine, for me to give you money as needed."

Lily opened her mouth to protest further, and I shushed her with a finger against her lips.

"I don't want to argue about this. Take the money, get the apartment, and let Lucy enjoy some of the perks of wealth. Why can't you just say thank you when someone does something nice for you? It's frustrating when you're always questioning my integrity."

"I wasn't questioning…" she began, but she stopped abruptly when our eyes met. "Thank you, Thomas," she said, waving the check in the air before folding it and slipping it into her back pocket.

My eyes followed the check, not because of the money, but because Lily wore jeans. Usually, she was dressed up after work, not wearing dark wash denim that clung to her curves like it was designed for her.

I drew in a breath that sounded like a hiss and forced myself to walk away.

Lily disappeared into the bathroom with Lucy, and when they both emerged, Lily began stacking up her papers.

After she left, I started to really think about it all. Why was I giving Lily checks anyway? She hated asking for money and I felt awkwardly like I was paying an allowance. It was complicated and messy.

Her appointment to sign the lease was at five. Band practice would prevent me from joining her, but I could go earlier in the day and simplify everything.

* * *

LILY

The bell beginning seventh period had just rung when Thomas messaged me.

"Don't sign the lease. Will explain later," was all he wrote.

I tried to decipher his meaning, but didn't have time. After my class, I texted back a single question mark, but he didn't respond. *Great.* After school, I tried calling him twice as I made my way to the apartment, but still no response.

When I arrived, the office manager I'd met with twice before greeted me with a smile, but clearly had not expected to see me. That surprised me, since we had an appointment.

"I'm sorry," she explained as she crossed the room towards me. "I assumed you wouldn't be coming. Was there something else?"

Else? "Well, about the lease," I began. Then I stopped myself. I still didn't know why Thomas didn't want me signing the lease, so I certainly couldn't go through with it today. But I also didn't want to lose the deposit. I groaned silently. "Is there any way you can hold my deposit one more day? I'm still interested in the unit, but…"

I stopped talking because the woman now looked so confused and was shaking her head.

"I'm sorry, but is there some problem? When Mr. Parker left, I was under the impression that everything had been finalized. The contract has already been signed, so…"

"Mr. Parker," I repeated. "Thomas Parker was here?"

She nodded, eying me as if I were completely insane. "To sign the lease."

"He signed the lease?" I felt ridiculous, repeating everything she said, but it was all so unbelievable. "There's nothing I need to sign?"

"No. He said only his name was to go on the lease, so…"

I blew out a sigh. "Sorry for the confusion. Clearly I need to talk with him and get caught up. Thanks for your time."

I turned and left before she could respond, not willing to further humiliate myself. Once outside, I dialed Thomas again. This time, when he didn't answer, I texted in all caps letting him know we needed to talk immediately.

By the time I reached the subway, he replied, apologizing but telling me they were in a middle of a meeting at Ari's office and that he'd call shortly. Not feeling particularly patient, I quickly looked up the address for Ari's office, ditched my subway plan, and hailed a cab.

The drive to Ari's office wasn't nearly long enough for me to calm down, so I hardly blamed the panicked expression of the receptionist who informed me they were closed.

My eyes scanned her, taking in the ridiculously short, tight skirt paired over her insanely long and skinny legs. Her top revealed more cleavage than it covered, and her bleach- blonde hair had been straightened so evenly that I wondered if the stylist came to the office so she wouldn't get windblown en route. She was exactly the type of woman Thomas used to date back when I was with Dylan. I instantly disliked her.

"Is Thomas Parker here?" I asked.

Her eyes widened. "I'm afraid I can't speak about clients, and um, like I said, we're closed, so…"

"He told me he is meeting with Ari and I need to talk with him urgently."

"I…I…" she stammered. She glanced towards a closed office door, so I assumed that was where they were meeting, but before I could decide whether to charge in like a crazy woman, the door swung open and out stumbled Dylan.

He was chuckling and shaking his head, and nearly made it to whatever room was across the hall when he glanced over and saw me.

"Uh-oh," he trilled, "someone is here to see us, and she doesn't look happy!" Then he walked closer, staring me up and down.

"I assume this wrath is for Thomas and not me?" he asked.

"I'm not," I began, but it was pointless. I was furious. What kind of a manipulative prick signed an apartment lease he knew someone else wanted?

"Ma'am," the receptionist began, placing her hand on my shoulder.

That was it. I swatted her hand free right as Dylan reached for my arm.

"Alright there, pretty lady. Let's go chat in the hall," he said, tugging me out of the office. "Holly, please tell Thomas to get his ass out here now," he called behind him.

"Holly?" I repeated. Of course her name started with an H. All of Thomas' girls had H names.

I took a breath and realized she wasn't exactly one of his girls. I was mad at him, not her.

"Before you kill my brother, is everything okay with Lucy?"

"She's great," I said. "Homeless, but great."

"Homeless?"

"Ask your brother," I spit. Luckily, Thomas joined us in the hall then.

"Right, so I'm going to tell Ari we need a quick break," Dylan said, turning to his brother. "Good luck."

The expression on Thomas' face was an even mix of concern and innocence, but I didn't have time to think about how that made me feel. Perhaps his obliviousness to his screwup should've earned him some sympathy, but I wasn't in the mood.

"What's wrong? Is Lucy…" He reached his hand for my shoulder as though I might run away, which was ridiculous since I'd just trekked all the way out there solely to chew him out.

"She's fine," I snapped. "I came straight from the leasing office."

His brows dipped lower. "I told you not to go."

I flung my hands in the air, accidentally knocking into his outreached arm. "You don't get to tell me what to do."

He took a step backwards as if facing an aggressive dog. "Poor choice of words. I wasn't forbidding you to go. I didn't want you to waste time going there when I already took care of it."

"How exactly do you think you took care of it?"

"I signed the lease for the apartment you wanted. I paid the fees for the full year, along with the first three months' rent. I will pay the rest in due time. The utilities will be in my name also, so I can take care of those directly as well."

"Oh. So you've just taken care of everything, haven't you?"

Thomas cocked his head to the side. "Is that a trick question?"

I focused on breathing so I didn't strangle him. "I told you I wanted to rent an apartment and you went and stole the apartment. What am I supposed to say?"

"Thank you, Thomas, would be a good start," he said.

I lunged for his throat. He smiled and caught my hands, holding them for a moment until he, apparently, no longer feared for his life.

"I didn't steal the apartment," he said. "I rented it for you and Lucy. What you said about overcomplicating things resonated with me. I realized it was simpler for me to rent the apartment in my own name. You and Lucy are listed on all the paperwork as residents, as am I, but that's only a technicality. I won't come over unless you invite me. I will give all copies of the key to you. This way you don't have to stress about asking me for money, Lucy has a good home, and your taxes are completely unaffected."

I considered his words, and tried to let his calm tone rub off on me. "So you rented it for Lucy?"

"And you, yes. My intention was to be nice, not to infuriate you."

"But my name isn't even on the lease," I said it like a statement, but I was looking for confirmation.

"Correct, but that certainly doesn't hurt you. If you trash the place, it's my ass on the line."

"Am I supposed to pay rent to you? Are you my landlord now?"

"No. You don't owe me anything."

"And how long do we keep this apartment?"

He shrugged. "As long as you want. I'm sure I have to give them some notice if we don't want to renew the lease, but I'll just keep renewing it until you let me know you're done with it."

"What if I've already changed my mind?"

"Then I s'pose I have an extra apartment for a year," he said dryly.

I didn't have a response for that.

His emerald eyes scanned over me. "Are you okay? You seem...agitated."

"It was important to me that we have our own place to live, Lucy and I. The last time I lived in a man's apartment, I ended up homeless when things went south. I can't risk that again."

Thomas sighed, his expression shifting back to pity.

"First off, you weren't homeless. You could've stayed at my place and you know it. Or you could've asked me to rent you another place then and I would've done it. Second, I'm not Dylan, so stop blaming me for things *he* did. And third, unless I missed the memo where we started dating, there's nothing here to go south."

He thrust his hand through his hair, tousling it in a way that he likely hadn't intended to be so damn sexy. "I'm not trying to control your life. I wanted to do something nice."

I listened to his points, but decided he still wasn't understanding my hang up. "So? When Dylan convinced me to quit work and move in with him, he was trying to be nice. He wanted to take care of me and spend more time with me. I'm not disputing that your intentions were pure, but the road to hell is paved with good intentions."

"Are you comparing your new apartment to hell?"

I closed my eyes, thinking until the perfect explanation came to me. "I wanted the apartment to be mine, to not have to worry about being dependent on someone else. I know you don't get that and I'm not even saying it's a rational fear, but it's important to me that I be independent. Okay?"

I waited for him to nod in agreement, but instead he just kept right on grimacing.

"No. It's not okay. You don't get to be Miss Independent now. We have a child together, so no matter how much you want nothing to do with me, you're connected to me for life because of her. You need to accept that I'm in this for the long haul. You can keep on rebuking my efforts to be nice, but I'm not going to stop helping you out because *you* are the mother of *my* child."

His voice had grown progressively louder as he spoke, and it occurred to me this was the first time he'd ever actually raised his voice with me.

"Do you understand?" he asked, ensuring that I felt like a petulant child.

I stepped backwards, leaning against the wall. I blew out a sigh and nodded.

Thomas inched closer. "I get that you're scared and that you don't trust people, but you have to start giving me a chance. I don't have years of parenting experience like you but I do have money. I want to give our daughter the benefit of what I do have."

"I said okay. I understand," I snapped.

He gazed at me for a moment, then breathed a laugh.

"What?"

"I thought only married couples fought about money," he said.

His bemused grin actually brought a smile to my face. I couldn't look at him and smile, though, so I glanced back into the office instead. Holly was watching us now, probably debating calling security to protect her precious Thomas.

"This wasn't a fight about money," I said, turning back to him. "This was about you going behind my back and doing something without discussing it with me first."

He appeared to consider that then nodded. "Okay, but in my defense, I didn't want you to lose your deposit. And I couldn't miss this meeting so I needed to take care of it beforehand." He paused, lifting his wrist to check his watch. "Although I've now missed a chunk of the meeting anyway…"

Holly was still staring at us from the receptionist desk. Shouldn't she have some work to do? What was so fascinating about Thomas' life that she had to spy on us? I stared back until she turned back to the computer in front of her.

"So about the apartment…I told them you'd pick up the keys Friday, but if you'd rather I do it, I can. I figured you'd want to take care of any cleaners or movers, but if you want me to arrange anything, I will."

"No thank you," I said, overflowing with maturity. "I'll take it from here." I snuck one last glimpse into the office.

"Why do you keep staring at Holly like that?" he asked, glancing in her direction.

I should've kept my mouth shut, but I wasn't really on a winning streak in that department at the moment. "I was just remembering how you always had a thing for leggy dumb blondes with H names."

He stared at me silently for a full moment, his expression unreadable. He glanced back at Holly, then turned to me and laughed. "Are you accusing me of sleeping with Ari's receptionist?"

"No. Of course not. Not my business. I don't care how many underage blondes you've been with." I trained my eyes to my shoes to hide my shame, but couldn't resist the temptation to sneak a glance at his expression.

His smirk told me I'd made a mistake in looking. "If you must know, I have not slept with Holly. Although, this conversation has stressed me out to the point that I might need someone to relax me later and if you're so certain she's my type…"

I rolled my eyes. "I'm going to pick up Lucy now," I said. I'd embarrassed myself enough for one day.

* * *

THOMAS

Lily moved into her apartment the following weekend. I came by in the morning to help occupy Lucy while Lily unpacked, but Lucy wanted nothing to do with me.

"Why doesn't she watch a movie and I'll help you," I suggested. "Moving is hard enough without being forced to play with the piano teacher."

Lily cringed. "Thomas, I'm sorry. I don't…"

I waved my hand dismissively. "Bad joke. Forget I said anything." I'd brought her a couple houseplants, which seemed like the perfect housewarming gift, but as I stepped into the kitchen, I saw a gorgeous bouquet of flowers on the countertop, surrounded by boxes.

"Those are pretty," I said.

"Thanks," she mumbled.

It didn't even occur to me that I was being nosy as I reached for the card, but I could barely suppress my gag when I read it. "Congrats on the new home! Looking forward to Monday. ~ Andy."

"Who is Andy?" I asked.

Lily scowled and snatched the card out of my hand. "Jill set me up on a blind date. It's in a couple days. I postponed once already because of the move."

"He hasn't even met you and he's sending you flowers?"

She nodded.

Geez. No wonder she wouldn't go out with me. I needed to step up my game to win her attention. "He sounds desperate," I said.

She gazed up at me, almost cracking a smile. I should've just stayed quiet and help with the boxes, but I couldn't resist.

"Cancel your date. Go out with me instead," I said, cringing as soon as the words left my mouth. Lily hated being told what to do.

She didn't try to strangle me or even swat me, though. Instead, she just stared at me, as though trying to find the answer to some question she hadn't asked aloud. Just as I was about to reach for her hand, she broke eye contact and reached into a box on the counter, pulling out a stack of plastic dishes.

"I can never tell when you're being serious lately," she mumbled.

What? I cleared my throat. "I'm serious now. I thought I'd been clear about my feelings for you, but if not, this is me, officially throwing my hat in the ring."

"The ring?"

"Uh-huh. The ring of men, vying for your heart."

"Right," she said curtly, continuing to unpack our daughter's dishes.

I waited a moment before pointing out she hadn't answered my question.

"Thomas, don't," she said. "I can't...there's Lucy, and..." she shook her head. "I'm going out with Andy."

I tapped my hand against the counter then left her alone in the kitchen. When Lucy's show ended, she happily agreed to accompany me to a nearby museum. When I returned her a few hours later, Lily was still unpacking, so I didn't mention her date.

CHAPTER EIGHT

*B*etween unpacking, work, and Lucy, my week was crazy enough without adding a date into the mix, but I didn't have the heart to reschedule again. We'd planned on drinks, the standard activity for blind dates.

Jill had been right about Andy. There wasn't any killer chemistry right off the bat, but he was a good-looking, well-mannered guy. He was nice and conversation flowed smoothly, so when he asked if I'd like to go out again, I had no reason to say no. We planned on the following Wednesday evening.

In the meantime, lots of unpacking remained, so I accepted Thomas' offer to spend Saturday afternoon with Lucy.

"She's still napping," I said apologetically when he arrived.

"I wanted to talk with you about something anyway," Thomas said, quietly pulling the door shut behind him. "I'm going to Europe in a few weeks, and I'd like you and Lucy to come."

I sunk into the chair nearest the couch. "England?"

"I have some business in France, Germany, and England. I

need to be there for at least a couple weeks, and then I thought we could stay in Ipswich for a while. I think Mum would enjoy spending time with Lucy."

"When would this be?"

"March."

"Thomas, school isn't out until the end of May. I can't go anywhere and miss work."

"You wouldn't have to stay the whole time. Just a couple weeks, maybe. If you're worried about the cost, obviously I'd pay for everything. You could stay in your own room."

I shook my head. "It's not the cost. I'm in my first year of teaching, so I really can't afford to miss any time at all."

His eyes narrowed. "You used to travel all the time with Dylan, even when you were working."

I sighed. He was right. Dylan could talk me into anything, and by the end of my relationship with him, he'd convinced me to leave both of my jobs to free up my time for him. He'd promised to support me financially and I'd never doubted that he would. But being unemployed had made it much harder to leave him.

"Don't turn this into a pissing contest with Dylan," I finally said. "I was young and stupid then. We both saw how that turned out, me ditching work for a guy."

"Fine, then what about Lucy? She's with your parents while you work anyway, right? So she could still come."

My breath caught in my throat and my palms started sweating at the mere thought of Lucy traveling overseas without me. "Thomas, you've never even had her overnight. You can't take her out of the country. What would you do with her when you were working?"

He shrugged. "I'll bring a nanny."

"Absolutely not. You are not taking my child out of the country without me."

"Our child," he said sharply. He stood abruptly and began pacing silently around the room. I couldn't see his face, so I wasn't sure if he was angry, hurt, or both. I hadn't meant to be so harsh, but he'd caught me off guard.

"Thomas, I'm sorry. Sit down."

He turned to me, but remained upright.

"You have to understand," I began, "the thought of being away from Lucy terrifies me. She's everything to me. When I left here, I wasn't just losing you and Dylan, but also my parents and friends and coworkers and everything familiar. For the past three years, she is all I've had."

"And you have to understand, Lily, that for the past three years, I've had nothing. Not you or Lucy." Thomas met my gaze momentarily, then started for the door. "I'll wait outside. I have work I can do in the car, so don't bother waking her early."

He shut the door behind him and I bit my lip to keep from crying.

Lucy awoke twenty minutes later. I wedged her blankie and stuffed dog into the backpack I'd already packed for her, watched her go to the bathroom, then helped her into her shoes. She held my hand as we started out the door, but as soon as she saw Thomas in the car, she squealed with delight and raced ahead of me.

He was on his phone but quickly climbed out of his car, greeted her warmly, and promised to call the person back later. He bent and picked her up, tossing her in the air before holding her at hip height.

"Hello, Mr. Thomas," Lucy murmured, twisting his hair around her little finger.

Thomas glanced at me as she said this and I knew exactly what he was irritated about now. I shrugged, defeated.

"You can tell her who you are whenever you want," I said.

"I think you should tell her, or at least be there when she finds out."

I nodded. "Have fun."

When Thomas brought her back promptly at 7:45, Lucy

looked happy but tired. And he still looked upset with me. He carried Lucy to the door and smiled warmly at her before handing her over to me.

"Goodnight, Lucy," he said, turning to leave.

"Thomas, wait. Let me tuck her in and then we can talk."

I saw his shoulders rise and fall with his breath, but he shook his head. "I have an early flight tomorrow. I should go."

"Flight? Where?"

"Los Angeles."

"Oh. How long will you be there?"

"Five days. Maybe a week. The whole band is going."

"I thought about what you said, I mean, about her knowing who you are. I can tell her tomorrow, unless you want to be here."

"No, that's fine."

"Goodnight," I said.

"Night."

Thomas had already changed her into her pajamas, even remembering the pull-up I'd told him she needed to wear overnight, so I just brushed her teeth, read her a few books, and then placed her in her bed. I was about to curl up beside Lucy like I did some nights and rub her back until she was almost asleep, when I heard my cell phone ringing.

I kissed her on the forehead and snuck out of the room. It was Thomas.

"Is Lucy in bed?" he asked, omitting any pleasantries.

"Yes, I just finished tucking her in."

"Has she ever asked about her father?"

This caught me off guard. "Well, yeah. She has. I mean, I don't know how much she really grasps yet, but she does see other kids with a mommy and a daddy."

"What did you tell her, when she asked?"

"I told her that her daddy lived in a faraway place called England, and that he was a very nice, handsome man."

"Were you describing Dylan or me?"

"Either."

He sighed. "She seems happy now. Maybe you shouldn't tell her."

"Thomas, she wants to have a dad. She's asked me countless times when she'll get to meet her dad, and I've always had to disappoint her with these vague answers. She's loved the time she's spent with you so far, and I think it'll mean a lot to her if she knows the truth."

"Oh," he said after a lengthy pause.

"Unless you're not going to be there," I added. "I mean, she's doing fine now without a dad, but once she knows, we can't take that away again. So if you can't commit to sticking around and continuing to be a part of her life…"

"Jesus, Lily. Is that what you think of me? That I'm just going to run off and never see her again?"

"Well, no, but…"

"The only reason I haven't been a part of her life before now is because I didn't know she existed. You didn't give me the choice of being with her. You are the reason she hasn't had a father up till now."

I cringed at the pain of his words and tried to hide the fact that I was crying. Thomas' voice had taken on a harsh tone he'd never used with me. He was right, of course. Everything he was saying was the truth. I couldn't trust myself around Dylan, so I deprived Lucy of a father. Thomas was justified in hating me.

"I'm sorry Thomas. I was trying to protect her. If I had known you were her father, I would've told you sooner."

"Bugger," he mumbled. "Lily, I understand why you left and why you didn't come back sooner," he finally said. "But that doesn't stop me from being pissed off. It's just a shitty situation. And Dylan knew the whole bloody time and didn't tell me." He sighed. "And I see why you don't want to send her to England alone with me, but how is this going to work if you won't trust me with her? My work involves a lot of travel. You say you want me to be a part of her life, and I'm trying, but if neither of us is willing to miss any work…"

"I'm sorry," I said. "I just need you to take it slow. Give her time to get comfortable with you and give me time to get used to the idea of her with someone who isn't me."

* * *

THOMAS

I felt terrible the entire flight to L.A. I'd blamed Lily for keeping Lucy from me, even though I knew in my heart it wasn't her fault. She'd been scared, and she'd done what she thought she had to. The person I should've blamed was Dylan. Except it was hard to blame Dylan when I was across the country recording select scenes for our new music video on location with him.

I texted Lily an apology in the morning after our flight landed, but nothing felt resolved. We needed a reset button for the last three years.

It was early evening Monday when Lily called again. "Did you tell her who I am?" I asked.

"I did."

I paused, waiting for more. When she said nothing else, I prodded. "Did she have questions?"

"Um, not really, no."

"What? Well, tell me how the conversation went."

"Okay, well, I said I wanted to talk to her about something important and then I asked her if she enjoyed spending time with you and getting to know you. When she said that she did, I said that was good because you were her daddy. I said that she was a lucky girl that had two parents who love her."

"That's it?"

"Well, yes. I mean, she's not yet four. I don't think she's ready for a more detailed explanation."

I blew out a sigh. I should've been there for that discussion, but I was a wuss. I'd make it up to her soon, though. "We'll finish with the video by Thursday at the latest, so I'll fly back Friday. Can I see Lucy Saturday?"

"Of course."

I wished I could think of a reason to keep her on the phone for longer, but I heard her yawn, and remembered it was late in New York. "Sweet dreams, Lily," I said, hanging up before she heard the regret in my voice.

The next day, I kept busy. I told Dylan that Lucy now knew me as her father, and as much as I should've been relieved that his expression was one of obvious happiness for me, I wasn't. It bothered me that he didn't feel guiltier, and that he wasn't more envious. I couldn't focus on that, though.

The moment we finished shooting for the day, I returned to my hotel and texted Lily. I asked about Lucy and how her day had been, then quickly moved on to Lily's day. We texted for the better part of an hour, and by the time I set my phone to the side to hit the gym, a feeling washed over me that I hadn't experienced for a while—hope.

* * *

LILY

For our second date, Andy took me to dinner. Halfway through the meal, my phone buzzed and I checked it instantly, in case my mom had a question about Lucy. But it was Thomas, not my mom. He'd gotten his picture taken in one of those touristy things that makes it look like you're posing over the famed Hollywood sign. It was hilarious and adorable, especially when he asked me to show it to Lucy and tell her he missed her.

I wrote back, explaining I was out at the moment but would show her first thing in the morning. He replied immediately, but I didn't respond.

"Is that your daughter?" Andy asked, interrupting my thoughts.

I peered up at him, certain I looked like a deer in headlights.

"You were smiling," he explained. "So I just figured."

"Sorry, I just have to check when I get a message, in case it's about her," I said, not exactly answering his question. My phone buzzed again, but I ignored it. Somehow, I now felt like I was betraying Thomas and Andy, and potentially missing important calls from my mom.

I reached for my wine, trying to focus on Andy. He was telling me more about his work, which wasn't exactly as fascinating as the television shows about lawyers made it seem. Still, Andy was a nice guy. He shared some funny stories about his nephew and seemed genuinely interested when I told him about Lucy.

At a break in the conversation, he smiled, then nervously fidgeted with his napkin. "So, I think Jill said you were never married?"

"No," I admitted, "I was engaged."

He nodded as though that were fascinating. "Is Lucy's father still in Michigan?"

I swallowed, not having wanted to get into this discussion, not yet, anyway. "No. He was, um, here, in New York."

Andy looked confused. "Oh. Sorry. I thought you said Lucy was born in Michigan."

I tried to find the right way to phrase my next statement. I didn't want to lie, but I certainly wasn't about to tell him the truth. "Lucy's father and I weren't together when she was born. I mean, it was over between us before then."

"Oh." He reached for his water glass, suddenly very thirsty. "So he's never been a part of her life?"

"Not the first three years, but he is now," I said, turning to the door as if mentally plotting my escape. "Is your ex-wife in town?"

Now he laughed, apparently appreciating my attempts to shift the direction of the world's most awkward discussion. "She remarried and moved to Connecticut, actually. We were college sweethearts, married after my first year of law school, and split before I graduated."

"Oh," I said.

"We were too young when we married, I think. But the nail in the coffin was that she started cheating on me."

I made a face.

"With the guy she married," he added, "So in a way that actually makes me feel better." He chuckled. "I'm glad it worked out the way it did. I have a better idea of what I want now."

Andy reached across the table and stroked my fingers, smiling softly.

My phone buzzed with what I assumed was another text from Thomas, and suddenly, all I could think about was his emerald eyes.

* * *

THOMAS

I awoke Thursday morning to see multiple texts from Lily. She said Lucy had giggled at the pictures I'd sent, and she replied to my other messages from the night before. She also apologized for not responding sooner, simply saying that she'd been "out."

As much as I loved reading messages from her before I'd even climbed out of bed, my stomach churned at the possibility that she'd been "out" with that guy, Andy. It wasn't my place to ask, certainly wasn't my place to comment, but damn if I didn't hate the thought.

That night, I called her at four o'clock west coast time, hoping to catch her before Lucy went to bed. I succeeded, and I was rewarded with the opportunity to say goodnight to my daughter. I half expected her to say something about her newfound knowledge that I was her father, but she didn't. Of course she didn't. She was young.

When she handed the phone back to Lily, I cursed myself for not having done a video call instead. I would've loved to have seen them both.

"So you fly back tomorrow?"

"Yeah, we get in around five, I think."

"What airline?" she asked.

I chuckled, wondering what prompted her to ask that. "It's a private plane, Lily."

"Oh. Right."

"So would you be able to see Lucy Saturday morning? Or like early afternoon?"

I cringed. Mornings weren't my best time of day to begin with, but add in the jet lag and I had no intention of waking before ten thirty Saturday morning. At least not if I could avoid it. "Does she have plans Saturday evening?" I asked, chuckling to myself at the thought of a preschooler having a packed social calendar.

The ensuing silence was so long that I almost wondered if the connection had failed. Then she spoke. "Well, no… but I do."

"That's okay. Can you drop her off at my place? Then just pick her up when you're done."

"I might be late."

I was having trouble understanding what she wanted me to do. Dylan was waving me back over to the sound stage. I shook my head. He could wait.

"Do you want me to watch her at your place? I can put her to bed then. I don't mind a late night."

There was another long silence.

"I have a date with Andy Saturday night."

"Oh," I said, suddenly nauseous. I didn't want anything to do with Lily seeing another man. I certainly wasn't going to enable her. Not again. Still, I wanted to see Lucy, and Lily was going on her stupid date regardless of who watched Lucy, so it might as well be me. "Do you think she'd spend the night at my place?"

"I mean…maybe? She really likes you. She's just, I don't know, sometimes sort of nervous in new places."

I tried to decipher her words. "Are you comfortable with her staying at my place?"

"You're her father," she replied.

I got the impression Lily didn't love the idea of Lucy staying overnight at my apartment, but she insisted, so that was the plan.

CHAPTER NINE

LILY

It was unseasonably warm Saturday, so Thomas had taken Lucy to a playground and then to one of those hibachi restaurants where they cooked right on the table. That left me with plenty of time to prepare for my date.

My closet was trashed by the time I found an outfit, but I told myself it was worth it. I'd chosen a simple black dress, sexy but elegant. I blasted music while selecting the perfect accessories, then finished off the look with a gorgeous pair of ridiculously tall high-heeled silver shoes. Now that I was on my feet at school then chasing Lucy around all day, I rarely had an opportunity to wear my fantastic shoes.

It wasn't until a few minutes before Andy was scheduled to pick me up that I started to panic. Historically, the third date was the earliest I'd sleep with a guy. Maybe that had been in my subconscious when I chose the dress, or maybe even when I asked my parents to keep Lucy overnight, but now that it was in the forefront of my mind, I had no idea what to do.

So far, we'd kissed, and that was it. Andy was the perfect gentleman, not even getting frisky with his hands when we made out.

I called Jill, and thankfully she answered on the first ring.

"Should I sleep with him?" I blurted out.

She laughed at my unusual greeting. "Oh right, it's your third date, isn't it?"

"Yep."

"Well, it has been a while, hasn't it?"

I cringed. It had been so long that I didn't even know exactly how long it had been. I really hadn't dated much in Michigan.

"And you like him, right?" she continued. "And he's hot."

I exhaled the breath I'd been holding. "So you think I should?"

"Yes. You need someone to take your mind off the damn Parker brothers."

"Shit, he's here," I said, peering out the window.

"Good luck!" she called before disconnecting.

I still hadn't made a decision when I answered the door.

Andy smiled widely when he saw me. "Good evening," he said, leaning in and planting a chaste kiss on my cheek. "You look beautiful."

"Thank you," I mumbled. I turned and reached for my purse, wedging my phone inside.

"So, I thought maybe we could do dinner and then head over to this club to hear some music, if that sounds okay. I remember you mentioned you like live music," he said as we got into the car.

"That sounds great. Which club?"

Andy had to think for a minute, which gave me time to pray it wasn't a certain one.

"Echo," he finally said, dashing my hopes.

I cleared my throat.

"Is…that okay? I looked into reviews and it supposedly is the best in town."

"Um…yeah," I said. The chances of anyone I knew still being

there were slim to none. But the memories…well, that was a different story. "It is absolutely the best. I used to work there, actually. Years ago. Before Lucy."

"Oh cool. I bet you got to hear a lot of great bands then. Ever meet anyone famous?"

I hadn't even begun to figure out how to answer that question when my phone rang. It was Thomas.

"Shit," I mumbled, gesturing to my phone when Andy glanced over. "I'm sorry, I have to take this."

"Is everything okay?" I asked Thomas.

"Well, yes. I mean, Lucy is fine," he began.

I held my breath, certain I could hear her fussing in the background.

"She's become quite agitated about a certain pink dog. She says she can't sleep without him, and I don't see him anywhere in her bag."

I swore under my breath. I had packed Barkie that morning, then unpacked him for nap. Had I seriously not remembered to put him back?

"Are you sure?" I asked.

"Quite positive. We've looked several times."

"Shit." I shook my head. "I'm so sorry. Umm…"

"We could go pick him up," he suggested, "Only I haven't got a key, so if you've already left…"

I didn't want him and Lucy wasting their time driving around anyway. "I'll drop him off soon," I promised, waiting till he confirmed to hang up.

Andy turned to me. "Sounds like we need to head back to get something from your apartment?"

"Yes. Sorry," I said, explaining what she'd forgotten and how critical it was. "Lucy is with her father tonight. His apartment is actually really close to Echo, so we could just leave it with the doorman. I hope this doesn't mess up the plans you made…"

He shook his head calmly. "The plans aren't important. I just wanted to spend time with you."

His sweet answer made me nervous. I chewed my lip, sneaking a side glance at him while he drove. He'd planned for us to eat at a restaurant near Echo anyway, so it all worked out. We'd just be a half hour behind schedule or so.

As we neared Thomas' building, I pointed for Andy to pull along the curb. "I'll just give this to the doorman and be right out," I said, starting out of the car right as he slowed to a stop.

The doorman approached and smiled.

"Hello there Ms. Mitchell. Mr. Parker said you and your friend could go on up."

I explained that I just wanted to leave the dog with him, but he repeated that Thomas wanted us to go up. I swore under my breath, but Andy seemed perfectly content with the detour. He handed his keys to the valet and walked with me through the opulent lobby.

"Nice place," he commented. "I'm guessing Lucy's father is rich?"

I squeezed my eyes shut, realizing I had to tell Andy the truth before we reached the penthouse. "I'm really sorry about this. We'll just be in and out."

"It's not a problem," he repeated, reaching for my hand. I squeezed the stuffed dog tightly in my other hand.

"So, um, yes, her father is rich. Also, um, have you heard of the band Sierra?"

"Yeah," Andy replied, as though it were a stupid question. Probably it was.

"Lucy's father is Thomas Parker."

Andy stared blankly at me for a moment. "Your ex is the lead singer for Sierra?"

The elevator rolled open before I could answer.

I dropped Andy's hand and knocked on the door. It opened quickly and I held out the dog. "Here you go." I took in the face looking back at me with surprise then glanced to make sure I'd knocked on the right door.

I had. "Hi, Dylan. I didn't know you were here."

He shrugged and motioned for us to come in. "Thomas called for backup."

I winced, then turned in time to see the two men sizing each other up.

"Hi, I'm Andrew Muller." Andy offered his hand to Dylan.

"Dylan Parker," Dylan replied. "Uncle and resident ex-fiancé."

Shit. I glared at Dylan then tried to force my face into a calm expression before turning to Andy. "It's a long story," I mumbled.

"Thomas, Lily's here with the dog," Dylan called. He turned back to Andy and held up the stuffed dog. "And an accountant," he added.

"He's not an accountant," I snipped.

"Well he's not a musician." Dylan replied as though Andy wasn't there.

"He's a lawyer," I clarified. "Can we go now, or did Thomas need to talk to me?"

"Oh, he'll want to see you," he replied with a mischievous grin. "Nice shoes," he added, plopping onto the couch and motioning for us to join.

"Thanks. We'll stand, though. Why are you here?"

"We're having band rehearsal here after the kid's asleep."

I felt my eyes widen in horror.

"Jesus, Lily, he's teasing," Thomas said, appearing like magic from the bedroom. He took the pink dog from Dylan. "Thanks."

Thomas introduced himself to Andy, then turned back to me. The heated look in his eyes as they scanned up my body made my heart flutter.

"Is she asleep?" I asked, following him down the hall away from Andy.

Thomas shook his head. He was visibly flustered. "She's just getting more and more hyper."

"What's she doing now?" I asked, confused by the silence in the bedroom.

"She's watching a movie on my iPad."

I sighed. I would go back and try to help get her to sleep, but I didn't want to leave poor Andy alone with Dylan and Thomas. "Have you tried singing to her?"

"Like a nursery song? I'm not sure I know any."

"You do, too, Thomas. But just sing her some of your songs." I glanced over at Dylan. "Seriously, if you both go in there and sing to her, rub her back a little, she'll be out like a light."

He looked skeptical.

"That's how she goes to sleep at home," I explained.

"You sing her our songs?" Dylan asked, now thoroughly amused by the discussion.

"No, you do. I play her a CD that I put together with a compilation of some of your quieter, more calming songs."

Thomas smiled. "Why would you do that? Why not just play her a regular kid lullaby CD?"

I rolled my eyes, since he obviously knew why. "I wanted her to know your voices. I always planned on letting her meet you someday and this way, I thought you'd be familiar to her. Just try it. You can call me if she still won't sleep."

Thomas gazed back into my eyes, his expression so filled with hunger and lust that I practically felt the need to fan myself. "I don't like him," he said.

"I didn't think you would."

"Then why are you with him?"

"Because *I* like him."

He narrowed his eyes. "Dump him, go out with me, and Dylan can babysit."

"Dylan will never babysit my child," I replied.

He grinned. "Our child," he whispered, kissing me on the forehead. "And you look so fucking hot tonight."

His voice was quiet, but I suspected I was now blushing so strongly that anyone who saw me could guess what he'd said.

"Have fun," Thomas called out to Andy.

I rejoined my date and we started out the door.

"Use protection!" Dylan called after us.

I tugged the door shut and took a moment to collect my breath before following Andy to the elevator.

"I am so, so sorry about that," I mumbled.

He shrugged.

"And I'm sorry you didn't get to meet Lucy. I just didn't want to risk getting her any more riled up."

"Seems like there's some history with those two," Andy said casually as we returned to the car.

"You could say that." I tried to read his face, then added, "It was a long time ago, though. I hadn't seen or spoken to either of them for almost four years when I moved back to Jersey."

"Did you, um, date both of them?"

I could've killed Dylan for telling Andy we were engaged. He did that solely to piss me off, and it worked. "You don't really want to hear this," I replied. "Or at least not before we have a drink."

He laughed. "Try me."

I took a deep breath. "Okay, I dated Dylan for a while," I began.

"You were engaged?"

"Yes. But it was not a good situation." I paused, not wanting to divulge Dylan's personal information, but painfully aware it was all widely available on the internet. "He had some problems with drugs and he wasn't the same guy when he was high."

"What drugs?"

"Cocaine," I said, immediately noticing the look of pity on Andy's face. "Anyway, I never actually dated Thomas. We were just friends and then one night we slept together. And when I found out I was pregnant, I left Dylan so he couldn't hurt the baby."

Andy patted my leg. "That's terrible. That must have been really hard for you."

I shrugged.

"I'm surprised you came back, that you even let them near Lucy after all that."

"Well, Dylan's drug free now, and Thomas was always fine. He's a good guy, actually."

Andy suddenly seemed uncomfortable. "Yeah, he seemed to like you, too."

"He's Lucy's dad. It's complicated." I glanced at Andy, and saw he still looked irritated. I quickly changed the subject.

* * *

THOMAS

Lily was right about the singing. When Dylan and I first launched into an a cappella version of one of our more popular, older songs, Lucy began giggling hysterically. But once she seemed to get over the fact that we actually knew the songs she liked, she snuggled right up with her doggy and went to sleep.

"Wow," Dylan mumbled as we tiptoed out of the room, echoing my exact thoughts.

I smiled. If I thought she was cute when awake, she was even more adorable asleep.

I left the bedroom door cracked in case she woke up, then went to the fridge to grab a beer. I needed it after seeing Andy. I offered one to Dylan, but he shook his head.

"I should head home soon. See if Patty is there."

I frowned, thinking it was odd that my brother didn't know what his wife was up to on a Saturday night. "Is everything okay with you guys?"

He bobbed his head from side to side before answering. "Not really."

I paused, not having expected him to admit that. "Do you… want to talk about it?"

"Not really."

"Does it have anything to do with Lily returning?"

Dylan stared at me for a full minute, his expression blank. "Maybe. I don't know," he finally said.

"Do you still have feelings for her?"

He lifted a finger and shook his head playfully, as though catching me trying to set a trap for him. "Do you?"

I raised the bottle to my lips, swirling the cool, bitter liquid over my tongue before swallowing, offering only the subtlest of nods in response. It didn't matter, Dylan already knew the answer to his question.

"Her date sure was a douche," Dylan said.

I nearly spit my beer at that.

"Can I give you some brotherly advice?" he asked.

"I'd rather you not."

He ignored my request.

"Fight for her. We both know you're the better man for her."

I thought about his words as I crawled into bed beside Lucy, desperate not to wake her. Lily had told me I could try to put her in the guest room, but that she'd probably sleep better next to me. I didn't want to risk her waking and being scared of her new surroundings, so we both slept in my room. She slept, well, like a baby. As far as I knew, she didn't wake once.

I, on the other hand, slept very little.

For a while, it was because I couldn't stop staring at her beautiful, precious face. But then, once I finally did drift off, I awoke often. Every one of Lucy's gentle movements, soft sighs, or tiny flutters woke me.

When Lucy awoke for the day, I had finally reached a deep sleep. I woke to the sensation of her literally jumping on me.

It was six thirty a.m.

No wonder Lily was always tired.

I waited until later to text her, not wanting to risk waking her if she was actually sleeping in. I tried not to think about whether she'd spent the night with Andy, instead focusing on making sure Lucy had the most fun morning imaginable.

It was nine o'clock when Lily called to check in. I told her about the night, said that Lucy and I had already colored, played the piano, and read several books, and that now she was eating a snack and watching cartoons.

Lily's soft laugh brought a smile to my face. "Did I forget to warn you that she's an early bird?"

"It's fine. I've loved every minute," I said, and I meant it. "How was your night?"

Now she responded with nervous laughter. "Fine."

"Are you home now?"

"I've been home since last night, Thomas Parker," she said.

I couldn't help but smile at that. "Well, Lucy and I might explore the town this morning if you don't have plans for her."

"You want to keep her longer?" her voice was filled with skepticism.

I chuckled. "Yes, if that's okay with you. You're welcome to join us, but I figured you might have things to do anyway."

She was quiet for a moment. "No, that's okay. I told my parents we'd come over after her nap and stay for dinner, so…"

"I could drop her off at their place," I offered.

Judging from the silence, she hadn't expected that. "Umm, I guess so. I actually was planning to tell my parents about you, so…"

"What about me?"

"Well, the fact that you're her father. They've always just assumed it was Dylan because…"

I laughed. "Yeah."

"But now that Lucy knows…"

"Oh, right. Well, sure. Text me their address again and I'll drop her off when she wakes up from nap."

She thanked me and hung up, leaving me free to tickle my other favorite girl.

* * *

LILY

My mother had just finished watering her mums when I approached.

"Hi, sweetie," she called, waving. "Could you be a dear and pop the rolls into the oven for me? The roast will be ready in ten minutes."

I nodded, relieved that she was distracted. I entered the house, immediately bombarded from the TV blasting a gold tournament. My dad was stretched out on a leather La-Z-Boy recliner. "Hi, kiddo. Where's the munchkin?"

"She's getting dropped off soon," I said, heading to the kitchen to complete my duties.

My mother came in, wiped the sweat off her forehead and washed her hands. Then she tied her apron around her waist and began carrying the food to the table.

"Where is Lucy?" she asked, as though she hadn't noticed earlier.

"Um, I actually wanted to talk to you guys alone, so…"

"Uh-oh," my mother interrupted. "Honey, you better get in here."

My father slowly made his way into the kitchen. He picked the corner off a roll and tossed it into his mouth despite my mother swatting at his hand.

I took a deep breath and immediately regretted my plan to tell both parents at once.

"I had some news about Lucy," I began.

"Oh my God. Is she okay? Is it cancer?"

"She's fine, Mom. Nothing like that." I cringed, wondering how I'd turned out even remotely normal if that was my mother's go-to assumption whenever someone professed to have news.

My parents were visibly relieved.

"I guess I should've said I have news about her father," I began again.

"Dylan has cancer?" my father said, without even a hint of alarm. I'd never told them exactly how bad things had gotten with Dylan, but they had accurately considered him the villain of my life story ever since I ran off to Michigan to evade him.

"No, and stop interrupting."

"Then spit it out, honey. The roast is getting cold."

I swallowed hard. "Dylan isn't Lucy's father."

My mother shook her head and continued setting the table. My father followed her into the dining room and plopped down at his usual seat.

"Did you hear me?"

Mom removed her apron and sat down, passing the potatoes to my father. "Yes, dear. But I don't see what the point of this is. Of course Dylan is Lucy's father. She looks just like him."

"Exactly like him," my father added, nodded. "The only way you could convince us he's not her father is if..."

"Oh God!" My mother dropped a ladle onto the table. She turned to me, aghast. "You didn't, Lily. You couldn't have."

I winced, assuming she figured it out.

She shook her head. "I don't even know what to say. We raised you better than that." She retrieved the ladle and dripped an excessive quantity of gravy over my potatoes before plopping it back into the gravy boat with a splash. "When you left Dylan the first time, he came to see me and said that you were upset because he accused you of cheating on him with his own brother. You assured me that wasn't the case."

Sadly, I remembered that exact conversation. "I was telling you the truth, at the time."

My father grimaced. "I don't want to hear any more about this. I'm trying to eat."

"What kind of a man does that with his own brother's fiancée?" my mother asked no one in particular.

I sighed. "Look, I don't really need a lecture and I'll spare you the details. Obviously, all parties involved know that mistakes were made. Dylan and I should've broken up by that point anyway."

"But you hadn't broken up, Lily. That's a pretty significant distinction."

"I get it, Mom. And I always knew there was a slight possibility that Lucy was actually Thomas' daughter but I never told you precisely because I wanted to avoid this awkward conversation. But I'm telling you now because we told Lucy the truth."

"So who does she think Dylan is? Hasn't she already met him too?"

"She knows he's her uncle. And she's fine with that."

My mother shook her head. "I can't believe this. Just when you think it can't get any worse…"

"It's actually a good thing, Mom. Thomas will be much better for Lucy than Dylan would have. He's a really good man."

My dad snorted. "A good man doesn't get a girl pregnant and then leave her."

I opened my mouth to respond but my phone interrupted me. Thomas had texted and they had arrived. Flustered, I stood up. "Well, Thomas is here with Lucy. I'll be right back with her."

"We don't get to meet him?" my mother asked.

That had been the plan, but with the way they were acting, I couldn't imagine it going well. "It doesn't seem like a good idea," I finally said.

"Oh, don't be ridiculous. If he really is our granddaughter's father, we deserve to meet him," my mom insisted.

"Unless he's too big of a coward to even come inside," my father added.

I rolled my eyes and prepared a protest, but my mother had already begun setting extra plates. I was fairly certain Thomas would not be hungry at 4:45, but for his sake, I hoped he faked it.

I hurried out to meet them before they got to the door. Lucy was already out of the car and running towards me when I got outside.

"Hi, sweetie!" I greeted her as she scampered past, eager to see her grandparents.

I smiled at Thomas and gave him a once-over as he waved back. He was wearing dark jeans, beat up boots, and a fitted long-sleeved gray tee shirt. His hair was ruffled and stubble coated his chin. He looked undeniably hot, but possibly not exactly father material.

He handed me Lucy's bag.

"How did it go?" I asked shivering as his fingers brushed against mine.

He grinned, heat flooding his eyes. "Fine. She didn't seem any different than normal. She still called me Mr. Thomas."

"It'll probably just take her some time."

He nodded and thrust his hands into his pockets. "Did you tell your parents?"

"Yep."

"And?"

"They want to meet you," I said. "But if you have to go…"

He glanced at his watch. "I've got time."

I hesitated, knowing nothing could prepare him for what would happen if he met my parents now. "Listen, Thomas, they weren't exactly happy with the news. They seem to think you're a…"

"Pig?" he supplied. "Yeah, I didn't figure they'd love me after what I did. Let's get this over with."

I nodded and led him to the house. My parents had filled a

plate for Lucy and were fawning over her when we walked in. My parents both stopped what they were doing and stared at Thomas for an awkwardly long moment.

"This is Thomas Parker," I said.

Thomas removed his dark sunglasses and stepped forward to shake hands. My parents each introduced themselves then stared back quietly.

"Right, so Thomas probably needs to be going," I said in my most enthusiastic tone. Lucy popped up to hug him again. He whispered something to her and she nodded giddily.

"Oh don't be silly, he should stay for a few minutes," my mother insisted. "We hardly know him."

Thomas sat politely in front of the plate of food my mother had served. He glanced at me nervously and I responded with a shrug. He took a polite bite of the food then turned to my mother. "Lily has told me you're an excellent cook. I have to say I agree."

"What do you do for a living, Thomas?" my father asked, ignoring Thomas' compliment.

"Dad, he's a singer and songwriter with the band Sierra. You know that."

My dad frowned. "Isn't that the band Dylan is in?"

Thomas nodded. "Yes, sir. We started the band together."

"And you're both still working together, even with all this?"

Thomas nodded again.

"I would've figured he'd stop talking to you, after what you did."

I panicked, but Thomas simply shrugged. "One would think, right?"

"So you boys just share everything?" my father went on.

Now Thomas laughed a little. "Generally not quite everything."

"Okay, that's enough, Dad."

"No, I want to know. What makes you think you're worthy of Lily here?"

My mother interpreted my glare and quickly whisked Lucy out of the room.

"Sir, I would never profess to be worthy of Lily," Thomas replied calmly. He took a slow sip of water. "In fact, I'd venture to say neither my brother nor I is deserving of your daughter, and fortunately for all, she's had the sense to tell me so quite frequently. I'm just hoping to do right by Lucy. She's such an amazing little girl, isn't she?"

I exhaled the mound of air I'd been holding, relieved Thomas could so deftly handle my father.

"Have you heard her play piano?" Thomas asked.

My parents quickly switched their focus to that and no longer worried about my dating life, thankfully.

CHAPTER TEN

"His heart danced upon her movements like a cork upon a tide.
He heard what her eyes said to him from beneath their cowl and
knew that in some dim past, whether in life or revery, he had
heard their tale before."
James Joyce, *A Portrait of the Artist as a Young Man*

LILY

I waited until Lucy was asleep to text Thomas, thanking
him for the way he'd handled my parents. He replied,
brushing off the compliment as though it had been nothing,
walking into the lion's den. I sent a response to that, then he
replied again. Before I knew it, two hours had passed and I was
long overdue for bed.

The next day was packed. I was preparing for the school's
Literacy Night, where a group of students from each of my
classes would share a sample of their writing and parents could
learn more about the books we'd read in class so far. It was part
fundraiser, part parent involvement and good publicity for the

school. Mostly, though, it was mandatory. The entire Humanities department participated, and as the newest teacher on the staff, I couldn't bow out.

By the time I'd gotten home, I was too exhausted even to make myself something to eat. I told Thomas as much when he called to say goodnight to Lucy, who'd eaten at my parents before I picked her up. But I was still surprised when the doorbell rang moments after I got her to sleep, and it was a delivery girl, bringing a sandwich, salad, and soup that had been prepaid, including tip.

When I texted Thomas to thank him, I had no intention of repeating the following night's pattern of texting back and forth for hours. Yet somehow, we did. It started innocently enough, with him telling me he'd canceled his trip to Europe. I'd assured him that he didn't have to, but he replied that he didn't want to be away from Lucy for that long. My chest tightened at the sweet statement.

"I hope it doesn't mess up things for the band," I said.

"It's fine. But I do need to be in England this summer."

That didn't surprise me, but I also didn't dare ask how much of the summer he'd be gone.

"I'd love to show Lucy where I grew up and introduce her to my mum," he added. "I'll pay for both of you to fly over, whatever dates work for you."

I smiled at the thought of taking Lucy to England. She'd love it. Heck, I'd love it. "She needs a passport. And mine's probably expired."

"I can take care of both," he offered.

I shook my head at the text. "No, I will," I'd said, before moving on to ask about his day.

The official Literacy Night event was the following night, and it promised to be my latest night yet. The event ran from 6-8:30, but it was well after 9 before the last of the attendees filtered out the door. After that, cleanup took a while. It was nearing eleven o'clock when I finally unlocked my apartment door, so I wasn't surprised that Lucy had long since fallen asleep. But I hadn't expected complete silence to greet me.

I tiptoed through each room in search of Thomas, finally giving up and checking on my daughter. Between her closet light and the nightlight beside her bed, there was more than enough light to make out her precious figure curled up in bed. But the moment I saw Thomas stretched out beside her, my heart ached with the desire to see the adorable scene even more clearly.

He'd removed his shoes, but still wore jeans and a long-sleeved shirt. He lay on his back, his legs crossed at the ankles, one hand clutching his phone off to his side, the other hand pressed against Lucy's back. Her stuffed dog, which I assumed had been in her hands as she fell asleep, now rested on Thomas' abdomen, inches away from Lucy's tiny fingers. She lay on her side, but her face was pressed against his side, her dark hair covering her eyes.

As I stood there watching them sleep, I forgot how tired I was. I forgot how impossible the last three years had been, forgot how badly Dylan had hurt me, forgot how much Thomas should hate me.

All I could focus on was my current happiness. The scene before me was absolute perfection. It was peace, comfort, and security.

I don't know how much time had passed when I decided to take out my phone and snap a picture. I wanted to memorialize the moment forever. As I set my phone back on the dresser, I gazed at them again. Seeing Thomas asleep reminded me of the night I'd spent with him. I'd gone to bed with him for comfort, and that was exactly what I'd found. That night I'd spent in his bed stood out in my mind still as the last night I'd slept undisturbed. I hadn't woken repeatedly, hadn't tossed and turned, hadn't laid awake stressing about whatever the next day might bring.

Logically, I knew it was the alcohol I'd consumed, but a part of me always wondered if it wasn't. If the awareness that, in Thomas' comforting embrace, nothing could hurt me, was actually what enabled me to sleep so soundly.

Clearly, he'd had that same effect on Lucy.

I considered not waking him. He was obviously exhausted, if he'd fallen asleep so early. But he likely hadn't intended to pass out and maybe had things to do, or places to be. It wasn't fair of me to keep him posed in my child's bed, no matter how heart-achingly perfect they looked. Besides, I'd never fall asleep knowing Thomas was in the room next door.

I stared indulgently for another minute, noting how his chest rose and fell evenly with each calm breath. He'd shaved that morning, and I longed to stroke his smooth cheeks and soft, warm lips. His hair, ruffled with sleep, looked exactly how they'd styled it for his recent music video when he climbed out of bed with some mystery model.

I swallowed hard, painfully aware of the dangerous way my body was reacting to him. My mouth watered, my breasts tingled, and a deep heaviness settled beneath my abdomen. I was doomed. To be this affected by a man who wasn't even trying to attract my attention—who was fully clothed and not in the slightest bit sexual in his current position—well, that was prob-lematic.

I clenched my teeth together. It was too late to call Jill, but surely she could talk reason into me the next day. Or, maybe not. Her last attempt to distract me from Thomas—the set-up with Andy—had failed miserably. Not because Andy was a bad guy, either. He was exactly the type of man a girl like me should be happy to end up with. Except that every moment I spent with him made me more acutely aware of how little I felt for him compared to Thomas. And besides, I couldn't exactly keep dating him after he learned what I'd done to Dylan during our engagement.

I knew what Jill would tell me when we spoke. She'd say my attraction was a normal chemical reaction. My body couldn't help but respond the way it did when I saw Thomas. He was a beautiful specimen of a human and had that effect on thousands of women. But my brain should know better. I'd matured enough now to recognize that indulging in things I wanted wasn't often good in the long term. Just like an adult knows better than a kid the negative impact of eating the full package of cookies, so, too, I knew better than to let myself enjoy a brief physical interaction with Thomas.

She'd tell me I was too emotional and too impulsive, that I needed to make rational decisions based on sound reasons—reasons I could enumerate, and not just describe as a feeling. Jill would remind me that I was still suffering the consequences of the mess I'd made of my life the last time I let myself get tangled up in the Parker brothers' web. She'd tell me to think of my daughter and how it would impact Lucy's long-term relationship with her father if I indulged in one last, brief fling with him.

She'd also probably tell me to go take a cold shower. And that, at least, I knew I could handle. But first, I needed to get the temptation out of my house.

Not trusting myself to get closer, I texted Thomas the photo I'd just taken. I hoped his phone would chime and wake him without requiring me to touch him. But of course, he'd switched it to vibrate. I heard the deep buzz as it rattled against his fingers. Thomas didn't even shift.

I blew out a breath and crept forward. Deciding his arm was the least innocuous place to touch him, I reached out and slowly patted his bicep. His shirt clung to the tightly coiled muscles in his upper arm, and I sucked in a deep breath to steel myself against the effects of touching his perfectly sculpted arm.

"Thomas," I whispered, flustered even by the way his name sounded on my lips.

I shook his arm harder, then finally, he flinched.

His dark eyelashes fluttered and then he slowly opened his eyes. His gaze settled on mine for a moment before his lips stretched into a wide grin.

I pressed a finger to my lips, cocking my head towards Lucy. Then, before I could do something stupid, I left the room.

I tried to find something in the kitchen to clean, but of course the jerk had done the dishes, leaving absolutely no menial task with which I could busy myself. Instead, I began gathering containers to use when packing Lucy's and my lunches for the next day. I tried to ignore Thomas as he made his way into the hall, softly pulling Lucy's door shut before extending his arms in an adorable yet disturbingly sexy stretch.

"I s'pose I fell asleep," he said, bending to pick up his shoes. "She asked me to stay with her for a few minutes, and next thing I knew…"

I smiled, having fallen into that exact trap multiple nights per week ever since Lucy stopped sleeping in a crib.

"How was Lit'racy Night?" he asked, his accent sending shivers up my arms. Over time, I'd grown somewhat immune to the way he spoke, but the accent was significantly more pronounced on some words than others. And whenever I heard such words…

"Lily? You okay?"

I raked my teeth across my bottom lip. The way he said my name was the most erotic of any word he spoke. I nodded.

"It went well. I'm tired, though. Thanks for watching her tonight."

I turned back to the fridge quickly, but felt his steady gaze hold firm on me. I assumed he was trying to figure out why I was behaving so strangely, but I could hardly explain it. So I just let him stare. Eventually, he made his way over to the couch and grabbed his coat.

"Sleep well," he said.

* * *

THOMAS

It wasn't until I got home that I saw the text from Lily. It was a photo of Lucy and me sleeping. Even though our daughter's face wasn't visible in the picture, it was adorable. I couldn't help but smile at the way her tiny little arm looked draped across my hip. I was still surprised I'd fallen asleep. I hadn't even felt tired before laying down beside her, but being that close to Lucy was just so calming. She had no expectations or demands about my album, the tour schedule, or how scandalous we made the next video. All she wanted was my warm body next to hers, helping her feel safe and comforted until her mother returned to her.

I didn't text Lily back, not wanting to wake her if she'd already fallen asleep. Instead, I posted the photo on my Instagram account, intentionally tagging my publicist so she'd see that I followed her instructions by finding a picture that wasn't professionally posed.

I didn't check my phone again until I was just about to head to bed for the night. In addition to thousands of Instagram notifications, I also had multiple missed calls from Stella, my publicist, along with a few all caps text messages instructing me to call her.

Oops.

It was nearing two a.m., far too late to call, but I did anyway, and she answered immediately.

"I did what you asked," I said before she could yell.

Stella sighed into the phone. "Thomas, you posted a picture of yourself in bed with a child. How is that what I said to do?"

I didn't know what to say. "I have literally no clue why you're upset."

Another sigh. "Is that your daughter in the picture?"

"Of course it's my daughter. You think I'm just in the habit of sleeping with random youngsters?"

"No, I don't. But maybe that is because I know you have a daughter. The rest of the world does not. Remember? You asked me to keep all news about Lucy out of the public eye. I've done an excellent job at that."

"You have," I agreed, cringing.

"But now, you need to tell the world that you have a daughter before they start to wonder why you're in bed with a toddler."

I swore under my breath. "I'll delete it."

"It's too late for that. You need to add a caption. Or a comment. Anything."

"Can't you do that?"

She sighed for a third time, but I suspected she was already on it. Stella had access to all of my accounts and could post as me anyway, so this seemed much more efficient. There was a pause, then she spoke. "Quality father daughter time is exhausting. How's that?"

"Well, fine, I s'pose. But don't I need to say something about being a father?"

"I'll handle that separately. On Twitter. We can talk tomorrow about whether you want to set up an interview."

"An interview? No. Definitely not. I don't even think…" I started to breathe as if I were lifting weights, suddenly picturing how Lily would react to all of this.

"Did you have permission from her mother to even post the picture?"

I hadn't asked Lily, but she had taken the photo. "We've never even discussed whether she was okay with the public knowing I was Lucy's father."

Stella groaned. "Might be a good time to have that discussion now, Thomas. Perhaps before she sues you."

She clicked off the call before I could respond. I rubbed my forehead. Then, I reached for my laptop, and braced myself to compose an email to Lily.

"I did a thing," I began. I then explained what I'd done, the call with my publicist, and how I'd fixed it. "Stella (publicist) recommended we talk about how you want to handle Lucy's appearance on social media. I wasn't thinking earlier when I posted the picture, and I'm sorry. There's no identifying details, so hopefully no damage has been done. I'm happy to keep her out of the public eye from here on out. I'll defer to your judgment on that. Again, deepest apologies. I'll be available tomorrow whenever you'd like to ring to chew me out."

I clicked send, then tried in vain to sleep.

It was the following evening before I heard back from Lily, and it was via text, not email. "Saw your email. It's ok," was all she wrote.

I replied, reiterating my apology, typing out a text so lengthy that my hand cramped up.

"Really, it's fine," she answered. A moment later, she added, "She's your daughter too, and it isn't fair of me to expect you to hide her from the world. I'd rather people not learn who she is or where she lives, but the basics are fine."

"Basics?" I replied.

"You could share her age, pictures that don't reveal her face, maybe even cute things she says."

"A photo of Barkie perhaps?"

"LOL," she replied.

I exhaled with relief. I wouldn't have blamed Lily for being upset. The fact that I hadn't even realized the potential minefield I was entering with my post told me how unprepared I was for this whole fatherhood task. Lily would never have done something like that. She always thought ten steps ahead about how every action would potentially impact our daughter. That was one of the many reasons she was such an amazing mother.

I told her as much in my next text and she thanked me. Then, she casually changed the topic. We wrote back and forth for another hour, our conversation somehow shifting into other topics.

As I waited for her next response, it hit me how inefficient texting was. Not to mention how woefully inadequate. I didn't want to picture Lily's voice in my head as I read her words, I wanted to hear her. I craved that sweetly seductive way her voice curled around each word when she was tired, like the effort of enunciating was just too great after ten p.m.

I called, expecting her to answer quickly. When she didn't, I considered that maybe she'd simply walked away from her phone for a moment, that I had epically bad timing. But then those little dots appeared, telling me she was there, holding her phone. That she'd likely considered answering my call, but hadn't.

"I'm sorry Thomas. I can't."

I cringed reading her message, hating that she bothered to write my name when that was my absolute favorite word to hear her say aloud. Who else did she think would be reading the text?

Staring at her words, I considered them more, my heart realizing the implication and beating wildly long before my brain caught on. If Lily couldn't bear to hear my voice right now, then I was right. I had to be. She had feelings for me and didn't want to succumb to them. Hearing my voice now would make her want things she didn't feel entitled to, might make her feel things she didn't think she should. While that awareness wasn't quite as good as hearing her voice, it was a fair consolation prize.

"I understand," I wrote.

"I doubt that," she replied.

I didn't have long to decipher her meaning before an image flashed on my screen. She'd sent me a selfie. It wasn't the scintillating highly erotic picture I'd yearned for, but in a way…maybe every way, it was better. I drank in every detail.

Lily was stretched out in bed, with Lucy draped over her abdomen. Lucy wore a nightgown with the likeness of some princess all over it, and her dark hair partially obscured my view of her face, but her adorable button nose poked between a part in her hair. I couldn't see as much of Lily, aside from a grey tank top covering her chest. Her hair was pulled up in a loose knot on the top of her head and her skin glowed, free of makeup.

Just from looking at the picture, I could imagine Lucy's warmth, feel the peace and comfort she must enjoy, curled against her favorite person in the world. Lily looked similarly relaxed and happy, her smile being natural, and not the forced over-the-top smile of a typical selfie. As I gazed at Lily's face longer, I nearly laughed aloud, wondering how I'd missed a tiny detail at first.

"You wear glasses now," I wrote.

"Yes, Thomas," she replied, and I could almost see her laughing into the phone as she continued. "You forget I'm old now. But I only wear them when I'm tired and reading in bed."

I wanted to tell her she looked gorgeous in them, but I didn't.

As I leaned back against the cold leather of my sofa, wishing I were snuggled beside them both, my chest burned with regret. I'd missed years of lounging with my girls. I could only imagine how it felt, the tiny flutter of hope that must spark when the child who has taken ages to settle finally stills and breathes the slow, steady rhythm of sleep.

Damn if I didn't miss them both.

"Wish I were there," I wrote, adding "With my two favorite people."

She replied with a smiley emoji, amplifying the ache in my chest. Not that I'd expected her to invite me, or even to say she, too, wished I were with them, but still...

"You should get some sleep, Lily."

"Goodnight," she wrote.

I sighed, gazing at the photo a minute longer before pulling myself off the couch.

CHAPTER ELEVEN

"Soul meets soul on lovers' lips."
Percy Bysshe Shelley, *Prometheus Unbound*

LILY

After the long work days due to Literacy Night, I wasn't thrilled to stay late two nights in a row the following week for second semester parent-teacher conferences. Lucy didn't seem to mind, getting to spend the first evening with her grandparents and the second evening with her father. By the second night, I, however, was exhausted, not to mention overwhelmed by the thought of everything I'd let slide while I was working late.

The fresh lemony aroma hit me the second I walked into the apartment. I hadn't left the place messy, but I was barely through the living room before I realized it was now sparkling clean. Not sure what to think, I pressed onward, hearing voices in the back of the apartment.

The kitchen shone as well, pristine, aside from the table,

which was set for two. A large vase of flowers marked the center of the table. A covered casserole dish rested atop an oven mitt adjacent to the stove.

I took in everything, without fully processing what I was seeing, and headed back to the bedroom. Thomas was seated on the fluffy, pink rug, and judging from the horn I recognized as the hood of Lucy's unicorn bathrobe, she was on his lap. I listened as he read the last few pages of Lucy's favorite book. The words were so familiar to me that I could recite the entire story by memory, yet it all sounded different, sweeter maybe, coming from his deep voice and thick British accent.

I waited until Thomas shut the book to greet them both. I'd expected Lucy to leap to her feet enthusiastically and hug me, but instead she shrieked and ducked under Thomas' arm. He swiveled around to face me.

"She wanted to surprise you by having her jim-jams on when you returned," he explained. "So if you could give us another minute…"

Still dazed, I nodded and stepped out, pausing beside the bathroom where Lucy had clearly been bathed. That explained the bathrobe. I returned to the kitchen, pressing my hands against my abdomen as my stomach growled hungrily.

I heard Lucy singing from her bedroom, so when I felt a presence behind me, I knew it was Thomas.

"You bathed Lucy and cooked and cleaned," I said, still not quite believing it all. I peered into the casserole dish, trying to guess its contents.

"I bathed Lily and cooked, but I paid someone to do the cleaning."

"You didn't have to do all that," I said, cringing and quickly adding, "Thank you."

"You're welcome," he said.

I stiffened, acutely aware that he had stepped closer. He smelled even better than the food, and unwanted images of me tracing my tongue along the side of his neck darted through my brain. I pushed the thoughts to the side and lifted the lid on the casserole, certain if I turned to face him, I'd do something I'd regret.

"It's risotto with chicken and asparagus," he said, his husky voice like music to my ears.

"I didn't realize you cooked."

"I love to cook."

"It looks delicious."

"It was," he said, quickly adding, "I ate earlier, with Lucy."

I wanted to know why there were two places set at the table if he'd already eaten, but that question was quickly bumped to the back of my mind. "Lucy ate this?"

"She did," he said with a soft chuckle. "I separated the rice and chicken and vegetables for her, but she ate it. She wasn't a fan of the asparagus."

That was impressive.

Suddenly, he was even closer. His fingers lightly grasped my hip, and his breath tickled the side of my neck. I could feel the heat of his entire body, likely less than an inch from mine. I was desperate to close that tiny gap, to lean back against him and feel his arms wrap around me. I craved the sensation of his lips on my neck.

I licked my lips at the salacious thoughts running through my mind, then forced myself to breathe. This was a bad idea. I was a strong, independent woman. I could not be swayed by a clean house and home-cooked meal.

"Thomas," I began, flustered that even his name flowing off my lips sounded erotic to me. "I appreciate this whole seduction scene, but…"

His laughter, like a low rumble from deep in his chest, interrupted me.

"If I were seducing you, you would know," he said, his lips brushing against my ear as he spoke.

I shivered right as he pressed a soft kiss right beside my ear. The gesture was so simple, so seemingly innocent, yet I was a tenth of a second away from turning into his arms and capturing his lips with my own.

But then Lucy scampered into the room and Thomas stepped a healthy distance away.

"Ta-da!" she squealed, smiling proudly, twirling around to show us that she'd successfully replaced her bathrobe with pajamas.

Thomas grinned at her, then me. He seemed completely unaffected by whatever had just transpired between us.

"I missed you today," I told Lucy, bending over to lift her up.

"Your mommy was so proud of you for eating such a good dinner," he said, kissing her cheek before walking away. He lifted his jacket off the back of a chair and slid his cell phone into his pocket before turning back to face us. "I told Lucy she could have her bedtime snack at the table with you while you ate. The risotto should still be hot."

I had no response.

"Goodnight ladies," he said, letting himself out.

Lucy plopped into her seat across from me and stared expectantly at her plate. I grabbed some graham crackers and her sippy cup of milk while she told me that Thomas taught her to set the table.

"Your daddy is pretty great, isn't he?" I asked.

She beamed, right as my phone buzzed. It was a text from Thomas.

"Forgot to tell you- opened a bottle of wine for the recipe. Bottle is in the fridge. Drink it. Too good to waste."

My eyebrow jutted up at his bossiness, but as soon as my eyes landed on the bottle of wine, any annoyance I'd felt dissipated. He'd clearly brought his own ingredients, since I certainly didn't own any wine that expensive. But after hours of listening to parents complain about my homework assignments ruining their entitled teen's little life, nothing sounded quite so good as a chilled glass of crisp, smooth white wine.

A groan escaped my lips as I swallowed the first sip while filling my plate. The food smelled as delicious as it looked, and when I sat down and sampled a bite, I couldn't help but groan again.

Lucy giggled. "Daddy's a good cook."

I nodded in agreement, then froze, realizing what she had just said. My heart squeezed uncomfortably as my lips parted in a wide smile. "Yes, he is," I agreed. *How had I never known that before?*

I brushed Lucy's teeth then tucked her into bed after her snack, getting away with only reading two books instead of our usual three since, apparently, the book Thomas read counted towards the total.

I loaded the plates into the dishwasher and poured myself a second glass of wine, gazing around my pristine apartment. I wanted to call Thomas, to tell him what Lucy said, but before that, I needed to get a second opinion on the situation.

I texted Jill. "Survived conferences. Came home to find Thomas had my entire apartment cleaned. He bathed Lucy and got her all ready for bed. And he cooked. A gourmet meal, which —by some miracle, he got Lucy to eat before I came home. Also, she called him Daddy."

At this hour, Jill was likely tucked into her comfy rocker, feeding baby Elise one more time before bed, so I anticipated a quick response. I wasn't disappointed.

"Is he still there?" she asked.

"No."

"How was it?"

"The food? Amazing."

"No, the sex."

"I didn't sleep with him." I shook my head at my phone. "I told you I wouldn't."

"You said that before he cooked and cleaned. Hell, if he cooked for me now, I'd sleep with him," she wrote.

"Not helping. Give Elise a kiss for me."

I took a few deep breaths, checked on Lucy, then called Thomas.

"Lily," he said upon answering.

"Hi," I replied, suddenly shy. "I wanted to thank you again for dinner, and the wine. It was very good. You might have to share your recipe."

"Never."

I wasn't sure what to say to that, so I paused.

"I'll make it for you anytime you want, though," he continued.

"Lucy called you Daddy," I said, jumping straight to the point. I retold the entire conversation to him, loving that he sounded as happy as I'd expected he would. As soon as we'd fully covered that topic, though, I quickly paved the way to exit the call.

"Well, I should probably get to sleep soon. Thanks again," I said.

"Sweet dreams, Lily," he said, giving me chills with the way my name rolled off his tongue.

* * *

THOMAS

I didn't see Lily the next day, but when she brought Lucy over the following evening, Lily looked even more breathtaking than usual. I wondered if she'd put extra effort into her appearance after school, or if I was just biased now that I was finally starting to think I had a chance with her.

Lucy immediately rushed into the guest room, eager to play with the toys I'd bought, granting Lily and me a moment alone to talk.

I stepped closer to her, eagerly anticipating the change in her posture when she gazed up. I'd noticed it the last time I'd seen her too, the distinct shift in her breathing and movements when we were close. She played it off as unease, but I knew her reaction to me was a sign that she felt exactly the same way about me as I did her.

"Your hair smells delicious," I said, my hand grazing her shoulder as I lifted a small section, tugging ever so slightly as I ran my fingers along the smooth, glossy locks. I could've sworn Lily shivered.

She gathered her hair over her other shoulder, probably to encourage me to keep my hands off of it, but in doing so, she bared the side of her neck, the precise patch of creamy skin that I'd been thinking about kissing and licking for days. I was instantly hard, then actually laughed aloud at how pathetic it was for me to be so turned on by a neck. God help me if I saw something truly erotic like her ankles or elbows.

"You alright?" she asked, furrowing her eyebrows together in an adorable way that reminded me of Lucy.

"Great. You?"

Her lips parted as if she just couldn't quite make out what to do with me. I felt my own mouth curve upwards into a smile.

"Listen, I wanted to talk to you about England this summer."

"Oh! Yes," she interrupted, her hands flying up. "I forgot to tell you I got our passports renewed. Lucy's and mine. Well, mine renewed, hers is obviously her first one. They should come in the mail soon. The photos are hilarious. Lucy looks precious, of course, but my photo is terrible."

"I doubt that."

She made a face.

"You know Lucy is technically a British citizen also," I said. "So eventually, once all that paperwork is finalized, she'll probably get a British passport as well."

"Is it legal to have two passports?"

I nodded, bemused by the way she was eying me as though I'd suggested turning our daughter into a terrorist.

Lily reached into her bag and pulled out a stack of papers. I assumed that was the work she planned to tackle while Lucy and I played piano. Her hand rose to the spot near her neck where her shoulder dipped, her fingers pressing into the skin. I peered at her bag, assuming she'd been carrying that, her purse, Lucy, and maybe even the booster seat.

"Turn around," I said.

She willingly complied, but she still jumped when I placed my hands on her shoulders. I delicately lifted her hair out of the way, then gently kneaded her shoulders, neck, and upper back.

"You need a lighter bag," I said, intentionally leaning close so my breath would reach her skin.

"Or stronger arms," she retorted.

"Your arms are perfect." To confirm, after focusing on her shoulders for another minute, I worked my way down the top half of her arms. It took all the self-restraint I had not to pull her against me. She was the ideal height for me to rest my head on her shoulder while hugging her from behind and I already knew we fit together perfectly, like two pieces of a puzzle.

Resisting the urge, I concentrated on my hands. I could feel her body start to relax even as her breathing grew ragged. I didn't have to hide my smile since she was facing away, but I did have to concentrate on maintaining control. The last thing I needed was to scare her off by pouncing on her in the middle of the kitchen when she was so close to finally admitting her feelings.

"About the trip to England," I said, my voice coming out husky and raw. I cleared my throat before continuing. "I really want to be able to give Lucy a taste of the entire country. Not just the touristy things, although of course we'll do all that, but I also want her to truly experience the real deal. London and the countryside."

"I figured we'd spend some time in your hometown," she chimed in.

"Yes. My mom is dying to get to know her. And you don't work this summer, right?"

"There are some training sessions over the summer, but I'm otherwise free for eleven whole weeks."

"Great. I think we should spend all of it in England."

She turned to face me so quickly that I didn't have a chance to move my hands. The result was that I was now holding her in a position so we could dance or, better yet, kiss.

"You want to take Lucy to England for eleven weeks?" Anger overflowed from her chocolate eyes.

"No. I want to take you *and* Lucy to England for eleven weeks. I don't want to separate you from her ever, not unless you need a break."

Her expression softened as she realized what I was saying.

I held my breath, appreciating her proximity, the feel of her arms beneath my hands, and the potential carried by that moment where she considered my proposal. Then she shook her head, predictably.

"We can't just stay in hotels all summer."

"I'm not asking you to. I have a home in London, you know. It's gorgeous and quite spacious. There's plenty of room for all of us. Separate rooms," I added, before she could accuse me of impure thoughts.

"What about your apartment here? And mine?"

I shrugged. "What about them?" I squeezed her arms. "Think about it, Lily. This could be a fantastic opportunity for Lucy."

"It would be just as great for her over a shorter trip, and then when she's older she could go for longer."

"Or maybe she'll be too busy when she's older. She'll have camps and sports and friends that she doesn't want to leave behind for that long."

Lily's gaze dipped to the ground, but I gripped her chin in my fingers and gently angled it back up so we were facing. I needed to see those beautiful eyes to know what she was thinking, and I hoped if she saw mine, she'd know my offer was sincere.

Our eyes met and time seemed to slow. Her lips parted, she drew in a slow, deliberate breath, and I began to lean closer.

She ducked out of my grasp and backed away. "I need to think about it, Thomas, and I can't think when you're…looking at me like that."

"Like what?"

She turned back to me, her eyes quickly scanning my body. "Like *that*. Like you want… me."

Watching her expression, it was clear. She wasn't bothered by her awareness of my desire, just distracted. She didn't trust herself to make the right decision when she was thinking with her heart and not her head. I understood that, but it wasn't going to work. Not in the long run. The sooner she'd accept what was between us, the better.

"Consider it, okay? And we'll talk later." I calmly walked away, finding our daughter and carrying her into the music room for our lesson.

Lily invited me over for dinner the next day. I offered to pick up Lucy from preschool on my way, which proved a much more daunting feat than I'd anticipated. I supposed it should've been a relief that there was such tight security to retrieve a child from a preschool, but the fact that my name was on the list and she called me "Daddy" seemed pretty conclusive to me.

Lily laughed when she heard the interrogation to which I'd been subjected, then willingly let me take over dinner preparations in the kitchen while she played with Lucy. Given that Lily's cooking repertoire seemed fairly limited, I decided that was definitely a good thing.

When she came in to check on the timing, I smiled. She'd clearly changed after work, since she was now wearing capri-length jeans and a sleeveless top, and I took comfort in the fact that she'd seemingly attempted to look good for me. If she was putting effort into her outfit rather than just changing into sweats and a tee shirt, surely my instincts were right about her feelings for me.

"Wine?" I offered, letting my eyes slowly drift up her body.

Her cheeks flushed. "Sure." She took the bottle from me and poured. "I wanted to talk with you about Lucy's birthday party."

I had assumed the dinner invitation was to talk about England, but I was more than happy to focus on Lucy's birthday. Since I'd missed her first three, I really wanted this one to be special.

"My parents offered to host, since they have the big yard."

"I could rent something at a park if you'd rather have it in the city," I offered.

"She doesn't have that many friends. I think everyone will be fine with driving." She scrolled through something on her phone. "Do either of these dates work for you?"

I nodded, but confirmed on my calendar. Nothing could keep me away from that day.

"If there's anyone you want to invite, let me know. My friend Jill and her family will come, so if you have any friends you'd like…"

I shook my head. My only friends were in the band. Inviting the entire band would likely create a distraction that would take some of the focus off of Lucy. Although, there was one person. I grimaced and gazed up.

"Dylan?" she said, always the mind reader.

I shrugged. He'd grown really attached to Lucy and was still a big hit with her. But given his history with Lily… "Your parents hate him."

"But Lucy doesn't. And it's her party. So I'll let you make the final call."

I supposed I could handle that. "Food's ready," I said.

After dinner, I read books to Lucy and got her ready for bed, but she wanted her mummy to actually tuck her in. When I returned to the kitchen, I saw that Lily had already cleaned up the dinner mess. I sighed, having planned to do that myself. Instead, I sat on the couch and looked into birthday party ideas for a four-year-old. By the time Lucy was asleep and Lily came out, I had a whole slew of ideas.

I turned at the sound of Lucy's bedroom door being shut, and couldn't help but smile at the sight of Lily. She looked a little surprised when she saw me, though.

"I thought maybe you'd left," she explained.

"I stayed in case you wanted to discuss the party more. I was thinking we should rent a pony."

Her lips parted and a myriad of expressions crossed her face before she finally laughed softly. "Let's come back to that thought. I actually wanted to talk with you more about this summer."

She turned as she spoke, heading back to the kitchen. My heart rate increased just at the thought of maybe getting an entire summer with her. She poured herself more wine and offered me some. I followed her into the kitchen but shook my head, sure I'd be leaving soon anyway.

Lily thumbed the cork back into the bottle and took a large swig of her wine.

"I spoke with Lucy about spending longer in England, and she seemed excited. And I do agree that your mom deserves some quality time with her."

I braced myself for the inevitable "but." I didn't have to wait long.

"But I guess I need more clarification. You said you want me to go the whole time too, right?"

I nodded, trying to guess where she was going with this. She fidgeted with her hair, then rapped her nails against her wine glass before setting it on the counter. Clearly, she was nervous.

"Well, I mean, in what capacity would I be joining you?"

A slight chuckle escaped my lips. "Pardon?"

"It matters for like, I don't know, sleeping arrangements and stuff. And I just need to know."

"I'm not certain I know what you mean about your capacity."

"Am I tagging along just because I'm Lucy's mom? Like because you don't want to separate us?" she paused, but not long enough for me to answer. "Did you invite me as a friend? Or did you envision us traveling together more as…um…more than friends?"

"More than friends?" I repeated, still completely mystified as to what she was asking. But then, as I pieced it together with her comment about sleeping arrangements, it all clicked. "You mean, like as lovers?"

Her cheeks flushed redder than I'd ever seen. *God* was it sexy. I stepped closer, aware that with her back against the countertop, she couldn't scoot further away. I waited to speak until she gazed up at me again, wanting to be certain she didn't misunderstand my answer.

"I would love to spend the summer with you in whatever capacity is amenable to you," I began, licking my lips to avoid laughing at the ridiculous terminology. "I would never ask you to spend time apart from Lucy, but no, I didn't just invite you as her mother. I do consider you a friend and I'd hate to go a week without seeing you, let alone a full summer."

Lily nodded as though she thought I was done. I raised my finger to her lips, not wanting her to speak before I'd finished my thought.

"As for the rest, that's up to you. I could think of nothing I'd like more than to spend the summer waking up with you in my bed." I paused, sliding my finger off her lips to graze the side of her cheek, stroking the line of her jaw. Her chin dipped towards my hand and she shivered. I inched closer, letting my body press against hers while twining my other hand around her fingers.

"You know exactly how I feel about you and how much I want

you. But I'm a patient man. If you're not ready for that, I'll play nice in England. I'll keep my hands to myself and respect whatever space you want. Just know that someday, when you come to your senses about us, you're going to regret having wasted so much time."

I tilted my head towards hers, moving ever so slowly so that she could protest if she wanted. When my lips finally reached hers, my heart thudded so vehemently that I was sure my whole body shook. Her lips were exactly as I'd remembered them-smooth, soft, and oh so sweet, just like she was. My tongue swept along the crease between her lips, but didn't press further. The slight taste of her was enough to drive me crazy, and it took all my control not to press forward, not to fully devour her.

I ended the kiss quickly, lingering with my lips a fraction of a centimeter from hers, then squeezed my eyes shut. I couldn't keep staring at her if I wanted to maintain the willpower to leave. And until she told me yes, I needed to hold back.

I dragged my thumb along her lip then pushed away from her. "You know what I want, Lily. The ball is in your court."

* * *

LILY

When Thomas left, I spent the next hour tracing my finger along my lip, trying to recreate the feeling of his mouth against my own. He had held back, I could tell he had, but still. That kiss was hot. A little too hot, maybe. He'd left ages ago and my heart was still racing.

It was good that he'd left when he did. If he'd pushed for more, I wouldn't have resisted. If he'd insisted on staying, I wouldn't have kicked him out. As it was, I was a little tempted to text him to come back and finish what he started.

I groaned and sank onto the couch. He'd answered my question about England, at least. He wanted me on the trip, and he wasn't going to pretend he was content to be only my friend. Now that we weren't dancing around the subject, it wouldn't be so awkward. I just needed to sort out my feelings. I could readily accept that I was attracted to Thomas. Well, that was putting it mildly. I couldn't recall ever wanting another human being as much as Thomas. My body craved him the way I'd needed licorice when I was pregnant.

On the one hand, I worried that my desperate yearning for him was a simple result of the fact that I couldn't have him. I didn't deserve him, not after what we'd done to Dylan, and I couldn't get involved with him and risk jeopardizing everything for Lucy. But on the other hand, it wasn't totally irrational for me to like him, either. The general consensus of females around the world was that Thomas Parker was hot, so I certainly wasn't in the minority in my attraction. From the chiseled torso and soft, tousled hair to the dreamy British accent and seductive voice, he was a common fantasy. Throw in the fact that he was amazing with Lucy and went out of his way to make my life easier, and of course I was falling for him.

What I needed to do was focus on the facts. He was Lucy's father, and he had missed several years of her life through no fault of his own. He deserved time to show her his home country, introduce her to his mother, and make memories. And I was a big girl. I could separate Thomas Parker, my baby daddy, from Thomas Parker my friend. And at the end of the day, I could completely avoid Thomas Parker, the romantic love interest. This might be the last summer that Lucy didn't mind leaving town for so long.

I pulled out my phone before I changed my mind. "We'll go to England for the whole summer, but I'm holding you to your promise to be a gentleman," I wrote.

"Duly noted," he replied.

CHAPTER TWELVE

THOMAS

*W*hen I picked up my girls that afternoon, we
stopped for ice cream before driving Lucy to her
grandparents'. I stayed in the car while Lily ran her inside, but
her expression as she returned was somber.

"What's wrong?" I asked.

"My parents are less than thrilled that I'm spending the afternoon with you."

Well, shit. I supposed that shouldn't have surprised me. Virtually all they knew about me was that I'd slept with my brother's
fiancée. Didn't exactly make me look like a stellar man. I was
beginning to realize how difficult it was to win someone over

when the first thing they learned about you was the worst thing you'd ever done.

"Did you tell them we're party planning and not drag racing or drug snorting or whatever illicit activities they think I'm into?"

Lily breathed a laugh. "They don't think that."

"What's their concern?"

"They're worried I'll get involved with you again and that when it ends horribly, I'll run halfway across the country to avoid you."

My stomach tensed. "Yes, that would be less than ideal."

By the time we arrived at the park, we'd both relaxed. It truly was an idyllic afternoon. The sun shone brightly amidst a cerulean sky, the air was warm but dry, and the slightest breeze danced across the treetops, making their newly grown leaves dance. Throughout the park, the early fragrant blooms of the flowering dogwood and Japanese magnolias decorated the winding paths. My senses were on high alert, satiated in every way except one.

I still needed her.

She walked beside me, her glossy hair bouncing as she walked, her vanilla lotion competing with the spring flowers invading my nostrils in the most delicious way possible, and her melodic voice soothed my soul even as she spoke of something as mundane as the menu for our daughter's upcoming birthday party.

God I loved this woman. I loved her so much that it hurt. It had hurt for years, and as much as having her in my life should've comforted me, it also made the pain of not quite having her that much more acute. I needed permission to touch her freely, desperately yearned to simply hold her in my arms, feeling her heart beat against my chest. I wanted to taste her...everywhere.

"Are you even listening?" she asked, stopping abruptly.

I cleared my throat, certain my salacious thoughts were

written all over my face. "Sorry. Yes. Cotton candy would be lovely."

Lily laughed. It wasn't a mocking laugh, more of an appreciative one. My word choice often amused her.

"Lucy asked if her Uncle Dylan could come to the party," I said, shifting the direction of the discussion.

Lily didn't appear surprised by that. "Yeah, I figured she would. He's your brother and best friend anyway. He should be there. And what about Patty?"

"She's still in Los Angeles."

Lily swallowed uncomfortably. We hadn't really discussed whatever was going on with Dylan's marriage. In part that was because I didn't fully know myself, but also because I was scared of what Lily would do or how she would feel if Dylan were single again. I assumed that relationship was over, but for the first time in our lives, Dylan and I weren't in a place where we openly shared such details. I could only guess that the reason for Patty's departure was that Dylan still had feelings for Lily, but I liked to believe she didn't share his affection. I wanted to believe Lily was only interested in me.

"We should invite her," I added. "But I doubt she'll come. I thought, though, that perhaps it would help make Dylan's presence less awkward for your parents if the whole band came. Owen has a son about Lucy's age, and…"

"That's a great idea." she interrupted.

I hadn't expected her to agree so quickly. "You don't think it would be too circus-like, with the entire band and their families attending?"

She shrugged. "We aren't inviting that many people. The families from Lucy's school probably don't know who you are, but…I don't think it'll be that big of a distraction. No more so than a unicorn you rented for the party." Lily turned and gazed up at me, her eyes sparkling and her lips curled into the purest, most heart-melting smile imaginable.

My chest squeezed and I thrust my hands into my pockets to avoid reaching for her hand.

"So, um, I was surprised to get your text about England. Thrilled, but surprised."

"Well, you were right. Lucy and I have nothing else we have to do this summer, and there might not be many years left that we can say that. I owe this experience to her—and you."

"So, your acceptance of my invitation had nothing to do with the rest of what I said to you?"

She cleared her throat, dropping her head. I followed her line of sight down to her shoes, which were lace-up athletic shoes. It hit me again how much she had changed. The old Lily lived for fun, designer shoes. She stayed up all hours of the night listening to new bands play and she spent her days daydreaming of travel and poring over classic romance novels. This Lily was practical. She'd grown into a phenomenal mother, and she rarely spared a thought for her own interests and desires. She lived for her child. For our child.

I had no interest in keeping my hands to myself any longer. I reached for her shoulder, lightly running my palm down the back of her arm and then across her back. She didn't shrug away from my touch, but I pulled back after a minute, not wanting to push my luck.

"I missed talking to you when I was gone," she finally said. "You'd become this comforting voice of wisdom, and until we were apart, I didn't realize how much I'd depended on your friendship. It was hard. I don't want to put myself in a position again where I could lose that, lose you, again. I like being your friend, though. I think it's great for Lucy to see us getting along and to have all of us spending time together. She's been so happy these last few weeks."

Suddenly, I felt emboldened. "I love being friends with you too. And I'm delighted Lucy is happy now, but as far as I can tell, she's always been happy. You've done such an amazing job raising her. It's you that I'm worried about. I know that being a parent means putting your child's needs first, but you've completely neglected yours. You need more than friendship. You need me in your life the same way I need you in mine."

Lily's pace slowed considerably and this time, when she spoke, her voice crackled with nervousness. "What I need is consistency. I need to know that you'll always be there for Lucy… and for me. That means I can't do anything that might push you away."

* * *

LILY

I didn't dare look at Thomas. I lacked confidence in my ability to keep my hands from myself if he was still looking at me that way, with that heated desire so obvious in his eyes. But he took so long to answer that I almost worried he hadn't heard me.

"I'm not going anywhere," he finally said.

I startled as his fingers brushed against mine, lightly at first, then fully clasping my hand while we slowly strolled.

"Nothing you could ever do can change that. You can date Andy, hell you can date Dylan…you can break my heart over and over, and I promise you that I will still be the best father I can possibly be. And that means that I will always be there for you, too. No matter what."

I tried to find words to respond, but I was at a loss.

"Do you really think I'm the kind of man that would ever leave you two?"

"No." I trusted him completely. I could totally see him staying by my side, helping raise Lucy and still paying for my apartment, even if I betrayed him in the worst way possible. He was just that kind of guy. But I didn't trust myself.

"I believe you," I added. "But that doesn't change who I am, or how I feel."

We abruptly stopped walking, and Thomas turned to face me. He took both of my hands in his, and just the gentle stroking of his thumbs across my palms was enough to send a spasm through my groin.

"Lily, you can't tell me you don't feel the same way. I know what you think about the timing and the logistics and all that, but you're wrong. This is right," he said.

I was too busy trying to think up a plausible response to notice him leaning forward. The second his lips touched mine, my mind went blank.

I was lost in the sensations instantaneously—the subtle scent of his cologne, the gentle tickle from his stubble, and the soothing warmth from his breath on my face. His lips were soft yet powerful, and his tongue…oh, his tongue.

I stumbled closer and released his hands as his arms pulled me tight against his firm body. I was panting, my entire body tingled with desire, and a soft moan escaped my lips. Thomas slid his hand up my back and through my hair, pressing my head to his as though he worried I'd pull away.

Thomas' breathing was becoming more frantic, matching my own, and my legs started to feel weak. As he deepened the kiss, I let my weight fall into his arm, not even caring if he supported me or if we both toppled over into the grass. His teeth scraped along my lip then our tongues clashed together. My hands pressed into his back, kneading from the curve of his hips up towards his shoulder blades, desperate to explore lower on his body.

And then a bird chirped and my mind switched back on.

We were outside. In public.

And I couldn't do this.

I tugged my mouth away, but kept my body against his, more

out of necessity than anything else. We were both quiet for a moment while our breathing slowed.

"Shit," I finally mumbled once I regained use of my legs. Still dizzy, I stepped back slowly.

Thomas stared back at me, surprised. "Excuse me?"

"What the fuck was that?"

He grinned, clearly not taking me seriously. "I thought that was obvious, but I could try it again if…"

"Don't you come any closer," I interrupted him. I collapsed onto the grass and he sat next to me. "Whatever happened to your promise that you'd be a gentleman?"

"Technically I said I'd be a gentleman in England. We're still on US soil."

I sighed loudly, several times in a row, since I couldn't think of what to say.

"I suppose this would be a bad time for me to say 'I told you so'?" Thomas asked quietly.

"What did you tell me?"

He shrugged and plucked a blade of grass. "Oh come on, you clearly enjoyed kissing me."

"Of course I enjoyed kissing you. You're a really good kisser." I was practically shouting at him, but I was frazzled, and it was his fault.

Thomas frowned. "So why are you mad at me?"

I flung my hands in the air. "I already knew I liked kissing you, Thomas. Remember, we've done that before?"

"That tiny peck last week hardly counted as a kiss."

I rolled my eyes. It sure had felt like one. "Well, there was a whole lot of kissing right around the time a certain almost-four-year-old was conceived."

He was clearly amused. "I didn't think you remembered that. You were drunk."

"I wasn't that drunk, and besides, you'd kissed me once before that."

Now I'd really piqued his curiosity. "Tell me, Lily, did you enjoy the other things you did with me that night?" he asked.

I felt my cheeks blush. "Thomas, that's not the point."

"I want to know," he said, his voice pushy.

"Yes. Are you happy? You're a good kisser and you are great in bed!"

An elderly couple strolling past grimaced at my statement then sped up considerably.

Thomas was quiet, then finally patted my leg. "I don't follow. Your words sound like we're on the same page here, but the way you're saying them makes me think we're not."

"Thomas, the problem has never been that I don't want to sleep with you. You're a sweet, sexy guy with really gifted fingers and lips, but we have a child together. We can't just hook up. There's too much potential for disaster."

"Let me get this straight. You're saying we can't have sex because we have a child together?"

I nodded.

"Lily, that's ridiculous! Most people who have a child together have sex, maybe not as often as before the child came along, but they do, and it all works out fine. The fact that we have a child together maybe means you shouldn't have sex with a guy like Andy, but…"

"I never slept with Andy."

"You didn't?"

I shook my head. "Are you kidding? After Dylan told him we were engaged? He thought I was a total slut. I couldn't sleep with him after that."

Thomas grinned. "I knew there was value to having Dylan around then."

"Thomas, if I go out with some random guy, and things don't work out, then so what? I'm back where I started. I never have to see the guy again. With you, no matter what happens between us, you'll still be in my life because of Lucy."

He was staring at me, but I couldn't tell if he really understood yet.

"Thomas, when Dylan and I broke up, I had to move halfway across the country. I couldn't stand seeing him for almost four years. I can't risk that kind of pain again and I don't want to jeopardize what you have with Lucy."

Thomas sighed now. "Lily, I'm not Dylan. I'm never going to use cocaine. I'm never going to drink so much that I knock you across the room. And I'm never going to give up and move on. Now that I've found you, I'm not letting you out of my life."

"Oh, Thomas," I murmured, turning to him. He opened his arms, pulling me close. I buried my face in the crook of his neck and cried.

"You know, Lily, lots of people get divorced these days, right? And lots of them have kids. And most of them end up figuring out a way to make things work okay for the kids after divorce, right?"

I pulled my face off of his shirt and shrugged, relieved that the dark fabric hid any traces of the mascara I'd likely smeared across his shoulder.

"Well, right now Lucy has two parents in her life, but they're not together. And even though every kid's dream is to have their parents together, all I'm saying is that if we give it a try and it doesn't work out, Lucy will be fine. I'm not going to run away or take it out on her and you won't either. She will be no worse off than she is now." Thomas turned to face me. "So you see, Lily, we have nothing to lose by giving it a shot."

I had to smile at his persistence. "What am I giving a shot?"

"Me, silly. You're going to give me a chance and see if you like being with me."

"I already know I like being with you. And kissing you. And the other stuff."

"Now you're just being stubborn."

"By saying I like you?"

He nodded seriously. "Come on, Lily. Go out with me. I'm not going to beg."

I raised an eyebrow.

"Okay, okay. I've been begging, for years, and I'll bloody well keep it up if you don't stop being so difficult."

"Thomas, you're my best friend. You're the only one I feel like I can talk to about anything lately. I don't want to ruin that. I'm too scared of losing you."

"Lily, you have to trust me, I'm not going to let you down," he took my hand and squeezed it. "Do you remember when I told you to leave Dylan?"

I nodded.

"You were scared then, too. You didn't want to lose him, you didn't want to tell anybody what was going on, and you didn't know what was going to happen. But you eventually left, and now you see that it was the right thing to do."

I stared back at him. "I'm sorry I've made this so difficult for you. It's not that I don't care about you…"

"I know how you feel about me," he interrupted.

"No, you don't, Thomas," I said, shaking my head and then taking a deep breath. "I love you. I just…"

He pressed his finger to my lips, shushing me. "I know that, Lily, and that's all I've ever needed, and it's all I'll ever need."

I took another deep breath, anxiously wiping a tear off my cheek. "What about what you want?"

"I want you," he said, and his eyes burned into me, over-flowing with desire.

I had no rebuttals left. I launched myself at him, kissing him so fervently that I knocked him onto his back in the grass.

I giggled, and he kissed me until we realized the scene we were surely making in the park. Thomas stood slowly, brushing the grass of his clothes, then reached for my hand to pull me up. I held tight to his hand once I was up and he smiled, his face looking more carefree than I'd ever seen it.

"What time do we need to pick up Lucy?" he asked, retrieving his cell phone with his free hand. "It's five o'clock."

I wrinkled my nose and took his phone. I'd left mine in the car, which was a first for me. I always kept my phone with me and on whenever Lucy and I were apart, just in case. I dialed my parents. When my mom answered, I released Thomas' hand and inched away so he couldn't hear her words.

I asked her about Lucy, then went in for the kill. "Listen, Mom, could you take Lucy home and put her to bed tonight?"

"I thought you were coming home before dinner."

"I know, but there's a lot more to discuss. It would really help me out, Mom."

She sighed and I could practically see her rolling her eyes. "Lily, I don't think it's a good idea for you to spend so much time with that Thomas."

"He's her father, Mom." Now I was the one sighing. "Never mind, we'll be back shortly." I hung up before she could irritate me further.

Thomas forced a smile for me. "Your mother hates me."

"She doesn't know you."

"She loved Dylan," he reminded me.

I laughed and reached for his hand. "See? That shows you what a crappy judge of character she is."

He kissed the side of my head. "So I'm taking you home now?"

"Why don't we pick up dinner on the way home and you can stay for a while? Lucy would love to see you."

CHAPTER THIRTEEN

LILY

We didn't talk much on the drive to get Lucy, and that was fine with me. I had too many thoughts zipping through my head to remember how to sit upright, let alone to make conversation. I ran inside for Lucy, dodging all conversation with my mom, then returned to the car, feeling my brief respite from panic cease the second I saw Thomas leaning against the car, looking all calm and sexy.

"I'll fasten her in," he offered, winking at me before lifting her into her carseat and tickling her.

With Lucy, it was easy to relax. Thomas and I both kept the focus on her while we drove home, made a lazy dinner of pasta and leftover vegetables, then ate. Lucy asked for Daddy to read her books, so I kept busy by clearing the dishes and tidying up. When I heard him start the last book, though, I suddenly felt breathless.

I'd wanted Thomas for years. Now that I'd finally told him that, I certainly couldn't back down. I didn't know what the rest of the night would hold in store, but I at least needed more time to kiss him.

When Thomas returned from tucking Lucy into bed, I was just filling our wine glasses.

"Guess I better be going," he said with a sly grin.

I made a face and he stepped closer.

"No fair. You brushed your hair and put on makeup."

I shrugged. "Benefit of being on home turf."

"You looked perfect before." He took a sip of his wine and waited while I did the same, then he pulled me close for a kiss.

My stomach fluttered and I became overly aware of the heat emanating from his body. I turned away to put the dishes from the drying rack back into the cabinet, desperate to distract myself.

He roped his arms around my waist and my body reflexively settled into his. I felt his warm breath on my ear before he spoke.

"Do you realize I am the happiest man alive when I'm with you?"

"You don't think that's a bit premature?"

"Not in the slightest. Lily, I've wanted you since the day you waltzed into my life in those shiny red shoes. I haven't stopped thinking about you for five years. "

His voice was soft and raspy, and it made my legs turn to gelatin. I resisted the urge to fall for his poetry. "I still have the red shoes," I said instead, "But they're getting worn out."

"Baby, if you let me, I'll buy you all the red shoes in the world," he whispered back, his lips tickling my flesh with each word.

I moaned, remembering exactly how his lips felt on mine at the park.

"How sound of a sleeper is she?" Thomas asked, his mouth hovering right outside mine.

Truth be told, she ended up in my room about fifty percent of the time since she'd stopped sleeping in a crib, and up to this point, it had never really bothered me. "My bedroom door locks," I said, dodging the question.

We were in my room in a flash, Thomas clicking the door locked and leaning me against it, kissing my neck. He released me after a moment and frowned, reaching into his pockets.

I raised an eyebrow in question.

"Condom," he replied, continuing to search until he located one in his wallet.

"What, you don't want more little Lucys?"

"Ooh, excellent point," he said with a grin, tossing it over his shoulder onto the floor.

He leaned into my neck again, his breath tickling my cheeks as he nibbled on my ear and traced his tongue down my neck and across my collarbone. He pulled back and lifted me up, carrying me across the room and placing me on the bed. I'd already removed my sandals, so he quickly progressed to my jeans and then my shirt.

Within a minute, I was stretched out wearing just my white lacy panties and matching bra. Thomas sat back and gazed at me admiringly. "You are perfect," he whispered.

I smiled. "No fair. You're still fully clothed."

Thomas ignored me and crouched on the bed by my feet. "Do you know how long I've been waiting for this? Wishing I could touch your body and worship every inch of you?" He kissed the tops of my feet then slowly worked his way up my legs, massaging one ankle while kissing the other and then switching sides. He rubbed both of my thighs simultaneously, then ran his warm tongue up the inside of one leg, then the other.

I groaned, aware that my body was trembling with desire. I wiggled my hips and reached for him, desperate to pull him up to me. The heat in my body was growing, and the pressure, what had started as a dull ache, was now nearly unbearable.

Thomas swung a leg over me so that he was straddling me and I moaned again, feeling his erection pushing against me through his jeans. "You're going to have to be patient," he said, lifting my arms above my head before securing them in one of his hands. He kissed each of my arms in turn, releasing my hands as he reached them, then dropped down to my chest.

My hands fell into his hair as he lightly stroked my breasts through the thin material of the bra. Now I moaned louder. He breathed a laugh, clearly not concerned that his little game was killing me. Thomas located my nipples through my bra and squeezed each one, then lowered the cups of my bra, gently freeing my breasts.

"Oh, Lily," he murmured, pausing to admire my bare chest.

I squirmed and arched my back, hoping he'd just remove the damn bra. He did, and I moved towards him, eagerly awaiting the touch of his lips on my skin.

"Patience, my dear," he whispered, his eyes locked on mine as he placed his hands back on my breasts, stroking them before gently tugging each nipple.

I bit my lip, embarrassed that I was already panting, already dizzy with pleasure. I opened my mouth to tell him to strip already, to hurry up and take me, but just as I did so, his mouth found my nipple and the only sound I could make was another moan. His hand focused on one breast while his mouth savored the other, and then he traded.

Just when I knew I couldn't take another moment of this sweet torture, he inched away and gently kissed my stomach. "Oh, Thomas, I want…you…now…" I panted.

Thomas dragged his tongue around my belly button before raising his eyes to mine. "Lily, I've waited for this for years. Surely you can give me five minutes."

As he returned to his soft, slow kisses on my stomach, I knew he was wrong. I couldn't wait. I was going to explode. He scooted to the side of my legs and my pelvis ached from the absence of the steady pressure I'd been enjoying from his groin against mine. But before I could protest, his hand slipped under the thin lace panties.

I moaned just as he looked up at me. "Oh Lily, you are eager," he said appreciatively. He swirled his fingers around the entrance to my sex before pressing one further, tracing a circle inside me. I squeezed my eyes shut, feeling my entire body surge like I was on fire. The pressure intensified and I was at my peak when suddenly, his finger disappeared.

I opened my eyes as Thomas slid my panties down my legs. He lifted my legs and knelt between them, pulling me closer to him and kissing me there. His tongue had just reached its goal when I couldn't stand it any longer. I cried out as my pelvis bucked towards him, thrusting his mouth against me even harder. His fingers grasped my thighs firmly and I lost myself to the swirling vortex of sensations.

When I came back to earth, I realized Thomas' hand was now pressed against my mouth. I stared at him, still dazed and tingling all over, and he slid his hand away.

"Can't have you waking our child before we get to the good part," he whispered.

I inhaled deeply, having forgotten with how good that orgasm had been that we hadn't even begun the main course. Thomas stepped away from the bed and grabbed the condom off the floor, tossing it to me. He slowly undressed down to his boxer briefs and I ripped open the small foil packet.

I stared unabashedly at his body while he stood before me. He'd always been fit, but he was even more muscular now than he had been years ago. I'd guessed that from his recent music videos, but seeing him in person, without the layers, it was even more obvious. I smiled and sat up, my head falling at his stomach level. I kissed his firm stomach before tugging his boxer briefs to the ground. His erection sprang free and I leaned closer, eager to take him in my mouth.

"Oh no you don't," he said, nudging me back onto the bed and snatching the condom out of my hand.

"That's not fair," I protested. "At least let me return the favor."

"Life's not fair, sweetheart," he mumbled, sliding the condom on and kneeling between my legs again.

I smiled and wrapped my arms around him, shifting my hips as he lay on top of me.

"Oh, Thomas," I whispered appreciatively, and he pushed into me.

I gasped, the fullness and warmth of him quickly bringing me back to the peak of my pleasure. Our bodies moved in sync, my hips rising to meet his, our mouths and hands desperately exploring each other's bodies. I felt the pressure mounting again with each thrust of his hips, as he stretched me and filled me again and again.

I opened my eyes, and as soon as I saw the bright green of his eyes gazing back at me, I lost all control. My fingers dug into his hips and I pressed my mouth against his thick bicep to muffle my cries as wave after wave of intensity washed through me, piercing all of my senses. Thomas thrust into me harder and called out my name, quickly finding his own release as well.

Our bodies stilled after a moment, but he didn't pull out of me.

"I wish we could stay like this forever," I mumbled once I'd found my voice.

"Fine by me," he replied.

But despite that, he slid away a moment later, tossed the condom in the trash, then lay beside me, stroking my hair purposefully.

"I do love you," I said finally.

"I know. You wouldn't have been so worried about getting hurt if you didn't already care so much."

I relaxed into his body and drifted off to sleep at some point.

When I awoke, I startled, surprised to feel another person in bed with me. I lifted my head and glanced at Thomas, and he smiled at me.

"I fell asleep," I said.

"Yes."

"Sorry."

He laughed. "Don't be. I love watching you sleep."

I sighed and tried to sit up. The clock read 12:30, so I hadn't been asleep for too long.

"I should go," he said, climbing out of bed and making his way to the bathroom.

"Why?"

He returned a minute later. "So you can get some sleep." He bent to retrieve his clothes.

"Clearly I can sleep with you here."

"What about Lucy? If she wakes up and I'm still here…"

I considered that. I'd never had a man sleep over since she'd been born because I didn't want to confuse or traumatize her if she woke up to find a stranger with her mother. But she knew Thomas. If she'd been older, I'd worry about her getting her hopes up about her parents reuniting, but at three, the chances of her understanding any of what was going on with Thomas and I were practically nil.

"She'd be happy to see you," I finally said.

"Are you sure?"

"If you want to stay, then yes."

Thomas smiled and climbed back into bed beside me, pulling the sheet up over us.

"I need to check on her first, though," I said, inching out of bed.

"Can I?"

I shook my head. "I always check on her before I go to sleep."

He simply nodded, so I grabbed my thin silk robe and left.

Lucy was sleeping peacefully, her tiny body sprawled across her bed instead of resting in the middle, with her head on the pillow and her feet beneath her like an adult would sleep. Her dark hair covered her eyes, but I could see her chest rising and falling with each quiet breath. I turned to leave and bumped into Thomas.

He was smiling at her, and just seeing in his face how much he loved her—this precious little girl he'd only met months before, made me love him even more. I pulled her door shut quietly.

"I always knew we were meant to be together," he said. "But she's proof of that. Without Lucy, who knows where we'd each be today. But since she came along, even you can't deny that we belong together. She's a miracle."

I nodded and kissed him softly, leading him back to the bedroom.

* * *

THOMAS

Waking up with Lily's fingers curled around my bicep, I smiled before even fully opening my eyes. When I did, I was overwhelmed by her beauty. Asleep, Lily reminded me of the old Lily, the calmer one who hadn't yet sacrificed so much of herself for our daughter. The last night we'd been together—the only other night, actually, I'd lain awake much of the night. It relaxed and amused me to watch Lily sleep, to see the tiny twitches and expressions she made then, much as it still did now.

The last night we were together, though, I'd felt an indescribable heaviness. I'd known she'd feel guilty for what we'd done when she woke, and, while I couldn't actually bring myself to feel bad about what I'd done to my brother at that time, I did feel terrible knowing my behavior would bring her guilt. I'd had the tiny dash of hope that she'd wake and choose me, but mostly I'd been afraid to sleep because I was fairly certain our time together would end when she woke.

I'd been right.

This time, the tables were turned. I wasn't completely confident that she'd wake with no regrets, but I mostly believed this wouldn't be our last night together. Still, even the fleeting thought that it might be my last chance with her made me panic. A gentleman would've let her sleep, but I wanted to make the most of our time together.

I leaned closer, inhaling the sweet scent of her hair, then lightly trailed kisses along her arm. She wiggled against me, only half awake, but I took the opportunity to lick my finger and slip it between her legs.

She moaned sleepily. I considered the possibility that she wanted to sleep, but then she shifted, opening herself up to my touch. I stroked her lightly, not wanting to rush her. But, only a minute or two passed before she turned to me, her lips crashing to mine. My hands shifted to her thighs, squeezing the muscles along the side of her legs, then moving to her breasts. She was so responsive when I played with her nipples, moaning at every gentle graze, pinch, and lick.

Lily reached down my torso, seeming surprised to find me already hard. As if I could've possibly avoided being turned on when in bed with her. She ran her hand up and down my shaft twice before I gripped her hand and moved it aside. After I'd spent the last half hour laying here replaying every moment of our last encounter in my brain, I wouldn't last two minutes if she kept touching me like that.

She nudged me onto my back, kissing my neck, chest, then abdomen. She gazed lower, smiling at my erection. When she brought her eyes back to mine, she raised an eyebrow. I knew what she was asking, knew exactly what she wanted to do, and as much as the thought of her beautiful mouth on my sensitive flesh appealed to me, I wanted all of her. So I shook my head. She pouted, but quickly recovered, positioning her hips over my torso. Emboldened, I gripped her thigh, sliding her up towards my face and lifting my tongue to meet her. She shrieked at the suddenness of my movements, then stilled, letting me stroke her only a couple times before pulling away.

This time when she straddled me, she positioned me right at her entrance. My eyes locked on her breasts as they hovered above me then moved on to her beautiful brown eyes. As beautifully breathtaking as Lily's body was, there was no more precious sight than her eyes gazing at me adoringly. She began to lower herself onto me, but as her eyes drifted shut, I remembered.

"Condom," I whispered.

Lily groaned and didn't climb off of me.

"Lily…"

She opened her eyes fully and let me slide out from under her. I had a second one in my wallet, but after that, I was out. I grabbed it quickly then rejoined her in bed.

"Do you have any here?" I asked, figuring I should know what we had on hand before getting my hopes up about a third round.

"I don't know. Maybe?" She groaned again. "I'm going on the pill tomorrow," she said, bringing a smile to my face.

I settled back against the pillow and lifted her onto me again, raising my head up so I could kiss her.

We both fell back asleep after this round.

A loud thumping awoke me shortly before seven. I was beyond exhausted, but the moment I saw Lily trying to sneak out of bed, it all came back to me.

"Oh no you don't," I said, tugging her back into bed.

She giggled and kissed me, then shook her head. "Lucy's up."

"You need more sleep, and I make fantastic pancakes. The best ever, according to Lucy."

Lily rolled her eyes. "That's because the only pancakes I've ever made her come frozen in a box."

"Go back to sleep," I ordered.

She crawled back under the covers, but her eyes stayed on me as I dressed. I pressed one last kiss on her lips before leaving the room.

* * *

LILY

By some miracle, I did fall back asleep, and when I woke later, the apartment was quiet. I pulled on a nightgown and my robe before slipping out of the bedroom. The kitchen still smelled of pancakes, but the mess had been cleaned. I gazed over to the couch where Lucy perched on Thomas' lap, looking at books with him.

He looked ridiculously hot, even in his clothes from the day before. And the way he was staring at me made my knees wobble. He whispered something to Lucy and she hopped off his lap and scampered over to me. I lifted her into my arms while she told me about the chocolate chip pancakes she'd eaten.

"Unfortunately, yours are just plain, but I have berries to put on top," Thomas said as the microwave beeped. He set a plate of pancakes on the table and poured a cup of coffee for me, thrusting it into my hands. "Good morning, gorgeous," he whispered.

Despite how intimate we'd been, the compliment made me blush. I turned to the table, not quite sure what to say.

"Eat!" Lucy commanded, so I did.

I didn't quite make it through the entire plate of pancakes, but they were delicious. And while I finished eating, Thomas dressed Lucy. She was begging him to play ponies with her, but he said he had a question for me first. He led me into the bedroom and partially closed the door.

His lips were on mine before I even registered what was happening. His kiss was intense and delicious and with his body pressed tightly against mine, I couldn't help but remember every detail of the night before. He broke apart our lips long before I was ready, leaving me breathless. I reached for his head, relishing the feel of his soft hair against my hands, and pulled him towards me. He resisted, then offered me a small peck on the lips.

"If you keep kissing me like that, I won't be able to stop," he said, his voice a sultry mix between a whisper and a growl.

"I don't want you to."

His chuckle came out like a deep rumble. "I don't want to either, but we'll probably have an audience in another minute."

I cringed. I'd completely forgotten Lucy was just playing in her bedroom. She could get bored and walk in on us any second. I groaned out loud. "She's lucky she's so cute."

Thomas chuckled, kissed my forehead, then released me. "That she is. And actually, I have to head out."

"What? No," the whine escaped my lips before I could stop myself. One night with him and already I was nagging. It was pathetic, but really, I needed more. I needed more time to kiss him, more time to touch him, more of everything. Last night had been amazing, but it hadn't even begun to satisfy my craving for Thomas. If anything, it had only sparked it more. "It's Sunday. What could possibly be so important?"

"I've got to go play a guitar with some guys," he said with a shrug, as though he were off to some garage band practice.

"Tonight?"

His grin widened. "You should get some sleep tonight. Practice might run late."

"I don't want sleep."

"And I promise I will give you exactly what you want, soon." He bent down, tipped my chin upwards, and kissed me one last time. "I love you," he whispered.

I watched from the edge of the bed as he left, listening to Lucy similarly protest his departure, then stood to go play with our daughter.

Later that afternoon, a package arrived by courier. I knew

without looking that it had to be from Thomas. While a normal girl would love receiving a thoughtful gift the morning after a night like I'd shared with Thomas, it filled me with unease. Back when I'd been with Dylan, he'd constantly showered me with gifts- jewelry when he'd accidentally hurt me, shoes to apologize for using drugs, a purse when he'd been a jerk. At the time, I'd found it sweet and romantic. Looking back, I realized it made me feel like he owned me, like he was buying my silence, or even like payment for sex.

Thomas was nothing like that, but still, I didn't want an expensive gift as a thank you for an intimate, mutually pleasurable night. I read the card first, but instead of some romantic musings, all it said was "open when alone." Lucy was happily entertained with modeling clay at the kitchen table, so I took the package into the bedroom and tore off the wrapping.

It was an economy size box of condoms. I laughed out loud, then stashed it in my nightstand drawer and texted Thomas a quick thank you.

"Figured you could use a stash at your place until that pill kicks in," he replied.

"Good timing. I have a date tonight so you saved me a trip to the store," I teased.

"Ouch. Well, I have a piano lesson tomorrow, but maybe after?"

It took me a moment to realize Lucy was the lesson he meant. Just as I figured it out though, he wrote more.

"What if I pick her up from school and we meet you at your place?"

I quickly agreed, then did a tiny happy dance in the corner of my room.

CHAPTER FOURTEEN

THOMAS

The next two weeks were like a dream. Lily and I spent several nights a week together, fulfilling my every bedroom fantasy. Each time that I awoke beside her, my chest constricted as I remembered I was the luckiest man alive. Every smile, every touch, every kiss from her was a precious gift. I wasn't taking any of it for granted.

Lily's parents didn't support her plan to spend the entire summer in England with me and Lucy, so she didn't want to tell them- or anyone else- that we were dating until after we were overseas. I had no problem with that, and I thought I'd done a good job of covering up the relationship, until the night before Lucy's party.

The band had practiced most of the day and well into the evening. I'd hoped I would finish in time to tuck Lucy into bed and then have some alone time with Lily, but no such luck. I knew Lily would still welcome my visit at that hour, but she had a big day the next day, hosting the party. I didn't want to deprive her of much needed sleep.

"You headed to Lily's now?" Dylan asked as he packed up his guitar, jolting me out of my thoughts about the exact question he was asking.

"No. Lucy's already in bed by now."

My brother eyed me warily. Six months ago, I could've deciphered exactly what that look meant. But now, we'd grown apart. I wasn't sure what thoughts were running through his mind. I turned away, finished zipping my own guitar case, then stood.

"You've been spending a lot of nights out lately," Dylan continued. "Coming home in the morning."

"You're spying on me?"

"It's the neighborly thing to do," he replied with a smile. "I assumed that meant you were finally with Lily."

I looked away.

"You're certainly seeing someone. Don't tell me I got the woman wrong. I can't stand another five years of you moping about her."

I blew out a sigh. "What would you say if I was with Lily now?"

"I'd say it's about fucking time."

"It wouldn't bother you?"

"Four and a half years after the affair is a little late to ask permission to sleep with my fiancée," he said. "You should've told me you were interested then."

"What would that have changed? You already knew, and besides, it's not like you would've stepped aside."

He raised his eyebrows, which I interpreted as a concession that my statement was true.

"Lily should have told me."

"You weren't exactly easy to talk to," I reminded him. "And she didn't want to risk you hurting yourself."

"We all made mistakes, I get it. But you don't need my permission to go out with her now. She's raising your child, and she's interested in you."

"And you're married," I reminded him.

"Mere technicality."

I glared. Dylan had a lot of nerve lecturing me on the proper way to end one relationship before starting another when he'd had women in his apartment at least twice over the last week alone.

"Fine. I'm just saying you have my blessing. Not that you needed it," he said. "I really do hope it works out with you two."

He sounded and looked sincere, but I didn't want to assume anything.

"So how long have you been sneaking around with her?"

I hesitated.

"Jesus, Tom, really? The jig is up. You're never home, and you smile incessantly. I haven't seen you this happy since…well, never."

"Two weeks," I finally admitted. "But she doesn't want anyone knowing before we leave for England, so keep it to yourself."

He nodded, still smugly grinning.

* * *

LILY

Every detail was perfect at Lucy's party. She loved the games and crafts we'd planned, and everyone enjoyed the light lunch that was served before the ridiculously over the top cake Thomas had ordered. We made it almost all the way through the meal before the guests from Lucy's school seemed to put together that all five members of the band Sierra were in attendance. One mom whispered to the mom beside her and then it spread like wildfire around the decorated lawn.

"So much for flying under the radar," I whispered to Thomas.

He didn't seem to mind, although there was a security team on standby.

As we all finished up lunch, Thomas placed his hand on the back of my chair and leaned close, his lips brushing against my ear. "I think we have time to sneak inside for a quickie if you're game. Lucy seems distracted by the cake and after all this food, there's only one thing I have an appetite for and it isn't frosting." He paused, then added. "Unless I'm licking that frosting off you."

I squeezed my eyes shut, trying to chase away the vivid imagery his dirty words had brought to my mind. My face flushed, and when I opened my eyes, Jill was staring at me. Actually, glaring was a more accurate term.

"You are bad," I said to Thomas. "Are you ready to sing?"

He chuckled. "I am always ready to sing. Do you mean the Happy Birthday song or did someone blow the surprise?"

"What surprise?"

"Never mind," he said. "Let's get to that cake!"

"What surprise?" I repeated.

He winked, flashing me his devilishly handsome grin that made my knees weak.

After cake, Thomas whispered something to Lucy and she grinned excitedly. I assumed he was going to get the unicorn, but instead, he gathered the rest of the band then carried Lucy to the patio. He placed her on a chair facing the back of the house, where she waited patiently. I watched, curiously wondering what he'd said to get her to sit so calmly at her own party. Within a few minutes, the entire band had reappeared on the back patio, three of them holding guitars, Dave with his drum set, and Owen facing his keyboard.

Thomas moved to the microphone. "Pardon the interruption, but as a special treat for the birthday girl, I've gathered a few of my friends to perform her favorite song."

A buzz washed over the crowd as all of our party guests rushed forward.

"Two songs!" shrieked Lucy over the commotion.

It was Dylan who leaned forward, presumably asking her what her second favorite was, then nodded briefly.

After a moment, they began playing and everyone fell under their spell.

"Did you know they were going to do this?" Jill asked, materializing by my side.

"I had no idea," I replied. I couldn't stop smiling. We'd invited the band as guests, not as hired entertainers, but it was obvious they were all more than happy to do this for Lucy. And to say she was thrilled was an understatement. After this performance, the unicorn would be a letdown.

"You're sleeping with him," Jill said.

I turned to her, feeling my eyes go wide.

"You don't have to be a mind reader to guess what he was saying to you earlier. And you two can't keep your hands off each other."

I cringed. I thought we'd done a good job of hiding our feelings. I'd given myself a headache trying to remember not to touch him. I tried to think of the best way to deny everything, when she continued.

"His hand was on your back when you held Lucy to sing to her."

"He wanted to be close to Lucy."

"His hand was on your leg during lunch, under the table. You fed him a bite of cake. You two are literally like nauseatingly sweet newlyweds. What I don't know is why you didn't tell me or how long it's been going on."

I winced. "Do you think my parents noticed?"

"Your father has been shooting him daggers for the last twenty minutes, so I'd say he has some guesses."

"Crap."

"So….?"

"A couple weeks, and I didn't tell you because we didn't want my parents to find out and murder him," I said, answering her questions. "Let's talk tomorrow."

She nodded just as Sierra moved on to their second song. The moment I heard the opening notes, my breath caught in my throat. They were playing *Lily Smiles*. It was the song that Dylan used to serenade me with. The song I thought he'd written for me until, shortly after Lucy was born, I'd read an interview where Dylan stated that Thomas had actually written that song.

I'd never known what to make of that little detail. The song was more Thomas' style and any other fan would've guessed from the start that he penned those lyrics. But what I didn't understand was why he'd write a song about his brother's girl-friend, or why his brother had no problem with that. I also couldn't help wondering if the song was what tipped off Dylan to his brother's feelings for me.

Lucy loved the song for the same reason all of Sierra's fans did—it had poetic, memorable lyrics combined with a heart-wrenchingly beautiful melody. But she also appreciated that my name appeared throughout the song, even though she'd never known the song was about me.

As the song rolled to an end, the pony paraded out to the crowd, on a lead held by its handler. As everyone oohed and ahhed over the "unicorn," I noticed the band members all slipped away except for Thomas. He grabbed Lucy and carried her to the animal, letting her pet its rainbow mane before finally mounting it.

He'd arranged for a professional to photograph the party, and for caterers to serve and clean up all of the food, so there was nothing for me to do but watch and enjoy my daughter's inno-cent smile.

* * *

THOMAS

Lucy was so exhausted that she fell asleep on the drive home from her grandparents' house. I managed to transfer her into her bed without waking her, then watched in awe as Lily wrangled her into pajamas.

"That's impressive," I said as we tiptoed out of the room.

She smiled. "I've got skills."

"Yeah you do," I agreed, swatting her butt as we both headed out to the kitchen.

She eyed the kitchen, probably noting the remnants of the breakfast dishes still in the sink, but made her way straight to the couch and collapsed onto her back. "I'm exhausted."

I was too, but I lifted her legs and sat beneath them, cradling her feet on my lap. I began massaging gently as she eyed me suspiciously.

"You're going to get lucky tonight. You don't have to do that."

"Noted," I said, biting back my smile. "But I want to." I wasn't about to pass up any opportunity to touch Lily.

"Lucy had a blast. The unicorn was amazing, but I bet her favorite part was seeing you sing. She's been telling her friends at school that her daddy sings songs, but I don't imagine they had any idea how well you really sing those songs."

I couldn't help but smile at the memory of how happy and proud Lucy looked when we sang. That moment would be hard to top.

"Hey, meant to tell you, but Jill figured out that we're dating."

Lily looked so concerned by her own statement that I couldn't help but tease her. "We're dating now? Oh geez. I thought this was just sex. Did I miss the part where I took you out on an actual date?"

She lifted her head to look at me, then frowned. "No, actually. You haven't taken me out on a real date. Why not?"

"That walk in the park didn't count?"

Lily swatted me with a pillow.

"I will take you on a date wherever and whenever you want. Just say the word. Will your parents still watch her if they know you're out with me?"

She cringed, covering her face with her hands. "I think my parents know, too. Jill figured it out just based on how we were acting today, so it's possible that…"

"That your parents hate me even more now?"

She shrugged. "Lucy and I like you enough to make up for anyone else who is too stubborn to see how amazing you are."

I wasn't exactly sure what that comment meant, but it seemed like a good time to tell her about Dylan. "Dylan guessed that we were together as well. He asked me about it the other day. I didn't want to stress you out before the party by telling you."

Now she wrinkled her nose. "How did he take it?"

"Fine. He actually said that we have his blessing."

She looked surprised, but pleased by this. "Jill seemed supportive too, which I wasn't expecting. But I'm supposed to meet her at the gym tomorrow, so we will talk more then."

"Be sure to tell her that my foot rubs are rivaled only by my bedroom skills," I teased.

She rolled her eyes but smiled.

I scooted her legs onto either side of my waist then pulled her close until she was on my lap. Her eyes still shimmered brightly despite her fatigue. I stroked my finger along her cheekbone and leaned closer. I loved watching her lips part, but I hadn't planned to kiss her. Not yet, anyway.

"You looked gorgeous today. You put on a brilliant party. And you are the most amazing mother Lucy could ask for. I'm so glad she has you, and I'm so, so glad you're letting me have a little part of you too," I said. I was going to kiss her then, but she tilted her head backwards and groaned.

"I already told you that I have every intention of letting you have your way with me tonight. You don't have to keep being so sweet."

I traced just the tip of my tongue along the salty sweet skin of her throat, relishing the taste of her more than an ice cream cone. She arched against me, then brought her face back to mine, clasping her hands behind my head.

"I spent nearly four years trying to forget you," she said. "I'm so glad I failed."

"Me too," I whispered, right as she breached the space between us and planted her lips on mine. I could've stayed right like that, kissing her until we both passed out, but I didn't want to traumatize our kid just yet. So I stood, gripping Lily's hips tightly with my hands, and awkwardly walked us both to the bedroom, plopping her onto the bed and climbing over her as she squealed.

* * *

LILY

I was even more exhausted the next day, but still managed to drag myself to the gym to meet Jill. Since her initial show of support for my relationship with Thomas, I was eager to share more juicy details with her. And, I realized I hadn't told her we were going to England for the full summer.

We met in the locker room about a half hour before our class was due to begin. Jill beat me there, and laughed when she saw me.

I glanced down at my outfit, trying to figure out what was so comical.

"I'm the one with an infant and you're the one who looks exhausted," she explained. "Did you have a lot of cleanup after the party? I'm sorry I couldn't stay and help."

I shook my head. "No, Thomas paid the caterers to clean

everything up. And then he took me home and gave me a foot rub."

"Nice. So why do you look like you haven't slept in a week?"

I felt myself blush, but this was Jill. We shared everything with each other. Well, or we used to. "I don't get a lot of sleep when Thomas stays over."

She nodded knowingly. "He's a snorer?"

Now I couldn't help but laugh. Hard. "No, he's actually a really quiet sleeper but we tend to do a lot more of other stuff and very little sleeping when we are in bed."

"Ohhh. You're sex tired," she said.

We both giggled.

"So, it's um, going well?" she asked.

"It's going great. As soon as I stopped trying so hard to convince myself I shouldn't be with him, I started seeing how perfect everything actually is. I don't think I've ever been this happy before. I mean, I knew he was good for Lucy, but he's been really good for me too."

Jill's smile was filled with warmth. "You deserve to be happy."

I lunged forward to hug my friend. She startled at first, then hugged me back.

"I'm so glad you're being supportive. I know you thought it was a bad idea at first, but I really did think it all through."

"I still think you should take it slow," she said when I finally released her.

"I absolutely agree."

She slammed her locker then started towards the door. I followed, averting my eyes from an older woman parading through the locker room completely naked from the waist up.

"Hey, so you know how I told you he wanted to take Lucy to England to meet his mom?"

She nodded.

"He invited me too. I mean, he invited me before we were…

involved. I think he realized I was too clingy to let Lucy leave the country without me."

"You should go," Jill agreed. "And Lucy will love that, I'm sure. It's not like you guys have had a lot of vacations, right?"

That was true. Yet another reason this was a good plan. "I hadn't even thought of that, but you're right. And this trip will more than make up for the lack of vacations thus far because we are leaving for the entire summer." I bent to tighten my shoelaces but kept talking. "We'll visit his family, travel the countryside some, and spend several weeks at his place in London."

"I'm sorry. What?"

I breathed a laugh, having expected my friend's disbelief. "You heard me right."

Jill's jaw dropped and her eyebrows wrinkled. "You've only begun dating him. I thought you were going to take things slowly!"

I shrugged. "We can take it slowly in England."

"Traveling overseas for an extended timeframe is the opposite of taking it slowly."

I had no response for that. Obviously, she was right, but at the same time…

"What about Lucy? Have you even considered her?"

Instantly, my blood was boiling. "Of course I've considered her. How could you even ask that?"

Jill's eyebrows raised pointedly. "You seem pretty focused on yourself."

"Every fucking thing I do involves considering Lucy. I don't get the luxury of ever being selfish because I'm all she has." I paused. "Except maybe now that has changed too. Or will, anyway. You do remember that Thomas is her father, right?"

"Yes. Exactly why you shouldn't jump into things with him. What if it doesn't work out?"

"He's still her dad, regardless of how things go with him and I. She won't lose him either way."

I saw the resolve wash over Jill's face as she clenched her jaw. I could tell she was trying to calm herself down. I knew she'd be surprised by my news, but hadn't exactly expected this level of panic.

"Look, I didn't expect you would immediately support my decision, but…"

"Support your decision?" She flung her hands dramatically into the air. "Lily this is insane. Have you already forgotten what happened last time? You rushed into things with Dylan and you got hurt. I don't want to lose you for another four years when things go sour this time."

"*If*, not *when*. And this is Thomas, not Dylan," I reminded her.

She made a face, which I supposed meant they weren't that different. Except they were. I squeezed my fingers tightly to my palms, willing my heart rate to slow even as the heat flooded my cheeks.

"You know, even if it were Dylan, he's different now. Yeah, he had a problem, but he got help, and he's better. He isn't on drugs anymore."

Her stone cold expression remained. "Don't be naïve, Lily. People don't change."

"But he has changed! And Thomas—he's so responsible. He's amazing with Lucy. He'd never let anything happen to her."

I stopped talking as Jill's eyes dropped to the ground. I sighed, and considered that maybe during my years away, we'd actually grown apart. Maybe our differences were too big to reconcile now, if she thought so little of the man I was very truly falling for.

"Never mind," I said. "I don't even know why I'm trying to defend them to you. I know what kind of a man Thomas is, and I know he and Dylan have both changed, and that's all that matters."

"I wasn't talking about Thomas or Dylan," Jill said evenly.

"When I said people don't change, I meant you. I don't think you've changed."

"But…I…then…" I stammered.

She shook her head. "You are so trusting and loving and you always see the best in people, Lily. Those are great qualities, except when you combine them with your tendency to rush into things…" Jill shrugged. "I just don't want to see you get hurt again. I know you think you love Thomas and everything is perfect now, but you have to admit your track record isn't so good."

Wow. So, clearly since I hadn't married straight out of college like her, my judgment couldn't be trusted when it came to men. I didn't even know what to say. I mean, yeah, I'd made mistakes. Obviously, all the men before Dylan reflected some serious errors in judgment, except maybe I'd learned something from each of those relationships. And as much as I knew Jill—and everyone else—seemed to think I should regret my time with Dylan, I wasn't sure I could say that I did.

Sure, things ended badly, and maybe could've ended even worse if I hadn't left when I had, but without that relationship, I wouldn't have met Thomas or had Lucy. And it hadn't been all bad, either. I'd had a blast with Dylan. When I was with Dylan, I felt interesting, loved, cherished. No other man had ever made me feel quite so sexy or important, except for Thomas.

"I didn't mean to upset you," Jill interrupted. "I just think it's a bad idea and I can't in good conscience keep my mouth shut about it. But now that I've told you what I think, let's just go into class and forget it."

I nodded. "Yeah."

I started to follow her into the spinning room, but the dim lights, the faint scent of sweat leftover from the last class, and the pulsating music all hit me at once. A wave of nausea washed over me and the claustrophobia threatened to sink in.

"Actually, I'm feeling a bit off now. You go on. I'll chat with you later," I said. I turned and left before she could protest. I knew she was watching me, but I didn't care. I couldn't sit through an hour long workout with her by my side knowing she thought so little of my judgment.

* * *

THOMAS

I had taken Lucy back to my apartment after her nap, thinking Lily wouldn't be back until after later. When she trudged in though, she was clearly annoyed.

"Bad class?" I asked.

She groaned. "I didn't go to class because Jill was being a jerk."

I pulled her into a tight embrace. I assumed her fight with Jill was because of me, but I wasn't sure whether she'd feel better with a glass of wine or the key to the private gym in my building. I offered both and she went for the wine.

"I don't think I could sit on a bike after last night anyway," she added, making me laugh.

She situated Lucy with some art supplies, then followed me into the bedroom to talk. As she recounted the entire conversation she'd had with Jill, I couldn't say I was surprised about any of it.

"You love people so fully, Lily, and that's not something you should ever feel bad about."

"Yeah, well, whatever it is about me, I nearly ruined my whole life doing it once before." She shook her head. "I look back now and I see my mistakes. I was young, impulsive, and naïve. I thought loving someone was enough."

"Who's to say it isn't?" I interrupted.

She made a face and continued her diatribe. "Everybody seems to think I'm making the same mistakes all over again."

I gripped her hands, desperate to calm her down. "Okay, slow down. What mistakes? Be specific."

"Rushing into a relationship."

"You've known me for years, Lily. I've loved you for literally years and you've just now let me take you on our first date. That is the opposite of rushing. Snails move faster."

Lily's mouth quirked at that, but she didn't fully smile. "I rushed into things with Dylan."

I shrugged. "Did you though? You're adults. You liked each other. It's not like you eloped on the first date." I paused. "And even if you did, so what?"

"So what? I ended up unemployed and homeless."

I flung my hands in the air. "You were too good for both of those jobs and you know it. You quit the travel agency to follow a dream of yours to travel the world. You can't possibly tell me you regret that. And if you hadn't quit waitressing at that club, you wouldn't be teaching. Are you seriously telling me you have any regrets about how your career has turned out?"

I heard her swallow uncomfortably.

"Well, no, but..."

"And you were hardly homeless. It's a big city. People move all the time. You could've just gotten a new apartment locally. Would you have truly stayed in your old apartment with that weird roommate of yours while raising a baby?"

Lily grimaced and shook her head. "She wasn't weird."

"Really? She would've been okay with night feedings and all the crying and poopy diapers?"

"Well no. But I got pregnant while my boyfriend was in rehab. Most people would consider that a mistake."

My body tensed at her words. I knew what she meant, but the implication wasn't something I wanted to hear. "Sure, the timing sucked. But...you got Lucy. You're counting that as a mistake?"

Her eyes fluttered shut and she shook her head. "No. Of course not. I didn't mean..."

"I know." I pressed a kiss against her forehead. "I'm not pretending you haven't faced some challenges these last few years, only that I don't necessarily think anything you did before was a mistake. Everything that happened, every choice you made, it brought you where you are today."

"Yeah, right back where I was five years ago."

"No. Today you're a strong, independent woman. You've got a great career that you love, one where people expect you to sit around and read your favorite books over and over again. You've got an amazing daughter that thinks the world of you and you're the absolute best mom out there even though you had to do it alone for the first few years." I paused to make sure she was truly hearing my words.

I squeezed her hands again as I continued. "And you have a super sexy, filthy rich boyfriend that literally tops the charts and wants nothing more than to love you the rest of your life."

She giggled at my cheeky comment.

"You have it all, Lily. You actually have it all. So whatever you did to get here, well, you must've done it right."

She sighed and drained the rest of her wine. "I should go start dinner."

I made a face. Lily was great at many things, but cooking was not one of them. "I'll handle dinner. You go take a bath and think about how your wretched choices have left you in that gorgeous oversized tub while a hot man entertains your angelic child and cooks dinner for you."

Lily giggled but headed towards the bathroom. "If that hot man brought me more wine, I wouldn't refuse," she said.

CHAPTER FIFTEEN

"Drink to me only with thine eyes,
And I will pledge with mine;
Or leave a kiss but in the cup,
And I'll not look for wine."
Ben Johnson, *Song: To Celia*

LILY

After Lucy's party, I only had a couple more weeks of school before we headed overseas. Since we flew on a private charter plane, the flight was spectacular, even though Dylan and Owen also accompanied us and overindulged in all the inflight beverages.

As much as I'd have liked a few days to relax and regroup in London at Thomas' apartment, we immediately went to Ipswich, where his mother, Kate, lived. I'd met her before, back when I was with Dylan, and she'd always liked me.

Now, I suspected she'd feel differently. Thomas said he'd told her I'd returned to town, and that my daughter was named after his sister Lucy, but he'd been intentionally vague on the other details. And, his mother had no idea we were dating. Thomas and I decided it would be easier to talk with his mother alone before bringing Lucy into the mix, especially since Lucy didn't actually know all the torrid details of her own conception yet.

Kate answered the door with unbridled enthusiasm. Her expression quickly turned to surprise.

"Thomas!" she exclaimed. "Where's Dylan?" she asked, pulling him in for a hug.

Thomas glanced down at his feet, clearly not eager to see his mother's expression as he answered. "He's with Lucy."

"Oh." Kate's disappointment was obvious. "I thought I was going to see my granddaughter."

"They'll be here after lunch."

"Well, compared to four years, what's another hour?" Kate sighed and glared at me pointedly.

I squeezed my lips together tightly and glanced at Thomas, nervously.

"We wanted to talk with you first. Can we come in?"

Kate nodded and swung the door open wider. She entered and went straight towards the kitchen. "Tea?"

"That'll be great, Mum. Thanks."

I exhaled the breath I'd been holding as soon as Thomas and I were alone in the small living room.

"She hates me," I murmured.

Thomas squeezed my hand. "I'll explain everything, love. I promise."

He leaned forward and kissed my forehead softly. The gesture calmed my racing heart, until there was a loud crash.

I turned in the direction of the noise and saw that Kate, having witnessed the intimate moment between Thomas and I, had dropped one of the mugs. Her face was red and she froze for a moment, clearly confused, before dropping to her knees to pick up the broken pieces of porcelain.

"I'll get it," Thomas offered, rushing forward. He grabbed a towel and crouched down, wiping the mess and collecting the broken pieces. "I'm sorry about the mug," he mumbled.

"I can make more tea," she said.

"No, Mum, wait. We wanted to talk to you. Just sit, we don't need tea."

Her eyes darted back and forth from Thomas to me then back to Thomas. "I know what you're going to say, so don't trouble yourselves. I can't say I'm surprised that she…" Kate paused to glare at me, "Would do something like that, but I did expect better from you. How could you do this to your brother?"

"He's married," Thomas answered.

"She's the mother of his child," Kate retorted.

Thomas glanced at me nervously and reached for my hand. I was tempted to run out of the cottage, but reluctantly accepted his hand instead.

"No, she's not, Mum. She's the mother of *my* child."

Kate remained still and expressionless for so long I began to wonder if she'd heard him. But then she silently dropped onto the sofa behind her.

Thomas motioned for me to sit on the chair adjacent to the sofa, and I gladly obeyed, not certain my knees would support me much longer anyway.

After a moment, Kate spoke. "I don't know what you expect me to say. Dylan is your brother. He's not perfect, but he's all you have. How could you do that to him?"

Thomas sat beside me. "It was a mistake, Mum." He glanced quickly at me, panicked, then turned back to his mom to clarify. "It was wrong and I didn't mean to hurt him, but…"

"And you!" Kate turned to me, her eyes wide with anger now. "It's bad enough you hide my grandchild from me, but you have to destroy my sons too? It wasn't enough to just break Dylan's heart, you had to try to ruin Thomas too?"

"Mother!" Thomas raised his voice and we both jumped, startled at his anger. "Do you remember what Dylan was like then? Do you have any bloody idea what life was like for Lily?"

"He had a problem, Thomas. I know that. But he wasn't a bad man. And he loved her."

Thomas nodded. "Yeah. He loved her. And he hit her. On more than one occasion. You see that scar above her eyebrow?"

He paused and I felt myself blush as his mother stared at me.

"Dylan did that. Only I got to drive her to the hospital because he was too high." Thomas shook his head, disgusted. "That wasn't even the worst."

I cringed as the details—still all too fresh in my mind—of that horrific night all flashed back through my memory.

Kate started crying, which made me feel even worse. I hadn't wanted her to know what Dylan had been like, and certainly hadn't anticipated Thomas telling her. I could've accepted the blame for my role in this mess without implicating Dylan at all.

Thomas looked flustered, his eyes flitting from his mom to me then back again. He squeezed my thigh.

Kate squeezed her eyes shut. "You can't tell him. Any of this. It'll kill him. He can't know."

"He already knows. Dylan has known about Lucy since she was born, and he knew Lucy was my child, but he didn't even tell me she existed."

Kate wiped her tears away but still didn't make eye contact.

"So if you want to be mad at someone for keeping your granddaughter away, be mad at Dylan, not Lily," he continued. "She did what she had to do to keep Lucy safe when the man she thought was her daughter's father was abusive and addicted to drugs."

"Don't talk about your brother that way," Kate begged. "He's better now."

Thomas nodded. "He is. That's why Lily came back. She didn't want to keep Lucy from any of us and now she doesn't have to. And she didn't have to come here today either but she wants this to work out. She wants all of us to be a family, for Lucy's sake."

She sighed and squeezed her eyes shut. "I'm sorry. This is just a lot to process."

I glanced at Thomas then stood. "Why don't I give you guys some time to catch up? I need some fresh air."

Thomas stood too, leaning close to say something. I beat him to it though, whispering, "You two need to talk alone. I'll be outside."

I meandered along the street for a bit before strolling down towards the clear stream behind the cottage, unable to resist smiling at the picturesque view in front of me. I casually tossed a few pebbles into the water then sat on the bank. A moment later, I heard the snapping of twigs and turned to see Dylan.

He crouched and selected a small stone. "You need a rock with a flat side. Then you have to flick your wrist more," he said, releasing the stone so that it skipped a handful of times across the stream before sinking.

"Impressive," I commented as he sat beside me.

"Forget someone?"

He feigned panic and then grinned. "Lucy is inside with Mum and Thomas. I'd give them some time if I were you."

I nodded, but tensed up remembering what Thomas had told Kate about Dylan.

"What is it?" he asked without looking up. It was eerie how well he still knew me after this long.

"Thomas told your mother you hit me."

Dylan's silence was telling.

"I'm sorry. He didn't—we didn't know how else to explain the situation."

Dylan rubbed his forehead. "You mean you didn't know how to explain how my brother having sex with my fiancée was *my* fault?"

I exhaled warily. "No one thinks it's your fault. I know I screwed up, Dylan. I hurt you, and I'm sorry. Thomas is too."

"This is a fucking mess, Lily. You were trouble from the moment you tripped in that damn drainage grate."

"But you rescued me," I reminded him.

"And then as it turned out I was the villain of the story, not the hero."

"Is that how you see it?"

"Don't you?"

I considered it then shrugged. "Does it matter now?"

Dylan turned to me. "I'm tired of always being the bad guy."

"Then don't be."

He snorted. "You don't think I'm too old to change?"

Dylan was hardly old. He was older than me, but younger than Thomas, and still startlingly young given all that he'd accomplished. "Where's Patty?" I asked in lieu of answering his question.

"She needed a break."

"A break from what?"

"I don't know. Me? This is all a bit much for her."

I gazed around. "It's a bit much for me too."

He laughed. "Yeah."

I swallowed awkwardly. "Do you think you'll patch things up with her?"

"Do you really want to hear about this?"

"Yes," I said, then I thought about it. "No. Well, I mean, I guess I feel guilty. It's my fault your life is complicated right now. I can't imagine she'd like you spending time with me."

Dylan shrugged. "That's probably true. But then again, I've never been one to do what women tell me to do."

"Even when the woman is your wife?" I paused. "I thought you were done being the bad guy."

"She chose not to come on this trip. I invited her."

I nodded.

"Did Patty know? About Lucy, I mean?"

Dylan turned to me, confused. "You mean before you returned to New York? No."

"Why didn't you tell her?"

"It wasn't her business. I told her after I told Thomas."

"She wasn't upset that you'd kept it from her?"

He paused awkwardly. "She doesn't know I knew about Lucy before she came to town."

"That's a pretty hefty lie of omission."

Dylan didn't answer, and I started to think of other important facts he'd neglected to tell me. "Does Patty know you're…I mean, that you can't have kids?"

"She would've never believed Lucy wasn't my child if she didn't."

I frowned, realizing his answer left a lot of ambiguity, particularly as to whether he told her before or after she saw Lucy, let alone whether he told her before they wed. I was tempted to ask, but it wasn't my business. My own relationship with him, however, was fair game.

"Would you ever have told me?"

"Of course."

"Then why didn't you? Seems like it should've come up before we got engaged."

He shuffled his feet around in the dirt and then lay back onto his elbows, squinting up at the sun. "It had never been an issue before. You were the only person I'd ever even considered maybe wanting to have children with some day. And it's not exactly the sort of thing you mention right off the bat."

I leaned back beside him. "How did we get engaged without ever discussing having children?"

"We were young and impulsive. And in love." He turned to me and grinned.

I rolled my eyes.

"I almost told you once," he said. "You were such a stickler for protection and we forgot that one time, and…"

"We hardly forgot," I interrupted, remembering the exact incident to which he was referring. "You were quite insistent."

"I can't help that you found me irresistible," he teased. "And after that, you were on the pill."

"Which I apparently didn't need to be on," I retorted.

"Yeah, and clearly you took them so faithfully," he replied.

I sat up. "You were in the hospital, Dylan! You nearly killed yourself because I left and the only reason I left is because I was terrified you were going to hurt me or your brother. I wasn't thinking clearly and yes, I missed a few pills."

"Sorry," he mumbled.

I was mentally exhausted. There was nothing left to say. We sat there in silence for a while.

"I'm glad," he said finally.

"About what?"

"You missing the pills."

Obviously, I was glad too. I wouldn't trade Lucy for anything, but it didn't make sense for Dylan to say that. If not for the unexpected pregnancy, I might have never left him.

"That's hard to believe," I said.

He looked hurt. "I love Lucy," he insisted.

I cringed. "I know. I'm sorry. I didn't mean it that way."

He rolled his eyes. "Yes you did."

We were quiet for a minute. "If not for Lucy, you might never have left me. I might have really hurt you. I might never have gotten help."

"You might never have married Patty," I added.

Dylan cringed.

Before I had time to dwell on the significance of his response, we heard a shrieking behind us.

"Mommy!" Lucy squealed, her long hair billowing behind her like a kite as she raced towards us.

I stood up, wiped the dirt off my jeans, and held out my arms for her. Unfortunately, she stumbled before she reached me, pitching headfirst into the weeds. Her happy squeals turned to cries.

Thomas winced and rushed forward, but I got to her first and scooped her up in my arms. "She's fine," I mouthed to Thomas, who appeared to have assumed she'd broken a bone, based on the tenor of her cries.

"What hurts?" I asked gently.

Lucy pointed to her knee, then sobbed louder when I gazed closer.

"Ow! Don't touch it. That hurts!" she screamed.

"Okay, it's okay," I said soothingly. "Thomas, can you get a bandage?"

"It's not bleeding," he replied.

I glared at him, trying to wordlessly convey the importance of my request. If there was one thing I'd learned as a parent, it was that bandages provided emotional support and fixed most preschool injuries, bloody or not.

He returned with the requested item a moment later, and though Lucy screamed as I applied the band-aid, once it was on, she quieted immediately.

Kate joined us outside then, watching Lucy as she played. Thanks to jet lag, though, Lucy was exhausted.

"I'll take her in and lie down with her so she can rest," Thomas offered.

I wanted to suggest we return to the hotel instead, where we could all rest, but that wasn't fair. Kate deserved time with her granddaughter, and Lucy would probably hit her second wind by the time we reached the hotel anyway.

I wouldn't have minded being alone to read, or even continuing to talk to Dylan, but he quickly pulled out his phone and walked away right as Kate approached.

I sucked in a deep breath, bracing myself for another lecture.

"Lily, I owe you an apology," Kate said.

I took a step back and shook my head, trying to mask my surprise. "It's fine. I understand why you hate me."

"I don't hate you," she insisted. Then she paused. "I was wary of you when I first met you. I had seen Dylan with many, many women before you came along. But he was so different with you that it was alarming."

"We were in love," I offered.

"It was more than that. He was obsessed with you. He was drawn to you. You had this magnetic pull on him."

"It was mutual." I declined to add that for me, it was like being swept up in an undertow, where the more I tried to swim against his current, the more I drifted back to him.

"I suspected about the drugs, but I had no idea he hurt you."

She paused, but I had nothing to say.

"Your sudden departure nearly killed Dylan. I went to him when you left, to help Thomas watch over him. As a mother, you have to understand that seeing my son in so much pain because of someone else, well, you have to hate that person." Kate sighed. "And it didn't help when you returned and Dylan told me about Lucy."

"It was Dylan who told you?" I interrupted, surprised.

She nodded. "He said you were back in town and that you had a daughter that you'd named Lucy. He invited me to come see her." She frowned after seeing my confused expression. "You didn't know that?"

"I assumed it was Thomas who told you."

"Afraid not." She smoothed her dress. "Thomas says he's in love with you."

I glanced down.

"That he has been, for years."

She was clearly waiting for a response from me, but I still didn't know what to say. I couldn't explain my complex feelings for her son in a way that would make sense or justify any of my past behavior.

"He loves Lucy too," I said instead. "He's a really good dad. We're trying to do what's best for her."

Kate nodded slowly before standing. "Well, God bless you for having a daughter. Boys are a challenge. I'll never understand the relationship between brothers."

We both watched as Dylan shoved his phone back into his pocket, thrust his fingers in his hair, then kicked a rock.

"Dylan tells me he enjoys being an uncle," Kate said.

I couldn't decide if that surprised me or not. "He's good at it," I finally said.

"I'm sure he's better at being the uncle than he would've been at being her father," Kate added. Before I could respond, she patted my shoulder and started to the house. "I'll check if Thomas needs any help."

Dylan joined me again as soon as she walked off.

"I can tell when she's talking about me," he confessed.

I shrugged. "It was nothing bad. We were agreeing that you've been a good uncle to Lucy."

"Not the first three years."

"Well, no." There was no getting around that truth. I slowly lowered myself to the grass, exhausted from the day already. Dylan followed suit. Neither of us spoke for a moment, until I remembered something from earlier. "Hey, Dylan, I know this is none of my business, but it sort of surprised me that your mom thought Lucy was your daughter."

"Everyone assumed that," he replied sardonically. "We were engaged at the time of her conception, you might recall."

"I know, but it seems like your own mother would know if you couldn't have kids."

He raised an eyebrow. "I don't share everything with her."

I bit my lip nervously but forged on with my awkward line of questioning. "Well how do you know for sure if you've never tried to get someone pregnant? I mean, everything seemed to work normally."

Now Dylan outright glared. "Everything does work normally, Lily. Better than average, I believe you once said." He shook his head. "I was in a motorcycle accident, Lily. About five years ago. There was some trauma to the vas deferens. It was essentially the same as a vasectomy."

"I'm sorry. So they said there was no chance of you ever having kids?"

He nodded. "Yes. They said it was highly unlikely."

I worked my teeth along my bottom lip, then froze as I realized what he'd said. "Highly unlikely? Dylan, that's not the same as impossible. What were the doctor's exact words?" I tried to make my voice sound calmer than I felt.

"He was really apologetic is all. He said I could talk to a specialist and see about some options and that I might be a good candidate for some of the newer procedures for getting a girl knocked up."

"Dylan, did he say it was impossible for you to conceive in the traditional way or highly unlikely? I need to know."

Dylan sighed and rolled his eyes. "Bloody hell, Lily. I wasn't fully with it at the time, if you gather what I'm saying, so I don't recall his exact terminology. Calm down!"

I rose to my feet to avoid slapping him. "Don't tell me to calm down, Dylan! I have a child who looks just like you and who was conceived at a time when I was with you and I assumed she was not your child because you said she was not your child. Now you're telling me there is a possibility you could impregnate someone."

I paced in a circle around myself. "How could you? This is not an innocent white lie, Dylan."

"I didn't lie, Lily. She's not mine. I'm certain."

"How can you be certain? Are you a doctor?"

Dylan stood and leaned close enough for me to smell his breath. "When I first saw pictures of Lucy, don't you think I wanted her to be mine?"

I didn't answer.

He continued through clenched jaw. "If I had thought there was any chance, Lily, and possibility there was something that still connected us, something that could maybe bring you back to me, don't you think I would've tried? Do you think I wanted confirmation of what you did when I was in rehab?"

I was so angry I could've hit him, but I willed myself to let him finish.

"From the moment I saw Lucy, I knew without a shadow of a doubt that my suspicions had been right all along. I don't need a bloody medical degree to tell me you fucked my goddamned brother!" Dylan's voice was deep and gravelly, and his eyes shone with the same fury I was feeling.

We stood there, glaring at each other, for several moments. I searched for something else to say, anything that would let me win this argument, but then it hit me. There was no winning this round. We were all losers.

I finally swallowed, took a deep breath, and spoke, taking great effort to keep my voice even and quiet. "I'm sorry we hurt you Dylan, but you should have told me there was a chance you're Lucy's father."

I turned to leave and slammed directly into Thomas. I froze, slowly peering up at his face and immediately registering the confirmation that he had heard my last statement.

His eyes were directly on Dylan, but he spoke to me. "What did you say, Lily?"

I glanced at Dylan, hoping for some guidance on how to proceed, but he was squaring off evenly with his brother. I grabbed Thomas' hand and tried to tug him away. "Nothing, Thomas. Just a misunderstanding. We can talk about it later, when we're alone."

Thomas stepped closer to his brother, but Dylan thankfully turned. He walked off across the field, silently.

CHAPTER SIXTEEN

THOMAS

I watched my brother walk away, trying to understand how he always did that…how he'd royally muck up everyone's lives then saunter off like it was nothing. Like the rest of us would move on as quickly as he could. As if we could.

God. Dylan was a sociopath. He didn't even think how his actions or words might affect others. Part of me wanted to chase him down, to pummel him with my fists until he bloody felt something. Pain, guilt, anger, remorse…whatever. Anything.

"Hey," Lily snapped, squeezing my hand so hard that my fingers felt sore.

I turned to her, abandoning all fantasies of beating my brother to a pulp when I saw her sweet, frowning face so close to mine.

"Let it go," she said. "It's been a long day for everyone. He just says stuff and he doesn't understand the significance."

I slumped to the ground, suddenly too tired to stand. Lily sat beside me, inching closer until I took the hint and wrapped my arm around her.

"Do you remember?" she asked. "When he had his accident?"

I nodded. He'd been speeding—or maybe drunk or high. I honestly couldn't recall which at this point, only that he'd been reckless and he'd tried to pass a car, hit a curve too fast and flown off his bike. He'd been battered and bruised, needed a short hospital stay and some physical therapy. He'd rejected his pain meds, opting for his personal drug of choice instead. And then, he'd recovered.

"I always assumed he was good as new after," I finally said.

"He told me just now that his doctor told him he couldn't have children, after the accident. But then he said maybe the doctor's exact words were that it was 'highly unlikely'." Lily rest her hand on my knee, squeezing lightly. "I honestly don't think there's even a slight chance she's not yours, but it wouldn't matter anyway. It doesn't change anything between you and Lucy or between you and me."

"It doesn't change anything for you because you're her mum either way."

"You're her father either way," she said.

I gazed at her, understanding what she meant, except it wasn't the truth. My throat grew dry as I considered everything that I stood to lose.

"Pretend he never said anything, Thomas. Let's go back to how we were an hour ago."

If only I could.

Unfortunately, I knew how my mind worked. The fear—the possibility—the sheer what if—it would plague me until I knew for certain. "I need to know," I finally said.

"Why? You're still going to sing to her over video chat every night that you aren't with her at bed time. You're still going to make her pancakes in the morning and rent unicorns for her birthday," Lily said.

That was true. Nothing that happened now could possibly keep me from being a part of Lucy's life. Except, still, it mattered.

"I'm not going to ask her to call someone else Daddy. Not now or ever," Lily said, her eyes pleading with mine now.

"I'm sorry," I said. And I was. "But I need to know."

Lily leaned her head against my shoulder, but she didn't say anything else.

* * *

LILY

It felt like I'd been awake for days on end by the time we reached the hotel, but the moment we pulled up to the curb, discomfort flooded my system. Ipswich wasn't a big city, so I shouldn't have been surprised we were staying at the same luxury hotel as the last time. I shuddered even thinking about that horrible night. The last time I'd stayed here, things had gotten so volatile with Dylan that Thomas had bought me a plane ticket home and arranged for me to leave without Dylan's knowledge.

I hesitated in the lobby and both brothers seemed to figured out why at the same time.

"Shit," Dylan murmured.

Thomas glared at him, gesturing to Lucy. Then Thomas turned to me. "We could stay somewhere else."

Lucy had grown limp in my arms. We didn't have time to find another hotel. "She needs to get to bed," I said.

"Let me carry her," Thomas offered. My arms were aching, so I handed her over to him, then we started upstairs with the bellman following behind. We took the elevator to the same floor where we'd stayed before, but thankfully a different room.

Dylan tipped the bellman and asked him to leave the luggage cart in the hall.

"You and Lucy can have this room; I'll be right there," Thomas explained, pointing to the room next door. We'd discussed it in advance, and decided it would be less confusing to Lucy if he and I weren't sharing the same bed in a hotel room with her. I nodded willingly in reply.

"Goodnight," Dylan mumbled, grabbing his suitcase and heading into a room across the hall.

I reached up for Lucy, taking her back from Thomas so he could bring the bags in. I carried her into the bedroom and began pulling the curtains shut to block out the lights along the exterior of the building. Thomas pulled the covers down on the bed.

"She's adjusting to the time zone quickly," he commented. I glanced to the clock and realized it was eight thirty local time, which was just after her regular bedtime at home.

I nodded wordlessly and began retrieving her pajamas from the suitcase. She barely woke as I changed her and tucked her into bed. Once she was asleep under the covers, I tiptoed out of the room, closing the door behind me. Thomas was seated on the couch.

"I didn't know if you wanted me to wait. I can go now if you're tired."

"Thank you," I murmured, glancing warily around the room. It was virtually identical to the one I'd stayed in with Dylan. I wasn't just scared and sad being back here, I could actually taste the blood in my mouth, feel his hands that I'd normally welcomed all over my body after I'd told him no.

"Hey," Thomas said suddenly, pulling me to him tightly. "You're shaking."

He was right, but I couldn't stop trembling.

"I'm sorry about the hotel," he said. "I didn't think…"

I sniffled, unable to keep myself from crying.

"Jesus, Lily, look at me. You're okay. It's okay now."

I squeezed my eyes shut tighter. "I know."

Thomas held me tighter. "I could kill him. I should've kicked the shit out of him that night. I should have never left you alone after what I saw."

"Thomas, it's over. I don't want to go through it again."

I forced myself to focus on happier thoughts. "I just need good memories of this place, especially if it's the hotel we will stay at every time we are here."

"I'll stay on the couch tonight. The separate rooms idea was stupid," he said.

That did actually appeal to me at the moment, but Thomas needed a good night's sleep and that wouldn't happen on the couch.

Thomas pulled me to the couch with him, practically forcing me onto his lap. "Okay," he began. "Why don't you focus on Lucy? She is snuggled up under the covers in there fast asleep. I still can't get over how adorable she is when she sleeps. That's a good memory."

I nodded, but needed something more distracting to keep my mind off the bad memories. "Why do you love me?"

Thomas frowned. "Why is the sky blue?"

I groaned. "There's some scientific explanation for that and I don't remember, but that's my point. There's a reason for everything, and I want to know why. You could have any girl, and you certainly didn't have to settle for me after I disappeared for years or after I chose your brother over you even when he was a monster to me."

"Gee, you make me sound rather pathetic."

"That's not what I mean. I just need to know."

He sighed. "Love isn't necessarily rational, Lily. I don't know if I can explain my feelings for you or justify them in light of everything we've been through. All I know is the way I feel about you. I want to be a part of you, of your life. You make me happy when I'm with you. You even make me happy when I'm not with you." He turned to stare at me, his green eyes softening. "You're a strong, independent, and passionate woman. You care deeply about others and you're an amazing mom to Lucy even though you had to do it alone for so long."

Looking into his eyes, I stopped shaking. Warmth had replaced the fear coursing through my veins and I realized the one thing that would definitely make my memories of the hotel better.

I leaned forward, gently pressing my lips to the corner of his mouth. He tilted his head, bringing our lips squarely together. Still, he moved slowly, forcing nothing. We kissed softly, our mouths barely touching each other. I enjoyed the feeling, even though it was nothing like our usual kisses, which went from zero to sixty in a nanosecond. My eyelids fluttered open, and I noticed Thomas had clasped his own hands together.

He was holding back. That sweet, wonderful man who'd never hurt me in his entire life, was terrified of pushing me. I lifted my hand to caress him, then stopped. Maybe he wasn't holding back for me. Maybe he was struggling with his own fears from that night. I still remembered the look in his eyes when he realized his brother had hurt me.

I reached for his hand instead, squeezing around his fist until his fingers unclenched and wrapped around my own. After a moment, I ended the kiss, angling my forehead to press against his.

"I love you," I whispered, "And it wasn't your fault."

He didn't respond, but he didn't move, either.

"It's late. I should shower," I finally said.

Thomas prepared to stand, clearly interpreting my words as his cue to leave.

"You could join me. I assume the bathroom door locks."

He gazed at me as though trying to decipher if I was sure. I was, and luckily he realized that, because he reached for my hand then walked towards the bathroom. He tugged his shirt over his head and unfastened his pants, then waited, again seeking confirmation. I breathed a laugh as I stripped off my clothes.

I checked that we'd locked the door before pressing my fingers against his abdomen, slowly tracing downward and taking the rest of his clothes with me. He helped me, stepping out of his pants and boxers, then ran his fingers through my hair. Cupping my cheek in his palm, he kissed me. Then he turned away and started the shower.

Neither of us spoke as the water warmed, and he made no attempt to touch me when we both climbed in. Maybe he wasn't in the mood. I should just let it drop.

Instead, I grabbed his hand and placed it between my legs. "I wish you'd make love to me."

Thomas licked his lips as though considering my request, then complied.

The water was still hot when we finished, but I reached for the shampoo quickly, aware that we might now have limited time to take care of our actual bathing needs before we ran out of warm water.

"Let me wash your hair," Thomas offered, interrupting my thoughts.

He squirted the shampoo into his palm, rubbed his hands together, then gently massaged the suds through my hair. He scraped his nails along my scalp and the back of my neck, then turned me delicately to rinse my hair.

"You really are beautiful, Lily."

"You are wonderful," I replied. "I still don't understand why you want me, but I'm smart enough to know that makes me the luckiest girl alive."

He kissed me chastely before washing his own hair. I watched the soap run down his contoured body and smiled appreciatively. It slid off his toned shoulders, clung to his well-defined pecs, then raced on to his perfect, rounded butt. Whatever he did in the gym was clearly paying off.

"Are you checking me out?" Thomas asked incredulously.

"Maybe."

"And?"

"And what?"

"Do I measure up? Am I as hot as you remember?"

"Hotter."

He looked skeptical.

"I'm serious. You look like you've put on a lot of muscle since I moved away."

"I had to do something with the pent-up stress. So, I filtered all of my sexual tension into weight lifting. That's better than sleeping with every groupie, right?"

I turned to face the water, stalling. Was he saying that was what Dylan did when I left? Or just what he could have done? And why did I care?

"You were in a magazine," I finally said, still hiding under the cascading shower. "You were shirtless on a beach somewhere. It was a top ten list of best celeb abs. You should be proud."

"That sounds like a tabloid, not a magazine. And I highly recommend you stop reading that smut."

"How many girls have there been since I left?" I blurted out, swiveling to face him.

"Are you asking about *my* sexual exploits?"

"Who else's would I be asking about?"

Thomas stared pointedly.

"What Dylan does or did is not my concern."

Thomas rinsed his face.

"I know I have no right to ask, since I was the one who left, but..." I said, nervously.

"Five," he said.

I had been gone for three years, so I wasn't sure if that was a reasonable number or not. Given his profession and lack of steady relationship in that time, at least as far as I could gauge from the "smut" I'd read in his absence, that seemed low. But I trusted his honesty.

"And you?" he asked.

"One."

"The accountant?"

I nodded.

Thomas snorted. "I bet he was a magician in the sack."

I giggled and did one final rinse of my hair. "So, um, any idea how many there were before me?"

"You want to know how many women I've slept with ever?" he repeated.

I nodded meekly.

Thomas outright laughed. "No, you don't. And suffice it to say I didn't keep track. But if I have it my way, there will be no more."

I frowned, totally confused. "What does that mean?"

He kissed the tip of my nose. "It means I want you, love. I want to make love to you as often as I can until the day I die. I don't want anyone else. Ever."

I sighed. "That's really romantic coming from someone who slept with half the women on each of two different continents."

Thomas swatted my behind and climbed out of the shower. I shrieked but followed him out.

"You better keep quiet or you'll wake my daughter," he teased.

I smiled. I would never grow tired of hearing him say that. But then, it hit me. What if it wasn't true? Maybe I needed confirmation too.

Thomas towel dried his hair then stepped back into his jeans and tee shirt. I tiptoed into the bedroom and retrieved my pajamas from the suitcase. Then we both went into the main room of the suite.

"I love watching her sleep," Thomas murmured, closing the door softly.

I nodded, and then I shivered.

"Are you cold?"

"No. I just…" I hesitated. We'd had such an amazing hour or so together, I didn't want Thomas to know that I was already starting to think about that other night again.

His face crumpled. "You're still frightened."

I nodded reluctantly.

"We'll find a different hotel tomorrow, but for tonight, I'll stay here."

As much as I wanted to spend the night curled up in Thomas' arms, I didn't want to have to explain that to Lucy. Not yet, anyway. And it wouldn't necessarily help. "That's not necessary," I said.

"Yes, it is. I should've insisted on staying with you the last time you were in this hotel and I didn't. You can't make me leave now."

"Thomas, nothing bad happened to me after you left last time."

"Yes it did. Dylan came back and apologized, remember? He weaseled back into your good graces." He shook his head. "Fucking asshole brother. I can't believe he did this to you."

I didn't say anything, but it was getting late, and we both needed to sleep. I was about to reiterate that Thomas should go, when he spoke again, this time more tersely.

"Lily, you know I love Dylan, but I love Lucy and you more. I don't want anything to do with a man that you're afraid of. We can leave tonight. We can move…"

"Thomas, stop," I interrupted. "I'm not afraid of Dylan. At all. I never really was." I sighed. "I probably should have been afraid of him all those years ago, but honestly at the time I was just concerned about letting him down or losing him. Now he's different and he's not on drugs. If that ever changes, we'll all leave right away. But for now, I'm not afraid of him. He won't hurt me or Lucy."

Thomas swallowed audibly. "You said you were frightened earlier."

"Yeah, but not of Dylan. Look, Thomas, it's hard to explain."

"Try."

"Being back here brings back all of those memories and all of the feelings. When you saw me that night, after Dylan left, I was scared of losing him. I was terrified that he'd start using more, that he'd accidentally overdose, or even that he'd just leave me. I wasn't scared of him coming back and hitting me again."

Thomas sat on the couch and thrust his head into his hands. "I don't understand, Lily. I remember that night pretty well too. I remember hearing you scream. I remember you refusing to open the door for ten minutes after I arrived because you were too scared. I remember seeing your shirt torn down the middle. I remember your cheek bleeding, your eye and lip swollen, and broken glass everywhere. Jesus, Lily, I guess I was scared for the both of us."

"Thomas, I'm not saying it is rational. I should have been scared of getting hurt, but I wasn't. And being here now reminds me of feeling that way—being terrified of losing someone I loved rather than concerned for my own safety. I don't want to feel that way again."

Thomas stared blankly ahead.

"I had a counselor in Michigan that helped me a lot," I explained. "It's pretty common in these kinds of situations, how I reacted, I mean."

"In what kind of situation?"

"Well, um, domestic violence and abusive relationships."

Thomas inhaled sharply, then stood. "I'm going to kill him," he announced calmly.

"No, you're not, because it wasn't your brother that did all that. It was the drugs. That part of him is gone. Now it's just the Dylan that you've always loved."

And the Dylan that I originally loved, I thought.

"Go. Lucy will be up at the crack of dawn, so I need sleep."

Thomas hesitated.

"Go!"

"Text me when she wakes up and I'll come over for breakfast."

"Okay." We kissed just long enough to bring back memories from the couch—and bathroom. I was grinning widely as I closed and locked the door behind Thomas.

The next morning, Thomas came over shortly after Lucy awakened, as promised. I was making coffee for myself and tea for him when he came in, and when I turned to face him, he was holding his hand awkwardly in front of his face. Lucy had greeted him warmly, but returned her attention to the television, playing Australian cartoons, of all things.

"What's wrong?" I asked.

"Nothing," he mumbled. "Shall I order room service? What sounds good?" He turned his back to me and reached for the phone.

I stepped closer and moved his hand. The corner of his lip was cut open and swollen. Bits of dried blood surrounded it. "Oh my God, Thomas. Did I do that?" I tried to remember biting him there, but all that came to mind was me biting his hand.

"No, I'm fine. Now about breakfast?"

I dragged him into the bedroom so we could talk in private. "You're not fine. Your perfect face is mangled. What happened?"

"Tiny little scuffle with Dylan," he replied, holding his fingers a half inch apart when saying "tiny."

"Dylan hit you?"

Thomas swallowed then nodded reluctantly.

"Why would he hit you?"

Thomas considered his response for a long time. "It was his knee-jerk reaction to an inadvertent comment I made about some of the activities you and I engaged in last night," he replied sheepishly.

"What? You told your brother what we did?"

"Not all the details, but I mean, Lily, he sort of knew what was going on anyway. Besides, he is married!"

"And he just hit you?"

Thomas nodded.

"This is ridiculous," I muttered. I stormed out of the bedroom, and headed to the door, grateful my pajamas were at least semi-decent.

"Lily, where are you going?" Thomas asked. Then as it became apparent what my intentions were, he said, "I wouldn't do that. He's still asleep."

I didn't care. I pounded on the door of the room Dylan had occupied the previous night.

I heard a muffled call from inside the room, presumably Dylan telling the knocker to go away, albeit in less polite terms, but I kept pounding.

After another minute, I heard the lock turning at the door.

"What the hell is so important?" Dylan asked, rubbing his eyes. "Oh, it's you," he said, surprised.

I was about to scold Dylan for hitting Thomas when I got a good look at him. His left eye was swollen and his right cheek was bruised. "What is wrong with you two?" I shrieked, turning to face Thomas. He shrugged.

"Why are you pounding on my door in your pajamas?" Dylan asked me.

"You punched Thomas," I said.

Dylan laughed. "And you're here to defend his honor? Geez. He hit me first."

"What the hell happened?"

They both stared at each other.

"A little scuffle," Thomas finally reiterated.

"Over what?"

Dylan laughed. "What do you think?"

"Me?"

He shrugged. "It was bound to happen sooner or later. Now it's out of our systems."

I frowned. "Wait, so you guys just beat the crap out of each other and then just went to sleep?"

"There was some drinking involved," Dylan added. "Can I go back to sleep now?"

* * *

THOMAS

We survived two more days in Ipswich with no drama, then brought my mum along to Norwich for a day of exploring there. Lucy, Lily and I then spent the next ten days working our way along the eastern coast of England as tourists. I should've been working, but the thought of anyone but me showing Lily the country I'd called home for so long made me cringe nearly as much as the sharp realization that we'd barely have a chance to explore a fraction of the nation during a single summer.

I'd always found Great Britain idyllic, but witnessing it all through the innocent eyes of my daughter renewed my impression. By the time we settled into my flat on the northwest side of London, I was even more enamored with the nation than before and more in love with Lily than I'd thought possible. We'd slept in separate beds during our travels so far, not wanting to confuse Lucy, but at my apartment, Lily dropped her bags in the master bedroom without a second thought.

"You're not taking the guest room?" I asked, hoping the teasing tone came through clearly.

She lifted her shoulders. "I miss you. And as long as I'm not sharing a bed with Lucy, I might as well be sharing with you."

"You miss me," I repeated, sinking into the plush mattress and inching backwards until I could lean comfortably against the upholstered headboard. "You've spent nearly every minute of every day with me."

"Yeah. But we've spent most of those minutes sightseeing. I

miss some of the other things we do," she said, crawling onto the bed. She straddled my thighs and roped her arms around my neck, but smiled instead of kissing me.

"I suppose I could make room for you in here tonight."

A dimple betrayed her efforts to not smile wider. "You suppose?"

I nodded. "But first, I'm taking Lucy to the shops for some toys. There's nothing for her to play with here."

Lily breathed a laugh before closing the distance between us and planting her soft lips on me. The kiss was short and sweet, and I'd barely registered her ending it by the time she was off my lap and out of the room.

I relaxed against the bed for a few more minutes, letting my body and mind settle after the whirlwind of activities the past two weeks. I loved New York City, and I loved the English countryside, but I felt happiest and most at home in London.

Lily had been here before. With Dylan. He hadn't shown her much of Great Britain outside the city, but they had toured London. So I didn't feel too terrible about leaving her and Lucy to explore on their own for the most part while I did a few publicity gigs with the band, worked on a music video, and tackled a couple of performances.

I snapped out of my daydream to the sound of my name. Lily was calling from another room. By the time I reached my feet, she appeared in the doorway, laughing.

"I got lost," she admitted. "Did you know this place is considerably larger than your New York apartment?"

I nodded, biting back a smile. It wasn't that big, really, but the it lacked the open floor plan of my other place, and the layout was different. In general, London real estate pricing was every bit as egregious as New York's, but I'd nabbed this place before the market had climbed in the neighborhood. When I'd been looking for a place years ago, I'd fallen in love with the way the light flooded the kitchen in the mornings and the music room in the evenings. I didn't need the space, but now, I couldn't help but hope we'd grow into it, and someday sooner rather than later.

"I apologize for not giving you the official tour," I teased, right as Lucy scampered into the room. Judging from her enthusiasm, her mum had told her the plan to shop for toys. I jotted down the address of the apartment for Lily so she wouldn't get lost returning from the store on her own errands, then left on foot with Lucy.

CHAPTER SEVENTEEN

LILY

Shopping in London was infinitely more complex than I'd imagined, with everything from the organization of the stores to the pricing of items stumping me. Still, I couldn't think of a more charming place to be disoriented. I made it home before Thomas and Lucy, unpacked her things, then threw together a simple dinner.

They were both in good spirits when they returned. We laughed around the table together at dinner and then Lucy arranged her new toys in her room while Thomas and I cleaned up. I couldn't get over how easy this was, for the three of us to just be together, like a family. For the first time in ages, everything felt right in my life. Absolutely nothing was missing.

"I've never seen someone look so happy to wash dishes," Thomas said, reaching for the wine glass I was rinsing.

I turned to gaze at him as he dried the glass. Even with the smirk on his face, Thomas was still the most handsome man I'd ever seen. His emerald eyes seemed darker than usual now, his stubble longer, and his hair slightly more unruly; yet he was still absolutely perfect. I began to salivate simply looking at him.

And yet, he wasn't just a pretty face (or incredible abs and a perfectly rounded ass, although he had those things too). He was also the charming, sweet man that helped with dishes, shopped with our child, and went out of his way to make sure I felt loved with every breath I took. And on top of all that, he was also a phenomenal singer, gifted songwriter, and talented performer. The man was literally perfect.

And somehow, he was mine.

"The way you're looking at me makes me think I should go put Lucy to bed," he said, licking his lips slowly.

It took all my self-restraint not to pounce on him. Instead, I shut off the faucet. "I'll do it," I said. I needed a distraction or I'd combust by the time I finished the dishes.

When I'd finished reading Lucy's books and tucked her into bed, I leaned against the wall outside her room. She was in an unfamiliar place, so I wanted to make sure she actually fell asleep before running off to ravish her father.

When I finally made my way into the living room, Thomas was seated on the couch, his laptop to one side and his guitar on his lap. I watched him for a moment as he scrolled through something on his laptop, then played a couple strings on the guitar. I laughed at his efforts to be quiet while playing guitar, and he glanced up.

"How long have you been standing there?"

"Just a moment. I didn't want to interrupt your work."

"I welcome the interruption," he replied, closing his laptop and moving it to the coffee table. He crooked his finger at me.

I approached slowly, watching him prop his guitar against the edge of the couch before pulling me closer.

"Being around you makes me want to write songs," he said.

I quirked an eyebrow.

"You've been my muse for years, but the lyrics and the melody ideas flow a lot faster when you're right here," he continued. "I love being able to spend all day and night with you."

"You're not sick of me yet?" I teased.

"Never. The more I have you, the more I want."

I leaned forward and kissed Thomas, tentatively at first, but then with more fervor as he kissed me back. His hand slid up my back, coming to a stop behind me head, as though he worried I'd pull away. Instead, I nudged him backwards, stretching out on top of him on the couch. His mouth was warm and eager, and the movement of his tongue made my heart race as I recalled what it could expertly do elsewhere.

I inched away just enough to lift my shirt awkwardly over my head. Thomas grinned drunkenly, admiring my body in a way that made me feel embarrassed and proud all at once. I lay back down beside him, slipping my hands up under his shirt and touching the firm ridges of his stomach as I made my way to his chest.

Thomas wriggled out of his shirt and kissed me harder, moving to my neck, behind my ear, and my collarbone. My body tingled with excitement, and the once dull ache deep in my belly grew stronger. His hand reached down my body, groping my buttocks, then sliding a little lower to cup my sex. I moaned softly, writhing against his hand. I wanted more, I needed more.

Thomas unfastened my bra with his other hand, and I leaned away to allow it to fall off my arms and onto the floor. When I pressed back against him, my nipples touched his bare flesh and my heart raced. I knelt above him, unfastening my jeans.

"What if she wakes?" he asked.

I didn't have a good answer for that. Fooling around with him on the couch, was irresponsible, but I couldn't help it. "We'll have to be fast," I replied.

Thomas gripped my waist firmly and flipped me onto my back, tugging my jeans off, and yanking his own pants off in quick succession. He kissed me longer, then worked his way downward, wrapping his lips around my left nipple. His tongue flicked it back and forth and I groaned again, this time saying his name.

"Shhh," he replied, and he pressed his hand playfully over my mouth. He moved his lips to my right nipple, and as soon as his tongue brushed across the sensitive tip, the pleasure was so intense that I clamped down on Thomas' hand.

"Hey," he murmured. "Naughty girl." He moved his hand and slid his boxer briefs down. I shimmied out of my panties while I waited.

Thomas raked his hand down my front, avoiding my breasts but tracing a circle around my belly button before coming to rest at the base of my sex. He ran his finger along the slit, the sensation so intense that I nearly cried out by the time he dipped his finger into my body then quickly removed it and retraced his path back up my body.

"You want me," he observed, seductively sucking the tip of the finger that had just been inside me. "You taste good."

I bit my lip in a desperate attempt not to smile at his lewd comment. "I thought we were going to be quick," I said, breathless, eager to reach the main course.

He grinned. "You don't think I can be fast, do you?"

I shrugged.

Thomas reached out with both hands, playfully pinching both of my nipples and sending ripples of sensation straight to my core. "Be careful what you wish for," he warned, his mouth so close to my ear that his breath tickled me.

A moment later, he reached behind my waist and hoisted my thighs in the air, his hands pressed against my buttocks. My head and upper back still rested against the couch, but my lower half was now raised to his stomach level while he knelt before me. Before I could question the position, Thomas rammed into me, filling me suddenly and completely.

A surprised cry escaped my lips and he paused, gauging my

expression. Once he was apparently convinced it was a cry of pleasure, he slowly inched out of me, pausing again, then pressing back in. He sped up, pounding into me faster and harder until I couldn't hold on any longer and I exploded into a symphony of sensation, my hips bucking uncontrollably against him. Thomas thrust into me twice more before finding his own release and collapsing quickly on top of me.

"Wow," I mumbled, still breathless.

"I told you so," he retorted, lifting his head off my chest and grinning at me.

We lay on the couch for a moment longer before I realized that we were still in quite the compromising position.

"I should shower," I said.

Thomas nodded and scooted off of me, beginning to dress. I snatched his undershirt before he could reach it and slipped it on. He paused, not yet done buckling his pants belt, and watched as I started back towards the bedroom.

"Come on," I whispered.

Thomas followed me into the bathroom. I closed the door quietly, locked it, then turned on the light. I lifted his shirt back over my head. His eyes widened with pleasure as he watched in the mirror while I undressed.

"I know I'm supposed to say how great your eyes are, and they really are, but you have the most amazing breasts I've ever seen, Lily. I could die now and be a happy man."

He stepped up behind me and cupped his hands around my breasts, leaving his thumbs free to rub gently back and forth across my nipples. I groaned and tilted my head slightly to the side, inadvertently inviting Thomas to kiss the side of my neck. I glanced in the mirrors and saw his eyes were wide open, watching me. I felt myself blush, then let my eyes drift shut again as the pressure in my groin intensified from his expert manual work.

"I want to see you," he whispered in my ear. "Please don't close your eyes."

I complied, hesitantly, choosing to focus on his peaceful and seductive face rather than my own naked body.

Thomas' left hand remained at my breast while his right hand slid down my body, gently teasing my clitoris before probing lightly into me. I resisted the urge to shut my eyes again for a moment, but then succumbed, unable to obey simple commands when my body felt this hungry for more.

"Open," he whispered, and then his right hand disappeared, prompting me to open my eyes more than his simple request. Right as I opened my eyes, he pressed his finger into my mouth. "See? I told you you taste good." It felt so wrong, but so hot. I tried to turn to kiss him, but he held me firmly in place.

"We could pleasure you like this," he said, still whispering.

I shook my head. "I want you," I said.

"You've got me," he replied.

"All of you," I clarified. I reached behind me as best I could with Thomas still holding me tightly and grabbed at his manhood.

He raised an eyebrow, then shuffled his pants to the ground. Thomas wrapped his right arm around my thigh, lifting it slightly to position himself at the entrance to my sex. "Eyes open or I'll stop," he teased.

I giggled and pressed my hips back against him.

"Eager, aren't we?" Thomas kissed my neck again, then raised his left hand to his mouth, licked his finger, and brought the damp finger back to my breast, the sensation now even more intense from the moisture. He slowly eased into me, and I felt raw and overly sensitive now from our recent lovemaking.

Thomas continued the slow movement, and I followed his lead with my hips. He slowly tilted me forward until my upper body was over the marble countertop. I supported my weight on my elbows and let my eyes drift shut as the sensations took over.

Suddenly, Thomas withdrew. My eyes flew open.

"I warned you," he whispered.

I groaned but opened my eyes. It felt strange to watch myself, so I craned my neck up to see Thomas. He smiled as our eyes met and I relaxed. I could tell he was enjoying watching my breasts rock back and forth as he thrust, and as his breathing became more ragged, I felt my own breath quicken.

I knew I was close, that the exquisite pleasure couldn't possibly get more intense without breaking me. As I gazed back up at Thomas, he mouthed the words "I love you," and that was my undoing. I spiraled into wave after wave of pure bliss.

By the time I could think coherently again, we were curled up on the bathroom floor. I glanced over at Thomas, trying to figure out how we ended up on the rug.

"You closed your eyes when you came," he said accusingly.

"Hmm…guess we'll have to practice more until I get it right," I replied sleepily.

"If we practice any more, you might not be walking straight tomorrow."

"I might be okay with that."

He kissed me and then stood up, offering his hand to help me up too. He turned the shower on then tested the water temperature. He stepped into the shower and motioned for me to join him.

I did, shivering as the not-yet-hot water hit my shoulders. Thomas laughed and nudged the faucet closer to "hot."

"I never knew you were so kinky," I said.

Thomas raised an eyebrow. "There's a lot you don't know about me yet."

"Oh really?"

He shrugged. "I might just surprise you."

You already have, I thought, but I didn't say it out loud. I didn't want Thomas to know that I still recalled snippets of intimate moments with his brother, that as much as I tried to resist, comparisons sometimes popped into my head unwittingly. I'd only been with one man since Dylan, other than Thomas, and the sex with him hadn't been memorable. I could easily now say that Thomas was the best I'd ever had, but it made me uneasy to realize that the runner up would always be his younger brother.

* * *

THOMAS

By some miracle, I woke before Lily or Lucy in the morning. I brewed the coffee and was about to scramble eggs for breakfast when I heard a thunk from the back bedroom. I hurried down the hall to find Lucy energetically bouncing on the oversized bed in her room.

Her eyes widened as she saw me and she collapsed onto the plush bedding, giggling.

"Good morning sweet princess," I said, leaning over to tickle her. "I think you like this bedroom."

She nodded. "Will we stay here another night?"

I sat on the bed beside her. "This is my house. Our house. We can stay here as much as we want."

"What about our other home?"

I cringed, not having intended to confuse her. "We will stay there lots too. But to answer your initial question, yes, we'll stay here another night." I gazed around the room. For years, I'd used it as a guest room, but my mother was the only frequent guest and she could always stay at Dylan's. The entire flat had been professionally decorated, and while this room did appear more feminine than the rest of the house, it didn't exactly seem childlike.

"We could decorate this room differently, if you'd like. Maybe paint the walls a different color?"

"This room is big. Is it all mine?"

"It is indeed. Now come help me make breakfast before your mum wakes."

By the time we made it back to the kitchen, I heard water running in the main bath, so I knew Lily was already up. Still, I brought her coffee then rejoined Lucy. I had business with the band, but not until ten o'clock. Dylan wasn't a morning person on any continent.

We met at a recording studio about a twenty-minute drive from my flat. Owen's wife and daughter arrived with him, which was a pleasant surprise. His daughter Elizabeth was nearly the same age as Lucy, and it always made me happy to see someone in my exact line of work with my precise touring schedule who was able to maintain a successful family life.

"We'll have to set up a playdate sometime," I said to Owen after he said goodbye to his wife and kid.

Ari snorted, spilling his coffee on the floor just as Dylan walked by.

"He's grown quite adept at playing house," Dylan explained. "You'll get used to it."

I narrowed my brows at my brother. "You gave us your blessing," I reminded him.

He shrugged.

Ari perked up like a dog who heard food being served. "Blessing for...?"

"He and Lily are together now," Dylan explained.

Ari turned to me for confirmation or clarification, perhaps, but there wasn't more to add. So I just nodded.

Ari pulled something up on his phone and held it up to me. "Care to comment?"

I grabbed his phone and carried it to my seat at the table, wincing as soon as I saw the first photo. It was a picture of me carrying Lucy as we walked between the shops the previous day. An oversized pink bear with a unicorn horn blocked her face, but if someone had taken this photo, it was quite possible other photos of us existed, too.

"I didn't even notice anyone with a camera," I said, handing back his phone after skimming the article. It didn't say anything too fascinating, simply that I was out for an afternoon of shopping with my daughter, all of which was true.

"People are asking who her mother is," Ari said, navigating off that website.

"No comment," I replied. I wasn't naïve enough to think I could fully protect Lucy's privacy and still be in her life, or even that I could keep the world from figuring out her true identity—and her mother's—but the longer I delayed, the better.

"If you're with her a lot now, you're going to be photographed. People might not pay attention in the rest of the country, but here they'll notice. And when you're at your shows…"

"No comment," I repeated. "Let them make their guesses. I'm not officially confirming anything until I have to."

Ari nodded, but he clearly didn't agree with my approach. I didn't care. It was hard enough to get Lily agree to give me a chance, and I sure didn't think she would be able to handle me, international travel and a paparazzi shit-show. Not yet, anyway.

"Well, if you're taking yourself out of the running for Britain's best bachelor, maybe let me know," Ari finally said in a half-teasing tone.

Gavin joined us, so now that the whole band was present, I'd hoped we'd begin band business. Instead, Dylan cleared his throat.

"I'd be happy to take over that role," he said. "Patty filed for divorce, so we'll still have one Parker brother playing the field."

A dull ringing thrummed through my ears as all the guys expressed their condolences to my brother. I was vaguely aware that several of them turned to me, as though seeking confirmation of Dylan's news or perhaps some sign as to how he was handling it, but I had nothing to say.

Dylan hadn't mentioned the divorce to me. I'd spent an entire cross-Atlantic flight with him, followed by several tedious days in our hometown, and he hadn't said a damn word.

"Can we get on with business?" I snapped, not realizing how harsh my tone must've sounded until I noticed the alarmed expressions on the faces of my band mates.

Ari gazed from Dylan to me then back to Dylan before nodding. "Sure. We need to go over the set lists," he said, shuffling some papers.

In the fall, we were heading out on our South American tour. Although we'd hit a couple of key spots in Mexico and Puerto Rico on our last world tour, we really hadn't ever performed in many locations in South or Central America. To help attract fans in the region, we'd recruited a wildly successful Latin rock band, Fuego Frio, as our opening act.

As a trial run, we were doing a few concerts with them throughout Great Britain over the next two weeks. We hadn't yet met, but I wasn't too concerned. We didn't need to become best friends and wouldn't even need to see each other's performances. Really, we'd just be traveling together some. We could manage.

We finished the meeting, ran through a few songs, then ordered in lunch before finishing the set.

When I made it home, Lily and Lucy were lounging out on the terrace, reading books in the sunshine.

I greeted them both with a kiss. "You know, London has some great bookstores," I said. "What if we went out for breakfast and then hit the shops tomorrow?"

Lucy squealed even though her mother was the one I thought would enjoy the books more. I felt bad for not having time to show them around the city at all today, though neither of them seemed to mind.

"Don't you have rehearsal tomorrow?" Lily asked.

I nodded. "Not until afternoon, though. You could come watch?" I paused, thinking. "And maybe we could do the zoo the next day."

Lily smiled.

"And if you're up for it after the zoo, there's a place I'd love to take you for dinner." I pointed at Lily even though Lucy had already lost focus on the conversation. "Owen's wife gave me the name of their babysitter and swore to me she's excellent."

Lily glanced at our daughter before nodding.

CHAPTER EIGHTEEN

"Ask me no more where these stars light,
That downwards fall in dead of night;
For in your eyes they sit, and there
Fixed become as in their sphere."
Thomas Carew, *Ask Me No More*

LILY

Our first week in London was fantastic. Thomas was still doing stuff with the band, but he managed to make it home by nap time most days. Back home, Lucy's weekend nap time was my chance to be productive. It was when I'd clean the apartment, work on my lesson plans, and do anything else that was tough to do while she was underfoot. Now that she was older, she wasn't even napping most days at home. But here, she seemed sleepier. Perhaps it was the time change or maybe just the exhausting life of international jetsetters. Whatever it was, Thomas and I weren't about to look the gift horse in the mouth.

As soon as she went to bed, so did we. And while we didn't

necessarily sleep or even do other typical bedroom activities, we did talk. A lot. The day before, he'd opened up about Dylan and how apparently, he and Patty were divorcing. He'd admitted he was scared that the divorce had something to do with me, and that he hated that Dylan hadn't even told him before the rest of the band. Today, he told me his worries about the paparazzi photographing Lucy.

Talking with Thomas, I realized how comfortable we felt with each other already. In such a short time, he'd become my best friend. I loved that he opened up to me about his fears—even when they involved topics that might rub me the wrong way, like his brother. I loved the way he held my hand when we talked, gently stroking my fingers. And I really loved the way he looked at me as though he'd never met someone as beautiful or fascinating or wise.

"I'm going to miss lying in bed with you in the middle of the day," I mused.

"Why would we ever have to stop? This is a lovely ritual."

I smiled and absentmindedly ran my fingers across the short, soft hairs on his chest. "Well, I have to go back to the U.S., you know? School starts in mid-August, and I've got meetings before."

Thomas frowned. "We could still spend nap time together on weekends," he reminded me.

"It won't be the same. And it's not just this, it's everything. Since we've been here, all of us in the same apartment, it's been nice. It feels like we're a family."

"We are a family."

"Oh, you know. It's just different when we're living separately."

Thomas quickly flipped over to his stomach so he could face me. "I assumed you and Lucy were going to move in with me when we returned."

That was news to me. "You never asked me."

"I did too," he insisted. "The offer's been on the table since you came back to town. You just keep saying no. I figured since you'd agreed to live together here, that we'd continue the arrangement back in the states."

"I didn't realize," I started. I contemplated this for a moment, although it wasn't like I hadn't thought about it before. His apartment was big enough, in an awesome neighborhood, was close to multiple preschools on my wish list, and probably wouldn't have a bad commute for me, since I'd always be going in the opposite direction of the rest of the traffic.

"We can't," I heard myself say before I'd realized I'd even reached a decision.

"Why not?"

"That's too big of a change for Lucy. If anything happened, then she would've gone through the stress of two moves."

"Lily, if you're worried about me leaving, don't. I told you, I'm not going anywhere. And if you're concerned you're going to want out, well, too bad. I'm not letting you run away from me again."

"It's just too risky, Thomas. The last time I moved in with someone, I ended up homeless. I can't chance that with Lucy."

"Then we'll keep your apartment."

"Oh, Thomas, I just can't help but be paranoid after everything that happened before."

"With Dylan," he supplied.

"I'm sorry. It's not fair that you have to pay the price for the damage he caused."

He kissed my shoulder gently instead of replying. I sensed the disappointment on his face and wanted to tell him I felt the same way, but I figured that would only confuse him more.

"When I told my mom I was moving in with Dylan, she thought I was insane. My roommate too. She told me it was too risky to move in together until you're at least engaged, and I didn't listen. No, no. I had to move right in and quit work."

"I'm not asking you to quit your job, though. I would never do that." He flashed another look of frustration and sat abruptly. "Lily, I rearranged my entire schedule so we could take this trip together, when you wouldn't have to miss work. What else do I have to do to show you I'm not Dylan?"

I shook my head and willed myself not to cry, but tears were already brimming in the corners of my eyes. "I know you're not Dylan. You have been nothing but wonderful to me and Lucy and I love you so much, Thomas. I just can't rush into this before we're at least…"

"Engaged?" he asked, wiping a tear off my cheek.

I shrugged. "Honestly I was going to say married. Being engaged doesn't necessarily mean you won't break up. I'm sure my ex-fiancé could remind you of that." Although, as I thought about it, I supposed being married didn't either, but it seemed like better odds.

Thomas appeared contemplative for a minute. Then he reached for my hand. "Then marry me."

I smiled even though he wasn't serious. "Thomas, do you have any idea how hard that would be to explain to my parents, to Lucy? Me saying I'm not going to rush anything and then getting engaged to you after, what, six weeks of dating?"

He grinned at me, that same seductive, mouthwatering grin that he flashed whenever he wanted me to take off my clothes. "Lily, you misunderstood. I'm not suggesting we get engaged. I'm suggesting we get married. I'm asking you to be my wife, not my fiancée."

All of a sudden, I released all the breath I didn't realize I'd been holding. "What?"

"Lily, will you marry me? Please?"

I giggled. Leave it to Thomas to be polite when proposing. "You're serious?"

He nodded. "We could arrange to be wed here before we leave town, and then we can plan some big party back in the states sometime down the road. If we're already married, you won't have to worry about me leaving."

"But…" So many thoughts were popping into my head that I wasn't sure where to begin.

Thomas kissed my forehead and then stood. "Just think about it," he said. "But don't think too long because I'll have to check into the requirements to make it official, what with you being a noncitizen and all. You already know it's a brilliant idea and that the minute everything is said and done, you'd finally be able to stop worrying about all these bloody hypotheticals once and for all."

He began to dress, then left the room.

I stayed in bed for another fifteen minutes, replaying the last few minutes in my mind. When I finally climbed out of bed and slipped into a pair of cutoff jean shorts and a tank top, I'd decided nothing.

I walked out of the bedroom and down the narrow hall. I spotted Thomas in the kitchen, Lucy perched on a barstool beside him. As I watched, she was carefully shaking a cinnamon-sugar mix onto a piece of toast he'd cut into the shape of a heart.

"Look, Mama!" she squealed with delight when she saw me.

Thomas turned and smiled. "Toast?"

I shook my head. He carried Lucy from her stool to a chair at the small table in the kitchen and plopped her down with a small cup of water and her plate of toast.

Suddenly, it came to me. "I would love to marry you," I blurted out.

Thomas eyed me warily. "But?"

"No but. My answer is yes."

He hesitated. I could nearly hear my heart pounding through my chest.

"Really? You mean that?"

"I'll marry you tomorrow if you can get it arranged that quickly."

He grinned. "I don't know if I can do that, but how does this weekend sound?"

I nodded. "That will be quite adequate, Mr. Parker," I replied, in my best British accent.

Thomas and Lucy both laughed. "Darling, I don't think you'll pass for a true Brit," he replied. He pulled me to him and wrapped his arms around my waist. We kissed, and I was overwhelmed with happiness.

That evening, we made love after Lucy went to bed, then soaked in his oversized bathtub together.

"I spoke with our solicitor," Thomas said, dragging the washcloth across my chest.

"Who?"

"Lawyer. About the marriage."

I smiled. "Yes?"

"He'll be by in the morning with some paperwork. Apparently, it's all a bit more complicated than I envisioned. There's a waiting period before we can be officially wed, so plenty of time to invite a few guests if you want."

I shook my head vehemently.

"You're certain? And you're sure you're fine with a simple official proceedings, no fancy ceremony or whatnot?"

"I just want to be yours, officially," I said. "We can have a big ceremony later."

He kissed the back of my head. "What about Lucy? Do you want her there?"

Selfishly, I didn't. Now that the idea of eloping with Thomas was on my brain, I didn't want to share the day with anyone. I wanted it to be a private, intimate affair. I certainly didn't want the drama or negativity that my parents, Thomas' mom, or even Dylan would bring. But Lucy was different. She was ours. She should be there.

"I suppose we should have her come," I said.

Thomas bit back a smile. "We don't have to. Most kids do not attend their parents' weddings."

"That's true," I conceded.

His bold green eyes seemed to pierce my soul with how intensely he was staring at me. "There's something romantic about it being just the two of us," he finally said.

"And we could involve her in every step of the big celebration later," I said.

I shivered, since the water was cooling off, and Thomas responded by pulling the drain. I stood and he handed me a towel after staring appreciatively at my body first.

"Will I be a British citizen after we're married?" I asked suddenly.

Thomas laughed. "Heavens no."

I feigned offense. "Hey, you say that like I'm not good enough to be British."

"I'm just remembering your accent from earlier." He helped dry my back, then moved on to his own damp body. "We'd have to live here for you to ever be eligible for citizenship, and even then, there's a lengthy waiting period."

"What about Lucy? Would she be a citizen if we lived here?"

"She is already a citizen."

"Really?"

He nodded. "From the moment you corrected her birth certificate, she's had dual citizenship."

"Even though you live in the U.S?"

"Yes. I'm still British, so my children all are too, regardless of where they're born or whether their mum is American."

"So you're still not a US citizen even though you've lived there for years?"

"And I probably never will be. I'm perfectly content with my green card."

My eyes widened. "But can't they deport you?"

Thomas laughed. "No. Not unless I commit some major

felony. I'm a permanent legal resident. Don't worry. And besides, if I did have to move back here permanently, my non-citizen wife could come with me. Promise."

I smiled.

We both got ready for bed, and since it was late, we were both exhausted. But I had one more question for Thomas before he fell asleep.

"Thomas, are you still awake?" I asked softly.

He lifted his head slightly off the pillow without answering.

"What if we didn't tell anyone back home that we got married?"

"What?"

"I mean, not keep it a secret for forever, just until…"

"Until you get the nerve to tell your parents?"

"No. Well, maybe that's part of it."

"I could call your father tomorrow and ask for his blessing. Then they'd already know."

"He'd say no," I snorted.

Thomas didn't reply, and then I felt bad.

I crawled closer to him and rest my head on his pillow. "Babe, my parents don't know you yet, and they're still holding a grudge because of Dylan. I want to marry you now because it's what I want, though, not because it's what they want. They'll be happy for us eventually."

"I don't understand why you want to keep it a secret if you'll tell them eventually."

"I want to spend our first few weeks as husband and wife happy and enjoying you, not defending our relationship to everyone we know." I paused. "And you know it's not just family and friends that will be skeptical. The tabloids will have a field day with this."

He sighed but rolled onto his side and stroked my arm and back with his free hand. "How long are we going to wait before telling people?"

"I don't know." I smiled, picturing the big reception we would have someday. "I've always liked the idea of a holiday wedding, but that seems awfully fast to throw something together. Maybe spring?"

"No, you'll already be pregnant by then."

"Thomas!"

He laughed. "What? We already know we make cute babies, and Lucy needs a sibling."

"Let's just rush into one thing at a time, okay?" Then I thought about what he'd said. "Is this because of Dylan? I mean, would you be okay with keeping the marriage a secret from everyone else if you could tell Dylan?"

"Well, yes," he said finally.

Maybe Lucy did need a sibling, eventually. Having grown up an only child, I never understood the bond between Thomas and Dylan. Even with everything they'd been through and everything they'd done to each other, they were still best friends.

"What if we wait to tell people anything until after a few weeks have gone by, and then we'll announce the engagement."

"You mean the marriage?"

"Well, I was sort of thinking I'd like another ceremony too. Not just a reception."

"I'm not made of money, doll," he teased.

"Just so my dad can walk me down the aisle and all that. And picture Lucy in a cute flower girl dress!"

"Okay."

"Anyway, so maybe we could just let people think that ceremony was the real thing, I mean, except your mom and Dylan."

"This is all very complicated for this late at night."

"I'm sorry, let's go to sleep."

"There's other things I can do well late at night," he replied.

"Good night," I said emphatically.

THOMAS

Thanks to the meeting we'd scheduled with Chris, the solicitor, it was the alarm clock which actually woke us up. I was confident he was the best person to ensure we crossed every T and dotted every I in making our union official. He'd handled everything for me so far, from my previous property purchases to business matters and even a few minor criminal charges from my younger, wilder days.

"You haven't changed your mind already, have you?" I asked, narrowing my eyes at Lily.

She smiled sleepily and shook her head. "Oddly, no. Have you?"

The fact that she even thought I could change my mind about her made me chuckle. I kissed her firmly, then headed out to grab coffee.

When he arrived, he congratulated us both, politely greeted Lucy, and then launched into mounds of documents. As the foreign national, Lily had a lot more paperwork and was still completing various forms when it was time for me to leave.

"I can stay," I insisted, hesitant to leave her to handle marriage details alone. "They can't start without me."

"It's not like I need you to watch me sign a bunch of papers," she replied.

I instructed Chris to call my cell phone with any questions and to keep me updated on the progress. Apparently, Lily needed some special visa to marry me in the UK, but as with most things in life, that application's approval could be expedited by paying a hefty sum. Chris didn't anticipate any issues, but he warned us that it would be close to the end of our time in England before we'd be eligible to wed. Apparently, my birth country didn't make it easy for people to rush into marriage.

By the time I reached the location for the photo shoot, I was whistling. Part of me worried I was a fool for celebrating before we actually sealed the deal, but the rest of me didn't care. The fact that Lily would even agree to marry me brought me such immense happiness that I couldn't stop smiling.

Even when the photographer told us to look serious.

"Christ, Tom. We're supposed to look moody here and you look like you just won the bloody lottery," Dylan snarled.

"Good night last night?" Gavin teased under his breath.

"Excellent," I replied. Then I turned to my brother. "I'll try harder to look miserable."

"Thank you. Since your life clearly isn't in shambles, maybe focus on all those puppies being tortured in the mills."

I wasn't sure what to make of his suggestion, but as I gazed down, I noticed the ring on Owen's finger and it hit me. I'd been dreaming of proposing to her from the moment she first let me kiss her, and yet somehow I hadn't bought Lily a ring. Maybe I should've focused more on the enormity of the fact that she actually agreed without a ring. Lily was far from materialistic, but she'd always loved jewelry. She could spend significantly more time deciding which bracelet or necklace to wear with a top than choosing the top itself.

Sadly, I didn't even know where to go to buy a ring in London. And I certainly couldn't ask anyone close to me because then they'd know about my plans with Lily.

Ari called for a short break and offered up his assistant, Vanessa, to get us drinks or snacks. The other guys made some simple requests, then scattered to relax, hit the loo, or catch up on calls. I saw my opening and took it.

"Vanessa, I have an unusual request that I was hoping you could help me out with," I began.

She made a face that suggested she'd grossly misinterpreted the nature of my request.

"I was hoping you could give me some recommendations on where one would go around here to buy nice jewelry," I said quickly, before her mind could wander too far.

Her expression relaxed. "Specifically what kind of jewelry? Is it for you or for your mother or…"

"I need an engagement ring. A nice one. And I need to pick it out in person, but I just don't know where to begin."

"Oh boy," she sighed.

"I understand this might not fall under the parameters of your job duties, but…"

"It's not that," she interrupted. "But you do realize you're literally a rock star, right? I mean, people know you around these parts. You can't just waltz into a jewelry store and pick out an engagement ring unless you want the whole world to know your plans before your girlfriend."

I swore under my breath. She was right.

"Also, Ari has asked me to keep an eye on things between you and your brother. He probably would appreciate me telling him if you plan to propose to Dylan's ex-fiancée."

"Ari doesn't need to know, and Dylan is fine."

"If you two kill each other, the tour is fucked."

"I realize that." I rubbed my forehead. Now I wouldn't have any trouble looking moody. I bloody felt it. "Look, can you make an appointment for me at a shop or two, maybe after hours?"

She considered that for a minute. "I'll see what I can do. How soon?"

"Today. Tomorrow at the latest."

This appeared to surprise her, but she nodded.

Comforted that I was making progress, I returned to the photo shoot, only to be interrupted a short while later by a phone call from Chris.

"I have to take this," I told the guys, wincing at their responsive groans.

"I'm sorry to tell you, but they've flagged your notice of intent to marry for review," Chris said.

"Why? What does that mean?"

"Well, I assume it's a combination of factors. Your income

disparity, the interest in rushing everything, her being a foreign national, perhaps even the age difference." He paused. "The government is going to great lengths lately to ensure that British men aren't bringing young girls into the country and forcing them to marry. Someone in the bureau would like to meet with you both, just to verify that everything is legit."

I supposed it made sense from the government's perspective, but I couldn't help but snap at Chris, even though technically he'd done nothing wrong. He promised to set a meeting for the following morning so we could progress without further delay.

As soon as I returned to the room where we were shooting, Dylan smiled. "There's the moody look we were going for!"

Lily took the news better than I did, although she did seem to be concerned that they'd quiz her over things she didn't even know about me yet. I couldn't imagine their investigation would be that thorough, though. Surely if they spoke with me for even a minute, they could see how sincere my love for her was. Still, I couldn't shake the bad mood. Nothing was going as I'd planned.

"We're getting married," Lily reminded me. "So why do you look miserable?"

"I wanted to take care of everything for you. Now you have to show up at some silly agency to meet with officials."

"I had nothing better to do in the morning," she insisted.

"My proposal was lame. And I don't even have a ring for you yet. You deserve so much more," I admitted.

Honestly, I half expected Lily to nod in agreement then storm out. Instead, she laughed.

"Thomas, did Dylan ever tell you how he proposed?"

I shook my head. Dylan told me almost everything about his life, including excessive details about even the most intimate moments with all of his other girlfriends. Except with Lily. From the first time I met her, Dylan had been uncharacteristically tight-lipped about everything having to do with her. That was how I'd surmised that he was aware of my feelings for her.

He hadn't even told me he was going to propose to her before he did it. Actually, he hadn't even told me after the fact. I'd seen the ring.

"No," I finally said."

"He took me away for the weekend. We stayed at some cottage in the Hamptons. Lobster dinners, breakfast in bed, a hot tub with candles…" she paused.

I made no attempt to hide my disgust. I wanted nothing less than to picture my Lily with my brother.

Lily reached for my hand. "Let me get to the point, okay?"

I winced, but nodded for her to continue.

"He took me on a walk along the beach and he'd written all these romantic messages in the sand, and then the actual proposal was cobbled together out of sticks."

"Jesus." I rolled my eyes, but I had to admit it was brilliant.

"If he had just sat there on the bed and asked me to be his wife, I would've said no. He needed the flowers, the poetry, the over-the-top romance. He was playing on my emotions and not my logic."

I cleared my throat. "If you're trying to tell me I don't need to step up my game, you've failed."

She cocked her head to the side, eying me much as one would an injured puppy. "Thomas, my point is that I don't need over-the-top romance with you. There's nothing missing between us that you're overcompensating for. You don't have to promise me the world because you've already delivered. You don't have to write me songs because you are there for me every time I need you."

I raised a finger and she paused, visibly annoyed at the interruption.

"I did technically write you a song," I reminded her. "It literally won awards, and…"

Lily bit her bottom lip, her hair flopping in front of her eyes. Unable to see her eyes, I couldn't decipher her expression anymore. I reached for her chin and gently tilted her face upward. She smiled sheepishly.

"I'm botching this," she said. "What I'm trying to say is that I love you and I can count on you. I don't need hot tubs and candles. I just need someone who will bring me coffee in bed and pick up soup when I'm sick."

I leaned in, brushing my lips against hers so lightly that I barely felt the contact. I didn't want to risk getting distracted by her sweet mouth before I said what I needed to say. "I love you. And I can actually make you soup," I whispered.

* * *

LILY

I tried not to let Thomas see how nervous I was about the interrogation by his government. He already felt bad enough about the entire proposal situation. His lawyer came with us, as did Lucy, but they asked to speak with me alone first. Thomas seemed hesitant to agree to this, but I reminded myself it wasn't a big deal. Worst case scenario they could only banish me from the country or something, right? And then he could simply come back to the States with me.

They led me to a messy office where one woman sat behind a desk. She was polite and promised not to take much of my time. Then she jumped right to the chase by asking when we planned to be married.

"As soon as possible," I replied.

"No set date?" she gazed up above the rim of her glasses.

"No."

She jotted something down before asking how long we'd been engaged.

I had a feeling my response to that question wasn't helping

our case any because her next question asked if there was any particular reason for the urgency.

"No," I said, assuming that was better than admitting we were each concerned the other would change their mind.

"And you don't intend to reside here after the marriage?"

I shook my head. "No. My home is in New York. I mean, Thomas and I both live in New York. His mother still lives here and he comes here a lot on tour, but…"

"Tour?" she interrupted.

"Yeah. He's in a band. Sierra?"

Her eyebrow rose, but that was the only sign I got that she actually knew who he was.

"Also, our daughter goes to school in New York."

"You have a daughter?"

"Yes. Her name is Lucy. She's four. She's outside with Thomas now…"

"Who is her father?" she asked, flipping through her stack of papers as though that should be on a form somewhere.

"Thomas. My uh fiancé."

"He's her biological father or…"

"Yes. Thomas Parker is her biological father."

She gazed at me for a moment, then nodded and stacked her papers neatly before shoving them in a folder and sliding it to the corner of her desk. "Okay, I think everything is in order here. We've expedited all of your applications so you should be free to wed at the end of the twenty-eight day notice period. If your intent to reside in the UK changes at some point, you'll of course have to leave the country to reapply for the appropriate visas."

"Okay," I mumbled.

She smiled curtly then motioned for me to leave.

CHAPTER NINETEEN

"When love with unconfinéd wings
Hovers within my gates,
And my divine Althea brings
To whisper at the grates;
When I lie tangled in her hair
And fettered to her eye
The birds that wanton in the air
Know no such liberty."
Richard Lovelace, *To Althea, from Prison*

LILY

The month flew by, and it felt like days rather than weeks had passed when our rings arrived. They were perfect, of course, so I didn't even tell Thomas that I'd had panic attacks about some horrific error in the rings symbolizing some deeper problem with our plan. We went out to dinner the night before we were to marry, all three of us, then we'd worked as a team to tuck Lucy into bed.

I thought I'd feel different, lying beside Thomas the night before he was to become my husband, but I didn't. When I asked him if he thought that was strange, he laughed.

"I'd think it were strange if you didn't worry about it."

"What does that mean?" I asked.

"You second guess everything that has to do with me. With us. It's like you just can't accept that life can actually be this good."

I considered that. "It is really good. That can't be normal, right?"

He laughed again. "Sleep well, my bride," he said, planting a chaste kiss on my forehead before wrapping his arm around me. I didn't expect to fall asleep anytime soon, but I did.

Thomas was already awake and helping Lucy pack when I woke. When Thomas asked Dylan if he would take Lucy for a night or two before he left to return to the States, he didn't bat an eye. He invited Kate up to stay with him too, and asked if it was okay for them to take Lucy to the London Transport Museum one day and the Natural History Museum the next. Having gotten my fill of touristy attractions early on in our adventures, I was fine with that plan.

Thomas told his brother we were headed to a bed and breakfast on the coast, which was true. But he'd omitted that we were swinging by a small chapel on our way. We'd agreed to keep everything as simple as possible. Thomas wore a suit, I'd chosen a long, flowy sundress a paler shade of the green from his eyes. I even styled my own hair. We wanted to save all the fanfare for the celebration back home.

We drove to the chapel, where we arrived fifteen minutes early. "Hmm. What should we do to pass the time?" he asked, wiggling his eyebrows.

I held him at bay. "I think I'll run to the restroom, maybe touch up my makeup."

He nodded. "Shall I leave the keys in the ignition, in case you decide to make a run for it?"

I stuck out my tongue and started towards the building. He'd already seen—and gushed over—the dress, but I still felt his eyes on me as I walked away.

Inside the small chapel, I introduced myself to the chaplain and receptionist, and a second woman showed me to the restroom. When I emerged, Thomas was speaking with the chaplain and the two women were seated in the front row pew. The chaplain greeted me with a pleasant smile.

Thomas' expression was … something else. Surprise, hunger, desire, gratitude and passion all mixed into one. Clearly, he'd been at least a little bit concerned that I would run, but it was equally apparent that he was now thinking about things that weren't supposed to happen until after the wedding.

I shook my head, letting my eyes widen to tell him I knew indecent thoughts were running through his mind. Thomas laughed, held out his hand, then nodded to the chaplain.

The man went through a short introductory speech, read a Bible verse about love, then asked for our vows. Thomas insisted on going first, which was fine by me, since the gravity of this moment had just hit me.

I was getting married. To Thomas.

We were actually doing it.

And I had no doubts.

"I've adored you since the moment I first saw you, which if you recall, was actually before the day with the red shoes." Thomas paused, his dimple popping as he winked in case I hadn't already remembered that I was completely disheveled the first time he'd seen me.

"Since that day, every word you've said to me, every look you've cast in my direction, it's all simply added fuel to the fire in my heart. But if I'm being completely honest, I think I dreamed of you even before we met. You fulfill my every fantasy about a wife, a partner, a lover, a friend, and a mother to my children," he said. His lengthy pauses between each title for me sent shivers up my spine.

"You make my soul feel alive in a way I never imagined possible. With you in it, my life is full. With you by my side, I'm complete, and I never before realized something was missing. You saved me when I didn't even know I needed rescuing."

He took a deep breath and squeezed my hands. The gesture made me realize I was trembling. Thomas stroked my hands for a moment, then raised each to his lips in turn. Somehow, that soothed my nerves.

His eyes locked on mine again as he continued. "The point is that I want nothing more than to be your husband, Lily. And I promise I will spend the rest of my life thanking you, supporting you, and loving you with all that I am."

As Thomas finished speaking, his lips curled into a half smile. It took me several breaths to even be able to muster the energy to speak, and when I did, it wasn't to launch into my vows.

"I should've known not to let the professional songwriter go first," I teased.

"You could recite your ABCs now and I'd still be smitten," he replied.

I licked my lips and started. "You once teased me about my love of tragic love stories. You couldn't understand why I'd go into a book already knowing my beloved characters would end up heartbroken. And the reason is that no matter how it ended up, I couldn't resist the chance to read about such a passionate romance. I didn't really believe such intense love existed in real life, and, even if it did, I assumed the closest I'd ever get to it was in those books."

Thomas' smile broadened and I could've sworn his eyes sparkled.

"I thought I knew what love was, but I was wrong. You showed me what true, unconditional love looks like. You taught me what it feels like." I paused to catch my breath. "Life with you is so easy that it scares me. It's so perfect that it doesn't feel real. But then whenever I start to have doubts, you're there, reminding me of everything we've overcome together, of everything we can do together. And at the end of the day, I know I can always count on you, and I wish there were more words to express how much that means to me. For now, it'll have to suffice for me to tell you I love you, more than I thought possible. And I always will."

I saw Thomas' chest rise and fall slowly. The past five years of our lives had culminated in this one moment, and it was utterly overwhelming. I needed more of him, more contact than just our hands. I craved the warmth of his arms roped tightly around me, the support of his torso pressed firmly against mine, and the ecstasy of his tongue dancing between my lips.

But of course, we weren't done yet.

Thomas bit back a smile, clearly reading my mind, and then he cleared his throat.

I turned and realized the chaplain was staring at me expectantly.

Shit. He'd obviously just asked me something, but since I hadn't heard how he phrased it, I wasn't sure how to respond. Did I say "yes" or "I do?" Or maybe "I will?"

I opted for the simplest. "Yes," I said, my voice a mere whisper.

He then turned to Thomas, presumably asking him the same question, to which Thomas replied "a thousand times yes."

"Showoff," I mouthed, rolling my eyes.

He smirked and pulled the rings from his pocket. Given the lack of pockets in my dress, I'd actually given him his own ring to hold on to as well. He dropped it into my palm, closing my fingers around it. The chaplain spoke about the symbolism behind the rings, then Thomas slipped mine on first, then held out his hand while I gently slid his into place.

"I now pronounce you husband and wife," the chaplain said. "Congratulations."

I was acutely aware that he hadn't said anything about

kissing the bride, but that sure didn't stop Thomas. He cupped my cheeks in his hands and kissed me so firmly that I nearly fell over. When he finally released me, the two women I supposed served as our witnesses were both clapping. We kissed again, then we signed some papers before we dashed out of the chapel.

* * *

THOMAS

I hadn't realized the enormity of the sacrifice when I'd told Lily we could keep the wedding a secret. Now that she was officially mine, I wanted nothing more than to shout it from the rooftops. I wanted to tell everyone we passed, text my entire family, notify the rest of the world by social media: Lily Mitchell was finally mine.

I was grateful that our inn was less than twenty minutes from the chapel, since I didn't think I'd be able to wait much longer before kissing my wife the way I really wanted to. But then, we passed a scenic grassy area where it seemed safe to pull over.

"Pit stop?" she asked, her eyebrow shooting up as I killed the ignition.

Chuckling, I unbuckled my belt and leaned over her. She met me half way, our lips crashing together. We didn't kiss as long as I'd have liked, we couldn't possibly have satisfied our desire for each other, but I felt slightly sated at least. I motioned for her to follow me, then I walked around the car to the boot. I retrieved my guitar, then reached for her hand and we walked further into the field.

"You're not seriously serenading me, are you?" she teased as we settled down against a tree.

I nodded, waited until her eyes locked on mine, then began singing the very vows I'd just proclaimed in the chapel.

"Why am I surprised that you wrote a song for me?" she said, smiling shyly.

"Do you recognize the lyrics?"

"Of course."

The moment my hand stilled after strumming the final chord, Lily reached for me. She nudged the guitar to the side, taking its place on my lap and propping my chin up with her fingertips. I gazed into her eyes, waiting for her to say something as her lips parted, but she simply shook her head then kissed me. I pulled her close to me, kissing her like I'd wanted to back in the church. With the weight of her body against mine, I truly felt the enormity of what we'd just done and I couldn't be happier.

I'd lost track of time, could've happily sat there kissing my bride for hours, when I felt her hand slip between us. She successfully unbuckled my belt before I realized what she intended. I swatted her hand away.

"We have a gorgeous private room awaiting our arrival," I told her.

"We can do this again there," she replied, breathless as she thrust her hand back towards my zipper.

This time I gripped her hand but didn't release it. "I won't have my first sexual experience as a married man take place in a field on the side of the road," I told her.

She giggled.

"We're ten minutes from the Inn."

"Yeah, but we'll have to check in, gather our bags, walk all the way into the room…"

"You are incorrigible. And impatient. You're going to have to wait."

Lily's ensuing pout was so adorable that I almost rethought my whole protest, but then she stood, helped me to my feet, and we made our way back to the car.

I'd confirmed our arrival time with the Inn earlier that day, so I hoped the room was ready and prepared as I'd requested. I didn't think I could handle any more delays. We unloaded our bags, not actually having much with us for only two nights, then went into the entrance of the charming building.

An older woman greeted us on arrival.

"Mr. Parker, I presume?"

I nodded. Lily stood behind me, wrapped her arms around my waist, and rested her head against my back as I checked us in.

The woman introduced herself as the owner, handed me a folio to sign to accept the room charges, then gave us the rundown about the Inn and breakfast. Then she turned towards a back room.

"Saige," she called. "Could you show this couple to their room please?"

A moment later, a girl who appeared to be about university age, probably her daughter, emerged. She froze mid-step, eyes wide and jaw dropped. The owner cleared her throat awkwardly, oblivious to why the young woman had reacted so strongly.

Lily's head popped up, and we exchanged a glance. Then she reached over and squeezed my left hand, covering my wedding band.

I cringed at the thought that, less than an hour after our nuptials, I'd blown my promise to keep it a secret.

"Listen," I said, leaning closer to the desk. "It is imperative that absolutely no one know we are here this weekend. I mean, at least until after we've left. Is that going to be a problem?"

I directed my question to the younger woman, but it was the owner who answered.

"Certainly not. We have a strict confidentiality policy here. We won't disclose the name of guests to anyone."

"Excellent. Thank you," I said, flashing my best smile. I reached for our bags and nodded to Saige, who still appeared shell-shocked.

She directed us to our room without issue, though, instructed us to call the front desk if we needed anything, then froze, still looking panicked.

As she unlocked the door, I confirmed that they'd followed my instructions. A bucket of ice held a bottle of champagne, and rose petals decorated the bed. I smiled as Lily walked into the room.

"Thank you," I said to Saige. "And, um, I'm happy to sign an autograph for you before we leave."

"That would be great," she stammered. "Thanks."

I chuckled at her nervousness then joined my bride in the room, closing the door behind us. Lily had already found the champagne and was filling both of our glasses. She gazed up at me and smiled. The moment distracted her enough to cause her to overfill the glass.

I lunged forward, taking the bottle from her and offering her a towel. She'd already raised her hand to her lips though, licking off the sticky sweet liquid. She offered me a glass and smiled expectantly.

"To secret weddings and the start of eternity together," I said, clinking my glass against hers. She sipped hesitantly and I thought she was about to kiss me, but then she turned. She trailed her fingers along the bedspread, rolling one of the rose petals between her thumb and forefinger before continuing her exploration of the room.

She lingered by the bathroom, smiling at the oversized jetted tub, and then she made her way to the window. She raised her champagne to her lips again, gazing outside pensively.

I took another swig of my drink before setting the flute on the table. Closing the distance between us, I swept her hair over to one shoulder then gently traced my lips along the other side of her neck. Lily shivered, angling closer to me. I reached around and took her glass from her and placed it beside mine. Then I slowly lowered her dress off one shoulder, then the other, planting soft kisses on each shoulder. I nudged her gown lower and she turned to face me, stepping out of it slowly.

I took a step backwards to get a better view of her as she dropped her bra onto the floor beside the dress. "Bloody hell," I mumbled. "You are the most gorgeous woman I've ever seen." She blushed but didn't speak, and I was still enjoying the view too much to move. "And now you're all mine."

"That I am, Mr. Parker," she replied. "So what do you plan to do with me?"

My laughter felt like a low rumble deep in my chest. I shucked my suit jacket, draping it over the back of a chair, then crooked my finger at my wife inviting her to finish undressing me. Nothing built anticipation more than feeling her eager hands fumble at each of the buttons along my shirt.

When she finally finished with my shirt, tugging it free from my pants before unbuckling them, she groaned. "You have so many layers."

I hadn't gone commando like my wife, and I did have on an undershirt, but that hardly seemed like an excess of clothing, particularly in light of the occasion. Still, I helped her finish undressing me. We kissed as long as we could stand upright, and then I guided her back onto the bed and made love to her on top of the flower petals.

* * *

LILY

I felt surprisingly well rested when I awoke the next morning. The previous night, I'd shared a relaxing bath with my new husband and then he'd dragged me out to a late dinner. When we'd gotten back to our room, we'd gone straight to bed, but hadn't actually gone to sleep for hours. And now that we were both up, Thomas seemed to be interested in working up an appetite before our full English breakfast was delivered to the room.

When they arrived with the food, Thomas slipped on a pair of trousers and an undershirt, but I hid in the bathroom. Whereas his fresh-out-of-bed look was sexy, from the stubbled chin to the tousled hair, I just looked sloppy.

"You'd better not be getting dressed in there," Thomas called through the door.

I opened it a crack, confirming we were alone again before coming out. I laughed, noting that he was already eating.

"Hungry?"

"Famished. Get over here or I won't save you any black pudding."

I gagged but joined him over at the small eating nook in the corner of the room. I sat on the chair beside him, but he quickly lifted my feet up onto his lap. There was an obscene amount of food on the table. I started with some eggs and then moved on to roasted tomatoes. I cringed watching Thomas take a bite of the aforementioned black pudding.

"It's just sausage," he said with a laugh.

"Sausage filled with blood," I replied.

He didn't dispute that, but cut a smaller piece. "When you eat your steak cooked medium, do you know what that red liquid is?" He poised the fork in front of my lips. "Marriage is all about trying new things."

"This is not what people mean when they say that," I replied. Despite my better judgment, I took the bite. I chewed and swallowed quickly, without truly tasting much or noting the texture. As I washed down the bite with coffee, I decided it reminded me more of meatloaf than sausage, but it wasn't as disgusting as I'd envisioned.

"Just you wait till I find something repulsive and new for you to try," I threatened.

He grinned.

"So what's the plan for today?" I asked.

"I thought we could let our food digest then head back to bed. Perhaps after that we could squeeze in a quick bath before lunch, and then return to bed until dinner."

"I like the way you think, but no. You dragged me all the way out here to the coast, so we're going to the beach today."

"All the way out here? You realize we're less than two hours from London."

I took a bite of toast and stood. "I'm getting my suit on. I bet they can make sandwiches or something we can take for lunch."

An hour later, we'd arrived at a gorgeous, virtually uninhabited beach. It was a picturesque day, with a vivid blue sky accented with the occasional fluffy white cloud.

With Thomas by my side at the beach, I didn't feel self-conscious like I usually did in a bikini. I felt beautiful, confident, and carefree.

Thomas spread out the thick picnic blanket and then we topped it with our towels. The beach was comprised of more pebbles than sand, but the blanket provided the perfect cushion. We set up the chairs, but as soon as I tugged off my cover up, I stretched out on my stomach on a towel. Between the breeze and the sunshine, I was ready for a nap.

"Could you spray my back?" I asked, smiling at the sight of my striking husband unbuttoning his shirt.

"You don't have any lotion I can rub on instead?" he teased. He sprayed my back then lay beside me on his side, his head propped up on his elbow.

"Are you just going to watch me?"

"Yep."

I laughed but closed my eyes anyway. When I awoke, he'd moved to a chair and was reading a book.

Thomas set down his book and smiled at me as I propped myself onto my elbows.

"The view is gorgeous from here," he said.

I craned my neck around to see the water, which did look rather idyllic, but he laughed. As I turned back to him, I realized he'd been talking about me, not the water. I supposed my position did give my cleavage a rather substantial boost.

"It's hard to tell where you're looking with those sunglasses on," I whined.

He tugged them off and tossed them on the towel beside me, locking his deep green eyes on me. "Better?"

I shivered, then wondered how long the intensity of his stare would have that effect on me.

"I was thinking I might dip my toes in the water. Care to join me?"

There were other people in the water, but it looked cold to me. And I was comfy.

"I'll watch from here," I promised.

He stood, slowly stretching his arms above his head. I couldn't help but smile. It was obvious why his abs had been pictured in multiple tabloids over the past few years. Thomas Parker was the best eye candy out there.

And he was all mine.

I flipped over, sitting upright so I could watch as he sauntered down to the water. He turned to face me, then hopped as though it were chilly when he actually made contact. After a moment, he turned back towards the sea. He waded out past his knees before returning, walking slowly to me in a way that made my heart thrum.

"It's refreshing, not cold," he said, stretching out beside me.

"Those are synonyms," I replied.

He growled his disagreement while kissing me. He gently lowered me to my back without moving his lips off mine, but he kept our exploits semi-appropriate by remaining on his side next to me. As he finally pulled away, I felt a twinge of regret that we hadn't spent the day in bed as he'd suggested.

He played with my hair for a minute, then grabbed his

sunglasses and slipped them back on his face. "Come here," he said, sitting upright and nudging me to the side so I could lay my head on his lap.

"You're all wet," I protested, but I didn't really care. He reached into the bag, pulled out the book I'd brought along, and began reading aloud to me. I sighed happily. There was no place I'd rather be than snuggled up against Thomas listening to his beautiful voice read aloud. My eyes drifted shut, soothed by his words as much as the rhythmic whispers of the sea. His left hand rested casually across my abdomen while he read, so I stroked his fingers, smiling wider when I reached his ring.

I opened my eyes, gazing at the ring. Thomas had never really been a fan of rings before, but this one looked perfect on him. It was masculine, unique, and gorgeous, just like him. I was equally pleased with my rings, though I'd already moved my wedding band to my right hand. Since we planned to tell people we'd gotten engaged right away, I wasn't worried about the sparkling diamond on my left hand.

I gazed further down the beach and noticed a group of teenaged girls staring in our direction. It wasn't until one of them pulled out a phone and seemed to be taking a picture that I gave it a second thought.

"Hey," I whispered.

Thomas stopped reading, but didn't move.

"You didn't switch fingers yet," I said, twisting and tugging at his ring. I placed it in his palm and curled his fingers around it, but he didn't move.

"You could put it on your right hand. I just…I think those girls down the beach maybe recognize you. It seemed like maybe they were taking a picture."

From his sigh, I knew that annoyed him, but he still didn't take the ring. "You put that ring on my finger. You're the only person who can take it off or switch it around," he finally said. He dropped the ring on my belly then offered me his other hand. I slid the ring in place then kissed his hand.

"We can go if you don't like the attention," he said.

I thought about that, but I was really comfortable. "It seems I'll have to get used to the attention eventually."

"You're not embarrassed to be photographed with me?" he teased.

I laughed. "You know those girls all hate me now."

He dipped his head down and kissed me upside down.

"You're not helping."

"Come on. Quick dip in the water and then we'll eat."

This time, I went with him. He held my hand as we walked to the water, kissed me as the waves hit, and even carried me when we went a little further. There'd be no doubt that we were together if there were photographs taken, and yet I didn't care. Thomas was worth more than my privacy.

We stayed at the beach until late afternoon, and I soaked up every moment of perfection.

CHAPTER TWENTY

THOMAS

*A*s soon as we returned to London, I took my brother out for a drink to thank him for watching Lucy during our absence. I planned to come up with a tactful way to tell him about the marriage, but he beat me to the punch.

"So she said yes," Dylan said, reaching for his beer.

My jaw dropped. "What do you…"

Dylan immediately went to his phone, making me wonder if he'd even heard my question. But then he dropped it down in front of me, open to a giant picture of Lily and I kissing in the water. Her arms were around my neck, and they'd enlarged the photo of her hand, showing what was undoubtedly a diamond engagement ring.

"Well, shit. That was fast. I knew there were some kids taking pictures, but…"

He shrugged. "They didn't actually blow the surprise. Vanessa did. She asked me if you'd liked either of the jewelry stores she recommended. Guess she thought you'd talked with me about it."

I cringed. It had felt wrong not telling Dylan before any of it, but we weren't sharing intimate details lately. Hell, he hadn't even told me about his recent divorce.

"It's alright. I figured that was what you wanted to tell me about today, and I appreciate the gesture."

I took a hefty swig of my beer. "That's actually not what I wanted to tell you." I pressed my hand against the table in front of him.

Dylan made a face, but clearly missed what I was trying to show him with my ring.

I sighed. "We didn't get engaged. We got married. That's my wedding band. She made me move it to my right hand because she doesn't want anyone to know."

Dylan gazed down at my hand then back to my face. He said nothing but reached for his beer. I waited patiently for him to respond.

"That's what you were doing when I babysat your kid? Eloping?"

I nodded, still holding my breath.

"Wow," he said with a laugh. "You've got balls I never knew about. Congratulations."

I hesitated, trying to decipher his true enthusiasm.

"I'm serious, Tom. Good job."

"Good job?"

"You and I both know she's had cold feet about anything to do with our family since…well, me. I'm impressed that you were able to make her see things clearly."

"Really? You aren't angry?"

My brother shrugged. "No. I'm not even going to think about what you spent the last two days doing while I was playing Chutes and Ladders."

My eyebrow shot up.

"Seriously. Time with Lucy is an excellent consolation prize."

"She isn't a prize. There wasn't a contest and nobody won or lost. You and Lily weren't right together and you know that."

Dylan cocked his head to the side. "Tom, calm down. I'm agreeing with you. You are the better man for Lily."

"You'll find someone who fits you. I know you thought you were happy when you were with her, but…"

"But I was a bloody junkie, I know. You don't have to remind me. Lily and I would've never had any sort of happy ever after. But you two could. And you don't have to worry about me. Just because I'm all alone doesn't mean I'm lonely."

He sounded sincere, but I wasn't really sure what to make of that comment.

"I don't think I'm the marrying type. Or at least not with Patty. She was great for a while and then it just got boring. Too much work. I missed playing the field."

I tipped the last few drops of my beer into my mouth then motioned to the waiter for another. "I'm sick of fighting with you. I want things to go back to the way they used to be between us. Is that even possible?"

"Is that why you're telling me about the wedding?"

"I don't know. Maybe. It doesn't feel real until you know about it." I shrugged. "Lily doesn't want anyone else to know. Not Mum, not Lucy, not her friends…"

"Secrets, secrets are no fun. Secrets, secrets hurt someone," Dylan chanted, snickering at his own rhyme.

I rolled my eyes then thanked the waiter for the new round of drinks.

"Seriously, though. It won't stay a secret for long. Especially if you're fornicating on a public beach."

"Nobody was…" I blew out a sigh, not even bothering to finish my sentence. "She's telling her parents we got engaged and we'll plan a ceremony in New York after the holidays."

Dylan nodded. "Alright. Good luck. I'll text you my availability for all best man duties."

I laughed and we shifted the discussion topic.

* * *

LILY

The next two weeks flew by, and before I knew it, we were packing up to head back to the States. I was excited to return to reality, but terrified to leave the surreal cocoon that England had offered Thomas and I. We'd arranged for movers to come the day after we returned so that Lucy and I could move directly into Thomas' apartment, hopefully avoiding an unnecessary transition step for her before school started back up in a week. She seemed excited about the move, so that was a plus.

I also knew I couldn't postpone talking to my parents in person any longer. I'd told them over the phone about the engagement and that we were moving, and they'd expressed their concern. Nothing they'd said surprised me, but it was still disappointing, even if predictable.

I left the apartment before Thomas and Lucy, planning to grab a bottle of wine to take to my parents, but as soon as I reached the lobby, I ran into Dylan.

I smiled warmly just as Dylan pulled me close. At first, I thought he was going to kiss me, but his lips moved towards my ear instead. "I hear you had a busy week back in England," he whispered. "Congratulations."

He released me from the hug and smiled. "You picked the right Parker brother this time," he added, winking.

Thomas had told me about their talk, and that he thought Dylan was genuinely happy for us and, seeing him in person, I agreed. I wished they could fully patch things up between them.

"Thank you. We're headed to my parents' tonight. They're not taking the news of the engagement very well, so…"

He shook his head dismissively. "Your mum's taste in men for you is rubbish. Tell Tom to get a thicker skin and shake it off."

I laughed.

When we arrived at my parents, they both focused their attention on Lucy, who was equally glad to see them. For a moment, I thought I could avoid any confrontation by using Lucy as a buffer, but then my mom suggested my dad and Thomas head out back with Lucy. I braced myself for the lecture. I didn't have to wait long.

"Your father was disappointed that Thomas never asked his permission."

I thought about telling her that was an antiquated tradition that suggested I was a possession to be passed from one man to the next, but instead I opted for a lie. "That's not something they do in England."

She was quiet for a moment as she worked on her next barb. "You could wait to move in with him. Lucy's just dealt with all the transition from spending the summer abroad and now you're uprooting her home, too."

"The movers already came. It's done."

"So now you live next door to Dylan? Won't that be awkward?"

"Lucy loves her Uncle Dylan. And he and Thomas let go of everything that happened in the past."

My mother kept glancing out the large window over the kitchen sink while she rinsed the dishes. Thomas and Lucy were outside, along with my father. I couldn't see them from where I stood drying dishes, but I could hear Lucy's happy shrieks and giggles.

"Well, he does seem good with Lucy," she said.

"He is," I replied. "He has so much fun with her too. He's teaching her sign language, piano, guitar, and even a little German and French."

"He looks an awful lot like his brother."

"You can't fault him for that. In fact, you can't blame him for anything Dylan did. He's nothing like his brother."

She sighed wearily. "It's just us women now, so you can tell me the truth. Are you pregnant again?"

"No!"

"I just think you're rushing into things, like always."

I rolled my eyes. "Mom, he's been in love with me for five years now. And he's been the only person I could trust and the best friend I've had for a good part of that time. He was the only one who was there for me when I was going through everything with Dylan."

"Then he should've stopped him," she snapped.

"He tried." I shook my head and stepped closer to the window so I could see my perfect husband playing with my perfect daughter. "Thomas defended me and took care of me as much as I'd let him. He was the one who gave me money to leave Dylan and encouraged me to go. And even though I chose to keep his daughter from him for three years, he forgave me."

My mom swallowed audibly but still didn't speak.

"Thomas rearranged his work schedule so Lucy and I could go with him to England. I chose to move in with him when we returned. He even offered to keep paying rent on my apartment if that would make me feel better. And it was Thomas who got Lucy into that preschool I loved."

She turned to me, a conciliatory smile on her face. "Okay, Lily, I can see that you love him and he loves you. I will be so happy for all of you if this all works out perfectly. But I just don't want you to rush into a marriage. What if we plan the ceremony for next summer? Four months just isn't long enough to plan a wedding."

"We've got a wedding planner. She's taking care of everything."

"But it's just not long enough," my mom insisted.

I sighed. "It is when we're already married."

She frowned. "What?"

Of course, that was the moment that Thomas returned to the kitchen with my father and Lucy.

I gazed over at Thomas, who could already sense something going on from the tension in the room. "I said that we're already married. We were married August 1."

Thomas dodged my father's glare and quickly crossed the room, placing his arm around my waist. The longest silence in the history of the Mitchell family ensued. Even poor Lucy looked concerned, glancing from person to person before finally sneaking another mini cupcake off the table.

"Congratulations," my father finally said, holding his hand out to Thomas.

My mother glared at him, and I realized she was about to cry. I turned to her quickly. "I'm sorry to keep this from you, Mom, but I had to do what felt right, and I didn't want to stress you out."

"You're my only daughter and I missed it," she whimpered.

I shook my head. "No, you didn't miss anything. We haven't had a formal ceremony or anything. It was just a paperwork sort of thing. We wanted to make everything secure for Lucy."

Thomas kissed the side of my head, his lips lingering there just long enough for me to start to feel his comforting power. Then he scooped up Lucy as she scampered over to us.

"You, my dear, are covered in frosting," he said, tickling her.

"I am happy for you," my mother finally said. "I think you've picked the right one this time."

Thomas and I exchanged glances. "We think so too, Mom," I said.

We emphasized that we weren't telling anyone else yet, then managed to use Lucy's impending bedtime as an excuse to sneak out quickly.

"You know, if we just told everyone the truth, you could save a lot of energy convincing people you haven't lost your mind by agreeing to marry me," Thomas said when we reached the car.

I sighed. Jill hadn't reacted well to news of the engagement either, and seemed determined to talk me out of it. But Alicia, my friend from school, had been nothing but supportive. "People don't know anything," I insisted. "How'd the rest of the band react?"

Thomas kept his eyes on the road. "They're all happy for us. Their only concern was Dylan going off the rails, but since he seems fine, everyone is happy."

"And your mom?"

"Hard to say, but she wasn't surprised."

There was an awkward silence before he spoke again. "Since you're already stressed out, I wanted to tell you that I sent the samples for the test."

I was about to ask what test he meant when it hit me. He was talking about the paternity test. I'd thought maybe he'd decided against going through with it, now that Lucy was officially his child in all records anyway. But apparently not.

"They'll analyze samples from me, Dylan, and Lucy. We'll get an answer within five days."

I stared out the window, unsure what to say to that.

CHAPTER TWENTY-ONE

LILY

I returned to school a full week before Lucy, but thanks to Thomas' flexible schedule, she didn't have to go to daycare or to my parents' house. It was strange, leaving the house on my own each day, knowing the two people I loved most were going to be off having adventures without me, but it was also refreshing in a way to return to my routine.

I spent the first three days setting up my classroom and preparing lesson plans, and then I had a full day of meetings before the students arrived. Parents and students were invited to the school to meet teachers the night before classes began, so it was late when I returned home. The apartment was silent except for Thomas softly crooning a lullaby to Lucy back in her room. I was tempted to go say goodnight, but I didn't want to get her all riled up after he'd clearly worked hard to get her to bed on time.

I went into the kitchen and poured myself a glass of wine, cutting my finger on the foil wrapped around the bottle. I didn't want to risk Lucy seeing me walk past her room to get to the bathroom medicine cabinet, and I thought I recalled seeing band-aids in the music room, so I went there. I pulled open the drawer on the side table and found the box. They were special round ones that apparently Thomas used for some sort of guitar-related blister or something. I sat down while fiddling with the wrapper, setting my wine glass on top of a paper. I hardly looked at the document until I saw the envelope beside it.

It was the paternity test results.

My breath caught in my throat as I slowly unfolded the paper. I squeezed my eyes shut, said a quick, silent prayer, then faced the paper. The bold-faced lettering indicated that Subject B was the match with Lucy. I frowned, flipping the paper over to see which subject was which. My heart sunk when I saw.

It was Dylan. Dylan Parker, Subject B, was the father of my child.

I felt nauseous and stood quickly, clutching my stomach. But as soon as I took a breath, the feeling passed. Sort of. I reached for my wine and downed half the glass.

Why had we done this stupid test anyway? Everything was perfect, and then we'd ruined it. We just had to know for sure, and now that we did, I'm sure we all wished we didn't know.

God. This meant Dylan would have some sort of rights to Lucy now. Would I have to tell him? Surely it would be too painful for Thomas. I couldn't even imagine what this would do to their relationship. They'd just repaired it and now…

I needed fresh air. I carried my wine back into the kitchen, grabbed my cell phone, and headed out. I didn't intend to walk very far, but the more worries that flurried around in my head, the more I lost track of time. When I finally stopped and turned around to head back, I realized I'd been gone for over a half hour already. I picked up the pace for the walk back, surprised that Thomas hadn't called or texted. He must have realized I'd come home when he saw the wine glass or my purse, and now he was probably worried.

I should've been there. He had obviously seen the results already, so he must be feeling even worse than I was. He needed me, and I wasn't there. I sucked at this whole marriage thing. The first time my husband really needed me and I took off on a damn walk to clear my head without even thinking about what he needed.

I was practically at a jog pace when I reached the apartment. I unlocked the apartment door then froze. Everything was exactly as I'd left it and the apartment was quiet. Too quiet, really.

I hurried down the hall and peered in Lucy's room. She was sound asleep curled up in her bed. Thomas lay beside her, his arm draped over her side, also asleep.

The whole scene was so sweet that it broke my heart. He must have read the letter and wanted nothing more than to be close to his daughter—the daughter who was his no matter what some stupid test said.

I wiped the tears off my cheeks and crept away slowly. My first day of school was in the morning, and I needed to shower.

* * *

THOMAS

I couldn't figure out why a stuffed animal was covering my face until I sat up. I was in bed with Lucy. I must have fallen asleep. I groaned silently, rubbing my head. It was four o'clock in the morning. Too late for me to still be drunk from the whisky I'd plowed through and too early for me to claim a hangover.

I slowly crept out of bed. The kitchen was clean and all the lights had been shut off. I noticed Lily's work bag perched beside her purse on the counter and I remembered. Tomorrow—well, today, was her first day of school with students.

What a shit I was, getting drunk and passing out while she was working late. A good husband would have poured her a drink, drawn her a bath, and sat down to ask her about how her day went. I tiptoed into the bedroom, but as expected, she was sound asleep.

I retreated to the kitchen, helped myself to a tall glass of water and a few pills to dull my headache. I made a sandwich for Lily, mixed together some veggies for a salad, and tossed them into a lunch bag with a handwritten note.

I told myself the results didn't matter. Lily wasn't with me because I was Lucy's father. She was with me because she loved me. And some stupid test didn't make Dylan Lucy's father anyway. I was the one who'd read all the damn books on potty training and preschool. I was the one who'd written essays and bribed the headmistress of the coveted nearby private preschool to enroll Lucy for pre-kindergarten. Dylan didn't pick all the tomatoes out of her chili, rub her back till his hand went numb, or sing silly songs while brushing her hair. That was all me. I was Lucy's father.

I was exhausted, but I didn't want to risk waking Lily by going to bed now. Instead, I stretched out on the couch, tugging a blanket over myself. It was surprisingly comfortable, and sleep found me quickly.

I woke a short while later to see Lily.

"I'm sorry to wake you, but I didn't see you last night and I had to kiss you before work," she said, whispering softly.

"I'm glad you did," I replied. I tugged her hand until she sat beside me on the couch. "Sorry I missed you last night. I wanted to hear about your day, and then I guess I fell asleep putting Lucy to bed."

She smiled softly. "Yeah, been there. Done that. You could've joined me when you woke up."

"Didn't want to wake you. You have a big day today." I sat up, wincing at my still-throbbing head.

"Are you okay?" she asked, the concern written all over her face.

"Yes. I'm great." I sure wasn't going to admit I'd drunk enough while watching our child to earn myself a hangover. "I made you a lunch. Nothing too fancy, but…"

She leaned in and kissed me again before I could even finish my sentence. "Thank you. I love you so much, Thomas. You are so good to me. And to Lucy. We're so lucky."

Her enthusiasm confused me, but I hoped she'd attribute my lack of response to the early hour. "I don't want you to be late," I said lamely.

She kissed me one last time before leaving.

I managed to drift back to sleep again for another hour before Lucy woke with an unprecedented amount of energy. We made it through breakfast okay, but then she wanted to do crafts. I suggested television instead, but she was insistent. I went to the music room to see if I had any craft supplies beyond the markers and crayons in her room. All I found was a bottle of sticky white correction fluid.

I went to Lucy's room and gathered her supplies, offered her some plain white paper, and watched as she drew what appeared to be a rainbow. My mind wandered back to the stupid test results. It was all my fault; I was the one who'd pushed for the test. And now, thanks to me, everyone would suffer. Lily wanted me to be Lucy's biological father. Dylan did, too. They both were much happier now, not knowing the truth.

Why was I going to make them both miserable over something they hadn't wanted to know in the first place?

I stood abruptly and returned to the music room. Grabbing the correction fluid, I painted the sticky liquid over a word on another paper. I waved it back and forth until it dried, then looked at the results. It was obvious I'd marked over something. I added another layer, let it dry longer this time, then wrote something else over it. Now it was slightly harder to decipher. Then, I realized the final step. I popped the paper into the printer and made a quick copy of it. I smiled when I looked at the results. It was nearly impossible to tell I'd changed the original, and that was with an entire word.

Without giving it a second thought, I snatched the test results. On the front page, where it identified Subject B as the biological father, I dabbed the white liquid over the letter B. I applied it as smoothly as possible, then left the room to check on Lucy while it dried. When I returned, I very carefully wrote an A over the white space, careful to copy the typeface of the rest of the letter. Then I stuck the document in the printer and made a copy. Once I confirmed the copy was acceptable, I shredded the original. I folded that page with the remaining pages of the test results and wedged it all back into the envelope.

I felt a tiny twinge of guilt as I returned to Lucy, but it passed quickly.

CHAPTER TWENTY-TWO

"O what can ail thee, Knight at arms,
Alone and palely loitering?
The sedge has withered from the Lake
And no birds sing!"
John Keats, *La Belle Dame Sans Merci*

LILY

I assumed Thomas would seem sad when I returned home. I considered that maybe he was planning to wait until the weekend to tell me about the results, so as not to interfere with my first week of school, but surely he'd still be a little melancholy.

I wasn't expecting him to have cooked a gourmet dinner, dressed Lucy in a fancy dress, and colored pictures of rainbows to tape all over the kitchen.

He greeted me with a kiss, and Lucy did a twirl and a curtsey.

"We thought you'd like to celebrate a successful first day of school," he said.

"What makes you think it was successful?"

"You're still standing and we didn't hear about any major explosions at the high school, so I'd call that a success."

I smiled and let them celebrate. They performed a duet on the piano they'd rehearsed. It sounded a bit like a recent hit from a princess movie but with silly lyrics. We ate dinner, and then Thomas insisted on giving Lucy her bath and putting her to bed. I would've liked to do it myself since I had barely seen her the past two days, but I let him. Spending extra time with her was clearly helping him cope with the test results.

I tugged the trash bag out of the kitchen trash and lugged it into the hall to throw into the chute, then stopped abruptly. Dylan sat in the hall, slumped against his door. I dropped the trash and rushed to him.

"Dylan! Are you okay?"

He swatted me away and the reek of alcohol washed over me.

"I'm fine. I just can't door the lock," he slurred, laughing at the end. "I mean, you know. The key's all wrong."

I gazed down at the key in his hand. It was the fob for his Porsche.

"Yeah, that's your car key, Dylan. Hang on."

I dumped the trash and then returned to my apartment, grabbed his key, then stepped over him to unlock the door.

"My hero," he said, faking a swoon that almost caused him to smack his head on the door frame.

"Crap," I mumbled. He was really, really drunk. "How did you get home?"

"I think a car."

"You drove?"

"No, some man did. I think my car is still out there somewhere."

"Well, that's good at least. Can you get yourself inside? Thomas is putting Lucy to bed now but I'll have him come help you in a few minutes. You need some water." I went into his apartment, opened his fridge in search of a bottle of water, and grimaced. He did have water, but other than that, it was just beer, old takeout and some expired condiments.

"You need to get groceries. Your fridge is bare."

"Doesn't matter," he replied. "No one else eats here. I'm all alone. No wife to cook for. No kids to feed. All alone."

He pulled himself to his feet and staggered in, collapsing on his couch. I untwisted the cap on the water and handed it to him.

"Careful," I cautioned as if he were a toddler. Despite my warning, more of the water ended up on his shirt than his mouth. *Whatever.* "I'm going to get Thomas. He can help you."

I started to stand and Dylan reached for my hand.

"Don't get Thomas. I'm fine. He's with Lucy. I don't need him. I'm really good at being alone. And now I get even more time to practice." He cackled as though he'd told a funny joke.

Sighing, I crouched beside him and held the bottle for him while he drank. "You're not alone, Dylan. You have the band, tons of friends, and you could have almost any woman you wanted. And you have Thomas, me and Lucy."

He nudged the bottle away, having actually swallowed a fair amount. "No, Thomas has you and Lucy. I have…maybe Ari?" He laughed again. "I should get a dog. Then I won't be alone."

I rose to my feet. "You should not get a dog," I said, unable to envision a person less suited for pet ownership. "I'm going home. I'll send Thomas back in a few."

When I returned to the apartment, Thomas had just started reading books to Lucy. I waited while he finished her three allotted books, then said I'd sing her song. He frowned but came over to talk when he saw the look in my eyes.

"I ran into your brother in the hall. He's upset and too drunk to walk. He keeps saying he's all alone in the world."

Thomas frowned. "Yeah, I think Patty moved the last of her stuff out yesterday."

"Can you just go check on him please?"

He nodded and left.

When I finished putting Lucy to bed, Thomas was already back.

"That was fast," I commented.

"He's fine. I got him more water, we talked for a minute, and he passed out. He just needs to sleep it off. It's been a rough week for him is all."

I gazed at Thomas, waiting for him to add that it had been a bad week for him too, but he didn't. "I wish there were some way we could make him feel less lonely. I mean, he really seemed upset. He kept saying how he was all alone in the world."

Thomas shrugged and lowered himself to the couch before turning his attention to his phone. "He'll be fine," he mumbled.

"Really? Because as his brother, it seems like it's your job to look out for him. And if there's anything at all you could say or do to help him be less lonely…"

Thomas looked up to me. "You want me to buy him a hooker? I don't understand what you think I can do, Lily. He's upset, but he just got divorced. It'll take some time and then he'll be fine. He always is."

I blew out a sigh and left the room.

* * *

THOMAS

The week couldn't possibly get any worse. The paternity results were enough to ruin it, but Dylan turning into a weeping bloody mess over his divorce sure didn't help, and I wasn't sure what to make of the way Lily jumped to his defense. Maybe she felt bad, thinking this was how he'd acted after she'd left him. I wasn't about to tell her he'd been a thousand times worse then.

Anyway, he would be fine. I talked with him again when he sobered up and he had no big regrets over Patty. In fact, he seemed happy to be single again. Dylan had never been big on responsibility, so that didn't surprise me. He wasn't mature enough for a wife, and he was eons away from being ready for a kid. Learning he had a child would probably push him over the edge at this point.

Ever since our sister's accident, Dylan had resisted taking any responsibility for other humans, and the smaller or more fragile the humans were, the more terrified he was. Telling him he was technically responsible for someone he already loved very much, someone who looked just like our deceased sister, and someone who was wholly dependent on those around her…that might actually kill him.

I'd intentionally waited until the weekend to tell Lily about the results of the paternity test. In part, I'd waited so it wouldn't seem like such a big deal. She'd never really worried that I wasn't Lucy's biological father, so she certainly hadn't been eagerly awaiting the results. But also, I didn't want to tell her when she was in the midst of her stressful first few days of school.

We'd arranged for her parents to watch Lucy Saturday night, so as soon as Lily returned from dropping Lucy off with her mom, I said I wanted to talk with her.

Her expression suggested she sensed the significance of what I was about to tell. She sat on the couch and I sat beside her, clutching the envelope with the results.

"I got the results back from the paternity test," I began.

"Oh?" she replied, her voice even and calm.

I pulled the papers out of the envelope and handed them to her. She glanced down, but not long enough to read anything.

"You were right. I'm her biological father," I said. "I'm sorry I made such a fuss about it, but I suppose it's good we now know and don't ever have to wonder what if."

She wrinkled her brow. "Wait…what?"

I laughed, tracing my fingers along her smooth cheek. "I said I'm Lucy's dad."

Her lips parted, and she turned to the papers. Now she read them closely, flipping from one page to the next, then starting over. She rubbed her forehead, then gazed up at me. "I don't understand. What is this?"

"It's the test results."

She shook her head. "No, it isn't. Did this just now come in the mail?" She reached for the envelope and stared at it.

"No," I admitted. "It actually came earlier this week but I didn't want to stress you out, so…"

Lily rose to her feet and walked into the music room. She tugged open the drawers beside my music stand and even looked through the piano bench.

"What are you looking for? Are you okay?" I asked.

She stopped and shook her head. "No, apparently I'm losing my mind."

I started to chuckle at that, but as she continued talking, I realized what she meant.

"I saw the results earlier, Thomas. I thought you just weren't ready to talk about them yet. And I'm a little surprised now because…"

"Fuck." The word rushed out of my like a breath as I sunk onto the piano bench.

When I finally garnered the courage to look back up at Lily, her expression had changed.

"I'm sorry. I didn't realize you'd seen it already. I thought…"

"You thought you'd just lie to me about my daughter?" she yelled. "For how long, Thomas? When would you have told me the truth?"

I winced, certain "never" was not the correct answer.

"Were you going to tell Dylan?" She flung her hands in the air. "Lucy? Jesus."

She stormed into Lucy's room and plopped down into the plush rocking chair in the corner of the room. She thrust her head between her hands, leaning forward as though she were about to be sick. I gave her a minute, then followed her in.

* * *

LILY

"You don't understand why I did what I did?" Thomas asked. His expression remained somber, but his tone was incredulous.

I shook my head. "No, Thomas, I really don't."

"You wanted Dylan to know the truth? You wanted to risk that for Lucy?"

What I wanted was for it not to be the truth. But it was what it was, and nothing I said or did now would change the reality of our situation. "He deserves to know, Thomas. Just like you deserved to know when he thought you were the father."

"Well he bloody well didn't tell us the truth then," Thomas retorted.

"But he should have. And even if Dylan didn't do the right thing, you still should."

He glared back. "No."

"He's your brother."

"No," he repeated, more forcefully this time.

It was clear we were at an impasse. He stepped forward and reached for my hand, but I tugged it away.

"No, Thomas. Even if I did agree with you lying to Dylan, which I don't, you lied to me too. You should have told me the truth immediately and we could've decided together whether to tell Dylan. But instead you went out of your way to conceal the truth from me too. How could you do that? She's my daughter. You really don't think I had a right to know? You said you loved me. Christ, Thomas, we're married now. How could you? How could you?" I was crying hysterically by the end and practically spit the words at him, but he remained firm.

"I do love you, and that's why I didn't tell you. You yourself said you wanted it to be me all along, that you were relieved when it was me. I did you a favor," he insisted.

"You bastard!" I shouted, chucking the nearest object, a small board book, at his chest.

"Oh, really mature Lily. Thanks."

I rolled my eyes and grabbed my keys. "I have to go. Don't expect me back tonight. I'll stay at Jill's."

Thomas grabbed my arm as I attempted to storm past. "And what about Lucy?"

I jerked free of his grasp and raised my shoulders with indifference, confident he'd keep her safe regardless of how we ended things. "I'll tell my parents you'll pick her up after dinner. If you can't handle her, you can see if they'll keep her." I started out the door, then added, "Or you could drop her off at her real dad's."

His eyes widened with fury. For a moment, he reminded me exactly of Dylan and I flinched, almost expecting him to slap me. But he didn't. His arms stayed firmly at his sides.

"This conversation isn't over. And don't you say a bloody word to Dylan. That's the last thing any of us need right now."

"I'll do whatever I want. She's my daughter, not yours." I slammed the door quickly, before he could react. I knew my words were harsh and without even seeing it, I could picture the hurt in his face. I pushed the image out of my mind, and started off down the hall. I was all dressed up, having thought I was going on a date with my husband, and now I had no idea where to go. I called my work friend Alicia, remembering she had actually invited me out for drinks this weekend to celebrate surviving the first week of school. When she didn't answer, I left a message then tried Jill.

Reliable to a fault, Jill quickly agreed to meet me. I ducked into the lobby bathroom to touch up my makeup so I didn't look as distraught as I felt, and then I asked the doorman to get me a cab. Alicia called back then, so I gave her the address of the restaurant where Jill and I were meeting. I beat them both there by nearly a half hour, but that gave me time to put in our name for a table and to glare at my cell phone.

Sure, I'd said some things I shouldn't have, but I couldn't believe Thomas hadn't yet called to apologize. That was so unlike him.

When Alicia and Jill arrived, we ordered dinner. I'd chosen a restaurant that was loud and crowded so we couldn't talk about anything serious. Next, we stopped at a bar down the street. I already felt buzzed, but an hour of dancing and another beverage or two would only improve my mental outlook.

"Okay, you said you were desperate for a night out," Jill said as we reached the bar. "So spill it. What's wrong?"

I shook my head. While I still firmly believed Thomas was wrong in keeping the truth from me and from Dylan, I had no interest in disclosing Lucy's paternity to anyone outside the triangle. "Thomas and I had our first fight," I finally said.

"First fight ever?" Alicia asked.

I nodded. When I had been with Dylan, we fought incessantly. Loud, passionate arguments with no rationality and lots of broken items. And then there'd been the makeup sex, equally loud and passionate. But with Thomas, everything was much more reserved. Until tonight.

"I really don't want to talk about it," I finally said. "I just want to get drunk."

We ordered a round of shots along with our first drinks, followed quickly by another round. Then we hit up the dance floor. When we finally took a breather back at our table, a waitress quickly approached with a steaming mug.

I peered into the mug, which appeared to contain tea. "I didn't order this," I said, turning back to my vodka tonic.

"It's from the gentleman at the bar," she said uncomfortably. "And he asked me to make sure you drank it."

Jill frowned and snatched the mug away, sniffing it. "What, is it roofied or something?"

I glanced over at the bar, knowing only one person who would send me tea at a bar. Thomas used tea as a cure for everything, and I'd always teased him about fitting that one stereotype of a Brit at least. But I didn't see him at the bar, so I turned back to the waitress. "Who did you say it was from?"

She pointed. "Him, in the gray tee shirt."

And as if on cue, Dylan turned around.

Jill gasped. "Is that…?"

He tipped his head casually at us, and I smiled. Inexplicably, I was relieved. He was probably the one person now that I felt comforted to see, now that Thomas had forced us into the same category of people he'd mislead about Lucy.

"Wow," Alicia mumbled. She'd met Dylan at Lucy's party, but he'd been dressed up and on his best behavior then. Now he looked rougher around the edges and, dare I say, sexier.

"I should thank him," I said, starting towards him.

Jill pulled me back. "Um, no, you should stay far away from him. Are you kidding, Lily? With your history and your current level of intoxication, you should run in the opposite direction."

I shook my head. "I'll be fine." I sipped my tea with a smile then made my way across the bar. "Evening, sir. Thanks for the drink."

Dylan flashed his charming grin. "You're pissed!"

For a moment, I thought he was referring to my present feelings about Thomas, but then he clarified.

"Drunk, Lily, you're quite drunk."

"Yeah, well…"

"That's why I bought you the tea. To sober you up. If Thomas knew I saw you this plastered and let you run off with your girls over there, he'd kill me."

I shrugged. "Well, he can fuck off."

Dylan was clearly taken aback by this, but didn't have time for a follow up before my friends arrived, presumably to rescue me.

"You thanked him, now let's go," Jill whispered, guiding me by the elbow.

"Nice to see you again," Dylan said, smiling at Jill.

She rolled her eyes. "Wish I could say the same."

Dylan's grin widened, and he turned to Alicia. Her face turned beet red. Dylan bent forward and delicately kissed her hand, and I thought she'd pee herself.

"What are you doing here?" I asked him.

"I needed to get out, do some people watching. Writer's block," he explained.

The old Dylan relied on cocaine to write, so I supposed drinking was an improvement.

"Alone?" I asked. Dylan never went anywhere alone. He was always surrounded by a flock of women. Although, as soon as the word left my mouth, I cringed, recalling his pity party from a couple nights back.

"Seems that way, yes," he replied. "Unless you need a ride home later."

"Nope, she doesn't," Jill answered.

I glared at her and she pulled me away, momentarily leaving Alicia alone with Dylan.

"Jill, I need to talk to him and he lives right down the hall from me, so he might as well drive me. You and Alicia can share a cab."

"Absolutely not. I am not leaving you with your abusive ex-fiancé when you're drunk and fuming over a fight with your new fiancé. You are in no position to make good decisions."

"I'm an adult, Jill. Good or bad, they're my decisions to make."

"Lily…"

"Stop! I'm tired of people telling me what to do tonight. I'm fine. You and Alicia can stay and hang out, or you can go, but enough with the judgment. If anyone can help with Thomas now, it's Dylan. I need to talk to him."

This explanation seemed to placate her. "Are you sure you want us to leave?"

"Yes."

"And you'll call my cell phone if you change your mind? Or if you need anything at all?"

I nodded, and they left.

Dylan looked awkwardly around us. "I guess that leaves me to see you home."

"I'm relieved to see you," I said. The waitress gestured to his empty beer and he glanced at me.

"Are we staying or going?"

"I need another," I admitted.

Dylan was silent as he finished his beer. When the new drinks arrived, he turned to me expectantly as I hurriedly sipped mine.

"Are we drinking in silence or are you planning to tell me what my brother has done that has sent you drinking?"

I sighed, eager to spill the entire story. Dylan was a great listener. That was what first made me fall in love with him. Well, that and his sexiness, unrivaled by anyone except his own damn brother.

"We need to talk, but not here," I finally said.

He turned towards me at the bar but didn't raise his eyes to meet mine. "You and Thomas or us?"

"You and me."

"I," he said.

"Huh?"

"It's you and I," he corrected. "Never mind."

I realized what he meant and a drunken giggle escaped my lips. Dylan looked like a run-of-the-mill illiterate rocker on the outside, but he was actually obnoxiously smart. And it struck me as hilariously ironic that the Rockstar was correcting the grammar of the English teacher.

"What do we need to discuss that can't be sorted out publicly?"

I buried my face in my drink to avoid his pressing stare. "Honestly the reason I was so eager to get drunk tonight with my friends was to forget about Thomas, but running into you was perfect. I'd have lost my nerve if I waited till tomorrow to tell you. Or Thomas would've gotten to me."

"So you want to tell me something that Thomas doesn't want me to know?"

I nodded and drained my drink and glanced to see if he was ready for another also. Dylan's beer was still mostly full, though. I motioned for the bartender but Dylan pressed down my hand.

"You're already drunk, Lily."

"So?"

He laughed at my brazenness. "Thomas will kill me."

I shrugged. "Seems inevitable that one of you will kill the other one of these days."

Dylan slowly sipped his beer, clearly contemplating something. My eyes were drawn to his mouth as he sipped. I remembered how talented he was with that mouth and suddenly wanted to kiss him. He may not have been the best boyfriend, he was good in bed.

"Okay, seriously, Lily. I think I should just take you home to Thomas now. Or, better yet, ring him to pick you up. We can talk later, when you're sober."

"No. It has to be now. It's really important, Dylan. Hurry up and finish your beer."

He stood reluctantly and offered me a hand. "If it's that important, I don't need to finish. Let's go."

He dropped some cash on the bar and helped me off the bar stool and out of the bar. As soon as the cold night air hit my face, I realized I had miscalculated my drunkenness. We walked silently towards a nearby parking garage and quickly located

Dylan's Porsche. He buckled me in and then angled into the driver's seat.

"We're not moving," I said after a moment.

"I thought you wanted to talk. If I start to drive, we'll be home before long."

"I'd rather talk at home."

"Isn't Thomas there?"

"Your home. I don't think you should be driving when I tell you this." And then I considered it further, remembering his violent history. What if he reacted worse than I expected to the news? What if he really did try to kill Thomas? They'd had some fights before, so it wasn't completely unreasonable to think I was at least setting up my poor spouse for a good ass-kicking by his brother. I didn't really want that, did I?

"This is really serious?"

"Yes. Thomas has done something horrible and you need to know." *Shit*. I hoped I hadn't said too much already.

"But you're okay, you and Lucy?" he asked as he switched the car into reverse.

"Yeah." Although I didn't know if I could say the same about my marriage. Could I ever forgive Thomas for deceiving me? Would he forgive me for telling Dylan?

The world was still spinning as I stepped out of the car and I stumbled, balancing myself on the hood of his car. Dylan wordlessly walked around the car and held on to me as we headed through the lobby to the elevator.

"You're sure?" he asked as the elevator doors opened and I was forced to pick a direction—left or right, Dylan or Thomas.

I shook my head, wishing I ever knew which I wanted. Really it was a matter of which I wanted more, because I couldn't deny that I loved both brothers at once, definitely in the past, and maybe still today. But Thomas had always been the right choice for me in so many ways, and learning Lucy was his biological daughter had simply confirmed that for me, like the universe telling me I had finally made the right choice. Now that I knew the truth, it raised so many questions and threw everything back into limbo.

Dylan escorted me into his apartment and locked the door, switching on the light.

"You might want a drink," I said, stalling.

He tossed his keys on the counter. "I'm fine."

"Well, you should at least sit."

He plopped onto the arm chair. I followed and sat on the couch. "Lily, spill it already."

I took a deep breath and opened my mouth but no words came out. I was still drunk, but apparently even that wasn't enough courage for me. Once I told Dylan, I couldn't go back. I couldn't undo whatever damage would be done. Was I okay pitting Dylan against Thomas, yet again?

"Maybe this was a bad idea," I mumbled.

"Lily, what are you so scared of?"

I laughed sardonically. What *wasn't* I scared of? I decided to pick one thing. "I'm afraid you'll hurt Thomas if I tell you."

Dylan frowned. "Jesus, Lily. What has he done?"

"Dylan, promise me. No fighting, no revenge, nothing. You don't have to forgive him, but you can't hurt him if I tell you."

He appeared to consider this. "Fine."

I hesitated. "I need you to say it."

"I promise I won't hurt Thomas," he said, clearly frustrated.

"I wouldn't even be telling you this, but I think you deserve to know. If it were me, I'd want to know." I laughed. "Well, it was me earlier this week, I guess, and I was happier when I didn't know, honestly, but I should've known. It just isn't right."

"Lily, you're not making any sense."

"It would make things so much easier to just never tell you, but I don't think I can look you in the eye knowing that I know and you don't know and…"

"Lily?"

I held up my hand. "Let me finish, Dylan. I just want you to know that I can tell you've changed lately and you deserve to be happy. I hate seeing how miserable you've been since Patty left."

He nodded, and I realized I hadn't even noticed the sadness in his eyes tonight. I looked now, and instantly saw the endless caverns that were his brown eyes.

"I want you to know you're not all alone," I finally said.

"Lily, really if that's all…"

"I know he told you about the paternity test, but what you don't know is that he changed the document." I blurted out, interrupting him.

"What document?"

"The paternity test results."

His lips parted and he frowned. "But I…"

"You are Lucy's father."

Dylan stood and immediately turned so his back was to me, running his fingers through his hair. I went to comfort him, but he instinctively swatted my outstretched hand away.

"Just give me a minute, okay?" His voice was gruff.

"Do you want me to go?" I asked as he started off towards the bedroom.

He shook his head, then closed the door behind him.

I paced around the living room, poured myself a glass of water, then resumed pacing. After maybe ten minutes, I heard a click and saw Dylan reemerge.

"How can you be sure?" he asked.

I swallowed hard then told him the whole story.

Dylan sighed. "He seemed so relieved."

I nodded.

"So you've known for days?"

I nodded again. "I'm sorry I didn't tell you sooner, Dylan. I figured it would be better if Thomas told you. But then he caught me off guard by changing those papers. It seemed completely out of character for him."

Dylan smirked.

"Dylan, he didn't just lie to you. He was perfectly content to lie to me the rest of our lives." I sniffled, feeling stupid that it was me crying when he was the one to receive the big news. "We're married, and he lied to me about my daughter." I collapsed into the couch, sobbing fully.

Dylan crouched next to me and rubbed my back soothingly. The warm touch was almost enough to distract me from my miserable situation.

"He loves you, Lily."

"He lied to me."

Dylan was silent, so I finally glanced up. He was watching me, his dark eyes misting. He ruffled his perfect brown hair again and I noticed his perpetual stubble, one of the many other differences between him and Thomas.

"I'm sorry, Lily. I hate seeing you so sad. Please stop crying."

"I can't. Why aren't you angrier?"

"Are you serious? How can I be? I did the same thing, Lily, remember? For years I was sure you had a baby with my brother and I never told him. But I did it to punish him, to punish both of you, for the affair. Thomas only lied because he's scared to lose you and Lucy. Yes, it was a terrible thing to do, but between the two of us, he's still the better man."

I realized Dylan spoke the truth, but it didn't help. And the calmness with which he was reacting was just upsetting me more.

"I shouldn't have married him," I whispered. "I always rush into things and I always fuck it up."

Dylan grabbed my hand and squeezed it. "Lily, you still love Thomas. You're just angry now and eventually you'll forgive him and you'll go on to lead the mundane, happy life you want."

I nearly giggled at the thought of my life ever being mundane. "He forbade me to tell you, Dylan. So even if I forgive him, that doesn't mean he'll forgive me."

"Yes, he will, Lily. And if not, well, you can always return to your fallback brother. Choice B."

I gazed up at him, unable to gauge the level of sarcasm in his voice. "Oh, Dylan, it's not like that. It never was. I loved you. I loved you so much I couldn't breathe sometimes. And then…"

"I remember," he interrupted. "We don't have to go back over it all. I know I hurt you."

"Thomas was just more reliable. He was always the one I could count on, and as soon as I had Lucy, dependability mattered more than anything."

Dylan cupped my chin to hold my head steady. "We should finish this discussion when you're sober. Can I get you some water?"

"No, Dylan, you don't get it. I picked Thomas because I could count on him, and now I can't." I paused and sniffled. "What if I picked the wrong brother?"

I stared into his eyes, the melted pools of chocolate, while I waited for him to answer. I could feel his warm breath. He parted his lips and slowly ran his tongue along the crease between his lips and I could practically feel the softness of his mouth. I remembered the taste of his tongue against mine, the pull of his fingers as they grasped at my hair, the full expression of devotion on his face whenever we made love.

And before I could stop myself, I leaned forward, pressing my lips against his, harder than I'd intended to. Any uncertainty I'd had disappeared as his mouth slid open, drawing me in closer. His tongue rolled against mine and I instantly felt the familiar aching in my core, the overwhelming need for him to possess me fully. Dylan's hand grasped the back of my head then slid down my body, sending delicious shivers throughout.

He turned, shifting onto his knees, and slowly laid me back against the couch. I pulled him to me and slid my hands under the thin material of his shirt, relishing the smoothness of his skin.

His kiss became hungrier, deeper, and more urgent and I arched my back toward him, desperate to feel him pressed against me.

"Oh fuck, Lily," Dylan moaned and abruptly sat up. I thought briefly he was pausing to remove his shirt, but instead he simply eyed me sorrowfully then collapsed back on top of me, his mouth buried deep into the emptiness between my neck and shoulder, his chest heaving in and out heavily with each breath.

CHAPTER TWENTY-THREE

LILY

J awoke the next morning to a furious headache and a terrible taste in my mouth. Thomas was humming softly beside me, but the bed was empty. As I turned to check the clock, I glimpsed Dylan, not Thomas. My breath caught in my throat.

He cringed when he saw me. "Shit, I'm sorry to wake you, but I just thought it would be better if you weren't here too late."

My mouth was unbearably dry and I couldn't even muster a breath. I glanced down to see that I was in my bra and panties, and my inability to breath morphed into panicked shallow breaths instead. The room was spinning, but I wasn't sure if it was the hangover or anxiety.

What had I done?

As if reading my mind, Dylan offered me a glass of water. "You must feel like rubbish," he said sympathetically.

"Where's my shirt?" I finally asked, my voice a hoarse shadow of its normal self.

"Uh, covered in vomit, I'm afraid. Yours, not mine," he said casually.

This raised more questions than it answered. I decided to skip the middle man. "What happened last night?"

"Well, how much do you remember?"

I rubbed my forehead. "Just tell me all of it and we'll see if it matches my memory."

"Okay." He sat beside me on the bed. "We ran into each other unexpectedly at a bar. You were drunk and begged me for a ride home so you could tell me something. We got here and you told me that Thomas lied to both of us about Lucy," he glanced at me uncertainly."

I nodded, and he continued. "And then you kissed me."

I cringed, but he went on.

"And then I stopped things before it got out of hand, you offered to leave, then you vomited on your shirt and so I let you sleep here, in my bed."

"So we didn't…"

Dylan locked eyes with me. "If we had, you'd remember."

Relief washed over me, followed quickly by embarrassment and the realization that I was still totally screwed. "I can't believe you turned me down," I mumbled, in lieu of focusing on the more serious issues.

He sighed. "It was your fault."

"I was really that offensively drunk?"

He shook his head. "Lily, you made me promise not to hurt Thomas once I heard the news. I certainly couldn't shag you without hurting him. You and I both know if we'd let things go further last night, it would've only been because of what he did."

I shrugged, unsure of how I felt at the moment. It was already eight o'clock. Thomas would be up. He'd know where I stayed, and it probably wouldn't matter at this point whether I'd slept with Dylan or not, especially given my lack of shirt.

"Go home, Lily. Talk to Thomas."

"And tell him what? That I slept at Jill's?"

"He knows where you slept, Lily. He saw me."

"What? Where?"

"I slept on the couch. At his place," Dylan explained. "Your place, I guess."

"You did?"

"You were a mess Lily, so upset over Thomas and losing him and crap. If he thought you spent the night with me, it would only make things worse."

I exhaled fully. "Thank you, Dylan."

He nodded, then slipped out of his shirt and into a fresh one.

I slumped back onto the bed and pressed the pillow over my face, groaning.

"What's wrong now?"

"Everything!" I shouted. "I'm still raising a child with a man who isn't her father. Even if we get past all the lies, what about Lucy? We just told her who her father was. What do we tell her now?"

Dylan tugged the pillow off of my face. "Nothing, Lily. Don't tell her anything. I'm glad you told me, but no one else needs to know."

"You don't mean that."

"Yes, I do. We both know I'd be a shit father and it's better for her to live with her mum and father in one nice, neat family. I'll always be there if she needs me, but for now, it's just a technical-ity, just a name on a paper. It doesn't mean anything."

"It means something, Dylan."

He smiled. "Yeah. You're right. But you've got to stop being so negative. Thomas and I both love Lucy, and we both love you. That's a good thing. Stop trying to turn it into something bad. It'll all work out fine."

He stood and tossed me a shirt. "Now go home to your husband and make him apologize. I told my niece I'd take her out to breakfast."

I pulled the shirt over my head, suddenly aware of the impropriety of my current state in front of my brother-in-law. "She's not your niece."

Dylan crouched down by the bed. "Yes, she is, Lily. I'm glad you told me the truth. I'm honored that you'd trust me with that information, honestly. But for all intents and purposes, Lucy is my niece. We don't need to change that based on some piece of paper. And I definitely don't want you telling her."

I swallowed hard. "Ever?"

He shook his head. "Never, Lily. It's a bloody fucking mess. No good could come from telling her, or anyone else, for that matter. Hold on to the copy of the test results that Thomas doctored. All three of us just need to go about our lives as though those are the real results. No matter what happens, none of us ever tells anyone otherwise."

I climbed out of bed, pulled on my jeans, and followed him out of the apartment and down the hall to my apartment. Thomas, standing in the kitchen with a coffee mug in his hand, glared silently at Dylan and me as we entered.

Lucy was curled up on the couch watching cartoons and barely noticed my entrance. I retrieved her purple princess-style hairbrush from the bathroom and knelt beside her.

"Hey sweetie, let me brush your hair and then you're going out to breakfast with Dylan," I said.

"Yippee!" she squealed, hopping off the couch and evading the hairbrush as she rushed to Dylan.

"Mine's all messy too," Dylan said ruffling his own hair. "Let's have a messy hair breakfast."

"Hold her hand on the sidewalk," Thomas barked at Dylan. "And you can't let her go into the bathroom alone." He paused. "Or with any strange ladies that approach you."

Dylan exhaled loudly. "Wave bye to Mummy and Daddy. We'll be back soon," he cooed to Lucy before shutting the door behind them.

I paused for a beat, then turned to Thomas. He glared at me, placed his coffee mug in the sink, and picked up the paper.

I brushed past him to pour myself a cup of coffee, then headed directly to the shower. I half expected him to join me in the bathroom, or at least to be waiting in the bedroom when I emerged, but he wasn't. I dressed, dried my hair, and downed some ibuprofen for my hangover, and then found Thomas in the exact same position as I'd left him, reading the paper.

I went into the kitchen and made myself some toast and another cup of coffee and ate in silence. Finally, I couldn't take it anymore.

"Are you just not speaking to me now?" I demanded.

Thomas glanced up from the paper. "What would you have me say?"

"You're obviously mad."

"True. Should I yell and scream at you? Maybe knock you across the room? That clearly is what you want in a man."

"I married you, not Dylan. Doesn't that mean anything?"

"I asked you not to tell him, and you did. I asked you not to leave last night, and you did. Not only that, but you went to *him*. You slept at *his* place. You picked my brother over me. Again. How did you think this would resolve itself?" He folded the paper and placed it on the couch.

"I told you. I'm done with all the lies. I deserved to know the truth and so did Dylan. I had to tell him. At least *I* didn't go behind *your* back. I was honest with you."

Thomas thrust his head between his hands. The silence stretched on for an eternity.

Finally, he was the one to speak. "I can't lose her again, Lily. Or you. And especially not to him."

I sat beside him, my anger dissipating. "Thomas, you won't. Did you talk to Dylan after he came over here?"

He shook his head.

"What did he say when he came over last night?"

"I thought he was you when I heard the key in the door. I was all ready to apologize. But instead it was my brother, informing me that my wife was passed out in his bed and that I was an arse."

"I didn't sleep with Dylan."

He rolled his eyes. "I know. But you can't run to him when you're mad at me."

"I didn't run to him because I was mad at you. I just happened to bump into him, and the only reason I even spoke with him was because I needed to tell him critical information that he had a right to know."

"But he didn't!" Thomas shouted. "He treated you like shit and he caused you to leave town for three years. He lost any rights he had." He shook his head with disgust. "He doesn't deserve you or Lucy."

"He doesn't want us," I said.

"What?"

"When I told him about Lucy, he thought about it for a while and said he didn't want her to know. He doesn't want anyone to know. He wants you to still be her father, on her birth certificate and in real life." I paused. "And he doesn't want me either."

"Bullshit. He's just biding his time."

I shook my head, hesitant to tell him the rest, but knowing I couldn't keep it from him while emphasizing the importance of full disclosure in our relationship. "I was drunk last night, Thomas."

"Yes, Dylan told me."

"Did he tell you that I kissed him?"

His eyes widened instantly.

"He told me no and left the apartment. So, I know for a fact he doesn't want me anymore."

Thomas stood and began pacing. "You're telling me you kissed my brother. Last night."

"Yes," I mumbled. "But only because I was really drunk and

mad at you and obviously it was a huge mistake. I'm so sorry Thomas."

"Fuck. I need to get out of here." He started for the door.

I leapt up and reached for his arm. "No, Thomas, don't. Please."

He turned to face me but said nothing.

"I don't want Dylan. I wish I hadn't kissed him last night. Hell, I'd wish I'd never dated him, except..." my voice trailed off.

"Except then you wouldn't have Lucy."

I squeezed his arm. "Lucy is your daughter. You are the one that is going to raise her with me. You will be at all the piano recitals, you'll be the one taking pictures before prom, and you'll be the one walking her down the aisle someday. Not Dylan. He's basically a sperm donor. And now that we all know, we can move on."

Thomas seemed calmer now, but there was still a distinct sadness in his eyes. "We can't move on when you still have feelings for my brother."

"But I don't."

"You wouldn't run to him every time there's a problem if you didn't. You certainly wouldn't kiss him."

"I was drunk and angry with you. I wanted to get back at you for betraying me and it seemed like a good way to do it at the time." I sighed. "One of the things I love about you is that you're so level-headed and honest and I don't have to worry about you lying to me about major things like our daughter's paternity. So when I found out that you had, it made me wonder if you're really the man I thought you were."

He sighed and started to the bedroom. "Sorry to be such a disappointment."

I followed, wincing when I saw he was already starting to pack for the South American tour even though they weren't leaving for four more days. "Thomas, come on. Can we just sit down and talk?"

He stepped into the closet and began gathering clothes.

"You can't leave town until you've forgiven me," I said.

"I have," he replied, without looking up from his multitude of shirts.

"Clearly," I mumbled sarcastically. "And Dylan?"

Thomas shrugged. "I was never mad at him. You were the one who told him about Lucy after I asked you not to. You were the one who kissed him. All he did was take you home and put you to bed when you drank too much."

I yanked a hanger out of his hands. "I'm so sorry, Thomas. I should've waited to tell Dylan until you were with me. And obviously I shouldn't have kissed him, but…"

Thomas pressed his finger over my lips, shushing me. "Please don't say that again. Every time those words come out of your mouth, I start picturing it and then I feel sick. Besides, this is unnecessary. I understand why you did everything you did and I'm not mad."

I sighed as he bent to retrieve the hanger.

"Then what are you? Something clearly is wrong."

Thomas shrugged. "I guess I'm not in a chatty mood."

"Then postpone your trip a few days. I can't stand the thought of us being apart when you're feeling this way."

He shook his head. "I can't postpone it. We have a schedule. And I'll feel fine when I'm gone. You know why? Because Dylan is traveling with me."

"What's that supposed to mean?

Thomas walked out of the closet. "Nothing." He glanced around the room before moving towards the door. "I need some air."

I felt the tears brimming in my eyes. "Thomas, don't!"

He grabbed his keys and reached for the doorknob. "I won't be long."

"Running out instead of talking to me is the exact thing I

would expect from Dylan," I muttered, hoping he didn't remember it was precisely what I'd done the previous night.

Thomas froze but didn't speak immediately. When he did, his voice was quiet and dry. "Is that a good thing or bad?"

I didn't know what to say.

"Nevermind," he said, and he left.

* * *

THOMAS

The entire week was absolute shit. I was about to leave on tour, and I had no clue where things stood with Lily. Sure I'd fucked up, but I'd apologized and meant it. I couldn't undo the past, and she didn't seem ready to move on. She kept accusing me of being mad at her, which I wasn't. If anything, I was mad at myself. I'd rushed her into marriage, and I'd done it intentionally. I'd known she wasn't ready, but I hadn't wanted to risk her changing her mind about me.

Maybe the time apart would be good for us. Maybe she needed the space to help remind her that we were good together, that we belonged together.

I didn't need distance to know what Lily meant to me. Every time I looked at her, I was painfully aware of what I'd lose if we couldn't fix things between us. If I had to live without her again, I wasn't sure I could survive.

The day before I left for tour, Lucy had her first day of school. Lily and I had dropped her off together, then I'd driven Lily to her school. Everything about that first—dropping my child off for her first day of pre-kindergarten—felt monumental. Somehow, it encouraged me that maybe everything would be okay with Lily, too.

That night, after I finished packing, Lily and I made love, but it wasn't the same. Usually we were in sync and it felt like the act itself was bringing us even closer together. But that night, I could still sense the distance between us even when we were as physically close as two people could be.

I held her close to me after, biding my time until the perfect words came to me.

"I'm sorry about everything," I finally said. "The truth is I'm scared. I'm terrified of losing you, of losing Lucy. And I'm jealous." My laugh sounded sardonic. "I was jealous of what Dylan had with you when he was with you, and I'm still jealous of that now."

"You're not going to lose me or Lucy," she said.

"You don't know that."

She pulled away, turning to face me. "I do know that." She reached for my wedding ring. "See that? We're married. You're stuck with me no matter what."

I shook my head. "You can't control your feelings, Lily. When you met Dylan, you loved him. You can't tell me that wasn't real." I paused, but there was nothing for her to say. "And then at some point down the road, you didn't anymore."

"It wasn't that simple," she said.

"It doesn't matter. Do you love him now?"

"No!"

"Do you love me?"

"Yes!"

"If someone had asked you four years ago, would you have acknowledged even the possibility that today, you'd be in love with me and not Dylan?"

She shrugged.

"Of course not. Because you didn't know you'd feel this way now," I continued. "Just like you don't know how you will feel in another five years. I want you to be with me because you love me, not because you feel obligated to stay. You stayed with Dylan after you started falling for me because you didn't want to hurt him. I don't want to be in that position."

I stroked her hand, intentionally avoiding contact with her ring.

"Lily, I saw firsthand how you felt about Dylan years ago. You guys still share that bond, you still have all that shared history, and now no matter what we tell people, you also share Lucy. That scares me."

She let me continue uninterrupted.

"Before we got the paternity results, I felt like the fact that we shared a daughter trumped any bond you had with Dylan. And then after, well I still felt like that could be true as long as neither you or he knew any better. But now," I shrugged. "I don't have that security."

She gazed at me for a moment before speaking. "I really love that you told me all of that. And no matter what happens with you and me or no matter how I feel in five, ten, or twenty years, you will never lose Lucy. That's just not even part of the equation. I could never do that to her, and you have to believe that."

I nodded slowly.

"And I understand why, given the circumstances and our history, you have some concerns about my loyalty, but I do love you. I want to be with you and I want you to be Lucy's father. You love me and Lucy and want us to be a family too. Dylan doesn't want to be with me and he doesn't want to be Lucy's father." She paused to catch her breath. "This conflict is all in your head. We all want the same thing here. You're not competing against anyone for me and Lucy."

I was still skeptical.

"What can I do to make you feel better? How can I assure you I'm not going anywhere?"

"Full body tattoos of my name?"

"Consider it done."

I laughed and kissed the back of her hand. "I couldn't tarnish your perfect skin." I pulled her onto my lap. "I think it's just going to take me some time. Although, I wish you were coming to meet me on tour sometime. Even if only for a weekend. You and Lucy both could…"

"I can't miss work. She can't miss school. You know that."

I nodded and said I understood, but it wasn't the truth. I would've felt a whole lot better about everything between us if we weren't about to be apart for a full month.

* * *

LILY

Thomas called every day when Lucy and I got home from school. She'd finally gotten the hang of video calls and looked forward to seeing him every afternoon. Sometimes, he'd call back at her bedtime too, but if he was traveling or getting ready to go on stage then, we only heard from him the one time. His concerts generally ran past my bedtime, though, and since he was sleeping when I woke up for work, we never chatted without Lucy in the room.

Still, it helped to see him when we talked, however G-rated our calls were. We swapped stories of the funny things that had happened to us the previous days and he'd amaze Lucy by telling her how many people attended each concert. He texted some pictures of the gorgeous scenery in South America and included sweet little comments, like 'wish you were here.'

It was meant to be flattering, but it filled me with guilt. Why wasn't I there? Sure, I had work, but so what? I was allowed to take a personal day every once in a while. It didn't help that I sensed Thomas was still holding back. He swore he wasn't mad at me and I believed him, but he certainly wasn't secure about our relationship either.

I texted him some ideas for the wedding, but his responses made me think he wasn't too confident we'd even go through with it all.

I was lonely without him in town, and I couldn't exactly open up to Jill. If she knew we'd eloped, she'd just tell me I was too impulsive. Out of habit, I told myself she was right. I was still too impulsive.

But the more I thought about it, the more I realized how being impulsive had led me to the husband of my dreams. I didn't regret marrying Thomas. Especially now. If we'd just been engaged, maybe one of us would've thrown in the towel when we'd fought over the test results. Maybe it was our impulsive wedding that had saved us both. Maybe what I needed wasn't to be less impulsive, but more.

* * *

THOMAS

I tried Lily's phone for a fourth time, and it went immediately to voice mail. Again. I hadn't spoken to her or my daughter yet today but our opening act was already on stage, so it clearly wasn't going to happen. I sighed, determined not to leave another pathetic voice mail. In my first one, I'd said how much I missed them both and wanted to talk with them. The typical cheesy stuff. In the second voice mail, I'd actually sung a goodnight song for Lucy.

Dylan offered a Mexican beer to me. I shook my head. I didn't know how he drank before concerts. I needed to be alert to perform. Now that I was getting older, singing at ten p.m. felt infinitely more taxing than it had in my twenties. Dylan started to say something, and I raised my hand, shushing him.

"You don't even have to say it," I said. "I'm grumpy. I know."

He chuckled at his own predictability.

"Not all of us have a different girl in our bed each night on this tour," I added, just in case he thought he'd been even remotely subtle with his escapades.

Now he grinned proudly. "You could, but you chose one girl, and you aren't fooling anyone if you pretend you aren't happy with your decision." He slapped his palm on the table and stood. "I wonder if I have time for another one before we take the stage," he mused, walking out of the main dressing room.

I rubbed my brow, unsure whether he meant another beer or another woman. Either way, it didn't bode well for our performance. I finished the rest of my water, then went to go warm up on my guitar.

* * *

LILY

I had forgotten how stressful it was to be impulsive. I'd thrown everything together so last minute that I hadn't thought through any of it. I didn't know what I'd do if Ari didn't answer.

"Hello?" he answered.

"Oh, thank God. Ari? It's Lily. Um, Thomas'..."

"I know who you are," he said with a laugh. "Thomas is in the dressing room now. The opening act is already starting, so he might not have time to chat before they take the stage."

I cringed. I hadn't realized I was that far behind. This had to be the worst plan ever. "No, um, I didn't even try to reach him. I wanted to surprise Thomas, actually. I, um, well, I'm in Lima. I planned to get in earlier so I could talk to him at the concert, but..."

"You're in Lima?" he repeated, his voice practically a shout. "Lima, Peru?"

"Yes. At the airport."

He was silent.

"I know it's a lot to ask, but if there's any way you could get me into the concert, I'd really like to see them tonight," I began.

Now he breathed a laugh. "You're asking me for tickets to the concert?"

"Yes. Well, just the one ticket, I guess," I clarified, adding, "If you could get me backstage access too, that would help."

"How do you plan to get here from the airport?"

I cringed again. "Cab?" I mean, that had been my plan. But seeing as how I was struggling to translate enough of the signs to even get myself to the baggage claim, I doubted my ability to find a cab or tell the driver where I needed to go. And where would I put all my stuff during the concert?

Ari sighed loudly. "Lily, Lily, Lily. What we are going to do with you?"

I waited a moment to see if he planned to say more, but when he didn't, I apologized. "It was a dumb idea. I will just head back to the hotel and wait to talk to him after the concert." Although, I actually didn't know the name or address of the hotel, either.

"Hang tight, Lily. I will send my assistant Vanessa with a car to come pick you up at the airport. Stay inside and I'll have her call when they arrive. They can take you by the hotel if you need to change or you can just keep your stuff in the car until after the concert."

I squeezed my eyes shut as relief flooded my system. "Thank you, Ari. I owe you."

He hung up right as an announcement came over the loud-speaker. A moment later, the announcement was repeated in English.

"Thank God," I mumbled aloud, turning towards the hallway the announcement indicated.

Once I located my suitcase, I lugged everything into the bathroom. I spent several minutes redoing the day's makeup from scratch. By the time I was done, I had to admit I didn't even look like I'd spent the last several hours on a plane.

Without more time, I was pretty limited on what I could do with my hair, but since I'd worn it in a loose braid on the flight, the situation wasn't totally hopeless. I tugged out the elastic, finger-combed the wavy tresses, then worked some Moroccan oil through the strands until some of the normal shine returned. I rinsed my fingers then spritzed hairspray over my head, eliciting a grimace from the woman at the sink next to me.

"Sorry," I said, wincing when I remembered that wasn't even the spoken language in Lima. She walked off before I could translate my apology though, so I resumed rummaging through my bag. This time I found deodorant and perfume. Finally, I pulled the outfit I'd planned to wear to the concert out of my carry on. It was a short, sleeveless, black dress. It was fitted, but not clingy, and while the v-neck did dip down fairly low, my booty was fully contained and my breasts weren't totally out.

My phone buzzed before I could change. I didn't recognize the number, but answered anyway.

"Is this Lily?" a woman's voice asked.

"Yes."

"Great. This is Vanessa. I'm standing in the baggage claim. Ari sent me to pick you up."

I draped the dress over my purse, then maneuvered past the other ladies in the bathroom to the exit. As soon as I'd walked a few yards, a woman waved.

She had a dark complexion, beautiful curly hair, and wore a black pants suit with a magenta blouse. I smiled politely.

"Vanessa?" I asked as I was close.

"Yes. How are you?"

"I'm…okay. Frazzled," I admitted.

She motioned for me to follow her, so I did.

"I'm sorry, have we met before?" I asked.

"I don't think so," she replied. "I recognized you from your picture. Thomas keeps it in his guitar case."

"Oh."

"And you're his screen saver."

I frowned, having thought Lucy was his latest screensaver.

Why on earth would he have replaced her picture? "On his phone?"

"Oh, no. On his computer. That giant one he uses for work stuff."

I didn't have the slightest idea what she was talking about, but we'd reached a black town car, so I let it drop. A driver got out and popped the trunk. I gripped my purse but let him pile everything else into the trunk and then followed Vanessa into the car.

"Do you want to stop off at the hotel first?" she asked, offering me a bottled water.

I accepted the beverage and drank greedily, chugging more than half of its contents before answering. "I did my makeup and hair at the airport, but I had planned to change," I said, gesturing to the dress. I checked my watch. "They're already on stage, aren't they?"

She shrugged. "Probably another five or ten minutes then they will be. They never start right on time."

I debated my options, then glanced down at my outfit. I'd worn leggings, a camisole, and a thin zip up shirt for the flight. With a little finagling, I could probably manage to change in the car.

"Actually, do you mind if I just…" I began.

Vanessa laughed. "Go for it," she said, turning towards the window.

I slipped off my top shirt and pulled the straps off the camisole, leaving it up over my breasts so nothing was uncovered. I then slipped the black dress over my head, hoping I didn't leave white streaks of deodorant all down the sides. Once I had it partway on, I tugged the camisole down the rest of the way. Adjusting my seat belt, I lifted my hips and pulled the dress the rest of the way on, then yanked my leggings and camisole down my thighs. Once they reached my knees, I used my foot to nudge it the rest of the way.

I wadded up my old outfit on the edge of the seat and reached into my purse for my concert jewelry.

Vanessa turned back to me slowly, giving me a surprised once over.

"Well that was impressive," she said, her voice genuine.

I supposed years of changing from my waitressing attire to true clubbing attire in the manager's office at the end of a long shift at Echo had taught me the important skill of discrete and speedy wardrobe changes.

"Do I look okay?" I asked.

She nodded. "You look amazing."

I blew out a nervous breath. "Thank you. Can I just leave all this in here until after the concert?"

"Yep." She handed me a plasticky wristband. "I'll walk you in through backstage so you won't need a ticket. You can hang out backstage the whole time if you want, or you can go out and watch the show in the front area where it's standing room only. The bracelet will get you back to the VIP section when you're ready."

I nodded and snapped the bracelet in place.

"Ari did ask that I, um, let you know that he'd rather Thomas not be distracted," Vanessa said, clearly uncomfortable now. "I mean, I'm sure Ari doesn't mind if Thomas sees you or whatever, he just wanted to be sure you realized that once the concert starts, they can't really take breaks or anything."

I rolled my eyes but nodded. "Yeah, I know." *Not my first rodeo,* I wanted to add.

The car slid to a stop and the driver swung open the back door. I followed Vanessa to a side entrance of the building, where she flashed a card at a security guard to gain entry.

I found myself in a cramped hallway, but I could already hear the opening notes to what I recognized as the second song on Sierra's playlist flooding the building.

"This way will lead you to the backstage area where I'll be, and if you want to go into Thomas' dressing room, that's fine. Make yourself at home."

"I want to go watch them," I said.

She pointed in the other direction. "End of the hall, then take a right."

"Okay, thanks."

She nodded and I started off down the hall. It opened up into a large atrium, where two security guards were posted. I smiled politely and they nodded, clearly bored. I assumed they were concerned with people heading into the backstage area, not out. I noticed the concessions and the restrooms lining the atrium, but made my way towards the music. As I started into the darkened stadium, I was impressed at how large the facility was.

I'd been to Sierra's arena shows before, but I hadn't realized they had this many fans in Peru. I smiled proudly. As I paused just inside the main concert area, letting my eyes adjust to the darkness for a moment, I reminded myself of why I was here. I needed to convince Thomas I was serious, that he alone was my future. I was not here to lose myself in the familiar melodies.

I lingered along the edge of the crowd at the front, waiting until the song ended to maneuver my way closer. At the moment, Dylan was singing, but he and Thomas were both off to the left side of the stage, so it was easier for me to inch forward on the opposite side.

I saw Owen and Gavin and was tempted to wave, but remembered that they couldn't see me, what with all the bright lights shining on the stage. Besides, what good would that do, disrupting the drummer and the bass guitarist in the middle of a song?

I relaxed and focused on the music. I'd honestly forgotten how good they were live, in their element. No matter how many times I was able to see Sierra perform, I would probably never cease to be amazed. The band—but especially Thomas—had an uncanny ability to read the audience, to sense precisely what to say to the crowd at precisely what time. While they began each tour with a basic set list, they adjusted it depending on the mood of the crowd. Occasionally, they'd simply swap the order of two or three songs, but other times they'd add a different song or two. A gal really could attend dozens of Sierra concerts and never experience the exact same show.

The lights flashed on the stage, then went dark as the audience roared with applause. When the stage brightened again, the brothers had returned to their spot in the middle of the stage, but I could've sworn Thomas glanced my way. I rose to my tiptoes and waved, feeling silly even as I continued the motion with my arm, painfully aware he was unlikely to see me.

This song had a quicker beat, and the crowd was growing rowdier, surging against me and nudging me closer to the front. As my purse nearly slipped off my shoulder, I remembered my other idea. I reached into my purse, first locating the wide black sharpie I'd packed. I pinched the marker between my lips, having no other place to stick it, then unfolded the oversized piece of card stock I'd folded into my purse. I uncapped the marker, pressed the paper against my thighs, and wrote my message as legibly as I could.

* * *

THOMAS

I peered into the crowd as we sang, but with the strobe lighting on this song, I couldn't see a damn thing past the security guard on the ground just off the stairs. Dylan was singing an acoustic track next, so if I had to, I could climb down the stairs and look for her then.

I told myself that Gavin was probably wrong, that it hadn't been Lily he'd seen. She was still in New York, not South America. And if she had changed her mind about coming, she certainly couldn't have come all the way—and gotten into the concert—without telling me.

Still, I wanted to believe it was true, that she was there. After my last guitar rift for the song, I pried my mic off the stand and started towards the edge of the stage. Dylan hit the last notes, and we both had a decent half-minute break as Owen finished off the song. Dylan dragged a chair towards the front of the stage while talking to the crowd, so I disappeared to the front of the stage right as the lights changed. The majority of the stage darkened, a spotlight honing in on my brother.

As the lights filtered, I scanned the crowd again, pleased that now I could see at least the first several rows of people. I didn't spot Lily on first glance, but as my eyes roamed back over the crowd again, I saw a familiar figure. A flimsy poster was covering the woman's face, and she seemed to be struggling to hold it up. I squinted to read the words, but her arms shifted again.

"Lily," I whispered, almost certain now that it was her, or if not, that this was the woman Gavin had mistaken for her. There was no child beside her, but then again, I couldn't imagine Lily would dream of bringing Lucy here, especially after her hesitation at letting our daughter even watch some of our smaller shows.

She shifted the poster directly in front of her face again, and this time, I could decipher the words.

It read: "I WILL FOLLOW U ANYWHERE. I LOVE U THOMAS."

I sucked in a deep breath, then crouched down, tapping the security guard closest to the stage. I pointed to Lily, then gestured for him to bring her closer. He looked confused, but then he pointed at her and I nodded.

Right then, she dropped the poster. She glanced to the ground, flustered, and I prayed she wouldn't bend and attempt to reach it, since she'd risk falling or being trampled for sure. As she gazed back up, our eyes locked. She froze, then waved like a giddy school girl. I shook my head, laughing, then crooked my finger at her, motioning for her to come closer.

She hesitated, then noticed the security guard had cleared a path for her. As soon as she was within a couple yards of the stage, she started speaking.

I pointed to my ear piece, shaking my head and mouthing the words "can't hear you." It was almost comical. You'd have thought with the number of concerts she'd attended she would know that my earbuds blocked out virtually everything aside from myself and my bandmates.

Lily bit her lip and nodded, now clearly saying "I'm sorry."

I wasn't sure why she was apologizing. I was the one who had been an ass. And looking at her now, I felt like one too. She was glowing, looking even more gorgeous than the day I first met her. Her hair cascaded over her shoulders, and she wore a tiny black dress that hugged her delicate curves perfectly. I could've stared at her all evening.

Except I was in the middle of a concert and Dylan's solo was quickly coming to an end.

Snapping out of my daze, I blew a kiss to Lily, mouthed "I love you," and motioned for her to stay put beside the guard. Then I stepped backwards on the stage, just as the lights changed in preparation for the next song.

My brother cast a knowing gaze in my direction, then grinned.

We segued into our next song, and I locked my eyes on Lily as I sang. She swayed gently to the music, her lips moving along to the lyrics she knew by heart. Watching my beautiful wife felt eerily poignant then, almost to the point where it was painful. I squeezed my eyes shut during the next line, then winked at Lily when I reopened them. I walked over towards Dylan so we could harmonize on the final notes.

As the stage darkened again, this time allowing crew members to slip onto stage and rearrange a few aspects of the set, Dylan turned to me. He nodded his head to the stairs.

"Go get her," he said.

I didn't have enough time to question his words before we launched into the next song, but it was one where I walked around and sang, leaving the instrumentals to the rest of the band. And sure, historically there had been times where I'd left the stage during such a song, although not as often as Dylan, the true attention whore of the band. The crowd always loved it.

I glanced back over at Lily and decided I couldn't wait until after the show to be closer to her. I made my way slowly down the stairs, then walked along the side of the stage just behind the security guards. The fans in the front surged forward, a slew of hands and posters and even some flowers flying in my direction. I waved and smiled despite my inability to actually make eye contact with anyone now that a spotlight had shifted to track my movements.

I eyed the security guard as I neared Lily, then stretched my hand out towards her. She hesitated, then reached back, her fingers lightly grasping my own. The crowd went wild as I tugged her closer, past the security guards. Thanks to the damn lights, I could now see Lily and nothing else. Her eyes locked on mine, and she smiled happily. She looked comfortable, so I suspected she had no clue that the cameras were likely projecting a massive image of our every move onto the large screen across the back of the stage and in the center of the arena.

The crowd continued to go wild as I sang, and I wondered if they assumed I'd chosen some random fan to serenade, not realizing that the words leaving my lips were not just being sung to her but had actually been written for her.

We were locked in our own little world together, the rest of the crowd simply disappearing into the background, almost like we were figures trapped inside a snow globe, perpetually oblivious to our audience.

As the song neared the end, I felt a pang in my chest, knowing I needed to return to the stage. At a break for a drum solo, I blew Lily another kiss, then squeezed her hand, slowly lifting it to my lips. My mouth lingered against her warm hand, and it took all of my self-control to pull away in time for my final line. Typically, Dylan would talk to the audience for a minute or two after this song anyway, to give me time to grab a drink before the next song.

Knowing that, I remained close to Lily for another minute. When Dylan began to speak, the crowd roared even louder. I tugged off my headset and leaned in to Lily.

"Come backstage," I whispered directly into her ear. "You can watch from the wings."

She smiled but shook her head as I repositioned my headset. Then she blushed, and I realized my brother was quickly approaching my side of the stage. I'd missed the first thing he'd said, but it was obvious he'd been talking about me.

"We'd start the next song, 'cept Thomas can't keep his hands off the fans here," he jeered. The audience shrieked louder.

I winked at my wife as I started back up to the stage.

"Oh come on now, bring her on stage," Dylan encouraged.

Certain Lily wouldn't be up for that, I made my way up the stairs more quickly.

Dylan shook his head at me before turning back to the crowd. "These two haven't had a proper reunion yet." He patted me on the back, harder than necessary. "I think tonight would be a good night to debut that new song we've been working on, don't you agree, Tom?"

My abdomen clenched. I'd written another song for Lily months ago. Well, maybe it was for Lucy. It was about both of them, about how their presence in my life changed everything. We hadn't even recorded the track yet, though we'd been practicing it for weeks before the tour. We'd planned to perform it at our final concert of this tour.

Initially, I resisted Dylan's idea, but the more I thought about it, the more it seemed like the perfect night for it. I certainly was feeling a lot for Lily now.

Dylan gazed at me expectantly, and after a moment, I nodded. He turned back to the band, and we received an enthusiastic thumbs up from both Gavin and Owen. As if they had a choice to resist at this point, now that Dylan had worked up the crowd.

Dylan paced around the stage longer, further working up the crowd. Finally, he spoke again.

"You can't really perform a love ballad without the object of your affection, though, can you?" he asked. He cocked his head towards me, but without waiting for a response, he hopped off the side of the stage—clearly too cool for the stairs—and made a beeline for Lily.

She shook her head vigorously, but he persisted, firmly gripping her hand and tugging her to the stairs. Panicked, I rushed forwards, meeting them at the stairs.

Lily's head drooped now that she realized everyone's eyes were on her, but she glanced up as she reached the stage.

"I'm so sorry," I mouthed.

Her eyes widened and she looked truly petrified.

A stagehand scooted a chair forward, angling it to face my mic from the side. Dylan released Lily's hand right as I reached for it. I escorted Lily to the chair, then repositioned my guitar right as the lights shifted.

The song started quietly, and my voice quivered in the second line. But as the song built, so did my confidence. I faced the audience, needing to sing into the mic on its stand, but gazed at Lily as often as I could. By the time we reached the chorus and the rest of the band joined in, the terror had left Lily's eyes.

As she relaxed, I could tell she was actually listening to the lyrics. Her eyes shimmered with the hint of tears, and she looked so gorgeous that I couldn't resist touching her. I finished my next guitar part, then shifted my instrument towards my back. I reached for Lily, lifting her out of her chair, and pulled her towards me. Her eyes briefly flared in panic, but I tugged her close, only wanting to dance.

I gripped her tightly, not willing to risk her falling—or running away. Together, we swayed while my brother strummed his guitar and sang the next line. As it neared the time for me to sing again, I tilted her chin upwards with my finger. Our eyes locked, and I briefly considered kissing her. But then the moment passed and I needed to sing again.

I managed my next line, then squeezed her hand and let her drop back into her chair. As the song ended, the lights dimmed, and I helped her to her feet again.

"Ladies and gentleman, I present to you the famous Lily," Dylan said, clapping dramatically in Lily's direction. Then, he turned to me. "If there's ever been a better example of the perfect soulmates, I sure haven't seen it. I love you both, and it's a bloody miracle you both finally came to your senses about each other. Now stop distracting my brother so he can sing a proper song," he finished.

I patted him on the back, appreciative of his words, then turned to Lily. She bit her lip and I nodded towards the side of the stage, where an assistant was waiting to help her.

I watched her exit behind the curtain, but I couldn't stop smiling.

"Sorry," I said to the crowd, despite my certainty that no one was protesting the surprise bonus song or performance. "I hadn't expected to see my wife in the audience," I said.

Dylan turned abruptly, eyes wide, and I realized what I'd done.

Now the whole world knew we were married. *Whoops*.

The audience took its time calming down after that revelation. Nervously, I turned to the side, where I could clearly see Lily watching from between two crew members. She shook her head and laughed, so I raised my hands and shrugged my shoulders.

Dylan chuckled into his mic. "Now he's gone and gotten himself in trouble with the Mrs. Not sure they were planning to share that happy news quite yet. Well, cat's out of the bag now, so who's ready for some more music?"

The crowd cheered, so we launched into our final two songs before the encore. As the lights dropped over the stage, I dashed toward Lily, nearly faceplanting over the cords and wires draping the side of the stage.

I kissed her without hesitation. We didn't have long before I had to return to stage.

"You came," I whispered as I pulled away. "You're actually in Peru."

She nodded and smiled.

"I'm sorry about…" I began, not certain how one even apologizes for prematurely telling the world about an elopement.

She waved her hand as if it was no big deal.

Someone thrust a bottle of water to me, so I accepted, drinking thirstily and nearly choking as a hand clapped onto my back.

"Glad you made it, Lily," Dylan said before turning to me. "Two more songs, brother, then she's all yours."

I nodded, then turned back to Lily. "You looked beautiful on stage," I told her.

Her cheeks flushed. I couldn't help but to kiss her again, this time, lingering longer.

It wasn't until I heard the deafening roar of the audience that I realized the rest of the band had already started back on stage. I pried myself away from her and jogged after them, grinning.

I tugged my guitar strap back over my head right as Owen began the opening lines of "Finders Keepers," our go-to encore. After that, we'd play another hit from our last album, and then we'd be done. Finally.

Usually, as we finished a concert, I'd take time to reflect. I'd really listen to the applause, soak in the appreciation from the audience and let it truly wash over me how blessed we were. It was easy to get caught up in the excitement of the concerts or the exhaustion of the unforgiving schedule—traveling and touring nonstop, so I tried to focus on the moment as the concert ended. We had enthusiastic, dedicated, and supportive fans, and for that, I would always be grateful. Without those fans, my dream never would've become reality.

But tonight, I was focused on a different dream. And I was starting to think I really could have it all.

Offstage, I grabbed Lily's hand and tugged her back to the dressing room. As much as I wanted to kiss her again, we'd be interrupted within minutes by the rest of the band. She gazed at me. Her expression was filled with such innocent adoration that I actually wondered if she was a little drunk.

"Have you been drinking?" I asked.

Lily rolled her eyes. "No, but I have been up for…twenty-two hours now."

"Shit, right. We should get you to bed." I glanced around, trying to figure out who could escort Lily back to the hotel. I had so many questions—like when she flew in and how she got to the concert venue.

"You need to at least make an appearance backstage, though, right?" she asked.

I cringed. I hadn't forgotten, but I still wasn't eager to be surrounded by more people.

"Yes. I'll find someone to drive you back to the hotel and you can sleep. I'll get back as soon as I can and we can talk in the morning." I paused. "How long are you staying?"

She shrugged. "I didn't book a return flight. But I don't want to leave Lucy for long."

"Of course," I agreed. That was sensible.

"I would've brought her, but…"

A knock on the door interrupted us.

"I've seen it all before, so I'm coming in," Dylan called out.

I rolled my eyes and opened the door for him.

A bemused grin passed his face, and then he leaned in to hug Lily. "Good to see you, as always. Where's my darling niece?"

"With my mom," Lily explained, turning and greeting the rest of the band politely.

I dragged my fingers through my hair, exasperated with the interruption and trying to figure out a plan.

Lily reached for my hand. "It's only an hour, right? I'll stay with you."

It was ninety minutes, but close enough. "You sure?"

She nodded.

We did this after almost every show. Selling backstage passes with access to a VIP after party with the band was lucrative these days, and generally, it wasn't a chore. The events offered us an opportunity to engage with fans, and since food and drink was provided, it wasn't much different than how we'd unwind after a concert anyway. I'd prefer to tackle some of those before concerts, but Dylan was pricklier.

"I'm sure the fans will be delighted to meet your wife," Dylan added, emphasizing the final word to remind me of my gaff.

CHAPTER TWENTY-FOUR

"You are my heart, my life, my one and only thought."
Arthur Conan Doyle, *The White Company*

LILY

The after party was a blur. I enjoyed watching Thomas in his element, though he barely left my side, instead clutching my hand while greeting and chatting with fans. He released me each time someone wanted a picture, but that was the extent of it.

After the long flight and the concert, I was famished, so when Thomas posed with one fan, I meandered over to the buffet, filling a plate for myself.

I felt his breath on the back of my neck a moment before his arm wrapped around my waist.

"I could order you takeout from the hotel," he offered. "Or we could stop someplace on the way back."

"I'm good with this," I said.

He laughed and shook his head. "I always forget how impossibly low maintenance you are."

"Would you rather I be more difficult?'

Thomas smiled and kissed my forehead. "No, Dylan is fussy enough for all of us."

I'd barely finished eating when it was time to go. After the short ride back to the hotel, I was finally alone with Thomas.

The entire time he'd been performing, all I'd wanted was to be alone with him. But now that we were…

I noticed my bags right inside the door. "Vanessa has a key to your room?" I asked, wincing as soon as I heard my words aloud. I hadn't meant to sound like I was accusing him of anything.

His lips parted as his eyes searched the room. "I imagine she just left it with the concierge and he brought it up."

I shook my head. "I'm sorry. I didn't mean…" *Shit*. "I'm just tired."

Thomas ran his fingers through his hair. "Right. We should get you to bed. I need to shower, but…"

"I should shower too," I quickly said.

He motioned across the cozy, yet well-appointed suite.

"Ladies first," he said.

I dropped my purse on the dresser then unfastened my bracelets and slipped out my earrings. I placed my jewelry beside my purse just as Thomas stepped behind me. He brushed my hair to the side and unclasped my necklace. His lips lightly fluttered across my neck, and I shivered in response.

Grateful he'd taken the first step in breaking the ice, I proceeded to slip my shoulder straps down off my shoulders. I watched Thomas' eyes widen as the dress dropped below my breasts, revealing my black bra. He helped the dress down the rest of the way, crouching down to allow me to step out of it.

I held my breath, unsure what he would do next, and equally uncertain of what I wanted him to do. He didn't move for a moment, but then he ran his hands up the back of my thighs, planted a chaste kiss on the side of my butt cheek, then stood. His eyes met mine in the mirror and I realized he was as uncertain about everything as I was.

Stupidly, I'd thought that by flying all day, following him to a different country, that he'd understand how sorry I was. He'd believe that he was the only Parker brother—the only man anywhere—for me. And I assumed he'd forgive me instantly when I made such a big gesture.

Clearly, I'd miscalculated somewhere along the line.

I turned, not trusting my ability to control my emotions after such a long, full day. The last thing I needed was to burst into tears and pressure him into comforting me. I wanted Thomas to forgive me, to love me the same way he did a month ago, not to pity me.

"We could shower together," I said, leading the way to the bathroom.

"You sure I can join you?" Thomas asked.

I nodded, and he followed me just as the water reached the ideal temperature.

It wasn't a small shower, yet still, his presence overwhelmed the space.

I turned away, focusing on shampooing my hair and washing my face. Thomas did the same, so I proceeded to finger comb conditioner through my hair. I felt my lips curl upwards as I spotted the body wash on the ledge. It wasn't the hotel's free bottle, but rather a full-size bottle of the same brand Thomas used at home. Of all the products for a man to be particular about, that struck me as funny.

"May I?" I asked, holding up the bottle.

He snatched the bottle back. "Let me," he said.

He worked the soap into a lather in his palms, then dropped down to wash my legs, his hands quickly passing over every inch of my skin in rapid circling motions. He worked his way up to my hips, then paused to get more soap on his hands. Mission accomplished, he then started with my shoulders, worked his way down my arms, and then reached around me to my back.

I gazed at him as he replenished the soap on his palms one more time, pleased that he planned to return to the key places he'd skipped. His hands then went to my abdomen, but quickly worked upwards, lightly massaging my breasts.

A soft moan escaped my lips, but apparently that was the reassurance he'd wanted because he immediately deepened his touch until he was groping me with a wilder abandon. His lips found mine and the force of his sudden kiss knocked me back against the wall. I startled from the sudden coolness of the tile against my hot skin, but as Thomas' tongue swept through my mouth, a new warmth spread through my body.

His right hand reached between us, briefly stroking between my thighs, then returned to my cheek, clutching me close for the kiss. I felt his arousal press firmly against my abdomen, but he made no attempt to move beyond the simple make-out session. I loved kissing him, had been craving his lips on mine for weeks now, but at the same time, I needed more to truly feel relieved.

I slipped my hand between us, and my fingers circled his erection. His breath hitched, but he said nothing as I attempted to position him towards my entrance. I maneuvered for a moment without any assistance on his part before he finally broke away from my lips.

"Are you sure?" he asked. "You want…"

"Yes," I breathed, my eyes finding his. "I always want you. You don't have to ask."

His gaze turned almost predatory and I was about to kiss him again when he quickly swiveled me around so my back was to him. Within seconds, his hands were on my breasts and he pressed into me.

I moaned when he thrust fully and he froze, clearly misinterpreting my relief for pain. I pressed back against him, urging him to continue, and within a moment, he did. I angled my head to try to see him and he kissed me. The intensity of the onslaught of sensations was incredible, from the heat of the shower, the relentless pounding of his hips, the delicious tugging and pinching at my nipples from his expert fingers, to the soft, desperate way his tongue sought mine.

Having gone without his touch for too long, my body could only handle so much. As I felt myself start to fall over the edge, I gripped his arms tightly, my fingers pressing into his flesh as exquisite convulsions wracked my insides. I'd barely recovered when I felt Thomas follow suit, clutching me tightly as his release overtook him.

He leaned against me for a moment, pressing my breasts against the tile wall as we both caught our breath. Before I could collect my thoughts enough to speak, though, Thomas swiveled me back around to face him. He stared at me for a moment, his eyes searching for something before he captured my mouth with his own.

We kissed like teenagers for what felt like an eternity. We switched positions a few times, rotating to fully share the generous spray of the shower. When the water finally ran tepid, then cool, Thomas shut off the shower, but kept kissing me.

By the time he finally pulled away, we were seated. He was on the floor of the shower, and I was on top of him, my legs wrapped around his torso and my arms hooked around his neck. Without his lips against mine, I realized the temperature had dropped. And I was wet.

"You're shivering," he said, gently nudging me off his lap.

I slowly stood, gripping his hand while he did the same. Thomas stepped out of the shower first, but wrapped a towel around me before reaching for his own.

Suddenly, I was exhausted.

I barely had the energy to wrap my damp hair into a loose braid and brush my teeth before collapsing into bed. It was late, but we needed to talk. There was so much to discuss.

"Sleep," Thomas commanded, as though reading my thoughts. "We have most of the day tomorrow here, then we'll fly out before dinner."

I wasn't sure where we were going, or even if we were both going, but I was too tired to question it now. Thomas rolled me onto my side, draped his arm across mine, and I acquiesced to the fatigue of my body.

* * *

THOMAS

Sun poured through the open blinds early—too early. I deeply regretted not having closed them, but I didn't dare move to do it now and risk waking Lily. It was already nine, so I'd gotten nearly six hours of sleep. I'd be fine, especially since we didn't have a concert until the following day. But Lily needed more sleep, and I needed time to think.

She'd said she was sorry, and that she loved me. But I wasn't positive that answered all of my questions. There were still too many factors—my brother, my touring, and most of all, Lucy. *My* daughter. I couldn't think of her as anything else without pangs of regret ripping through my chest. She was mine. She wasn't Dylan's. He didn't want her and he certainly didn't deserve her. But genetically…

I blew out a sigh and stared at Lily. She was so peaceful while she slept. The first few times we'd spent the night together, I'd panicked, worried something had happened to her. She was so still in her sleep that she truly appeared frozen. I had to stare closely at her torso to see the subtle movements of her breathing.

I stayed in bed until ten a.m., then I slid slowly out from under the covers and successfully made it out of the room without waking Lily. I brushed my teeth while making coffee, then perused the room service menu while waiting for her to wake. I glanced in on Lily again, then ducked into the bathroom and switched on the exhaust fan to mask the sound of my phone call.

The operator greeted me by name and in English, making the call infinitely easier. I hung up and poured a second cup of coffee while reading the news on my tablet. I texted my brother to confirm our travel plans for later that day, but he didn't respond. I wondered how late he'd stayed out after the concert, or what trouble he'd gotten into after we left.

I startled as the bedroom door inched open. Lily stood there, a bathrobe wrapped loosely around her.

I couldn't help but smile. She looked beautiful first thing in the morning, all soft and warm and still loopy from sleep.

"Good morning," I said. I set my coffee mug on the table beside me and rose to pour her a cup. I walked the coffee over to her but she accepted it tentatively.

"My clothes are in my suitcase," she said, eying her luggage.

"Oh. Right." I grabbed her suitcase and dragged it into the bedroom. After last night, though, I couldn't pretend I wasn't disappointed that she felt this uncomfortable around me without her clothes.

A knock at the door interrupted my thoughts before I could say anything to her.

"I ordered breakfast," I explained, ducking quickly out of the bedroom and shutting the door behind me.

When I returned to the bedroom, Lily had opened her suitcase on top of the bed but still wore the bathrobe.

"I wasn't sure what our plans were for today," she explained. "I didn't know what to wear."

"Our flight is at five. I arranged for late checkout, but we're supposed to be out of here by 3ish." I paused. "Why don't you keep that on to eat and then we'll decide?"

She hesitantly wandered out of the bedroom. She took in the spread on the table, then laughed. "Hungry?"

I grinned. I had ordered a lot. I'd initially asked for the traditional foods I knew Lily liked—like toast and fruit, along with the eggs and meat I wanted. But then they mentioned that their oatmeal was a popular selection, so I'd asked for a bowl of that. And they had a couple different items labeled as the traditional Peruvian breakfasts, so I figured we had to try that.

After a moment, she grabbed the oatmeal. She spooned some toppings over it from a small saucer along with a splash of milk. I started with the tamale-looking dish and some eggs.

We made casual small talk as we ate, and Lily seemed to loosen up more with each passing moment.

"Ooh is that fresh papaya?" she asked.

"Looks like it," I replied, scooting the plate closer to her.

I watched as she eagerly bit into the succulent fruit. Her tongue darted across her lips, catching a drop of juice and drawing my eyes to her mouth.

"You're just so beautiful," I said, startled to hear I'd spoken the words out loud.

Her cheeks turned a rosy hue, then she smiled. "Lucy was upset that I didn't bring her," she said. "She misses you."

My chest tightened. "I miss her too," I said.

"I know. I'm sorry."

We'd both mostly finished eating, so I stood and reached for her hand.

"We have a lot to talk about," she said.

"Yes. It's more comfortable in here, though," I replied, leading her into the bedroom. I crawled onto the bed and she followed suit, snuggling under the covers while still gripping her coffee mug in both hands. Then, we just stared at each other.

"You're still mad at me," Lily blurted out.

"What? No, I'm really not."

Her eyebrows rose and she tilted her head to the side. "You left the country to get away from me."

"I left the country because I had to. This tour has been planned for nearly a year. It had nothing to do with us."

She still looked skeptical.

"What am I even supposed to be angry about now? That you wouldn't miss school to come with me? That you wouldn't let Lucy come along?"

She winced as I spoke and I realized—too late—that those hadn't been the reasons she imagined.

"I'm here now. I'm missing work now," she said.

I nodded. "I know. And I appreciate that. I am happy you're here." I cleared my throat, hating the awkward distance between us now. "I understand why you didn't want to come. It's your job, and it's important to you."

"You're important to me too."

I chuckled at that.

"You are!"

"Lily, I know. That's why I laughed."

She inhaled deeply through her nose, then bit her lip. "Are you still mad that I kissed Dylan?"

I turned my head, a rancid taste in my mouth. "No, but I thought we agreed not to bring it up any more." I waited a moment, then asked her what I'd been wondering. "Are you still mad about what I did?"

She took her time but shook her head. "No. I mean, I wish you'd just been honest with me, but I understand why you did it." She yanked the elastic out of her hair and started separating the sections of her hair from the braid. "Before that, you were still perfect in my mind. You always did and said exactly the right thing. I could count on you to always exercise impeccable judgment."

"And now you realize I'm no better than my brother," I supplied.

Her response took longer than I would've liked. "No. You are better. You did that because you were scared of losing Lucy.

You weren't being vengeful and you weren't trying to hurt anyone."

"It isn't just Lucy I'm scared to lose," I said.

She frowned. "I'm here, with you. I married you. And you're Lucy's dad no matter what her genetics say."

I started to voice my other protests but she shushed me.

"I'm not with you because of Lucy, I'm with you despite her. Have you seriously forgotten all my concerns from when you first tried to convince me to go out with you? It would be so much easier for me to be with someone else. With someone who didn't have a lifelong connection to Lucy regardless of what happened between us."

"I don't," I reminded her.

"You do!" she shouted, true annoyance in her voice this time. Her eyebrows furrowed tightly. "I would never take her from you again, Thomas. How can you even question that? Is that what you think of me? Jesus. She calls you 'Daddy' now. No matter what happens between us, you will always be her dad. Don't you get that?"

A moment passed, then she flew out of bed, slamming the bathroom door behind her.

Fuck.

I waited a minute, but when it was clear she had no intention of coming back out, I followed. I leaned against the door, imagining her right on the other side.

"I'm sorry, Lily. I know that, I do. I will always be there for Lucy. I only meant that I felt more security before, when I had actual rights I could enforce if it came to that. But I know you'd never try to take Lucy away from me."

I paused, but there was so much more I needed to say.

"I love you so much, Lily. I've loved you since the day I met you, and I'm sorry that I keep messing this up. I want Lucy in my life, but I also want you. I want you so much that it hurts. And I want you by my side no matter what that looks like on a day to day basis. I'll take as much time with you as you'll give me, but if we're apart when I tour, that's fine. I still want to be your husband."

I paused again, praying she could actually hear me and that I wasn't wasting my breath pouring my heart out to her now, with a door in between us.

"If you want me to stop touring, I'll do it. If you want me to leave the band, I'll do it. There is nothing I wouldn't do for you, Lily. I just need you to talk to me."

The door opened so abruptly that I nearly fell onto Lily.

Her eyes were glazed and red, so I knew she'd been crying. But I wasn't sure if she'd heard my entire spiel until she spoke.

"You can't leave the band. Or stop touring," she said. "I love watching you perform. I'd forgotten how…mesmerizing you are. And I want Lucy to see that. She's already so proud of you, but if she could see you in your element…"

"She's seen us perform."

"Not really. And that's my fault, too. I was just scared. It seems like the wrong thing to do, taking a preschooler to a rock concert." She paused and laughed. "But she can wear headphones, and we'll go on a day where she can nap the next day. It's not fair to deprive her of the chance to see you impressing a huge audience."

I felt a smile twitch against my lips. "You don't have to say that. I'm okay with waiting until she's older to bring her along on tour." I inched forward, waiting until she fully acquiesced to me to pull her into a hug.

When I finally released her, Lily appeared deep in thought for a moment.

"I need to change my mindset," she said. "I've spent so long keeping my focus on protecting Lucy from everyone who isn't me. It's hard for me to start remembering that you're looking out for her now, too."

I nodded. Obviously, she'd done a great job with Lucy. But it would be better for all of us if Lily stopped acting like she was on her own.

"I forgot how much I loved watching you perform," she repeated. "But I also love teaching, and I want Lucy to be proud of me. I want her to see her mom working."

"Me too. And she is proud of you, you know? So am I. But I also want her to see her mom being happy. I want Lucy to know you really can have it all."

Lily's eyebrow raised. "Oh?"

I crooked a finger, motioning for her to follow. I sank onto the couch where I'd left my tablet and notepad. I patted the cushion beside me until she sat.

"This whole adulting thing is hard," I began.

She burst into laughter. "Yeah. And clearly we both suck at it."

I shrugged. "But you can have it all. We both can." I clicked on my calendar and scrolled through it, month by month. "What do you see?"

I turned to Lily to confirm she was looking at my calendar. By the confused expression on her face, though, she wasn't getting my point. "An unusually high number of dental appointments?" she finally said.

I shook my head. "No. Look." I clicked on the daily schedule. "This tour is over in another month. Lucy and you are both off a whole week for fall break, right?"

She nodded slowly.

"So you can both come tour with me then. And then another week will pass and I'll be home with you" I kept scrolling through my calendar to show her.

"Until Christmas," she said, tapping the screen to pause my movements.

"We're going to England for Christmas," I said. "You, me, and Lucy. Remember? For fun, not for work."

She nodded slowly, so I resumed scrolling. "I have nothing planned for January, February, March, or April," I said.

"Nothing?" she looked skeptical.

"Okay, I mean, we'll still be practicing and maybe recording. Possibly the odd interview or two out of town, but I can say no to any of those. Or you can."

"Then what?"

I pursed my lips. She knew what happened next summer, but apparently I needed to say it out loud. "Well, then we tour. But only in the US. And it's a summer tour, so you and Lucy can come with us. We can get a separate RV, just for our family. It'll be like the dream vacation every family wants but can't afford. Lucy will get to see the country, we'll all spend so much time together that we'll actually get sick of each other, and you won't have to miss work."

"I'd love to get sick of you," she teased.

I kissed the tip of her nose. "My point is, this can work. It's not even that hard."

Now she rolled her eyes. "When you're stuck in an RV for twelve weeks with an energetic five-year old, you might change your opinion on that."

"We don't have any tours scheduled past that. I don't even know if we will keep touring after that."

"Really?" her voice dripped with skepticism.

"Okay, so realistically we'll probably still have opportunities after that, but I'm not committed to anything at this point. I can say no to it all or I can insist everything happens over the summer."

"After this year, I'll have more personal time from school," she said. "I could miss a few more days here and there without getting into trouble."

"We can do this," I repeated.

She bit her lip but smiled.

I leaned in to kiss her, then paused. "I'm sorry I blabbed about our marriage," I said.

Lily cupped my cheeks in her hands and tugged me to her,

tracking her tongue over my top lip before gently kissing me. I smiled, feeling her smiling against my mouth.

"I'm glad you did," she replied. "I want the world to know you're mine." She nudged me back and reached for my ring. It took her a moment of tugging and twisting before she was able to pull it free, but then she slipped it onto the ring finger of my left hand, where she'd initially placed it one month before. Then she wiggled her hand at me until I did the same with her wedding band.

"I love you so much," I said, capturing her lips with another kiss.

"I love you too," she replied, when we both paused for air. "And we're still having a huge formal wedding ceremony with all our friends and family and then a real honeymoon."

"I wouldn't dream of skipping any of that."

EPILOGUE

LILY

$\mathcal{I}$ fussed over Lucy's dress one last time before brushing a kiss across the top of her head. She looked positively cherubic, with her dark hair curled into adorable ringlets and a soft, white band of flowers circling her head like a crown. Shockingly, she'd not only cooperated during the forty-five minutes it had taken to style her hair; she'd actually relished the attention and pampering. Her dress—trimmed in lace, tulle, and crystals—was already her most beloved outfit, although I couldn't imagine where she'd ever wear it again. The sleeveless lace bodice was white, the tulle skirt was a pale pinkish hue, and the crystals coated the small train of the gown. A silk ribbon in a gorgeous rust color trimmed the waist and matched the majority of the flower petals in her small basket.

"You are the most beautiful flower girl I've ever seen," I cooed, tapping her nose gently right as the wedding planner flitted up behind us.

"It's almost time!" she chirped to Lucy, nudging me towards the aisle.

I took the hint and stepped outside, smiling as the warm ocean air hit my cheeks. I'd expected sweltering heat in Barbados, or at least a suffocating humidity, but today we'd been blessed with blissfully warm temperatures and a delightful breeze. The still, turquoise water just past the canopy glistened serenely. Everything about my surroundings was calming.

I startled as warm breath hit the back of my neck.

"You look gorgeous," the familiar voice whispered gruffly as he pressed his torso against my back, wrapping his hands around my abdomen.

I bit back a smile, relaxing against his comforting embrace. I could've stayed just like that for hours, gazing at the ocean while secured in Thomas' arms, but then I remembered why we were here.

I swiveled to face him. "The ceremony is about to start. Aren't you supposed to be out there?"

"I s'pose I am," he said with a chuckle. He kissed my cheek and then delicately stroked his hands across my stomach again before releasing me and offering his elbow instead.

I let him walk me down the aisle and deposit me at my seat in the first row. Then I watched him saunter off to his place at the front, appreciating the way his tux fit his deliciously toned figure.

Dylan was already there, waiting patiently for his bride. He greeted his brother with a hug, then calmly clasped his hands in front of him and gazed towards the lobby where the processional was lining up. On his other side stood Davi and Miguel, the bride's older brothers. I'd only just met them, but they seemed nice, and with none of the drama that seemed to plague Thomas and Dylan's relationship.

Thomas caught my gaze and winked, his smile wide. Seeing him in a tuxedo, beaming like the happiest man on earth, I couldn't help but think back to our wedding day. Well, the day of our renewal ceremony and reception. Even though the secret had gotten out that we'd eloped in England, we'd still enjoyed a second ceremony. My dad had a chance to walk me down the aisle, my mother wore her dream mother-of-the-bride dress, and Lucy was able to participate.

We'd enjoyed an intimate reception in Manhattan with our closest friends and family, then had jetted off to an all-inclusive resort in the Caribbean to avoid the paparazzi and enjoy each other's company without distractions. Every aspect of the wedding, reception, and honeymoon was perfect.

Music began, breaking the spell locking my gaze on Thomas. We both turned towards the aisle as Lucy made her appearance. Thanks to the length of her gown, she appeared to float across the satiny aisle runner. She beamed proudly at her father, then turned to me and giggled with joy as she passed. Judging from the coos from the audience, we weren't alone in our belief that she was the most adorably perfect flower girl ever.

As Lucy reached the canopy at the front, Dylan crouched down and said something to her before giving her a big hug and a kiss on the cheek. Then Thomas reached for her hand and escorted her to her chair, right beside mine. She squeezed my hand as she sat, swinging her legs back and forth excitedly as we watched the rest of the procession before we all stood to watch the bride.

Isabella looked stunning, which surprised no one since she was a supermodel. She had long, dark hair, fiercely green eyes, and perpetually bronzed skin. She was nearly as tall as Dylan, and she had the sultry cheekbones, legs for days, and perky breasts you'd expect from a model. She was younger—not yet 29, but that, too, seemed appropriate for Dylan, since he wasn't exactly known for his maturity. Though she'd lived in New York for years, she'd actually met Dylan in her hometown in Brazil, when Sierra was on their South American tour. They'd chosen

Barbados for their wedding due to its position between New York, London, and Brazil, although the British attendees still clearly had the longest flight.

I didn't know Isabella well, but my impression of her was positive. She was kind, delighted with Lucy, and clearly enamored with Dylan. She didn't strike me as Dylan's equal on an intellectual basis, but maybe that was my own biased assumptions based on her line of work. Regardless, they were clearly happy together. I'd never seen Dylan with Patty outside of the tabloids, so I couldn't truly compare, but this relationship struck me as more genuine, and Thomas agreed. We were confident that Dylan had finally found his true match.

Hopefully, this marriage would last.

The happier Thomas and I grew, the more aware I was when others around me weren't so blissful. And since life was looking up and up for us, well, Dylan's union was good timing.

The ceremony was short, and as the wedding party made their way back down the aisle to hide out inside the resort lobby for a few minutes before the reception, Thomas paused, offering Lucy one hand, and me the other. We smiled for the photographers on both sides of the aisle, and I tried- in vain- to suck in my stomach.

I was not even a full five months pregnant yet, but I looked about the same as I had at seven months with Lucy. Thomas adored my changing body, and for the most part, I wasn't too self-conscious, except when I knew my photo would end up in tabloids. The paparazzi was blocked from the wedding and private resort, but Dylan had warned us that Isabella had already sold the photos to a prominent gossip magazine.

Jill, who'd delivered her second child mere weeks earlier, had warned me that I'd get bigger much faster with the second pregnancy. But in my case, there was an additional explanation for my quick growth. I was carrying not one baby, but two.

Twins.

Boys.

The next set of Parker brothers were already in existence, and from the feel of things, already fighting in utero. Thomas was over the moon. Lucy was thrilled. I was…terrified, but also very, very happy. With no twins in either of our families, we hadn't expected it, and yet it was the perfect solution. Thomas really wanted three children and I wasn't keen on three pregnancies.

"Can we borrow her for a few photos with the happy couple?" the wedding planner asked, tugging Lucy away before I could answer.

"You are stunning," Thomas said, shaking his head in disbelief.

"You don't look too shabby yourself," I replied. I had just enough time for my eyes to wander all the way down then back up his torso before he pulled me close, holding me as though we were about to slow dance.

"I've got some news," he whispered.

My heart pounded instantly. There was only one thing his news could be about. We'd put an offer on a new apartment the previous day. "We got it?"

He nodded, pressing his mouth to mine. His tongue brushed across the crease between my lips, darting in just enough to make me forget where I was.

The sound of someone clearing his throat caused us to separate.

We turned simultaneously to see Dylan. He chuckled, raising an eyebrow. "Isabella and I should be the ones making a scene today. Not you," he teased.

"Sorry," Thomas mumbled. "Congratulations."

"Thank you. My bride would like you both to join us for some photos," Dylan replied.

We spent the better part of the next hour posing and smiling. After photos, there would be dinner and dancing. In the morning, we'd join the happy couple for brunch and then they would jet off to a smaller island nearby to enjoy their honeymoon in private. Thomas and I were staying the rest of the week in one room. Lucy and her grandma Kate were in a separate room.

Thinking about the new apartment made it easy to smile through the photos. It was our absolute dream home. It was close to Lucy's elementary school, and its four-bedroom layout promised plenty of space for us, the twins, and for a music room. Between the pregnancy and my desire to travel more with Thomas before the babies came, I'd decided to take the year off from teaching. With the boys set to arrive early spring, I'd left my options open for returning that fall if I was up for it.

The band had just finished recording their fifth album, and Ari was pressuring them to think about another world tour the next year, but no decisions had been made yet. I couldn't imagine Thomas would be too eager to travel the world unless Lucy and I —and the twins—came along, but I was open to that possibility, too.

"I've always wanted a sister," Isabella gushed, interrupting my daydream.

"Me too," I said, realizing as I looked at her warm, sincere smile that it was actually the truth. A white-gloved waiter distributed tall champagne flutes to each of us. I was about to reject mine when I realized that the contents of my glass and Lucy's were a slightly different color.

"Sparkling juice," Isabella explained.

"Sisters are a whole lot easier than brothers," Dylan chimed in, winking at Thomas.

Thomas knelt down in front of me, pressed his palms gently against my abdomen, then kissed right above my belly button. "Actually, I can't imagine a better gift we could give to our boys than a brother," he said, rising back to his feet and clapping Dylan on the back.

Dylan laughed and raised his glass in the air. "To brothers," he said.

"To brothers," we all repeated.

The End

ACKNOWLEDGMENTS

I'm filled with gratitude for my editor Kim, my cover artist JD Designs, and all of my beta reviewers. I also truly appreciate all those hours my mom babysat so I could write and all those times my husband did more than his fair share of driving our kids around so I could edit. Finally, a huge thank you to my readers!

ABOUT THE AUTHOR

Liza Malloy writes contemporary romance and women's fiction. She's a sucker for alpha males, bad boys, dimples, and muscles, and she can't resist a man in uniform. Liza loves creating worlds where her heroine discovers her own strength and finds her Happily Ever After. When Liza isn't reading or writing torrid love stories, she's a practicing attorney. Her other passions include gummy bears, jelly beans, and the occasional marathon. She lives in the Midwest with her four daughters and her own Prince Charming. *The Brothers' Band: The Next Track* is her eighth novel.

Visit her website at www.LizaMalloy.com

Join her email list at http://eepurl.com/gnuROD

Sixty Days for Love

For Love and Italian

Forbidden Ink

The Brothers' Band

Hollywood Endings

Legacy: The Awakening

Legacy: The Revelation